CROSSCURRENTS / MODERN FICTION

HARRY T. MOORE, *General Editor*
MATTHEW J. BRUCCOLI, *Textual Editor*

PREFACE BY

HARRY T. MOORE

THE
LAND OF PLENTY

Robert Cantwell

SOUTHERN ILLINOIS UNIVERSITY PRESS

CARBONDALE AND EDWARDSVILLE

FEFFER & SIMONS, INC.

LONDON AND AMSTERDAM

For Nina Cantwell

Preface

BY HARRY T. MOORE

ROBERT CANTWELL is one of the finest American novelists who began writing during the depression, and his 1934 book, *The Land of Plenty*, remains one of the strongest fictional expressions of that age. We are pleased to present it in the Crosscurrents/Modern Fiction series.

This series has brought back into print a number of novels which have not been available for a number of years, as well as two which it has published for the first time. We have been fortunate in securing the reprint rights to Kay Boyle's first two novels, to two of D. H. Lawrence's books, to H. D.'s *Palimpsest,* to Bernard Shaw's *Cashel Byron's Profession,* to Zelda Fitzgerald's *Save Me the Waltz,* and to Richard Aldington's collection of satirical stories, *Soft Answers.* We have also first published H. G. Wells's *The Wealth of Mr. Waddy*—not altogether a finished work, but we included Wells's notes toward completion. And now, at the same time as Cantwell's *The Land of Plenty,* we are bringing back the too-long neglected novel by D. H. Lawrence and M. L. Skinner, *The Boy in the Bush,* as well as Francis Stuart's hitherto unpublished novel, *Black List, Section H.*

Robert Cantwell's *The Land of Plenty* is a particularly timely reprint when interest in the 1930s is becoming intense. In our other series, Crosscurrents/Modern Critiques, we have published David Madden's two critical anthologies of the period, *The Proletarian Writers of the 1930s* and *The Tough Guy Writers of the 1930s.*

Those of us who remember that decade recall it as a pretty grim time, particularly as we watched fascism rising in Europe, with everyone sitting quietly by as the Nazis took over Germany not by

[vii]

their street-corner and torture-basement brutality, of both of which there was plenty, but rather because their voting power was great enough to put Hitler in high place, the Hitler so many of us were later willing to oppose in the rare thing, a justifiable war.

Over here in the 1930s, we watched with some horror as ku-klux elements in the community who didn't bother to wear white robes (or brown or black shirts) began to show themselves in everyday American clothes. Their tendencies were dramatized in a rather gruesome, half-satirical novel by Sinclair Lewis. Two years after Cantwell's *The Land of Plenty,* Lewis published the ironically named *It Can't Happen Here,* which still makes for good reading and was recently reissued in paperback. Huey Long, who before he was assassinated in 1935 was looked upon with dread by some American liberals, once cheerfully said, "Sure we'll have fascism in America—only it'll come in the disguise of Americanism." Then as now, many citizens linked Americanism to anti-communism and tried to impose on free speech an embargo of the kind that operates in Soviet Russia.

By 1931, the depression had already become a painfully serious matter: that year saw the emergence of Robert Cantwell as a novelist, with his *Laugh and Lie Down.* This was not exactly a "labor novel" like its successor three years later, but was rather the story of young people of the middle class and their disillusionment with "the system."

The year was 1931: on the side of a freight car in Kentucky, I saw printed in chalk, HOOVER—CAPLIST DOG. In Chicago I saw well-dressed young married people, the husbands having lost what seemed to be good jobs, trying to sleep under newspapers on benches in Jackson Park; when some of us who were undergraduates at the University of Chicago attended performances at Samuel Insull's big new white opera house, before we arrived there we saw the groups of unemployed men lingering in despair along Wacker Drive. Those of us who were studying literature, and had for the most part neglected political science, didn't quite know what was wrong, but we felt that Herbert Hoover—caught unhappily in the trap of history at exactly the wrong moment—was to blame.

In Los Angeles the next year, I read on a windshield,

COOLIDGE BLEW THE WHISTLE
MELLON RANG THE BELL
HOOVER PULLED THE THROTTLE
AND THE COUNTRY WENT TO HELL.

Some of us didn't know much about Roosevelt, but his resonant confidence was reassuring. Nevertheless, we could see that things continued to be wrong, and we didn't always feel that "big business" was helping anyone or things in general very effectively. We read most of the proletarian novels in those years (I reviewed a number of them), but life on the surface semed to change very little in the early 1930s; though when we read *Mein Kampf* we began to understand what was taking place in Germany, in accordance with a plan announced in a kind of cold hysteria.

In 1935, I wrote up the University of Chicago "red hearings" for the *New Republic* in March, and saw the drugstore magnate Charles E. Walgreen try to bring a "case" against the University of Chicago for supposedly converting his niece (attending the school on a Walgreen scholarship) to communism. The University was in danger of losing its tax exemptions, and this was a serious matter. President Robert Maynard Hutchins and several professors—including Paul Douglas, Robert Morss Lovett, and Frederick L. Schumann (who had recently written a penetrating book on the rise of Nazism)—defended the university and its right to academic freedom; so did Professor Harry Gideonse, a noted anti-Communist who was soon, as president of Brooklyn College, to be routing out "reds." Walgreen seemed to feel that Marxism shouldn't even be discussed in political-science classes which studied it objectively and critically. Walgreen lost his "case" in the hearings, which were conducted by a committee from the state legislature; and in any event he wasn't so frightening as some of those who testified against the university, including the "superpatriot" Harry E. Jung and Mrs. Elizabeth Dilling, author of *The Red Network*. We university students for the most part distrusted such people as the Jungs and the Dillings, and looked hopefully toward Franklin D. Roosevelt and toward John L. Lewis, who in that year of 1935 formed the Committee for Industrial Organization, designed to help labor (two years later it became the independent

[ix]

Congress of Industrial Organization, the C.I.O.) and to help repel fascism.

Robert Cantwell, in his *Laugh and Lie Down,* had been several years ahead of so many of us in showing youth shedding its illusions about what was soon to be widely known as bourgeois society (the book was the work of a young man who was only twenty-three). And in *The Land of Plenty* he was prophetic indeed in foreshadowing the strikes which were to become so common after the middle 1930s, with workers often seizing and occupying the plants. But the novel is much more than that; it is an important creation in its own right.

Cantwell was born in Little Falls (which is now Vader), Washington, was graduated from high school there in 1924, and spent a rather unhappy year at the state university. From 1925 to '29 he was a veneer-clipper operator at a plywood factory, the setting of *The Land of Plenty.* He later worked on a pipeline construction crew in the Texas desert. He had been writing in his spare time, and when one of his stories was printed in the *American Caravan* (an annual volume of distinguished new literature edited by Lewis Mumford and others), he decided to become a full-time author.

After *The Land of Plenty* he virtually completed a novel about the San Francisco waterfront strike of 1934, but although the book was announced it never appeared. Cantwell served on the editorial staffs of *Time, Fortune,* and *Life,* later becoming literary editor of *Newsweek.* He has since 1961 been managing editor of *Sports Illustrated.*

His *Nathaniel Hawthorne: The American Years,* is a monument of American scholarly research, presenting a new view of Hawthorne as a man more *engagé* than he is usually considered. In 1951 Cantwell edited *The Humorous Side of Erskine Caldwell,* and in 1961 further demonstrated his interest in scholarly biography with *Alexander Wilson: Naturalist and Pioneer.*

In *The Land of Plenty,* Robert Cantwell showed that a novel about the working class didn't necessarily have to be lacking in literary distinction. Cantwell was aware of what literary distinction was, as he showed in articles on Henry James written for the *New Republic* and other periodicals in the middle 1930s. Indeed, in calling the attention of liberal intellectuals to the skill of the then neglected James, Cantwell was importantly instrumental in starting the James "revival." He pointed out that James didn't really celebrate the "idle rich" (popular cliché in those days) but rather showed up their weaknesses, and that James's approach to fiction could be used by authors of proletarian literature as well as by those who wrote other kinds. Cantwell was clear and forceful in these statements, and his influence on the renewal of interest in James should be noted; in 1945 it was shocking not to find him included among the contributors to F. W. Dupee's *The Question of Henry James*.

In *The Radical Novel in the United States, 1900–1954* (1956), Walter B. Rideout mentioned sixteen novels about "class battles." For the sake of the record, here they are, in the order he gives them: *Strike!, Lumber, Beyond Desire, Call Home the Heart, To Make My Bread, Gathering Storm, S.S. Utah, Parched Earth, The Land of Plenty, The Shadow Before, A Stone Came Rolling, Marching! Marching!, A Time to Remember, Another Such Victory, Jordanstown, The Stricklands.* Some of these are read today or are familiar from bibliographies—Sherwood Anderson's *Beyond Desire,* for example. But of the large group, Professor Rideout finds that Robert Cantwell's *The Land of Plenty* is "the best from most points of view."

As Rideout also notes, Cantwell, shortly after the novel appeared, deprecated it in the *New Masses* (July 3, 1934), largely because he had written it as "quite simply, a work of propaganda." He felt that the ending was weak: "I couldn't imagine clearly what would happen, and the novel suffers as a result." But Rideout defends the book against its author's strictures at the time, for it so skillfully adumbrated the 1936–37 sit-down strikes.

Professor Rideout, in this and in his general praise for the novel, is perfectly right; coming as it does out of the mists of the past, *The Land of Plenty* looms up as a remarkable production. And if it shows here and there the influence of Henry James upon Cantwell, it is an influence helpfully assimilated.

Growing up in mill towns—though as the member of an important pioneer family, not as a proletarian—and working in a factory, Cantwell knew his people, their thoughts, the effects of their environment. And his portraits of the middle class are more

[xi]

than stereotypes. His projection of workers taking over a plant, dramatically sound, also proved to be prophetically sound. The characters, particularly the laborer Hagen and his son, are vitally presented, and young Hagen's first love-experience becomes an important part of the vivid action. The picket lines, the scabs, the owners, the police, the townspeople—all are put forth in a series of stirring episodes, ending with the workers' battle with the police. If we hold in abeyance the ideology of 1934, the ending may be seen to be dramatically powerful, not tragic in the classical sense perhaps, but tragic in the social concept of the word.

The writing throughout has just the right cadences and colors to bring everything in the story to life. The book begins abruptly, with a strong paragraph starting with a strong sentence that pitches the reader abruptly into the action: "Suddenly the lights went out."

The reader can take it from there.

Southern Illinois University
April 6, 1971

"The Bureau of the Census announces that, according to a preliminary tabulation of data collected in the Census of Manufactures taken in 1932, the value of the output of timber products and lumber in the United States in 1933 by establishments engaged primarily in the manufacture of this class of products amounted to $441,587,203, a decrease of 65.2 per cent as compared with $1,267,373,693 reported for 1929. The total production of lumber reported for 1931 amounted to 16,522,643 M feet, board measure, a decrease of 36.6 per cent as compared with . . . 1930 and of 55.2 per cent as compared with 1929 . . . "

Census of Manufactures, 1931.

Power and Light

PART ONE: POWER AND LIGHT

1. CARL

SUDDENLY the lights went out. He was standing in a cleared space toward the head end of the mill, trying to decide what he should do, when the lights went out and left him groping for the wall behind him. There was no warning fading or flickering of the bulbs; there was only a swift blotting out of the visible world. At one moment there were things he could see, there were familiar objects and people and walls; and at the next there was nothing, nothing but darkness streaming from the empty bulbs.

For a time he stood motionless, waiting for the light to come back. He was conscious of a dull, growing exasperation, a feeling like that he experienced if he was kept waiting by someone he did not like. He said "Hell," somewhat plaintively, and then waited, occasionally turning his head to see if somewhere a flare of light would not break out in a signal that the brief night was over. In the darkness the motors began whining down to silence. The operators could no longer see, but they moved blindly and automatically to stop the machines that were already stopping. No current was passing through the switch boxes, but at each machine the operator stepped back to press the switch that stopped his motor, finding it at once in spite of the darkness. When no current was passing through the wires the sound of the switch releasing was hollow, a dull throb, somewhat like the sound of a rock dropped into a well. For a time this was the only sound in the factory, this dull throb of switches cutting a current that had already ceased to flow.

[3]

Then the voices began to bubble up in the darkness, faint and wordless at first, growing to a slight shuffle of release. . . . At the far end of the factory someone shouted, *Yahoo! Yahoo!* over and over again. Listen to that, he thought. Listen to that.

He stepped back indecisively, feeling his way to the wall he knew was not far behind him. He knew where he was. He knew that all around him the floor was clear and solid. But as soon as he started to move he could not be sure; he could not remember whether there wasn't a drop through the floor somewhere near him, or whether he wasn't nearer the sloping walls of a conveyor than he had thought. So he shuffled along uneasily, his feet sliding and testing each plank before he placed his weight upon it. He was skating along with great caution when he heard someone running past him.

He stopped incredulously. He heard the steps coming a long way off, long steps coming down hard on the fragile plank floor, leaping over the pits and gullies where the refuse was spilled, the sound splashing up from the leather meeting the wood. He stood listening in amazement with his own feet still delicately testing the planks that the darkness had turned to tissue-paper.

You crazy fool, he said silently. Do you want to get killed? The movement passed him as he reached the wall.

He reached the wall and held it for its sightless guidance, waiting now for the lights to come back without wondering why they had gone off or what he should do. He was surprised to find that his heart was pounding and that his fright had drained the strength from his knees. He leaned against the wall to get his breath, listening to the darkness without wondering what he should do or what had happened, without expecting anything except the light to come back, and in the blindness of no light he could only wait helplessly and believe that the miracle that had robbed him of his sight would soon give it back to him again.

Outside, the tideflat on which the factory stood was almost as dark. There was no moon and the summer sky was clouded with the film of smoke drifting toward the sea from the forest fires in the mountains. In this part of the country, at the edge of the last great forests between the mountains and the Pacific, the hills burn each summer between the rains, the fires starting in the logged-off land and spreading into the green timber where nothing can stop them but a river or a patch of bare ground or a storm. A fire had broken out and in two days was out of human control. Before that the weather had been fine and dry, rare for the Northwest where there is a saying that it is a lucky year if summer comes on a Sunday, and the timber, the last great forest that stretches for a hundred miles to the north and fifty miles to the east, was seasoned and waiting. The loggers had had to stop work because the woods were so inflammable. A cable might grind against a stump, or a spark fly from a donkey-engine, and in an instant an area a hundred feet across would be in flames, almost as though the underbrush had exploded. Two weeks before, the fire had started. It could be seen from town, looking at first like a new mountain pushing its way up beyond the nearer hills. The great glaciers of smoke piled up and rolled in silent avalanches down its sides. As the days passed the peak dissolved and the rolls of smoke, heavier and thicker than clouds, drifted behind the wind. At night an indefinite red light showed somewhere behind the smoke, coloring it dimly; sometimes the fire itself rose over the hills. During the hot days the smoke seemed like a great tan canvas stretched tight from one horizon to the other, and underneath it the world looked dull and strange, the sharp colors and outlines disappearing or running into one another like objects under water.

This film of smoke covered the sky. The factory was a good mile from town and there were no lights on the tideflat. There were a few lights marking the ship channels in the harbor, and the reflection of the lights over the main streets of the town, but that was all. Once the tideflat around the factory had been a marsh, until bulkheads had been built around it and mud from the bottom of the harbor pumped in behind the bulkheads. Gradually the tideflat had been drained and packed, and as the bunch grass and bulrushes had taken root in it, and the scrub willows that grew beside the drainage canals had spread, a small prairie had formed around the factory. Only one road connected it with the highway, and a spur with the main line of the railroad. There were a few empty freight cars on the siding, and a few automobiles huddled in the parking space at the entrance of the factory.

All the way across the tideflat and across town there was felt an accident at the power house. One of the men moving behind the switchboard, for some reason that was never known, brushed against the deadly wires and in an instant half the town was dark. The street cars ran blindly for a few feet and stopped; the people looked toward their companions who had so suddenly become invisible. In the houses the darkness settled like a weight. At the factory the very nerves and muscles of the machines were cut, the motors began whining down to silence, the men moved automatically to press the control buttons. Thousands of great and small precautions were taken, thousands of dangers avoided, casually, as part of the moment's work, and then the men settled themselves to wait. The crew on the presses worked feverishly in the dark trying to save the doors that were partly finished. The electricians hurried through the building, trying to find the break; in the fireroom the fireman cut the steam that was going to the kilns. In the factory a man climbed under the roof, feeling his way up a ladder that seemed to lean outwards, crawled over a shaky plank bridge to set a valve, finding it by burning his hands along the pipe. And out at the head end of the mill, where the logs were lifted from the steam vats, a man was hurt when the hoist that lifted the logs suddenly stopped.

The factory was a large rectangular building with a long peninsula thrust out from it, to the edge of the water, like the handle of a frying pan. The long peninsula was a relic of its early days, when the logs had been moved in from the vats on trucks that ran on a narrow-gauge track. The logs were sawed into lengths while they still floated in the water of an inlet, lifted into vats and steamed for two days under pressure. Then they were taken into the mill through the long corridor that thrust out from the factory, washed and cleaned and peeled into veneer; moving on, then, through the complicated processes that transformed them into doors and desks, into panels for walls and furniture.

The man who was hurt worked at the far end of the peninsula, where he was running the hoist that lifted the logs into the factory. He was a new man and, since he worked off by himself and the accident happened swiftly and silently, it was a long time before anyone found him. When the lights went out the log had lifted enough to be free to swing. It was a large log, six feet through and nine feet long, the butt log of an enormous fir. It lifted very slowly, for the motor of the hoist was geared down to give it greater power. There was a strained singing sound from the motor as the cable tightened and the hooks buried themselves in the wood at each end of the log, and the sap and water spurted out around the hooks as they sank into the wood. Then the log stirred in the shadow of its own steam, rising like some great awkward beast awakened at night, rising and swaying until it was almost clear of the ground.

The motor stopped when the power was cut. A brake prevented the log from dropping back, but it began to swing, very slowly, until the uneven track let it go. Slowly and silently it moved through the darkness to where the hoist man was staring at the darkened lights, picked him up and pressed him against the foundations. For a time it held him there, crushing through the brief defense he made against it, breaking through his arms, his clothing, the frail protection of his flesh. Then it settled back slightly, leaving him jammed against the piling.

[7]

This happened in the instant that Carl was groping his way toward the wall. He did not know it. He knew only that there was a tremendous amount of work that had to be done and that it could not be done as long as the factory was dark. When he realized that the lights were not coming on again a wave of despair, almost of physical sickness, swept over him, and when he thought of how he was going to answer the manager about the orders that had to be got out, his hands clenched and unclenched nervously. He was a new foreman. A year before he had come to the factory as an efficiency engineer with a contract to cut operating costs and power to weed out the incompetent men, and before the year was over he had been given charge of the night shift to show what he could do. Nothing like this had happened since he came into the factory. He knew what to do in case of a fire, and he had learned what men to give the cutting orders to when the shift started and where to check up when the stock seemed to be running short, but nothing had ever happened to make him wonder what to do when the lights went out.

He shifted his hold on the wall and wiped his moist palm on his overalls. The factory rocked when he released the wall. He grabbed it again, his fingers clamping on one of the cross-pieces. He felt the sweat on his forehead.

Oh, Christ, he said silently. Come back on.

Tomorrow he would have to face the manager. Every afternoon, when he came to the factory, he went at once to the office where MacMahon sat behind his polished desk reading the order sheets and checking them with the records of the output of the night before. There was an order sheet on MacMahon's desk now, he knew, marked with the three red stars that meant urgent and headed with the code symbols that told where it was going. An export order, five thousand doors for Sydney, and the cars were on the track, the ship was loading. Here in the factory they were half through and there was a holiday tomorrow and the men did not want to work tonight. The precious time passed. He knew what MacMahon would say. He could imagine MacMahon trembling with nervousness and worry and pacing back and forth in his office saying, Carl, that's your problem. I can't help you with that. All I know is it's got to get out. Over and over, thinking of the cars on the track, the demurrage piling up and the ship's loading, the penalties for delay. It's your problem, Carl, while his secretary Miss Hazen tiptoed around the office not wanting to notice while he was being bawled out and afraid of MacMahon's temper when the work was jammed up.

Somebody yelled again, a long *yow!* dragged out like the whistle at the end of the shift.

Listen to that, he said to the darkness. Listen to that.

"Morley!" he called out. "Morley!"

There was a stir in the darkness. He could hear Morley skating over the thin planks and hear the papers rustle while he moved. The gnawing sound of Morley's feet stopped.

"Morley!" he called again.

He could hear Morley turn around. Jesus, he said silently, you crippled?

"Yes?"

"Where the hell are you?"

"Here I am."

"Where?"

"Here. Over here."

"What the hell you doing over there?"

"I—" Morley said.

For Christ's sake. You see? he asked the wall. Is it any wonder?

"I got turned around," Morley said. He heard an edge of panic in his voice. "I must have got turned around."

"Well, come here."

He heard Morley skate over the thin floor, testing each plank before he put his weight on it. His shoes made a dragging, tired sound in the darkness. Take your time, he said silently.

We got all night. "Don't take all night," he said. The scraping sound speeded up. He could hear the rustle of the papers and picture Morley wading through the dark, swinging his arms in wide circles ahead of him. Then he heard Morley bump into the wall.

"I got turned around," Morley said breathlessly. "I must have got turned around somehow. I was surprised when you called me. I was going the wrong way. I thought you were ahead of me. So I was surprised when you called me and here you was behind me. I thought the conveyor was right here. I was all turned around."

Carl nodded. You're always turned around, he said silently. Wouldn't be the first time.

Morley gave a sigh of relief. "What happened?" he asked in a low voice. "What's the matter?"

He held to the wall. Morley's voice sounded odd and frightened. It was almost a whisper.

"The lights," he said briefly. "The lights went out."

There was no shouting for a while. His breath went out and he found that he had been holding his breath. He released the wall with one hand and drew his handkerchief from his pocket to dry his face. As he did so he thought, The fans have stopped. The panic in Morley's voice infected him slowly. The guy who ran past, the long steps coming down hard on the floor, running like hell; the long yell in the darkness.

"That guy that ran past," he asked. "Who was that?"

"What?"

"Running like that. He'll break his fool neck."

He pushed the handkerchief back in his pocket. The heat crept up over his neck and face and the blisters of sweat stung like insects. The fans, he thought. They've stopped too. When he breathed it was like drinking hot water.

"Ran past me like a bat out of hell. It looks like a man ought to have better sense than to run around like that. Especially when he can't see where he's going."

[10]

There was a pause while Morley edged down the wall toward him. After a long time Morley said, "I should think he'd want to be able to see before he goes running around, all right."

"Reckless son of a bitch," he said. "Serve him right."

Then he said nervously, "You see how it goes? What I got to put up with? Now Mac will give me hell." His voice dropped. "If it's Hagen again, he goes. I don't give a damn if he's been here fifty years. I'm not going to nurse him any longer."

Morley did not answer. Carl brooded for a moment, bitterness with MacMahon's interference infecting him slowly; the thought of the electrician and MacMahon's defense of him robbed him of his strength. Ever since he had come into the factory, it had been his deepest source of trouble. From the very first, long before he had taken over the night shift and had only tried to find out how Hagen spent his time when he was not oiling the motors, when he had gone to Hagen in a perfectly friendly way and asked him so he would have it down on his records—from that time they had never got along and Hagen had never told him. When he complained to Mac-Mahon, MacMahon had told him to go easy, Hagen was an old hand, longer in the factory than anyone else; and it had taken Carl a long time to see that MacMahon was afraid of Hagen, afraid of the bad feeling that would grow up if he was fired. Carl could not get over it. Whenever it came up he thought he saw a kind of insolence and serenity in Hagen, as though he knew that he was safe. Whenever Carl's back was turned he knew that Hagen loafed, and bragged about his loafing, and through all the ways he got his information he knew that Hagen ridiculed him and lied about what he was doing.

Beyond them, in the darkness, there was a slight crash. A voice said mildly, "Why don't you watch where you're going?" Morley giggled, the brief chatter of nervousness bursting from him and stopping abruptly, as though he had clapped his hands loudly at the wrong time before it was over and nobody else clapped. A voice said, "Ain't there a flashlight in this God-damned laundry?" Then somebody let out a yell again and there was a loud horse laugh at the other end, up near the glue room.

"Listen," he said contemptuously. "Listen to that."

They listened. The darkness quieted down. Sometimes the yells and stray bursts of laughter broke on the silence like shots. He did not answer; their irresponsibility sickened him and he did not want to waste his voice. He tried to settle himself more comfortably to the wall. His fingers had clamped on the cross-piece. Sweat streamed down over his eyes and he could feel the tweed suit under his overalls sticking to his sweaty legs. *That's your problem,* he thought. *We pay you damn good money for just that problem.* It's easy, he said to the darkness, thinking of MacMahon sitting comfortably in his office and believing that he knew more about running the factory than anybody else in the world, giving orders and watching Miss Hazen flag her ass around the office, watching her bend over the low files, and at this very moment finishing a banquet with the officers from the destroyers stationed in the harbor over the Fourth of July.

He pulled at his pants' leg again, giving a smothered grunt of irritation.

"What?" Morley said.

"My suit. It binds me."

He lifted his leg and tried to twist around inside his overalls to get his pants more comfortable.

"I don't see how you do it," Morley whispered. "Wearing a suit under your overalls. I'm hot enough the way it is."

"I don't want to look like a tramp when I get out of here. I take off my overalls, I'm a new man. I don't suffer from the heat, only these pants bind on me. It's worth it to leave here feeling like a white man."

In a far part of the factory somebody gave a cheerful yell. Take it easy, he said. He pictured them stretched out flat on

[12]

their cans, the young punks trying to tear off a piece, and the crew taking it easy, the old women sitting down, everybody sneaking outside, glad of a chance to rest, glad of a chance to chew the rag while he took the responsibility and MacMahon beat it off to get drunk with the officers—all the grief, he thought. Nothing but grief.

How long? Christ, how long? Three hundred and fifty men at sixty cents an hour, cent a minute, three dollars and fifty cents a minute. Five minutes $= 5 \times 0 = 0, 5 \times 5 = 25$, carry two, $5 \times 3 = 15 + 2 = 17$—$17.50. Jesus Christ. Half an hour: 6×17.50: $6 \times 0 = 0, 6 \times 5 = 30, 00$; $6 \times 7 = 42 + 3 = 45$; $6 \times 1 = 6 + 4 = 10$. $105.00. Thrown away.

He cried out: "Christ! What the hell's the matter?"

"What? what?" Morley said. "What?"

"I can't stand this. What the hell happened?"

"I don't know," Morley replied. "I don't know."

What are you here for? His foot tapped restlessly on the floor. The factory seemed larger; the voices and the occasional sounds of activity came from a long way off. I can't stand this, he said silently. I can't stand to sit around and wait, always have to be doing something. Not my nature. He listened to the long swelling cry, somebody trying to test the echo, the sound bouncing back and forth under the roof.

"Bastard, I'll put a stop to that. Yelling like that. What sense? Tell me what sense is there in that?"

"Darn nut."

For a moment he wondered why he had ever agreed to take Morley when MacMahon suggested it. Someone he could depend on, MacMahon had said. A man he could trust. Now he suffered while Morley sneaked around the factory always looking as though he thought someone was going to plant a knife between his shoulders.

Morley said "I tell you I don't see why they do it. Yelling like that— Some of those fellows, by George, they yell like that every chance they get. What sense is there in that?"

[13]

I need some young guy, Carl thought. Somebody with nerve. "Yell, yell, yell," Morley said, "that's all they do." With a real interest in the work. I could say, Go tell Hagen to get them lights on or get the hell out of here. Tell him what I said. They'd stall if their mother was dying. Tell him to get the lead out. Weed them out—*the prevention of duplication and unnecessary effort and the weeding out of incompetent and careless workmen*—some young guy. Who? He thought over the names of some of the men he knew, keeping away from MacMahon's pets, Hagen and all the crowd that hung around him, the half-breed Ed Winters and the kiln man Frank Dwyer, Sorenson and the nut Gil Ahab and a bunch of new men whose names he could not keep straight—there wasn't one of them he could trust. There was Jug Bullett and Prentiss Fisher, but neither of them could keep his mouth shut, and Bullett was always running to MacMahon.

There was no decrease in the darkness; his eyes did not grow accustomed to it. He turned blindly toward the lights that had perished so suddenly, sighing with restlessness and turning his irritation against the empty globes. The rustle of voices rose like the sound of some underground river sliding through a cavern; there was a dim shuffle as the men moved casually through the dark, sure of their footing, knowing the floor around their machines as they knew their own houses even when the lights were out.

"It's that God-damned Hagen," he said bitterly. He dropped his voice to get away from the eavesdropping darkness. "What can I do if he can't keep the lights on? What chance have I got when I never know if we're going to lose an hour or two every night?"

"Shame," Morley murmured.

"My hands are tied. As long as Mac sticks up for him my hands are tied. From the very first," he said bitterly, "from the minute I came here. God knows I tried to get along with him. I went down to his shop. Let's bury the hatchet, I said. What did he do? He didn't have the decency. I don't believe in bearing a grudge, I said, I want to get along with the men. Maybe I fly off the handle, I said, I'm only human, I said, nobody's perfect. Son of a bitch just looked at me. Mouth hanging open."

He saw himself in Hagen's dim shop, putting his cards on the table, talking it over, man to man. I turned in a report, he had said frankly. All right. That's what I'm here for. I timed you. That's what I'm paid for, just like you're paid for watching the motors. We're in the same boat. I want to get along with the men. He remembered the smell of insulation; Hagen leaning over the bench, filing a bearing, his contemptuous nod; no answer.

"He's got it in for you," Morley said.

He remembered going to Hagen to try to make friends with him. He had put his cards on the table and said, I want to talk to you, man to man. I don't believe in bearing grudges. Hagen had looked at him, his large beefy face dulled and expressionless and sly, a look of cunning and insolence coming into his narrow eyes. . . . And MacMahon stood up for him. *You don't want to stir up trouble,* he had said, *Hagen's an old hand.* Bitterness seized him again. Someone passed on the far side of the conveyors. He could hear the firm decisive steps. A voice said casually, "My Old Lady wants to go to the beach. I don't give a damn where we go." Then the voices passed. He sighed and sank back against the wall.

"I wish I knew what happened to him," he said.

"Probably smoking," Morley said. "Probably he don't even know they're off."

Carl nodded. He felt a moment of wonder at the abyss of difficulties that went with his work, the millions of details he had to take care of and for which no one gave him credit, the hardships that were put in his way when MacMahon interfered or reversed his orders, and the slyness of men like Hagen going around behind his back and never coming out in the open. How

[15]

much he had to put up with! For a moment he was proud of his own endurance and strength, the kind of pride he sometimes felt when he came home late at night, exhausted because the logs had been bad or the work jammed up, and saw the tenderness and pity in his wife's features and got a sense of how dangerous and exacting his work seemed to her. He heard Morley murmuring about Hagen, but he did not pay any attention, too absorbed in his thoughts of the hardships that went with his work to listen, and sure that he knew beforehand everything Morley could say.

The factory had grown sultrier; there was no life in the air. Most of the little things that had to be done were taken care of, and now, at the head end of the mill, the hoist man had been found, and the few men who worked there were trying to get him free. It was the boom man, a large, red-faced man named Henderson, and a little Italian who tended the vats, who found him, and while one of them raced to the office to telephone for an ambulance the other collected the small crew that worked near the head end of the mill. They did not call through the factory; they were too far away from the main part of the building and too intent on the first attempts to get the hoist man free to call the whole crew to help them. Nevertheless the sense that something had happened spread through the building. The men at the far part of the factory recognized some unusual stir and movement or they were warned in a negative sense, because they did not hear the casual and relaxed sounds their experiences had led them to expect.

There was nothing strange in this. When the manager or some of the investigators from the Eastern office came to the factory it was known almost before they had stepped inside by the people in the most distant parts of the building. The spreading of a warning in these cases was a responsibility which almost everyone accepted. But the fact that it was a warning was usually disguised, for neither the worker who circulated such news or the one who received it and passed it on wanted to admit that he was disturbed because the boss or some spy had showed up at the factory. Casually, someone would remark, "The Old Man just got here," or would say, "It must be getting tough—I heard even the Old Man came down," and in a few moments almost everyone in the factory would be on his guard. In somewhat the same way, though it was a long time before the crew at the head end realized they could not free the hoist man alone, the sense that something had happened sped through the plant; there was a slow drain of workers from all over the factory to the scene of the accident, some drawn by curiosity or awakening alarm and some merely because the others were going.

Then there was another way in which the knowledge of anything unusual spread among the workers. Working there eight or ten or twelve hours a day they came to be as familiar with the factory as with their own homes, and so they became aware of minute differences that no one else could detect, and learned to recognize the fine shadings, the nuances of sounds that were only confused or terrifying to anyone who came in for the first time. They became aware too of the variations in what their experience had led them to expect; they became aware of the absence of usual impressions and this absence too had its meaning, and again without knowing why, they became restless and uncertain, the restlessness and uncertainty also communicating itself to others who did not know where it came from or why they felt it. Each worker was aware of the men on both sides of him, and when the drain of the workers toward the tideflat and the head end of the mill began, those who were left responded by being conscious of the absence of those who were ordinarily near them. A silence and intensity settled over the factory as a response to the accident, a kind of tightening up and expectancy that touched and influenced even those who did not know that the hoist man was hurt, who had never seen him, who did not even know who he was. It had its effects on the fleeting moods of the people who were waiting for the

[17]

lights to come back on, who were sitting back absorbed in their own thoughts and who did not know the reasons for the uneasiness that suddenly touched them, which forced them to look from side to side in the darkness, or led them to wander about vaguely wondering what had happened. It had its effects too on the conversations that were still going on all over the factory; the pauses between the words became longer, and the casual sentences lost their small importance. The life went out of those talks, the little opinions and anecdotes lost their meaning and the groups broke up or became silent. These silences and pauses were also contagious, coloring the thoughts, the words, the impressions of those who were less sensitive and who responded more slowly to the general uneasiness.

So the consequences of the accident circulated swiftly and silently throughout the factory, and there was no one who did not, in some way, respond to it. There were those who were irritated because some trivial conversation went on and on after they felt—although they did not know why—that it should stop, and there were some who did not know why confused and troubled thoughts drove back irresistibly on them, who could not understand why their restlessness became acute, or why the heat and the waiting suddenly seemed unendurable. So the movement toward the head end of the mill began, and even though some of the workers went in the opposite direction, out on the tideflat or into the stockroom, they revolved steadily nearer the place where the greatest crowd had gathered and where the activity seemed most intense.

Carl continued to listen to Morley's murmuring, and the bitterness with his own hard lot grew as he listened; it was true, he thought darkly, it was an easy life Hagen led, knowing that he was safe and no one could touch him. . . . "A sorehead," Morley said softly, and Carl replied, "Yes, he's a sorehead." But he was irritated with Morley too, conscious that Morley echoed him in everything and conscious that Morley could not

[18]

help him, not even in the slightest thing that demanded any courage or responsibility. There was only one thing Morley was good for, and that was writing out the order sheets and carrying them to the men; he wrote them beautifully, marking the rush orders in red ink and the numerals with a neat accountant's precision. Otherwise he was useless; the factory terrified him and he never became accustomed to the sudden screams from the saws or an abrupt roar from the hog that cut the scraps into fuel; his nerves were always on edge and at times the muscles in his cheek would flutter convulsively from some nervous disorder that had bothered him all his life. When Carl came into the factory for the first time Morley had been assigned to help him because, as timekeeper, he knew the names of the men, how much they were paid and what they did. He had stayed because Carl had not found anyone else to take his place, even though Carl himself was sometimes puzzled as to why he kept him, and Morley had never accustomed himself to the better job he had through Carl's inertia. When he hurried through the factory, carrying the sheaf of orders that made him look important and official, his eyes would dart from side to side as though he feared an ambush behind every machine, and the men, who had shortened his name to Molly years before, would hail him with merciless ridicule whenever he came in sight.

Carl frowned restlessly, trying to guess at the precious time that was lost. Time was real to him. The minutes had value and when he thought of them slipping away it was as though wealth he had in his hand was escaping; three dollars and fifty cents a minute was thrown away with intolerable extravagance and that was only part of the loss. He turned on Morley abruptly.

"Did this ever happen before?"

Morley whispered back, "What?"

"The lights. Did they ever go out before? Before I came here?"

Morley fussed around in the darkness.

"Well?" he asked sharply. "Did they?"

"I don't remember. . . . You see I was never out here. In the office we never heard. If they did go off," Morley said, "I never heard of it."

He asked impatiently, without expecting to be answered, "What do you think? What made them go?"

Morley searched for a reason. He did not know. While he tried to think of something to say, Carl listened to the stray sounds of the building, thinking of Morley as another trial that went with his job, a weakling when there were so many good men who could do it. But whom could he get? A dozen times a day he thought of it, checking over names and measuring the friendliness that some of the men showed; Sorenson, the clipperman, but he was an oldtimer too, and Carl knew that if he got anyone who had a lot of friends in the factory he would be too easy on the men, he would try to protect them when they stalled or made serious mistakes, and besides, Sorenson was Hagen's friend. There was Winters on the saw crew but he was a half-breed and though he knew the factory like a book he was morose and temperamental and there was no trusting him; there was Walt Connor but he was new to the factory and he was young and too easy-going for the kind of thing Carl wanted.

"I don't know," Morley said at last.

"It must be something."

"It's Hagen's job," Morley said, and presently Carl replied gloomily:

"The son of a bitch."

There were a few simple tricks that Morley used. Lifted out of a quiet job he had not thought of escaping, he never got over regarding Carl with awe, hanging on his words and learning his moods until he could sense what Carl was thinking, reading in small gestures or expressions a depth of meaning that no one else could see, in the way that fishermen read the

[20]

weather from faint discolorations in the sky. And as he remembered everything that Carl told him, he had a great advantage, for he had no similar importance in Carl's eyes so that Carl never remembered what he had said to Morley or, even more markedly, never remembered what Morley said to him. When Carl came out of the office after his interview with Mac-Mahon every afternoon, Morley would guess what had been said from Carl's mannerisms, and if it seemed that Carl was angry at having been bawled out, Morley could prevent this anger from being turned against himself with a few simple words; he could remind Carl of Hagen or tell him of trouble on the day shift, and these two subjects never lost their power to distract him. When Carl thought of Hagen all his bitterness came to life, and when he heard of some new trouble that the day foreman had had he was gratified with the knowledge that others had as much trouble as he did. Like a prospector searching for nuggets Morley sifted the day's happenings until he found these stories; he heard something that suggested that the day foreman was in bad with MacMahon, or that Hagen or someone else was loafing, and he saved these little episodes, in which like no one else could have seen any value, polished them, refined them and gave them to Carl when Carl was distressed. So when Carl stormed out of MacMahon's office, his self-esteem raw and swollen, and spoke harshly to Morley to revenge himself, Morley would whisper, "They burnt up a motor on the day shift!" and it would save him. There were always enough of these stories to keep Morley's pockets filled, and he gave them away generously, often when he was in no danger and did not need to buy his way out. And often Carl gave them back; often Carl told Morley the stories with which, later on, Morley would save himself. After a year of this Morley had learned that there were some subjects, such as those revolving around Hagen, which could be saved for emergencies, and these were not so much like gifts as like

[21]

charms that warded off danger when everything else had failed, or like coins which could be spent again and again.

"Probably smoking," Carl said bitterly. "Probably sitting on his can somewhere sneaking a smoke."

Someone stirred in the darkness near them. He felt a swift shock of alarm and irritation. Eavesdropping. All ears and no brains, he thought. The factory's full of them. He turned his back to the wall and faced the darkness that stretched from here to nowhere. There was no sign of light. The little windows under the roof were crusted over with pitch and dust, and the fans had stopped and the blades were stopping the light and air.

Morley said loudly, "He had trouble before you came here, two years ago I remember. . . ."

"*Shut up.*"

Morley gasped in bewilderment. Carl moved toward him and whispered, "Not so loud. You don't know who's listening."

"What?"

"You don't know who's listening."

"I don't know?" Morley stammered. "He had trouble. Two years ago. Before you came. . . ."

"Well, not so loud."

They became silent again. He could hear Morley trying to figure it out. The order sheets rustled and Morley moved nervously with his hands still on the wall. He would be looking up with a dazed uncomprehending expression, the muscles in his cheek fluttering.

Carl said, "Maybe a fuse plug blew out."

"What?"

"Maybe a fuse plug blew out."

After a moment Morley said, "Maybe."

"Why don't he fix it? Where the hell is he?"

Morley whispered, "Probably he don't even know they're out. Probably he's sneaking a smoke."

Carl said bitterly, "The son of a bitch."

[22]

He tapped his foot on the floor. Beside him Morley sighed with the release from his bewilderment.

Morley said, "Son of a bitch."

Carl said, "A fuse plug. That's what it is."

"He always crabs."

"That's why he was running."

"What?"

"That fellow," Carl said. "Came running past here. When they first went out."

There was a long silence.

"Who?" Morley said. "What?"

"Maybe that fellow who came running past," Carl explained. "Maybe he knew what broke down. Maybe he was looking for Hagen."

After a time Morley replied, "Maybe."

"When they first went out."

"The crazy fool," Morley said quickly. "Running around like that. When he can't see where he's going. I'd think he'd have better sense. . . ."

He said in a fury, "Christ! We'll be here all night."

"If it's a fuse plug," Morley said nervously, "I don't see why he don't fix it."

"How long does it take?"

"What?"

"To put in a new fuse plug?"

"I don't know," Morley said. "I. . . ."

Carl rested against the wall. He's scared, he thought. He's yellow. He's no good to me. I wouldn't have him if Mac-Mahon wasn't shoving off his deadheads on me. I don't have to stand for it.

Morley cleared his throat.

"The other night the lights went out at home," he began. "A fuse plug blew out. We got one of these electric percolators, and as soon as my wife turned it on, every blame light in the house blew out."

[23]

He was interested. He raised his voice. "Fuse plug?" he asked. "Was it a fuse plug?"

"Yes. A fuse plug blew out."

They became silent again. Presently Carl said, "That's what it is."

"Yes," Morley said. "Something was the matter with the percolator." After a moment he continued, "I never got it fixed either. Brand-new percolator, silver plated, got a big eagle on top of it. Cost me nine dollars."

He thought of Morley paying nine dollars for a percolator.

"Something was the matter with it," Morley said.

"That's what it is," Carl said. "Why don't he fix it?"

"What?"

"Hagen. What the hell's the matter with him?"

"Son of a bitch," Morley said.

"Where the hell is he?"

"Hagen?"

"Yeah. Where is he?"

"Well," Morley said, after a moment, "I really don't know. But he must know by this time. He must know they're off."

"Go find him, Morley. Find out what the hell's wrong. I'll wait here."

Morley stuttered for a few moments. The factory was quiet. Only now and then some sort of commotion spluttered meaninglessly like the chatter and blur of sparks leaping across a live wire. When the voices rose they were disembodied and unreal; the words drained off into the dark as though they did not care whether they were heard or not.

"I. . . ." Morley said. "Where do you think he'll be?"

"That's your problem, Morley. You'll just have to look for him. . . ." He added kindly, "I'll stay here. So if they come back on. . . ."

"I—" Morley said.

"Maybe he's in his shop. Look there."

Morley did not move. You paralyzed? Carl asked the dark-

[24]

ness. You crippled? He could hear the men stirring around, able to find their way in the dark, the familiar floor solid under their feet. Aloud, he asked, "You think he'll be in his shop?"

"You can't tell." After a pause Morley added cautiously, "He might very well be in his shop."

They waited.

Morley said desperately, "He's generally in his shop about this time, as a rule. Sometimes he's there and sometimes he ain't there."

"Look there first, then."

Morley skated away. His shoes on the planks made a low gnawing sound. Useless, Carl said to the wall. Afraid of his shadow. Then he heard Morley bump into the wall. There was a faint grunt, and the papers rustled as Morley waved his arms to ward off the sunken beams and timbers. The darkness pulled at his feet like quicksand. The heat increased; the hot air hurt Carl's throat; he could hear the steam pipes humming under the factory. He'll never find him, he thought, and then he thought: I can't depend on him. For anything.

"Morley!" he called.

The scraping stopped.

"Wait. I'll go with you."

Morley stirred. The scraping sound made him think of a rat gnawing on a piece of wood in the darkness. Then Morley said, unexpectedly, "Sometimes he's there and sometimes he ain't there."

"What?"

"Sometimes," Morley said.

"I might as well go with you," Carl said. "No use hanging around here."

"Might as well, I guess."

"I figure I might as well. No use hanging around here all night. Might be off an hour."

"Maybe," Morley replied.

They stayed by the wall.

[25]

"The way I look at it," Carl said, "if that son of a bitch can't keep us in light, there's no use my doing anything."

"That's the way I look at it too," Morley said. "That's what I thought from the first."

"The way I look at it, if a man hasn't got light, he's screwed. I do my part. What the hell do they expect me to do? Do everything? I told Mac, I said, you're going to have trouble, I said, and by God don't say I didn't warn you. I can smell trouble," Carl said. "I can smell it a mile off. I can smell it when the ordinary person don't know what the hell's the matter."

"That's the way I look at it," Morley replied.

They were silent for some time. There were no longer any voices near them, but they could hear the low rustle of talk in the parts of the factory where the workers were close together, a hundred casual voices rising softly in the dark.

Then Morley said suddenly, "Carl?"

"What?"

"What's the matter?"

"My pants," Carl said. "They bind me."

"I don't see how you do it," Morley said. "Two suits. Whew."

"I like to look like a white man. When I leave here I look like a white man."

"Yes, but the heat," Morley said. "It's bad enough with just one suit."

"The way I look at it, I'm clean when I come here and I'm clean when I leave. While I'm here I may be as dirty as the next one, but when I leave I can hold my head up with anybody."

"What I think is," Morley said, "I don't see how you can stand the heat."

"The heat don't bother me. It's only these pants. They bind me," Carl said.

They waited.

"These God-damn lights," Carl said. "I wonder what's wrong."

"Fuse plug," Morley replied. "Maybe it's a fuse plug."

"We can't stay here all night. The way it looks now, we'll be here all night."

"If it's a fuse plug, I don't see why he don't fix it."

"Well," Carl said, "I'll be damned if I'll wait here any longer." He waded off recklessly into the dark and immediately ran into the wall. He was swinging his arms widely and he slapped his hand against the wood. The slight pain calmed him. He held to the wood and mopped his face. Within the shell of his coveralls his clothing was drenched with sweat. At the far end of the factory someone shouted. He drew a deep breath and let them have it: *"Pipe down, you guys! What do you think this is!"*

There was a sudden silence. The exertion of shouting had left him weak. He was surprised to find himself trembling. Then the answer came back like an echo. "You kiss my ass!"

In a moment of astonishment he held the wall. He did not trust himself to speak. Well, he kept thinking, so that's it. So that's the way you feel. They're brave, he said silently, when the light's out and you can't tell who it is. He heard a little splutter of laughter not far away. "All right," he said in a stern executive voice. "That's enough." Still speaking in a stern voice he turned to Morley again. "Come on," he said. "Let's get a move on." Then somebody tripped him; something cracked across his shins and brought him down.

He fell hunched over, not knowing where he was falling, barely conscious of the blow on his shins. He thought somebody had hit him. Falling, he waited for another blow, in a panic too sudden to give him time to cry out. The darkness blazed with the shock, and his hands began to sting as they slapped the floor.

"You hurt?" Morley whispered.

There was a scuffling sound as Carl thrashed around in the

darkness. Lying on the floor, Carl straightened his legs until his feet touched the scrap iron he had fallen over. His feet studied the iron. His hands were stinging, his chest ached, and he pulled up his knees, caressing his shins that he was sure were now dented like fenders. Morley began tugging at his shoulder, saying, "Oh!" in a sympathetic voice.

"Let loose!" Carl said. The words sounded low and strangled. "Let loose, you God-damned fool!"

Morley backed away. Carl rubbed his shins while he got to his feet and danced around for a while. The tears crowded to his eyes. "You God-damned fool," he kept saying. "Oh, my God, my God." He went around and around with his hands clamped on his shins. "Oh, my God," he kept saying. "Oh, my God, my God."

Finally he gave up and leaned against the wall. When he breathed the wind whistled between his clamped teeth. "Oh, my God, my God." Gradually he stopped threshing around and his cries of pain subsided, the roaring to God sinking down and down until it became a dim little whimper. When Morley made a noise intended to imply sympathy, Carl said soundlessly, Go to hell. He did not have strength enough left to say it aloud. As his pain subsided a deep and savage hatred of Morley began storming up inside him, and the words, You useless son of a bitch, began to swing through his mind. "You God-damned fool," he said blindly. "Leaving that stuff there. Where somebody's sure to fall over it. Right in the way. Where you might know. I've told you. I've said it a dozen times. Somebody'll get hurt. What good does it do?"

"I—" Morley began.

Carl put his hands over his eyes. With his eyes closed the pain streamed up from his bruised legs, up over his knees and hips and spine until he leaned against the wall thinking he could not stand it any longer, his face twisting and the desire to talk to Morley going away. All the grief, he thought. All the grief.

"I—" Morley said again.

[28]

They were silent for quite a while. "Morley," Carl said at last, "I can't do everything here. I can't notice everything."

He spoke in a despondent voice, all his anger dissolving into a sort of patient resignation. Morley stirred uncomfortably.

"Try as I will, Morley," Carl said sadly, "there's bound to be some things I'll overlook. Try as I will."

They became silent. The factory had grown quiet after the slight commotion caused by Carl's fall.

"I—" Morley said.

"I know, Morley," Carl interrupted him. "You do your best."

I might have broken my leg, he thought.

Morley did not try again. Someone moved up out of the darkness. "Carl?" a voice asked.

"What?"

"What's wrong?"

"The lights went out," Carl said. "Didn't you notice?"

Walt Connor came up to him uncertainly. After a moment Carl recognized his voice, and a sense of relief lifted him; he was sorry he had been sarcastic. Walt was one of the college boys who had come to work during the summer vacation and stayed on instead of going back to school, a good kid, a good worker, anxious to please and anxious to learn the business. "Oh, Walt," Carl said gruffly. "I didn't recognize you."

"You hurt?" Walt asked.

"No. I just skinned my leg."

Walt said uncertainly, "I been wondering what I ought to do. . . . I just been standing here and waiting."

"I can't find Hagen," Carl said. "I don't know what's happened to him. I can't do anything till I find him. . . . This is going to raise hell with me. Mac will raise hell. We got to get that God-damned export out. And I can't do a thing till I find Hagen. Mac's going to jump all over me."

"For God's sake," Walt said. "You can't work with the lights off."

"Mac don't know it."

"He sure can't expect you to work in the dark."

"You can say it. You don't have to listen to him."

Walt laughed. He moved over toward the wall. "You take that old son of a gun too serious. He don't give a damn. It's just habit with him. Besides, he don't want to pay demurrage on the cars. Three-four days won't make any difference."

"Tell him that."

"If I had your job I would." Then Walt Connor became serious. "What are you going to do? What happened?"

"Probably just a fuse plug," Carl said lightly. "It looks like a fuse plug to me. . . . Only I can't locate Hagen and get it fixed."

Walt Connor bumped into Morley. "Hi, Molly," he said. Then he said in a low voice, "Can you hear me?" Immediately afterwards he raised his voice and said loudly to Morley, "Move over, Molly! Quit pushing me!" There was a scattered sound of movement as he scuffled with Morley.

In the darkness Carl felt Walt seize his arm. "Listen," Walt said, close to his ear. "Send them home. They're sore as hell. Blow the whistle. I'm telling you."

"Go on," Morley said. "Cut it out."

Walt Connor released his arm and began talking to Morley again. Carl stayed by the wall. His leg hurt him; the sweat poured down his face; there was a steady ringing in his ears. The sound of the men moving around and the occasional voices came from a long way off. He repeated it to himself: *Send them home. They're sore as hell.* To me, he thought dully. Telling me.

"You're nuts," Walt Connor said to Morley. "You're crazy as hell."

"Crazy," Morley said. "You're the one that's crazy."

Walt Connor began to laugh again. "Jesus, Molly," he said. "You want to watch out some big bogey man don't jump out

[30]

and booger hell out of you. . . . *What do you say?"* he said to Carl. *"I'm telling you."*

"What?" Carl whispered. *"How can I?"*

Walt Connor said loudly, "You want me to get Hagen? I can find him. Why don't you send Molly after him?"

Carl said, "Go look for him, Morley. Tell him I said I'd wait here."

Morley hesitated. "Hurry up," Carl said.

Morley skated off over the planks. The factory seemed extraordinarily quiet. They listened to the gnawing sound of Morley's shoes sliding over the rough floor. Carl said nervously, "Sure as I did the lights would come back. Mac would give me hell. . . . I got to find out what's wrong first. That Goddamned Hagen."

Walt Connor did not reply. He edged up the wall toward Carl. Presently he said, "Christ, it's hot in here." His voice was natural and unstrained. "Morley won't find him. He's probably digging around the switchboard. Morley won't know where to look." His voice dropped, *"Use your own judgment. I'm just telling you. They're sore as hell."*

"Sore?"

"What did you expect?"

"What about it?"

"Why work 'em tonight? Why raise hell? Why take a chance?"

"It's got to get out. It's overdue. It was a rush two weeks ago."

"Then why didn't they wait to put it through till after the order was out? Why give them a cut and make them work tonight on top of it? Jesus God," Walt Connor said. "MacMahon is nuts. He's nuts. What does he think we are?"

Carl drew a deep breath. In the darkness the worries swarmed around him like bats; the winged rats of worry crowded the air. He tried to think clearly, to figure out what he would say to MacMahon, fearful that if he had the whistle blown the

[31]

light would return a moment later, too late to get the crew back to work. Then he remembered the voice out of the darkness, the way they answered when he told them to be quiet. . . .

"Walt," he whispered.

"Yeah."

"*I'll wait a while. If they raise hell I'll let them go.*"

Walt did not answer.

He whispered, "*What do you think?*"

"*Why wait? Why take a chance?*"

"*Mac. He don't understand. If they come back on.*"

"All right." Then he said loudly, "I'll look for Hagen. Molly'll never find him."

"Yeah," Carl said. "I'll go with you."

"Stick around. We'll come back here."

Walt Connor began yelling for Hagen. He called his name several times. The factory seemed to suspend while everyone waited for an answer. There was no answer, and Carl asked irritably, "Where the hell is he?"

A voice answered, surprisingly near them, "He went out in the fireroom."

"The fireroom?"

"Yeah."

"I'll see you later," Walt Connor said. He slipped away from the wall like a man slipping silently into water, groping his way through the tangle of the machines, the sound of his movement disappearing in an instant. Carl dried his face with his handkerchief. His heart was pounding after his talk with Connor. Trouble, Walt Connor said. Trouble. All they needed was somebody to start it. His leg began to pain him again and he reached down and rolled up his pants leg and ran his fingertips delicately over the ruined flesh. *That's your problem.* Then all at once reassurance began to come back to him again and he said to his leg, He's a nice kid, proud of Walt for coming up to him, impressed because Walt had known someone was listening and had whispered. Reassured, he

[32]

thought that Walt exaggerated; he was only a kid and too easy-going and too easily impressed and too willing to send them home because they were beefing. There was a hum of voices and in the far reaches of the factory somebody threw some-thing—a lunch bucket—against the wall, and it rang first against the wall and then on the floor.

"*You guys!*" he yelled. "*Cut it out!*"

He thought of Morley and Walt moving through the dark, doing what he told them to do.

A voice said softly, "I'm stiff as a God-damn board."

"Tomorrow I sleep."

"Jesus! do I sleep tomorrow."

"My Old Woman wants to go to the beach," a voice said. "I don't give a damn where we go."

The voices came up all around him. The darkness seemed crowded.

"I'll be outside," a voice said. "I want to see Dippy."

"Come on outside."

Morley and Connor moving secretly through the dark. I better get hold of Jug Bullett, he thought, thinking of getting them quiet and having no trouble.

He said in an executive voice, "Where's Jug?"

There was no answer.

"Anybody seen him?"

"He's in the can."

"Tell him I'm looking for him."

The voices stopped.

"I'll be up by the kiln."

They did not reply, and he felt them trying to determine where he was and if he could hear what they had been saying.

"Tell him," he said.

Presently a voice replied, "I'll tell him."

"Be on your toes, you men," he said. "They'll be on in a minute."

There was no more talking. The silence spread like ripples going over a pool.

He felt his way along the wall, carrying the silence with him. Whenever he passed the voices stopped. Jug, Connor, Morley, Bishop, Anderson, he said to himself, repeating the names of the people he could depend on.

Morley whispered, "He ain't there." His voice came up right at his elbow, a thin whisper.

"What?"

"He ain't in his shop."

"Did you look?"

"Yeah."

"He ain't there?"

"No," Morley said. "He wasn't there when I looked."

"Son of a bitch. . . . We can't wait for him. Wait'll I tell MacMahon." He pulled at the crotch of his suit. "We got to do something. Get started, anyway."

"Yeah," Morley said.

"I can't depend on these guys."

They moved on up the wall. It became hotter as they approached the kiln. Carl walked ahead, his hand touching the wall, his feet sliding over the floor, his bruised leg warning him to be careful. He could hear Morley panting along behind him and the throb of the steam pumps in the fireroom. It was quiet; the men had moved away from the heat.

Seventeen dollars and fifty cents a minute, he thought. Maybe if they knew how much it cost they'd try to get started.

"I got to do something," he said. "I can't just sit back and leave it to somebody else the way these birds do."

"How's your leg," Morley replied.

"Like hell. It'll have to wait."

In the darkness, someone began calling him. The voice sounded half-hearted: *"Carl! Hey, Carl!"* Calling me, he thought. Now what?

"Carl!" the voice said again. It was nearer.

[34]

"Somebody's calling you," Morley suggested.

Before Carl could say anything a dim funnel of light sprayed up from a flashlight and grazed over the factory, sending back the wide waving shadows to dissolve into the darkness. All the pits and hollows, all the razor edges of the darkness disappeared; the floor became smooth and the sharp projections rounded down under the light like icicles swiftly melting. He could see. He headed toward the light, his thirsty eyes spotting all the dangers that lay in wait beside his path. The light was some distance away. Before he reached it, a voice said impatiently, "Quit horsing. Where's that God-damned efficiency expert."

"What?"

"Where's Carl?"

A few men crowded around the flashlight. Carl pushed his way through them. They looked around in surprise as he pushed them back and said, "All right fellows," in a stern executive voice. "Here I am," he said. "What do you want?"

Hagen was holding the flashlight. In the reflected light he looked enormous, his face dull and expressionless, his mouth hanging open stupidly. Efficiency expert, Carl said silently. All right. Hagen turned the light toward him.

All right, Carl said silently. Now what?

2. Hagen

WHEN the lights went out Hagen was in the saw room where his son had just started to work. One of Hagen's duties was to oil the motors, as they used a finer grade of oil than the heavier bearings on the machines and too much was at stake with them for the manager to trust anyone who might be careless or waste oil or let a motor burn up. So every night he sandwiched the oiling in when he could, trying to catch the brief periods when the machines were stopped so that he would not hold up the work. In the saw room he waited until they changed the panel size and had to re-set the saws, and then, while Winters bent over the shaft, moving the saw along the steel rule, Hagen climbed over the guard to the motor and let the rich oil drain into the cup on the bearing. He ran his fingers over the bearing and motor to feel its heat.

His son stood back and waited, watching Winters and trying to figure out what he was doing. All around them the saws were ringing; the bright panels spurted out under the rolls and the strips of waste fell into the conveyor. Under the hard light the men worked intently, the sawyers feeding the panels swiftly into the rolls, never taking time to do more than glance from the loads of panels to the ones they shoved into the rolls, while at the other end of each machine the off-bearer lifted them as they poured out, dropped them on the trucks in neat piles and reached up for another. The piercing *swing swing swing* of the saws shook the air and the nutlike smell of fresh sawdust rose in the heat. The pipes that sucked the sawdust

[36]

to the fireroom trembled and crackled as the grains beat against the metal. Hagen could see that they were far behind; the trucks of wood waiting to be sawed filled the saw room and every few minutes a man came from the grading room and pushed out one of the loaded trucks. Hagen's boy had stepped back and wiped the sweat off his face when Winters stopped to change the dimensions of the panels they were cutting. He gave a brief, embarrassed look at his father and then turned to study Winters' involved efforts again.

Hagen finished the oiling and stepped back beside Winters. The Indian was sweating; his black hair looked oiled and was plastered to his head with sweat. There were large circles of sweat at each side of his shirt and the fine powdered dust that was too light to be drawn off by the fans had settled in a frost-like coat over his clothing and hair. He gave a brief grunt of acknowledgment when Hagen stepped beside him. He was trying to re-set the saws to trim the panels down to fourteen and one-eighth inches on some fresh order, and he forced the saw along its shaft, tapping it with the heel of his palm as he watched the steel rule, easing it just fourteen and a quarter and then back when he urged it too far, his movements quick and sure.

"Pounding you on the tail," Hagen said.

Winters gave a brief nod. "Christ."

"How's the wife?"

Winters set the saw where he wanted it, stepped back and started the motor. He sent a panel through, shut off the motor and came around to measure it. It was short. He tossed it into the conveyor. While he measured it he said, "She's no better." He glanced up at the waiting panels and said bitterly, "Look at that. We'll never get out of here." Then when he climbed back to set the saw he grinned toward Johnny standing uncertainly beside the guard. "The kid's all right," he said. "He's been working like an oldtimer."

Hagen looked at his son as if he had not seen him before.

"You getting the idea of it?" he asked.

Johnny nodded in embarrassment. "Yeah, I guess so," he said. "I guess. . . ."

His overalls were too large for him. The waist line came at his hips. His round face was flushed and tired and his blond hair rose straight up over his forehead; sweat and sawdust streaked his cheeks and there were heavy circles under his eyes.

Winters set the saw again. "I will say he got a God-damn good week to begin on," Winters said. "It's a madhouse; it's a madhouse." He glanced up at Hagen and jerked his head toward Johnny. "That's a man's job," he said contemptuously. "That ain't no kid's job. That's too God-damn heavy when we got this stuff."

Hagen looked uncomfortable. He was still holding the two oil cans and looking around the saw room to see if another machine was stopping. For a moment he did not reply; then he said uneasily, "I know it is. But by God, Ed, I just can't help myself. . . . I'm in a hell of a hole. . . ."

The Indian interrupted. "I didn't mean that. You don't have to tell me. That ain't what I meant. But they ought to give us some help. God Almighty. If we haven't got half the crew we used to have in here. . . ." He got tangled up trying to explain to Hagen that he had not meant that Johnny was too young to be working, trying to make it clear that he was kicking about the way they were loading work on kids; but there was no relief for Hagen, the shame and bitterness stayed on his face and all that Winters said only dug more deeply into the sore. Winters bent over the rule and moved the saw back, his features expressionless again. One of the off-bearers shouted *"All set!"* and a man appeared from the grading room, wheeling the loaded truck away and putting an empty one in its place while the off-bearer timed his movements to drop the next load on the empty truck.

When Winters began tightening the saw in place Hagen said slowly, "A year ago I figured I'd have him in school. Now

[38]

I got my daughter and her two kids living with me. Now we got word my oldest daughter's husband's out of work."

Winters said, "It's hell, ain't it?"

Hagen jerked his head toward the boy. "It's hell for him."

Winters stepped back and ran another panel through. This time it was right. In a moment he was back and the saw was running steadily. Winters fed the panels into it with swift, accurate movements, like a man dealing a deck of cards, and they whipped through the machine to where Johnny stood waiting, and catching them as they came out. There was a stream of bright wood from one truck to the other; the panels followed one another with scarcely a break between them and the air trembled with the noise of the saws. The sweat began to stream down Johnny's face as he stooped and straightened methodically. For a moment Hagen watched him, seeing the weariness and uncertainty so clearly written on his son's features, the embarrassed awareness he showed at his father's presence and the eagerness with which he tried to show himself dexterous and capable. "No," Hagen wanted to say, "don't try so hard." But he said nothing, only wiping the oil carefully from his hands, staring at the roaring machine and glancing again at Winters who was already lost to everything else in his effort to keep up with it. The Indian's face was set and his eyes were half closed under the bright hanging light. The effort to keep up with the racing saws drove everything else out of his mind: thought of his wife, who was dying, his concern because Hagen had misunderstood him and his desire to ease the work of his off-bearer; there was nothing left for him now but the straight-edge against which he lined the panels and the rolls that drew them in. Gradually his features emptied of any life, only his swiftly moving hands and his intent eyes revealing the spirit in him.

Suddenly the lights went out. The saws stopped abruptly, a terrible roar rising as the teeth choked against the wood. Hagen had time to think of how hard that sudden stopping was on the bearings and shafts before he raced through the dark factory to his shop. There he grabbed a flashlight and ran outside to the fireroom. It was on another circuit and if it was dark too, he'd be sure it was a break outside the factory. Outside it was dark, but he could see there was still light in town by the light on the smoke that hung over the streets. There was the string of lights on the harbor and no signs of light on the tideflat. He could see the conveyor that led up to the fuel bin and the cars in the parking strip and the empties on the siding. The motors were whining down to silence.

Norfolk and Western, he read on a box car. O.K. for Grain.

The flashlight flickered with each step. He could hear the machines slowing down, the switches being cut. Somebody yelled. The fireroom too was dark, and he fought down a growing uneasiness, thinking of Carl and knowing that Carl would blame him. The blower on the roof was stopping; the fans were stopping, the sawdust was settling and clogging the pipes. The ground around the fireroom was red with the re-flected fire from inside. There was no wind; the steam floated straight up. All at once a rocket from one of the boats in the harbor lifted over town, sailed up and up and exploded against the low clouds.

He hurried to the office on the chance that someone might be there, someone who could call the power house to find out what had happened. In an instant he foresaw that Carl would find some way to twist this accident to discredit him, and with-out a conscious plan, with increasing anxiety, he began to think of his defense. The office was set across the track from the factory, a neat little colonial dwelling with a square patch of lawn around it. Smoke from the factory had laid a heavy smudge on the white paint and in daylight the ragged spots of cinder were apparent, but now the building looked bright and clean, the most conspicuous object on the tideflat. Hagen hurried toward it, thinking of MacMahon's insisting on the little patch of grass under his windows, trying to think of some way to protect himself, noting that the grass looked gray under the flashlight. . . . The door was locked. He said "Hell," and after a moment went back to the track to call the fireman. Presently Mike appeared at the opening on the second floor of the fireroom, his body red with the light from the fires.

"What you want?"

"You seen Carl?"

"No." Then Mike asked, "Is that you, Hagen?"

"Yeah."

"Where is it?"

"Power house. It ain't here."

Mike raised his voice and yelled out toward the flashlight. "Had I better pull my fires? How long'll we be down?"

"I don't know yet. I got to call the power house. I got to find Carl so I can get a key to the office. . . . You better wait. Till we find out how long it'll be."

"I got all kinds of steam."

"You better wait."

There was a moment of silence. Then Mike called, "Hagen?"

"Yeah?"

"Can you come here a minute?"

He said "Hell," under his breath, and hurried toward the fireroom. Mike climbed down the ladder to meet him. Inside the fireroom the fireman's two helpers were sitting down close to the open door to get away from the heat. They were both stripped to the waist and their faces were caked with sweat and dust. When Hagen came in the older helper nodded to him and then leaned forward, his arms resting on his knees, his naked back toward the fire. He sat motionless, his eyes fixed on the concrete floor, conserving his energy now that he could. The other helper, Waino, a Finnish boy, greeted Hagen when he came in and questioned him with his eyes, excited at something unusual happening and trying to guess the reason for what Hagen and the fireman did. He had the high cheek bones and the clear skin of the Finns; he was part of a large colony of them that had settled on the harbor. His new work could not exhaust him; even on the bad nights when the fuel was low and they had to feed the fires by hand from the fuel bin he drove himself carelessly and spent the time when they were caught up pumping Mike of everything there was to learn about the fireroom, studying the complex arrangements of valves and pipes and trying to discover their order. The little fireman was a cripple, a grouchy, self-conscious man, weakened with shame over his lameness and his belief that his wife was unfaithful to him; but he knew the fireroom and what he could expect of his boilers, and he had had an involved and exciting life. He had fought in the Boer War and had lived in Australia and India, and when he unbent he would go on about this, or give some elaborate proof that he had been where he claimed—naming the streets of Sydney, for example, while Waino sat back and tried to visualize the reality behind his words. Hagen spoke to them when he came in, calling out the senseless words that served as a sort of formal salutation: "Hiyah," he said. "——— the dog, eh?" He spoke swiftly, breathing heavily from having hurried, and when he and Mike talked their voices were sharp and impatient, the words of people who took everything for granted except the essential task.

"Both fires are way up," Mike said. He lifted a hook that was hanging by the wall and limped rapidly across the fireroom to open the door of one of the fire boxes. The heat and light streamed out against the bricks. "See?" he said. He replaced the hook, his dark wizened face still twisted with the heat that had poured out when he opened the door of the fire box. He leaned against the wall, keeping his weight off his bad leg, and stared at Hagen questioningly.

"Well?"

"If I pull them and the lights come on, he'll murder me. . . . I ought to pull them. It'll be getting hot as oh Jesus in there."

Hagen said, "Look at me. If I stay in my shop he'll say I was loafing. If I don't, he'll say he couldn't find me."

Mike grinned. "He'll say it anyway."

"I know he will. But I don't want to give him any excuse."

"Look," Mike said. "I got to protect myself. Suppose the sprinklers blow. If they do he'll pin it on me. If they do I might as well go down the road."

"If you pull your fires and the lights come on you might just as well go down the road."

"Well?"

"Protect yourself!" Hagen said sharply. "Make him tell you to pull your fires!"

The Finnish boy was watching them uncertainly, his eyes darting from one to the other as he tried to figure out what they were talking about.

"I cut off the kiln," Mike said. "I turned it all in the vats. . . . Even so it'll be getting hot if the fans are off for long. He's been pounding us on the tail all night and we've had both fires way up."

"He can make trouble," Hagen said. "I didn't know one man could make so damn much trouble." Then he said to the new helper, "You know Carl?"

"Yeah."

"Listen, Waino," Mike said. "We ought to pull the fires. See? It'll be getting hot as hell in there—it's hot anyway and now the fans have stopped. But if I pull the fires and the lights come right on, Carl'll raise hell with me. You see? There won't be any steam. So go find him and ask him what I should do. Tell him the sprinklers may blow."

Hagen said, "He won't know what that is."

"Who? Waino?"

"Carl."

Mike limped across the fireroom and pointed to one of the sprinklers near the fuel bin. "Fire prevention," he said. "You see? These little bastards melt when it gets too hot. But now it's getting so hot they may pop off anyway. Fans off; the thermometer must be going up like a God-damn elevator . . . I don't think there's a chance of it. But I got to protect myself in case. You see?"

Waino nodded.

"Go in this end," Hagen said. "I'll go around the other end. Follow right under the conveyor—there's a ladder there where the conveyor comes out. When you get inside holler for him. Somebody'll know where he is."

Waino pulled on his sweater and started toward the door. As he disappeared Mike limped across the fireroom and called after him.

"Waino!"

"Yeah?"

"If he tells you to cut off the sprinkler system, tell him he can't do it without written permission from the insurance company. You understand? There's some kind of a tie-up with the insurance company; the rate drops when they put in the sprinklers. You got it?"

Waino called back, "I'll tell him."

Hagen started back toward the main entrance of the factory. He said to Mike, "If he shows up here, tell him to call up the power house and find out how long we'll be down. Tell him I'm looking for him."

"Yeah," Mike said. He motioned toward the fires. "All that heat," he said, "going to waste." He turned to the darkness again. "Waino!"

"Yeah?"

"*If he says for me to use my own judgment, tell him in that case I'll pull the fires. Make sure somebody else hears you say it!*"

"All right."

Hagen walked toward the main entrance of the factory. The funnel of light from the flashlight washed over the packed cinders around the fireroom. When he came near the factory somebody standing behind one of the cars lit a cigarette. The light flared for an instant before the flame was hurriedly snapped out. Right over the main entrance of the factory there was a sign that read: *Carrying cigarettes, pipes or matches anywhere on these premises will be punishable by instant discharge.*

"Watch it," Hagen said. "He'll be out here in a minute."

Reckless bastard, he thought. These guys never learn. The flashlight swung; as he walked through the stockroom the light washed up on the walls and ebbed swiftly back.

He yelled at the darkness, "Carl been here?"

"No." Then somebody said, "Thank God."

Somebody else said, "How long they be off?"

"I don't know yet."

A voice said, "Leave 'em off, Hagen. Give us a rest."

He called back, "Tell him I'm looking for him."

"Tell him hell." He recognized Bullett's voice and wondered: What's he doing out here?

"No; tell him," he said sharply. "Tell him to call the power house and find out how long we'll be down. I got to find him so I can get his key—I can't get in the office to phone."

Jug Bullett asked in his heavy voice, "Who you want to phone to, Hagen?"

He replied, "What are you doing out here?"

"Listening to these guys crab. It puts me to sleep."

He frowned at the weak wash of light from the flashlight, disturbed at the thought of Bullett's snooping around, knowing he carried everything to Carl and MacMahon, even a lot that wasn't true. Then he said, "I got to call the power house. Tell Carl Mike's got to see him."

The piles of doors in the stockroom narrowed the light. It was cooler than in the factory and the voices echoed in the airy spaces under the roof. He hurried on, occasionally calling for Carl, still disturbed at the thought of Bullett's listening in while the men of the loading crew said innocently what they thought and he took it down. The voices rose up from the shadows as he passed.

"How long they be off?"

He answered them hurriedly, "Don't know yet," and asked in turn, "Seen Carl?"

"He ain't been here."

At the far end of the stockroom Winters caught up with him, calling from behind him in a low urgent voice, calling his name and giving a brief hissing whistle through his teeth to stop him. Sweat poured down his thin face; his black hair was plastered to his forehead. Hagen let his finger slip from the switch on the flashlight, and they stood in the darkness for a moment.

"Listen," Winters said.

"Yeah?"

"Nuts, huh?" Winters said. "What a break."

"You seen him?"

"No."

"I'm protected. It ain't in the factory."

Winters grunted skeptically. "He'll pin it on you."

"If I let him. . . . I can't get in the office. He's got the key. Somebody's got to call the power house." They walked on slowly, Hagen leaving the flashlight off. "That's the hell of it. He can hang us up here half an hour. Then lay it on me. I figure maybe I can tie his hands. Mike's looking for him— sent his new helper out. Fifty guys will know he's a liar if he says I wasn't in the plant."

"He'll say it anyway."

"Maybe."

They were silent. Then Winters said blindly, "The son of a bitch. Ah, the son of a bitch."

The kids in the dark factory were yelling. The crew from the stockroom swarmed around the girls; he could hear the shrill cheerful laughing, the brief cries as the girls ran or were touched. I'll be here all night, he thought, and hell to pay at home. "Watch it," he said, and switched on the light for a

[46]

moment, revealing a truckload of doors standing in the alley, cutting the light again as they went around it.

Winters said, "We're here for nothing. The stock's no good. We haven't done enough to pay for the logs. We're working our heads off for nothing. That's why I know he'll pin it on you. He'll have to pin it on somebody and this has played in his hands."

Somebody said, "How long we be down?"

"I don't know yet. Carl been around?"

"Not up here."

"He must have been sneaking a smoke."

"Maybe he's out on the log deck."

"You see," Winters asked. "You see what I mean?"

"Yeah. I think you're right."

"What are you going to do?"

He said grimly, "I yelled all over the tail end for him. Now I'll yell all over up here. What else can I do? He'll try to say I was on my can. He can't say it if everybody in the factory knows I wasn't."

He was touched that Winters had come after him. For a moment he thought of Winters' troubles, his sick wife and the nervousness that sometimes showed on his dark face, and then he thought the politics seemed strange to Winters, and he said, "I'm used to it. You get used to it." He turned the light again on the floor and the piles of doors. The stench from the glue room struck them as they went into the main factory. He wanted to switch off the flashlight, knowing that if they ran into Carl the first thing Carl would do would be to ask Winters why he was so far from where he worked—not in so many words, but by asking Winters if something had broken down in the saw room or by telling him that he expected the lights would be on any moment.

"I hate that son of a bitch," Winters said quietly. "He caused me enough misery."

He's in hell, he thought, responding to Winters bitterness.

He's in hell. He ran the light across the open spaces of the glue room. The white faces turned inquiringly. *"Has anybody seen Carl? I been looking all over hell for him." He ain't been here.*

Hagen was stirred at Winters' voice. He ditched the light for a moment. "Winters, I hate his guts. He's been trying to get me out of here ever since he's been in here. He's got me in every kind of trouble he could think of. Now he's put that kid of mine on every dirty job in the mill. . . . But don't let him get you down. He's a little bastard. Mac's riding him and somebody else is riding Mac. I've seen twenty guys like Carl here since I been here and two-three guys in Mac's job."

"Yeah," Winters said. "That's a big help."

"He don't amount to nothing."

The heat rolled out from the kilns; the fans were stopped, the heavy blades blocking the air.

Winters said, "I'm getting twenty bucks a week. I been cut three times since he's been here. Now he comes around sticking that God-damn stop watch against the back of my neck like a gun."

In hell, he thought. He said softly, "Don't tell me. But take it easy. Don't let him ride you."

"How can a man live on it? I still owe them a hundred and twenty and they take out ten dollars a month and I can't get a place to live in for less than twenty."

Hell.

The girls yelled *Don't! Don't! Don't!* the sharp cries broken with laughing and the scuffling in the darkness. *Hagen! How long we been down!* Oh, Christ! *I don't know!* Winters leaned against the truckload of doors, his dark Indian face fixed and expressionless.

"Don't tell me," Hagen repeated. He looked around impatiently, thinking that he had to locate Carl or break in the office, and Winters saw the thought before he moved; asked, "You want me to look for him?"

[48]

"No. He'll see the light. Sooner or later."

"He'll pin it on you."

Hagen grinned, "He'll try to."

How long?

Winters said heavily, "I'm going outside. It's getting too hot in here."

"Watch yourself. I run into Jug way out in the stockroom, getting his earful." Winters nodded briefly, his set face unrelaxing. Hagen watched him go, saw the jerky, awkward walk before he left the circle of light. In hell, he thought. He don't know what he's doing.

Hagen walked toward the kilns. Here silence; the heat had driven them away. Here when the lights went out a hundred men moved to press the switches that stopped their motors, finding them at once in spite of the dark, moved without orders to cut the switches so when the power came back the load would not be too heavy. A hundred men moved without orders, checking the thousands of dangers, the thousands of dangers no foreman could ever see, had ever heard of, could not even imagine. Here Hagen walked, the flashlight swinging loosely at his side, the gray light washing across the floor. He did not need it. He knew the factory; he could find his way around it in the dark. The minute rises in the floor were blue-printed in his mind, and the narrow trails between the machines were so much a part of his way of thinking that he could not have forgotten them, even if he had wanted to.

The heat increased. Great fans drew off the hot air from the driers, and now with their stopping the smoke and steam from the drying wood rolled back into the factory. There was a faint pulse beat of the pumps in the fireroom, sounding through the pipes under the factory, the drain of hot water under the kiln, the drone of exhaust steam. But there was a rustle of movements as the workers formed into groups or moved through the factory, and the sounds that were hidden when the machines were running soared up strong and full, in the way that foot-

[49]

steps that are inaudible in a crowded street seem loud and strange in the middle of the night. There was a stir of talk, no louder than the pull of some slow river at its banks, or the rustle of telephone wires along a country road. All over, in the factory and on the tideflat around the factory, the groups formed and broke up and formed again, and the murmur of talk rose in its slow patient sentences, in those tiny distilled drops of experience given in words so rich and so varied and inadequate. Hagen could hear it. These were the sounds, this low murmur and the steady shuffling and re-grouping, that he expected to hear when a breakdown stopped work, and although he did not think of it consciously, he would have known if anything unusual was happening in the factory anywhere near him; there would have been some sort of commotion, some new and unusual cluster of sounds that did not fit into the patterns of his experience.

Five minutes had passed. No more. He asked the few men he met if they had seen Carl, and then walked on, feeling himself protected as more and more knew of his search. There was nothing else he could do. He passed the men lying down beside their machines, trying to capture the moment's rest before it passed, and others moving toward the cool air of the tideflat, and small groups that had gathered naturally when the lights went out, talking things over while they had a chance. Sometimes he lifted the light in the hope that Carl would see it, and occasionally he called out for him, reluctantly, hating to be doing Carl's work as well as his own. The meeting with Winters oppressed him, and he could not throw off the dull sense of hopelessness that gripped him when he thought of Winters' bitterness, his wife sweating and dying in the hospital, the baby dead, the nervousness and strain of Winters' speech. The misery weighed him down, blinded him to the people who called to him or answered his questions. He'll crack, he thought, he won't be able to stand it; and he tried to think of what he ought to do.

[50]

A girl came running up behind him, called to him—
Hagen!—in a sharp urgent voice.

He recognized her as she came into the light: Ellen Turner,
recognizing her by the band she always wore around her forehead and then by her voice.

"Yeah?"

"How long will we be down?"

"I don't know." She was watching him intently, her features
pulled out of shape by her anxiety, her mouth pressed tightly
shut.

"I don't know yet."

"Ten minutes—will they be off ten minutes?"

Why? He turned the light full on her, her intensity sur-
prising, faintly alarming him. The ribbon pulled tight across
her hair was covered with flakes of sawdust. There were drops
of sweat on her white face; her eyes were hollow and sleepless.

"What's wrong?"

She said nervously, "You think? Ten minutes?"

"I don't know yet. It's at the power house." The light on
her face made her nervous. He turned it to the floor. "What's
the matter, Ellen?"

"Marie."

"Marie?"

"Yeah," Ellen said. "She ought to go home; she's sick; she
can't hardly stand up. . . . So I thought if they'd be off she
could go home, if they'd be off long enough. Maybe somebody
could take her to the bus line. . . ." Her voice trailed off
indecisively. He thought of Marie, vaguely remembering that
he hadn't seen her in the factory, wondering at Ellen's tense
voice.

Scared of me, he thought.

"If it was ten minutes," Ellen said.

"Why didn't she just punch out? Why'd she show up?"

"Carl said if we didn't come tonight he'd pull our cards.
He'll think she just wants to get off because it's tonight."

[51]

He nodded. Ellen watched him, almost pleading with him to tell her the lights would be off a long time. He hesitated. "I don't know. They may come on any minute. If I can ever find Carl I'll find out." He turned to roar at the darkness. *"Carl! Where the hell's that God-damned foreman?"*

"Hagen," Ellen said.

"Yeah."

"What shall I do?"

"That old son of a bitch," Hagen said. "He can make more trouble. . . ." He drew his hand over his face. Sweat and corruption. Doing his work, he thought. Cleaning up after him. The key to the office, Mike waiting, the crew standing around, and if any sane man had charge he'd blow the whistle, pull the fires and drain off the heat and send them home to get some sleep.

"He made a rule," Ellen said. "He was afraid nobody would show up tonight. And he wants to fire her anyway."

Someone barged in out of the shadow. "I lost my nerve," Frankie Dwyer said. "I climbed up there to cut the heat to the drier and I'm a son of a bitch if I didn't lose my nerve. Look at my hands."

He thrust his hands, palm out, into the ray of the flashlight. The skin was reddened; there was a white raised blister across each palm.

"Jesus," Hagen said.

"I climbed up on that plank, I thought I was a hundred feet off the ground. I was shaking like a God-damn leaf. You think it's hot down here. You ought to climb up there. I had to feel for the valve and when I found it I half burnt my hands off trying to close it," Frankie Dwyer said.

"Mike turned all the steam to the vats."

"Yeah, I know. But I figured I ought to cut it anyway. The heat was way up before they went off. But look at them hands," Frankie Dwyer said. "You ever see anything like it? I tell you, I was so shaky by the time I found the valve I didn't

[52]

feel how hot it was. It don't seem like anything to climb up there when it's light but you'd think it was ten stories up when you can't see the bottom and it's as hot as it is now."

"Hagen," Ellen said.

"Won't he find out she's gone?" Hagen asked. "Even if she sneaks out? Even if they're off half an hour?"

"I can punch her card," Ellen said nervously. "We can say she's in the toilet if he comes by and asks where she is."

Frankie Dwyer edged in, pulled by their low voices. Somebody yelled, *"Hagen! How long? I got time to sneak a smoke?"* He yelled back, *"I don't know yet!"*

Frankie said, "What's the matter?"

"Marie's sick," Hagen explained. "Carl don't believe her. He thinks she just wants to get off because it's the Fourth. So Ellen wants to sneak her out and punch her card herself."

"She can't hardly stand up," Ellen said. "If I can't get anybody to take her to the bus it'd be better for her to walk than wait here."

"To hell with him," Frankie said. "Tell her to go ahead."

"Suppose he comes snooping around."

"He'll be tied up when they come back on. You see? If he does come around, tell him I'm looking for him. Then when he comes to find out what it is I'll tell him something's gone haywire—I'll think of something, I'll keep him busy. You see?"

Ellen nodded. She glanced indecisively at Hagen and then at Frankie, at the long jaw with its stubble of reddish beard, the eyes permanently narrowed because of the heat where he worked.

"Yeah," Hagen said. "Go ahead."

"All right."

She started away. Frankie stepped after her. "Listen, Ellen," he said. "Don't punch her card yourself. Get somebody else to do it. If he thinks she's sneaked out he's liable to be watching you."

He came back. Hagen mopped his face dry and tried to get a deep breath. The factory had grown less noisy; the girls had quieted down; there was only an occasional loud burst of talking from the cooler head end. "He won't notice," Frankie said. "If they do come on he'll be so rattled he won't know his —— from a hole in the ground."

"Molly'll know it."

"Somebody ought to konk that son of a bitch."

"I run into Jug way out in the stockroom getting his earful."

"Bastard," Frankie Dwyer said. "Somebody ought to konk him."

"Somebody told them the guys were taking motor oil and using it for their cars," Hagen said. "I wish I knew who that was." Frankie did not say anything for a moment. The oil for the motors was kept in a fire-proof storeroom that was locked with a padlock for which only the oilers had the key. But years before, when some of the men had been able to buy second-hand cars, the oilers had made duplicate keys and given them to the crew so the men could get oil for their cars. For years they had gotten oil that way and no one except the workers had known it. Presently Frankie asked, "Who you think?"

"I don't know . . . Carl's snooped around. He's looking for things like that. It gives him something to report."

"Jug's been sucking around him."

"I don't believe Jug would do it . . . "

"Bastard," Frankie said. *"Hagen!"* somebody yelled. *"You looking for Carl?"*

"Yeah!"

"He's down toward the log deck!"

"My hands are like boils," Frankie said. "Has Mike pulled his fires?"

"No. He's trying to locate Carl. So he'll be protected if the lights come on."

[54]

"Look, Hagen," Frankie said. "I'll be outside; I'm going to grab a smoke. If you want me. Right outside the kiln."

He nodded and headed toward the log deck, past the frozen machines and the hot steam pipes and the dead tubes of wires that dropped down the walls to the motors. Trouble followed him: Mike trying to protect himself and Winters sinking into quicksand debt with his wife dying and his kid dead and stumbling around the dark factory like a drunk. You can't talk to anybody without getting a load of trouble, he thought; and then he thought, here I am, the world's prize, loading myself with everybody's grief and doing his work and my own too.

"*Carl!*" he yelled. "*Hey, Carl!*"

Where is that son of a bitch?

A squeaky voice answered him, out of the dark, "*Yoo-hoo. Here I am!*"

There was a sputter of laughter. The men began moving toward the light. He said impatiently, "Quit horsing. Where's that God-damned efficiency expert?"

Then he saw him behind the circle of faces.

The men stepped aside. Carl did not like to see them hanging around with nothing to do. After he had turned around and given them a dirty look he motioned for Hagen to step aside and talk to him alone. Some time passed before Hagen understood what was wanted; he could not imagine that Carl wanted to get away from the men. He watched Carl in perplexity while Carl edged toward the darkness, jerked his head sideways, and made grimaces and motions which he thought were suggestive. After Carl said, "Step over here, Hagen," the electrician got the idea. He led the way across a plank bridge over the conveyor.

Hagen walked slowly, with a curious lumbering sideways motion. Carl clenched his fists with impatience at the slow dray-horse pace. He became aware that some of the men were following them.

"All right!" he shouted. "You fellows stay where you are.

[55]

They'll be on in a minute. Don't get excited." Hagen stopped when Carl started talking. He turned the flashlight back against the men. In the watery light their faces looked strange and pale, and although there were only a few of them it seemed that everybody who worked in the factory was there, out of the light, behind the first pale figures. Carl had shouted impatiently, but now his voice dropped and he smiled. "All right, fellows," he said. "There's no use running around." Morley had dropped back with the others. "Come on, Morley," Carl said, in a natural tone of voice.

They went on. The light dropped at Hagen's feet, spread across the floor and dropped back as he moved, wavering and unsteady, outlining shapes and letting them sink back into the darkness. Machines and tables came up for a moment, lived at the dim edges of the light and disappeared soundlessly as if sinking into water that closed over them without a ripple. Occasionally they heard voices and the pounding of the steam pipes that trembled under their hard inner weight.

Hagen said, "I've checked it all the way through. We're all right. You better call the power house."

"By God," Carl replied. "You can't do anything around here without fifty people trying to horn in. I've worked with some nosey crews, but I'm a son of a bitch if I've ever worked in a place where everybody was always hanging around, hanging around, the way they do here. What good does that do? God damn," he said, "I can't see it."

Morley crowded up. Hagen reached over and pressed the switch of a motor beside them. There was a little hollow throb in the switch box. "It's dead," Hagen said. He pressed it several times. Each time there was the same dead throb.

When he stopped, Carl leaned over and pressed the switch. There was another dead throb.

Carl looked at Hagen. He shook his head from side to side, responsibility creasing his forehead and deepening his voice. "God," he said. "I hate to have this happen."

Morley too stared at the floor. Wrinkles appeared in his forehead; the muscles in his cheek began to twitch. The flashlight was now directed toward his feet, and as he stared at the floor he thought that his shoes looked funny and dead, like two brown rocks in the pool of light. The floor here was well laid, and the oil that had drained from the machine had saturated the floor. Where the operator of the machine stood, the planks were polished like a dance floor, the oil bringing out the grain in the wood. Morley moved his shoes over the floor to feel how slippery it was. "Gosh," he murmured.

He reached over and pressed the switch. There was a dull answering throb.

"It's all right, Morley," Carl said in a businesslike voice. "It's dead all right."

Morley straightened self-consciously, wiping his fingers against his trousers. "Dead," he repeated. "Sure is dead."

For a time nothing more was said, and Carl resumed his scrutiny of the floor, beating his fist against the palm of his hand. He paced back and forth, murmuring "Fuse?" somewhat apologetically, and glancing at Hagen. He was afraid to say any more, because he was afraid that it might not be the fuse plug, and in that case the electrician would think he did not know what was wrong. As Hagen's expression did not change, Carl went on hastily, "Reason I ask. A fellow ran past us. I thought maybe." Still Hagen made no response, his features not even indicating that he had heard. "It's what I get," Carl ended. "All the grief."

The flashlight was directed toward his legs. He bent down and rolled up his trousers. "Another thing," he said quickly. "I nearly broke my neck." He ran his fingers over the blue dent in his flesh. The skin had not been broken, but the blue spaces of the bruise were spreading. Squeezing the skin gently, Carl located the far margins of the places that hurt. He held his leg up to the light, balancing on one foot, while Hagen brought the light down so he could see more clearly.

[57]

"You ought to put something on it," Morley murmured.

Presently Carl rolled down his trouser leg. He tested his leg cautiously, barely putting his weight on it, and flinching as he did so. Then he asked, "How long do you think we'll be down?"

"I don't know. You better call the power house."

"Power house!" Carl cried. "Power house!" He stared at Hagen in dismay. Hagen continued to run his hand over his face. "Those fellows," Carl said. "They never tell you anything."

"There's nothing we can do."

Carl gave him a sharp look. "We *can* do something," he said. "We've *got* to do something." The frown reappeared on Carl's forehead, and he began smashing his fist against the palm of his hand as he paced back and forth. When he spoke again his voice had a slight edge of accusation. "You're sure it's not here," he said. Hagen did not answer him. "What I mean is," Carl went on, "you're sure no power is reaching us. Because if none is there's nothing we can do."

Hagen nodded.

"Damn," Carl said. "They won't tell me anything."

The electrician said, "You better call them and tell them the lights are out. Anyway."

"Yes," Carl said. "I suppose I better."

They waited.

"Can you get in the office?" Hagen asked. "Have you got a key?"

The telephone was in the office. Carl began searching absently through his pockets. He knew that he had a key somewhere. Someone was hurrying toward them. A voice said weakly, *Hey!* and *Wait!* Hagen turned the light back toward the voice. At the far reach of the light they could see a man moving around the machines.

Carl waited until he came nearer. Then he said to Morley, "See what he wants."

The fireman's helper came into the light.

He was breathing heavily and his clothes were plastered to him with sweat. For a moment, when he came into the light, he looked around in bewilderment, turning away from the flashlight Hagen directed toward him to the small group of men.

Morley asked politely, "What do you want?"

"The foreman?" Waino asked.

Morley gestured toward Carl.

Waino said rapidly, "Mike wants to know if you want him to pull his fires. He says he ought to know how long we'll be down because it's getting so hot he's afraid the sprinklers'll blow and he said to ask you what you wanted him to do."

Carl stared at him. Then he said quietly, "What in Jesus' name are you talking about?"

Waino flushed. Hagen started to interrupt, but Waino started over again, talking very rapidly, Carl's incomprehension bewildering him and making him wonder if he had the message right. His lips drew back from his teeth in an expression of acute discomfort and the red climbed up his face, over his high cheek bones, even to his forehead. "So he's afraid the sprinklers'll blow," he said painfully. "So he said *what do you want him to do?*"

"Talk slower!" Carl yelled. "For God's sake! How can I understand what you're saying? Talk to him, Morley," he said. "Find out what he wants. Take care of it. . . . I got to call them guys."

"Wait," Hagen said. "Listen."

Morley stepped up to the foreigner. "Now," he said firmly. "Tell me what is it you want."

"Listen," Hagen said. "For Christ's sake. Mike's got to know how long we'll be down. . . ."

Carl said quickly, turning to Waino, "Tell him we don't know. That's what we're trying to find out. We don't know. You *sabe?*" He stood before the foreigner and lifted his

[59]

shoulders and shook his head violently from side to side. "No can tell. No *sabe.*"

The foreigner nodded that he understood. An embarrassed look came on his face. "Then he said . . . if you said that . . . to ask you, *what do you want him to do?*"

Carl walked away impatiently. "Tell him to go to hell. I ain't got time to screw around with him now."

"Wait," Hagen said again. He turned the flashlight up toward the roof. The light cut through the dust, focused on the cluster of pipes and wires on the inside of the roof. Carl looked up in annoyance. He was getting sick of all this wasted time. He saw a tangle of wires and pipes, the spotty whitewash on the inside of the roof, the blur of dust that moved in a funnel of light. He had seen it before. He frowned and tried to indicate his impatience.

Hagen said, "Mike has to know what to do, Carl. If we're down much longer he'll have to pull his fires. It's getting too hot here; sprinklers may blow."

"Sprinklers?" Carl repeated.

"Yes."

Carl frowned. "What about them?"

"They're liable to blow. If it gets much hotter."

"Blow."

Carl looked up into the darkness. The fire-prevention system consisted of a network of pipes, tapped every few feet with automatic valves that melted at a certain heat, throwing water all around and putting out the fire that opened them.

"The fans have stopped," Hagen explained. "If it gets much hotter in here some of the valves may pop off."

Carl rejected the possibility the way a man does when he finds out something he does not want to know.

"They won't," he said quickly. "They take care of that. When they put them in. Unless there's a fire."

Hagen shrugged and started to walk on. Waino waited while Carl tried to reassure himself. "There has to be fire," he explained to the darkness. "I forget how hot it has to get. But there has to be a fire. . . . *Morley!* How hot does it have to get before the sprinklers melt? How hot?"

The light moved obediently and concentrated on Morley. He looked up in bewilderment. He had been listening to Carl and Hagen without understanding them, hearing the rustle of their talk in the way that he turned the pages of a newspaper without remembering what he had just read. Now he put his hand to his chin and stared at the floor. His fingers squeezed his cheek steadily, as if trying to force out some item of information that was lodged there.

"I used to know," he muttered, after a long time.

Carl said, "A hell of a lot of good that does." He moved around nervously. All at once his voice rose. "God damn it, Morley, what do you know? You run all over this factory. You're here all day. Don't you ever learn anything? What the hell do you learn? You used to know. For God's sake! You *used* to know. Will you tell me what the hell good that does? Do you think we got all night?"

Morley backed away under this attack. His features fixed themselves into an apologetic grin. Hagen turned the light away from him. Carl was well under way now; the words were bubbling up of their own accord; he did not know what he was saying. The men shuffled uneasily and Morley backed still deeper into the darkness. "God Almighty, Morley!" Carl cried. "If I can't depend on you, who can I depend on?"

Waino grunted inaudibly at the outer fringe of light.

Carl turned on him, "Now what do you want?"

Hagen said again, "Do you want Mike to pull his fires?"

Carl ran his hand across his forehead. "It won't get that hot," he said. But even as he said it he felt the sweat on his forehead, and the thought of what would happen if the fire-prevention system did blow settled on his mind like a weight, stirring up the cloudy sediment of all the things he did not want to think about, the heat, his bruised leg, the orders that had to

[61]

be got out, the time that was being forever lost. In a brief moment of imagination he pictured the pipes overhead suddenly opening and letting their waters drain out upon the factory; the men running for shelter, the ruin spreading a foot deep on the floor. Surely they thought of that, he thought. Surely they thought of that when the factory was built. But it was no comfort; he had already learned that there were a hell of a lot of things they hadn't thought of when the factory was built.

The pool of light they were in made the rest of the factory seem darker. Most of the time it was quiet. Once in a while voices reached them, and sometimes a vague carefree shout. Hagen waited a moment and walked on impatiently. Carl followed him. After a moment of indecision the foreigner tagged along.

"You!" Carl said. "Tell Mike I don't care what he does. Tell him to pull his fires if he has to and don't do it if he don't have to! You hear? Ask him how the hell should I know?"

Waino had dropped back into the darkness. Now he shouted, *"He said if you said that to tell you that he'd pull his fires!"*

"Ah, God!" Carl cried in a stricken voice. He moved his arms. *"Tell him I said,"* he shouted at the empty dark. *"Tell him how should I?"* He began to run after Hagen. "I told him!" he shouted. "I said for him!" He could see the men following them, attracted by the light and the shouting, keeping out of the direct beams of the flashlight. He caught up with Hagen and wiped the sweat off his face nervously, leaning against a saw guard while he got his breath and composed himself. "All the grief," he murmured.

"By God, Belcher," Hagen said. "You ought to call the power house and tell them the power's off. Anyway."

Carl nodded. "Yeah," he said. "I will. That Polack," he said. "How do those fellows get in here? Why do they turn over all the dumb ones to the night shift?"

Hagen bent over a small chest set back against the wall. It

was a wooden chest with a padlock holding the lid down. Hagen knelt beside it, clamping the light between his knees while he opened the lock. He said through his teeth, "I'll get you a flashlight. *Then you can get to the office and call them yourself.*"

"I guess I better call them," Carl replied. "Maybe they don't know our lights are out. Only I hate to call them fellows. You never do get any satisfaction out of them. I remember last year I had to call them. I couldn't get any satisfaction."

Hagen opened the chest. There were a few tools scattered around, and a long extension cord coiled in a neat roll with the bulb at the end looking like the swollen head of a snake. Leaning over the box, Carl could smell the rubbery electrical supplies, the complicated hardware-store smell of tape and insulation.

"A tool chest!" Carl said. "You know I've seen this box here lots of times, and I wondered what was in it."

Hagen nodded. "I keep some stuff in it."

"Yes. I've seen it here and I wondered what it was for."

Hagen said bitterly, "I keep it here so when there's any trouble in this end I won't have to go all the way back to the shop."

"I see," Carl said. "A sort of emergency tool chest."

Morley saw them peering into the box. As he peeked over their shoulders Carl explained kindly. "It's a tool chest. He keeps some stuff here so he won't have to go all the way back to the shop."

"I see, I see," Morley whispered.

"Here," Hagen said. He gave Carl the light and locked the box. Carl tried the light. The switch would not stay down. Carl tried to fix it, but his hands were too slippery and sweaty, and he stood for a long time with the flashlight pressed against his shirt while he dug at the catch with his fingernail. "Screwdriver . . ." he muttered. "If I had a. . . ." All at once the flashlight bounced out of his hand and dropped to the floor. The case rolled out of sight. Carl and Morley got down on their

[63]

knees to look for it. Hagen gave his light to Carl, saying, "Here. Take this one. I'll get it."

On his hands and knees, Carl looked up and took the flashlight.

"The switch don't work," he explained. "It keeps flickering on and off all the time."

"I know. I'll fix it."

Hagen picked up the flashlight. Carl practiced with the one Hagen had given him. He switched if off and on to see how it worked. It worked well. He swung it around to focus the light on different parts of the wall. At his feet the light became a bright circle about a foot in diameter. When he moved his hand slightly the light washed across the floor like a stream of water from a hose. Everything looked changed under the light. The machines seemed stiff and paralyzed, frozen into inactivity as soon as the light touched them, moving again when the light moved away. The light caught the cluster of pipes and wires that crawled like vines over the inside of the roof. There was a fat pipe like a stalk going up the wall, and from it the smaller pipes jutted out in right-angle branches. Every few feet there was an ominous blossom of a valve.

"Those must be the things that melt," Carl said.

"Ah, God," Hagen said.

Carl and Morley stared at the pipes, thinking of the water on the inside trying to get out.

"It's hotter," Carl said. "Maybe he better pull his fires."

He looked at Hagen. He wanted Hagen to tell him what to do. But Hagen knew that if he advised Carl to have the fires pulled, and the lights came on again a few minutes later, Carl would blame him. He would report that Hagen had caused the loss of time. He would probably say that anyway, no matter what happened, but Hagen did not want to give him any reason to do so. Hagen pretended that he did not hear.

"You see, Morley," Carl said, "if it gets too hot that little jigger melts and the valve opens. Then if there's a fire it melts

[64]

and the water comes out. But maybe it'll melt anyway. . . . I told them," he said. "I said the other day."

"It must be hotter up there than it is here," Morley replied.

"By God that's right," Carl said. "Hot air rises."

Surprised, Morley whispered, "Cold air is heavier. It's better ventilation if you open a window at the top."

"By God, that's right."

Carl looked up at the pipes again. There was something deep and scientific about the thought of hot air rising that stirred him. He could imagine the hot air rising like a thief in the night and trying to open the valve. Inside the pipe the water waited and pushed and strained and tried to get free. The good cold air stayed close to the ground; it could not rise. He wished that it was the cold air that rose, and the hot air that was heavier; then there wouldn't be anything to worry about. . . . Small drops of steam had condensed on the outside of the pipe.

The men were standing on the transfer tables and machine platforms, back out of the light, watching them. He swung the light until it focused on a boy near him, Hagen's boy, sitting on a sawyer's table with his feet drawn up under him and his back resting against the saw guard. "You!" Carl yelled. *"Go out in the fireroom and tell Mike to watch his fires and if it gets too hot for the sprinklers tell him to pull his fires! You hear?"*

Johnny gawked at him.

"You hear?" Carl yelled again.

Johnny looked from side to side, trying to see if Carl wasn't talking to someone else. Then he looked embarrassed. "Me?" he asked.

"Yes, you!" Carl was shouting. "Can't you hear? Tell Mike to pull his fires if it gets too hot and he thinks there's any danger of the sprinklers blowing! Can't you understand that, for God's sake?"

Johnny jumped off the table. He started toward Carl. When

[65]

he moved he almost fell over. His foot had gone to sleep. When he moved it seemed to follow him with a separate, dragging motion. Johnny stopped and looked down at his foot in astonishment. Then he leaned over and began slapping at his knee.

"No!" Carl was shouting. "No! Not here! The fireroom!" He waved the flashlight in a wide circle. The boy kept on slapping his knee while he stared at Carl and then looked in the different directions Carl pointed. He made a little run in one direction, only to turn around and run back the other way. "The fireroom" Carl yelled. "Tell the fireman, you dummy!"

But before Johnny could get started, Carl changed his mind again. "*No, wait!* Go up in the other end and tell Dwyer to see it don't get too hot for the sprinklers. Tell him to watch the heat. Frankie Dwyer!"

Johnny started off into the darkness. He did not know where he was going, or what he was supposed to do. He only wanted to get away from the light, and to act as if he understood what Carl wanted. He almost dove into the shadows. After a moment he called back, "*Who shall I ask?*"

"Frankie! Frankie Dwyer! You know him? Ask somebody. He's up there!"

There was a little silence.

"What," Johnny said. "What shall I tell him?"

"Tell him," Carl began loudly. Then he turned around and slammed his gloves on the floor. "Oh, God," he said in despair. He went stamping back and forth, mumbling to himself like an old man. "Oh God, oh Jesus, oh, son of a bitchen hell. I can't stand this; son of a bitch, I can't stand this."

Hagen came over to where Johnny was standing. He did not turn his flashlight on. "Listen, son," he said, "go right straight across till you hit the wall. Follow it till you come to a door. Frankie's outside. Just tell him Carl told you to tell him to keep his eye on the heat. That's all. You understand?"

Johnny said, "I know, I'll tell him." He was trembling.
"Take it easy," Hagen said shortly. "Don't try to break your neck."

Johnny started off in a blind, reckless sprint. He almost dove into the shadows again. First he bumped into one of the cut-off saws. He jumped and scurried around it like a rabbit. *"Take it easy!"* Hagen yelled angrily. "You want to kill yourself?"

But Johnny was already far on his way. Hagen turned back on Carl and Morley. Carl was storming at the darkness. He lifted his voice; he was bawling out the whole factory. Sometimes he bawled out the whole world. "I can't get any co-operation around here!" he cried. "How can I get anything done when everybody's dead from the tail both ways? How can we get anywhere if nobody pays any attention to what I say? By Jesus God I'm not going to screw around with it any longer. You fellows listen to me, you listen to me, there'll be some changes here—there'll be some changes! And somebody will be God-damn surprised some day when they try to come to work!"

Hagen turned on him. "Hell, I've had enough! Are you going to call the power house?"

"How can I call the power house when every son of a bitch and his brother is hanging around my neck? Everybody here is outside smoking or stretched out flat on his can. I been trying to call the power house for half an hour! What do you think I been trying to do?"

"Who's stopping you?"

"I know who's stopping me! I know God-damn well who is!"

There was a moment's silence. Then Hagen said, "Well, Carl, if you don't like the way I work, you know what there is to do about it."

The crowd had grown around the light. Carl glanced up before he spoke. "I didn't say I didn't like the way you worked!" he said. He tried to say it angrily but his voice faltered.

[67]

"If you don't like the way I work," Hagen repeated, "go pull my card."

There was a moment of silence. Carl made a brief interrupted gesture of contempt. "I'm not pulling anybody's card," he said. "I just want to say. . . . I'm trying to get the lights back on. I ain't got time to screw around here all night with everything else."

They waited.

"You hear?" he shouted suddenly. "You hear?" Then he stamped off toward the stockroom, the light bobbing at his feet, and Morley trudging along behind him.

3. MARIE

THE lights went out and the girls straightening the veneer on the long grading tables stood listening to the dying motors and the long wail of the fans as they stopped. Darting in quick, adroit movements, they lifted the pieces of veneer as the chains carried them along, separated them into their grades and widths and turned back to lift another piece without pausing. And now the chains stopped. Slowly, as if reluctant to stop, they moved for a moment longer, gave a last spasmodic jerk before they became motionless.

She stayed in her place. Her hands in their cotton gloves braced her against the table. She saw Hagen's flashlight graze across the factory and heard the long-way-off voices after he called the foreman.

Wait, she begged him. Don't hurry.

Hello, Bilious, a voice said, *can you feel that?*

One of the kids from the stockroom.

"Oh, get out of here," she heard a girl's voice, wearily, not in anger but disgust, "keep your hands to yourself."

And old Mrs. Humphrey said, sternly, "You boys get right out of here. Now I mean it. Now git."

They gave a long raucous laugh.

"Git!"

She felt her way to the wall and sat down. The spasms of weakness cut through her. Shaking in this heat, she thought, my teeth chattering. And yet there was no pain, but the aching dizziness that deafened her to the sounds around her and

[69]

dulled her to the heat and thick air. Without thinking anything she worked and wondered how much time was left and how long, how long, before the whistle blows and lets me go.

She slept on her feet. The chains pounded and the stream of wood passed endlessly under the low bright light. Beside her the grader marked each piece, his face set and expressionless and his eyes darkened under the green eyeshade.

Oh yes! the kid's voice, *Who said?*

"Now you git. You hear me?"

The sheets of wood floated down the chains, past the graders and the girls who stood watching, all the way down the table and out of sight. They came up out of the haze at the end of the kiln, hot and dry, dropped over a slight waterfall where one chain ended and another began, and where she stood straightening them as they passed. She was thirsty, but each time she got a drink the water was hard and acid in her mouth, the taste of the rust on the inside of the pipes.

While she worked she made up long and complicated bets with herself, forgetting whether she had won or lost. A part of her would say that an hour had passed, a part would say that only five minutes had gone by since she had looked at her watch. Then she would bet with herself—that she could wait for half an hour before looking to see what time it was, that she could count to a thousand before looking around. Sometimes she would count the dead pieces of wood that floated so gravely under the lights, giving them quick names and numbers as they passed with their eyes closed and their hands folded beside them. And sometimes it would seem that the chains had stopped, and that the factory was moving in the other direction . . . and then it was like sitting in a train stopped at a station, when a train on another track begins to move. The chains would stop and without a jar the factory would begin to slide the other way, the floor and the lights and the people sliding past the motionless pieces of wood.

What time is it? All night long she made up games and

bets with herself, trying to spur on the slow hands of the watch. She began to hate the stiff priggish little hand that barely moved, that held back so stubbornly from one figure to the next, her heart warming to the minute hand that tried to hurry. There was a small precious ration of the things she could do: get a drink of water and go to the toilet; look at her watch and count the pieces of wood as they passed. She tried to concentrate on the games she played with herself, on the bets that one part of her mind made against another part. The good part of her mind bet that an hour had passed, and the dark and unpleasant part bet that only a few minutes had gone by. She tried to concentrate on what was before her eyes, the appearance of each piece of wood, struggling not to remember the pain of the last few days, the waves of anguish that threatened her and almost overwhelmed her.

Sometimes the things she did not want to remember were stronger, driving the games and bets out of her mind. Then she gave up and the dark cloud of things she did not want to think about blinded her and made her hands clench and her eyes close involuntarily; she gave up and remembered all the things she did not want to remember: the hot stench in the doctor's office and the sweat on his face as he leaned over her; a girl who had died a long time ago, and somebody who had told her it was harder on a woman than having a baby; the pain and the feeling that she was broken inside; the rush of secret blood. Over and over as she stood by the table the dark rush of memories poured over her, and she went down and down, the games and bets shattered and forgotten. Then when she could not endure the memories any longer she would build up another game to try to drive them away.

"Marie," someone said.

Here I am.

She had a nightmare feeling that she only dreamed it and no words were said. *"Marie!"* the voice said again, *"where are you?"*

"Here I am."

Ellen settled beside her by the wall. "Oh, God, it's hot in here," Ellen said.

Now I want to tell you boys this, Mrs. Humphrey said, as long as I'm in charge of these girls I'm not going to have you coming in here and acting smart and I've told you for the last time. If I hear one more complaint I'm going to turn in your names, and not only that—I'm going to slap you down so hard you won't know what hit you.

Wow!

Some of the men passed on their way outside. The old women gathered somewhere near them and their complaints rose in a weary murmur.

I told you, Ellen would say. *I told you not to come to work.*

I'm all right now.

You're not all right.

I am all right.

You're not! You're not!

Standing in the littered room at home with Ellen's voice low and anxious so her mother could not hear them.

You're not. Do you think I'm crazy? Do you think I'm blind?

I ought to know how I feel.

You'll kill yourself.

The dark thoughts began coming back like cats after a bird. She saw them prowling behind the near fringes of darkness like cats, all the dark savage thoughts waiting to pounce on her and tear her apart. *It's your own fault,* Ellen would say unless she stopped her, *I told you.* Unless I stop her.

She braced herself with a dull aching resentment against anything Ellen could say out of the remoteness of her strength and free mind. She braced herself against Ellen's fierce affectionate gloating and her *Marie, I told you, I told you,* when she thought she was being kind.

[72]

"Say Myrtle," someone said. "Come here a minute. I want to tell you something."

"Oh, yes?"

"Ellen," she said.

"Yes?"

"What time is it?"

"About ten I guess."

"Ten?"

"Listen, Marie," Ellen said.

Here it is.

"I asked Hagen how long we'd be down."

"What?"

"He said he didn't know—maybe half an hour. So I said would you have a chance to get out and he said yes, and Frankie Dwyer said if Carl came around to tell him Frankie Dwyer was looking for him and he'd tell Carl something was wrong so Carl would keep busy and wouldn't have a chance to snoop."

Tell them all, she thought. "What about Mrs. Humphrey?"

"She won't say anything."

"No?"

"She won't! You know she won't!"

"Won't she."

Ellen began stammering, "You don't want to do. . . . You just say. . . . Because you think he'll come after us. And you know you can't depend on him."

She braced herself, the savage thoughts circling around her in the dark. "Why don't you ask me how I feel?"

"Why?" Ellen said. "Why don't I ask you how you feel?"

"You always ask me. You never let me alone."

"Oh, hard!" Ellen cried. "Oh, Marie, you make it so hard for me! Why don't you go home? Why can't you take care of yourself? You can't stand up and everybody knows it; everybody can see. . . . You're supposed to be home. You know what he said. Do you want to kill yourself?"

Marie smiled into the dark. The thoughts were driven back.

[73]

She felt the sweat on her face, and I must look like the wrath of God, she thought.

"Don't get excited," she said in relief. "I can take care of myself."

"Yes, you can take care of yourself."

She heard the boys from the stockroom teasing the girls, the sarcastic cries *oh, yes!* and the incomprehensible shouts of laughter. Nearer to them the old women's voices rose in the tired complaints, I did a big washing before I came to work, it's a wonder to me how they expect us to get along.

"You'll pretend it's all right," Ellen said. "Just to show me. . . . I don't care. It's none of my business. But I despise him. I don't see how you stand him. You're a fool to put up with him. . . ."

Marie closed her eyes. Behind the dry lids the colors moved and flashed in their soundless explosions. She could see the pieces of wood passing endlessly before her under the bright explosive lights, the marker beside her checking each piece, the chains stopping and the factory beginning to slide the other way. For a time, talking to Ellen, she had forgotten. Now all the things she did not want to think about began crowding up on her again, as if with renewed strength because they had been away so long, and she remembered the hot, hot stench in the doctor's office, the scythe-shaped instrument, the stirrups that cut her bound ankles. The memories pressed on her like a weight she could not carry any longer, and she turned almost frantically to Ellen, saying, *"What time is it?"* in a harsh strained voice, not knowing that she had asked it before, not remembering that Ellen had already answered her.

4. WINTERS

L ISTEN, the voice said dully and he said, I'm listening. I don't want to argue, the voice said. I want to tell you the truth.

Don't listen to that goofy bastard, the other voice said.

Goofy, the first voice said coldly. Goofy, you goofy son of a bitch, you're goofy.

What?

I'd like to get that guy here. I'd like to have him juggling them hundred-fifty-pound irons on the press for a week. I'd give him his three weeks in six weeks and let him look at forty-six ahead of him.

Listen, the voice said. See if I'm right.

Winters said, Why? What are you arguing about?

A match flared somewhere down the wall. On the harbor the string of channel lights and the intermittent flash from the lighthouse of the jetty. No wind on the slate water. It's cooler, he thought, and then he thought of the hot room where the fan swung and Ann gasped for her breath. *Open the window!* Blind in the heat and the fan humming like an insect and the sweat on her face and the muscles in her throat like wires. *Ed,* she said, *open the window!* and the girl wiping her face and the fan reaching the end of its swing and starting back.

Don't listen to him, the voice said with dull passion. His ass is out.

Tide in, the tugboats headed for the bar-bound ships. Forget it. Somewhere down the wall a match flared. *Listen.* Cool on the still water, the fresh air she'll never taste.

[75]

What? he cried. What is it?
We're having an argument.
Argument hell.
Listen, Winters.
Let me tell him.
So all right I can't stand it and her eyeballs turned back in her head. I can't stay here. I can't stay here. Hands clench and unclench and the girl reading and the fan buzzing like a fly. Stopped now. I wonder.

Believe it or not the voice said. You seen the cartoon. You know Ripley, them believe it or not cartoons, he had one proving that if you worked twenty-four hours a day you'd only have to work three weeks to work as many hours as you do in a year working eight hours a day. Three weeks! I looked at that, I said, if you was here you'd learn something, baby, besides how to draw cartoons.

Tell me this.

He says you work three weeks out of the year. If you work twenty-four hours a day. Three weeks! How does he get it? He figures five and a half days a week.

Forty-four hours.

You're nuts, the voice said. Nuts.

I didn't say it! I'm telling you what it said in the paper!

Forty-four hours. Fifty-two weeks.

It still makes better than three months. And he figured you got Hallowe'en off and a week for Christmas and two weeks' vacation and ten days besides.

He did it by days.

I don't give a damn how he did it.

He said, I don't get it. I don't see what you're driving at.

Listen, the voice said. We're having an argument.

A voice corrected him. His idea of an argument.

Listen, the voice said. You see how he got it. Three hundred and sixty-five days. Take off fifty-two Sundays.

Yeah.

[76]

Take off twenty-six Saturdays.

Yeah.

Take off fourteen days' vacation and ten days for holidays.

Ed? a voice said. Ed?

Connor's voice.

Yes.

What's up?

I don't know. They're having an argument.

Connor moved up by him, kicking through the long grass that grew beside the building. The sound of his feet in the grass like water. The voices moved down. Here in fresh air no deep enough breath. Connor grunted as he eased himself against the building. "Christ, I'm tired," he said. He rummaged through his pockets, squirming his large body as he searched.

"I believe what I read, Winters," he said. "If they say no matches I don't carry any."

"I haven't got any."

Connor went back to the group, saying "Matches? Who's breaking the iron-clad rules?" The match flared, revealing his square clean face, the high forehead and light hair, the figures grouped around him.

"Ditch it," a voice said. "He could tell who you were."

The cigarette glowed as he returned. Red beneath the fragile ash. No deep enough breath. Like a deep mounting pain in his chest that no deep breath could answer. The drenched bed and suffering.

"How is she, Ed?"

"No better."

The warm voice touched him. Mounting through pain like staying too long under water, the lungs begging for air. He took a deep breath. The drenched bed, the sweat on her face, the fan buzzing like an insect under the sick orange light.

Silence. Connor cleared his throat, gravely thoughtful, drew

[77]

at his cigarette. Doesn't know what to say, Winters thought. He wants to say something.

A voice said bitterly, "If he worked here he'd find out you work longer than three weeks."

"She suffering?" Connor asked.

"They keep her doped up." Then he said with an effort, "She's got a good chance. It ain't hopeless . . . I couldn't stay home! I thought I would but I couldn't stand it. Besides they won't let me see her after five."

"They won't let you see her?"

"Not at night." He spoke with a gauging calm. "Besides, she don't know me."

Silence again. Walt stirred restlessly, said *Jesus!* and drew at his cigarette. Farther down the wall the voices died away, became only slow lazy sentences broken with occasional sharp cries of doubt or indignation. Winters listened, trying to keep his mind here on the factory and the tideflat, but stirred and deeply moved that Walt had looked for him and asked him how she was. Think of something else, he thought, force myself, and brought his mind back to the tideflat, to the hot factory, to Walt and the words of the men. *I can't live on it,* he heard. *How do they expect?* And he thought, They won't take it. That's one thing. Very slowly he drew his mind back from the thought of Ann, slowly and patiently, as though making a physical effort that took all his strength and left him exhausted. "She'll get all right," Walt said awkwardly, and then, as though conscious of the awkwardness and hollowness of what he said, went on hurriedly, "I was supposed to be looking for Hagen. Carl sent me and they told me he was out in the fireroom but I couldn't locate him."

"He was looking for Carl. Up by Carl's desk."

This brings me down to three bucks a day. Last year I made four and a quarter and there's only three of us left on the crew. Last year there was five. We do twice as much.

They won't take it, Winters thought. They won't take that

last cut. The knowledge pulled his thoughts back to them and he thought of going to them and joining in their talk.

Walt said, "He sure must be taking his time."

He heard the indifferent complaint, impatience, a sort of smothered accusation. Why? Walt ground his cigarette under his heel. "I yelled all over for him. Then I thought, to hell with it. Why should I be doing his work? Carl's sore as hell."

When I looked at the check I said, Listen, I said, when are you guys going to begin paying us off in buttons?

He roused himself again. *Forget it!* he thought. *Forget it! Does it do her any good?* The long spears of bulrush crumpled in his hand. Someone moved out on the tideflat, wading through the grass that reached to his knees. He threw the broken spears of bulrush away, irritated with himself that he had held and broken them without knowing it.

"I think Hagen's done for," Winters said. "From now on, Carl won't give him a chance. He'll pin this on him. See. He'll find some way."

They think they're a bunch of missionaries. All they need is a string of heads and some strips of red calico. I looked at the check and Jesus, I said, how you throw away money.

Walt said uneasily, "Hell, be fair. He ain't so bad."

"No?"

You'll learn, he thought. Wait till you been here another year. He thought of Walt coming into the factory, looking over the crew with a college-boy uneasiness, getting in the way and trying to brag about school while he worked.

"It's Hagen's fault. Carl tried to make up with him. He told me himself. He went down to Hagen and said he'd put his cards on the table and Hagen wouldn't even talk to him."

"Yeah. He wanted Hagen to suck around."

Walt stirred uncomfortably. "It'd be all right," he began vaguely, "if all of the guys. . . . But that Polack I work with. He shoves off everything on me. . . . Hagen's sour. He can't get along with anybody. It makes a lot of trouble. . . ."

[79]

The tightness returned in his chest. I'm tired, he thought, with a dull surprise, how long since I slept? Arms and legs heavy, a weight in his lungs that a deep breath did not lift. By Ann's bed, still tired, watching the fan swing while she slept. Only her heavy breathing and the buzzing of the fan. The smell of antiseptics and the sick smell from her bed and the girl reading, the fresh ink smell of the magazine as she opened the pages. THE CASE FOR FROZEN FOODS. WHAT PRICE COMPLEXION? The sweat on her ravaged face.

What good does it do her? If I sit here eating my heart out?

He opened his eyes and looked hard at the shadows beyond his feet. Think about it. He could see his own feet and the faint outline of Walt beside him. Walt's new overalls, his clean white shirt. Beyond, the empty flat and the few lights on the harbor and the faint gray reflection of the lights in town. Low sky, smoke from the fires.

"I don't blame Carl," Walt said. "Hagen don't try. He's been here so long he thinks he owns the place."

"That's what he'll say."

"Who?"

"Carl."

"I don't blame him."

But why try? Oh, why, why? The waves of grief rolled over him. What I could do, he thought, all I could have thought of! In the narrow room she watched him, crying, and he said it: *Christ, I didn't want to marry you. I'm sick of your God-damn whining.* Her face gray and her eyes clouding over. Say it, say it, no excuse. In the narrow room, the rain outside and the window shade torn and Ann sitting on the bed, her face swollen and her mouth hanging open watching me. *Nobody else would have you. Nobody else would have you.*

Why I said it. The dull urge of no reason. Oh, Ann! Racked and tender; listen, darling, listen!

He got up and walked blindly to the group down the wall.

"He won't work together," Walt was saying, quietly, so the

men could not hear. "When a man's that sour. Why do you put all the blame on Carl? He's all right if you get to know him."

A voice said passionately, *What did they do with the glue crew. They put them on piecework. All right. They made good money. They worked themselves to death. Whenever we got bad stock they'd all get sore at us—they'd say we weren't giving them any stock. So what happened? As soon as they found out how much the crew could do they cut out the piecework. They'd give them a cut and then sweeten it a little if they squawked and then cut them again and now they're doing twice as much as they did before they went on piecework. Now with this they'll get ten per cent less.*

"Listen," Walt said. "What's the matter?"

"What?"

"What's the matter. Jesus, I just said. . . ."

He looked around, seeing the white shirt and the blurred outlines of Walt's face. The voice sore and puzzled. "What's eating you?" Walt said. "Just because. . . ."

"Nothing."

"Well why. . . ."

Whatever they do we get the dirty end of the stick. To hell with it. I've had enough of it. Ten per cent. That means thirty-five cents for me and multiply that by a thousand and you see what it means to them. Three hundred and fifty bucks a day. Right here in this one plant.

Because I walked off. Thought I was sore. "No," Winters said, "I was thinking about something else." He waked up slowly to Walt's puzzled resentment, tried wearily to think of something to say. *I won't take it,* the hot voice said. *I'll go down the road before I'll take it.* Walt moved about uneasily, wading through the long grass, mumbling something that he could not hear.

"Hell," Walt said. "He has to earn a living. Like anybody else."

A skyrocket sailed over town, exploding into thousands of green and red balls of light. The sky turned the color of milk. He could see Walt's square face, questioning, distrustful, young, and he came back to earth, driving the thought of Ann out of his mind, feeling ashamed of himself because he had forgotten what he was doing. Sticking up for Carl, he thought. You'll learn.

The muffled chatter of the skyrocket reached them: an explosion and then a rush of diminishing sound, a ball rolling downstairs.

They got it worse at the Superior, a voice said. *Fifteen per cent.*

Yeah, and they won't take it. They're talking strike and they won't talk anything else.

He took Walt by the arm. "For God's sake don't swallow that stuff," he said. "You start sticking up for that son of a bitch and you got your hands full. The hardest guy to stick up for I ever run into." They walked toward the door to the factory. He felt the effort of talking and tried to keep away from an argument; he felt a vague irritation that Walt was so stupid and at the same time a friendly response to Walt's own friendship for him. "You haven't been here long enough," he said. "Wait till you been here another year. Wait till he makes you work yourself to death and then turns around and gives you hell for doing what he said to do."

Walt said, "Hell, they all jump on him."

For God's sake! "Listen," he said sharply, "do you stick up for every son of a bitch you see just because he's a son of a bitch? Do you know what that guy's here for? Fifty men have lost their jobs since he's been here. We've all got two cuts. What do you think he carries a stop watch for? A race! You think he's going to time a race?"

Walt said unexpectedly, "I get along with you but these guys make me sick. They never do anything but beef. You're the only guy I ever worked with I got along with. That Polack

[82]

I work with now drives me nuts. He gives me the heavy end of every truck and whenever I crab about it he says we're all members of the working class."

Winters laughed. Walt rushed on, confused and aggrieved by his laughter, "You don't believe me. I'm telling you the truth. He does it every night. And when I was working with Frank Dwyer he used to give me every dirty job that came along. He'd make me clean up the crap under the kiln when the heat was on, just for the hell of it. They got it in for anybody that's got any education trying to get along. It's no way," Walt said bitterly. "No way to treat a white man."

What do we stand to lose! the voice cried. *We can't live on it! Nobody can live on it! I don't want any trouble but I'm so damn far in debt now I'll never get out.*

"Listen, Walt," Winters said.

"If I hadn't got along with you I'd think it was my fault. But we worked all right. Just because a man has a college education. . . ."

Even then I did your work, Winters thought. I tried to break you in. "Take it easy," he said. "They all got all they can do. Dwyer's got his hands full. . . ." He was listening to the harsh passionate voices of the men, their anger evoking a stir of elation, breaking the numb despondency that had paralyzed him. "Listen!" he said sharply, when Walt started to answer him. *I'll go out,* a voice said. *Any time anybody says the word.*

Say the word, a voice repeated. *Just say the word.*

"Then they wonder," Walt said bitterly. "They act like that—then they wonder."

Are we going to take it? Is there a law we have to take it?

Wake up, he said silently to Walt. Wake up for God's sake. He saw the white blur of Walt's face and sensed his anger and bewilderment, feeling an irritated friendliness. He doesn't know what it's all about, he thought, and touched Walt's arm briefly. "Come on inside," he said. "Let's see what's up."

[83]

"Why?" Walt said.

"Come on," Winters said impatiently. "I want to talk to you."

There was a moment of silence.

"No," Walt said. "I'm going to wait here."

Stubborn, Winters said silently. Wake up. "O.K." He walked toward the door.

Say the word! the voice said. *Just say the word!*

Wake up, he thought.

He got inside a few moments before Carl and Hagen quarreled. He heard the passionate voices as Carl sent Johnny after Frankie and then, when Hagen called him, when he told Carl to pull his card, his heart began to pound with excitement; here it is, he thought, and he knew that if Hagen left he would leave too. The men began crowding around him. *Fight!* somebody said exultantly. He boosted himself up on a pile of lumber. In the dim light he saw Carl glance nervously at the crowd, worried, indignant at this fresh worry, the ground slipping out from under him. Then Hagen called his bluff and Winters got ready to jump down, never thinking of anything but of walking out when Hagen walked out, and then he saw the fleeting panic on Carl's face, heard him stammer hotly, his voice loaded with contempt, *I'm not pulling anybody's card. I just want to say . . . I'm trying to get the lights back on. I ain't got time to screw around here all night with everything else.* He watched Carl and Molly wade off into the darkness, saw them diminish to a little blob of light and disappear. Hagen switched off his flashlight. There was a vague stir in the darkness.

Hagen said flatly, "I won't take anything more off that son of a bitch."

Someone said skeptically, "What'll you do?"

"I don't know. But I know this: I'll drive that son of a bitch out of here. Or I'll get out."

[84]

Winters was stirred; he was impatient when the same voice said again, wearily, "What the hell difference does it make? If it ain't Carl it'll be somebody else. Why worry with him?"

Hagen said sharply, "To hell with that. That's what I used to think." He lifted his voice. "I worked here ever since they built this place. I've seen twenty foremen in here. But we never had anybody as bad as that fat little bastard. I mean it. Never been anybody in here like that little son of a bitch."

When Hagen settled back against the wall, someone said briefly, "He sure gave your kid hell."

"To hell with him," Hagen said. "I don't care about him bawling out the kid. But he's so damn useless. He can't walk around without falling down. I spend half my time pulling Molly out of a conveyor. He couldn't even operate a flashlight. I gave him a flashlight and he didn't know how to turn it on. Asked me if a fuse blew out. For God's sake. A fuse. Look. Mike sent a kid in here to ask Carl if he ought to pull his fires. Now you known God-damn well that Mike knew he ought to pull his fires. But he had to send the kid in here to tell Carl to protect himself. And what did Carl do? He flew off the handle, raised all kinds of hell, and finally sent the kid back to tell Mike what Mike told him. *We can't do our work as long as that guy is here. He gets us in one mess after another!*"

A voice said, "You can't tell me anything. I remember one time when I first came to work I showed him where the floor was loose and somebody was liable to fall through and break their God-damned neck, so he better get it fixed. The next night, *the next night!* he came along, he said, 'Look here, Madison, God damn it, you better watch this floor,' he said, 'you better watch this floor or you're liable to fall through and break your God-damned neck!' "

There was a silence. Presently another voice said thoughtfully, "Son of a bitch takes credit for everything."

Hagen asked, "Why do we have so much trouble on the night shift? Because he's always got his nose up it. He tells you

[85]

one thing and five minutes later he turns around and tells you something else. Then he gives you hell for not doing something entirely different. If we get anything done he thinks it's because he did it. Then when we have any trouble he thinks it's because nobody did what he told them."

Someone pushed Winters aside. "Move over," a voice said. "I want to lay down and I hate to lay down on the floor because I get grease in my hair if I lay down on the floor."

Winters shifted over on the pile of lumber. The newcomer stretched out, grunting and sighing as he tried to get comfortable. "I'm stiff as a board," he said. "I had to get up at six o'clock this morning and reline the brakes on my car. Took me all morning. Finally I got them relined."

No one said anything. The newcomer yawned, exhaling a series of mournful, wordless sighs. "Oh, I got the yellow dog," he groaned. "I think I'll die. . . . Hagen, you big bastard, if you turn the lights on again, I'll kill you. They been pounding me on the tail so hard I didn't know what I was doing. When the lights went out, Jesus, I put my hand on my forehead, Jesus, I thought, my eyes are sure getting bad."

Hagen said bitterly, "When he first came here he used to carry a stop watch around, little bitty rig, fit right in the palm of his hand. Then he used to follow everybody around, see how long it took to do anything. If you went to get a drink, there he'd be, working his little clock. If you wanted to take a crap, there he'd be. It gave you the creeps, having him stick that watch up against the back of your neck like a gun. Took twice as long to do anything."

"You know what he did before he came here?" a voice asked. "He used to sell shoes. I run into a guy that knew him. He was a dick for the company. He'd go around, checking up on all the clerks to see if they was getting a rake-off. Then he'd see if the clerks was wearing the same kind of shoes they sold in the store and if they wore new shoes."

[86]

"How can a guy work if some son of a bitch has got a stop watch pointed at him?"

"Yeah," the voice said, "this guy told me Carl knew all the stock so he'd find out if the clerks knew the stock by asking for some funny-sized shoe. All the clerks was supposed to try to sell some high-priced shoe—if you said you wanted something for five dollars they was supposed to sell you something for six. So when Carl would go into a store, letting on he was a customer, he'd ask for something for five dollars and if the clerk didn't show him something for six he'd turn in a report and the clerk would be bounced."

"I believe it."

"Yeah. So this guy told me that when Carl would leave one of the stores there'd be shoe boxes all over the place and all the clerks would be run ragged and they'd think they'd been selling shoes to some poor loony bastard that didn't know what he wanted. And all Carl would do, he'd take the shoes back to the main office and turn them in and they'd go right back on the shelves. Then Carl would turn in a couple names to show he was working, the guys would get fired, so then he got to be an efficiency expert."

Somebody said, "Hell! You know what he did to me? He never could catch me ——— the dog, so you know what he did? He used to stop me when I was working, ask me a lot of dumb questions and start chewing the fat, and all the time he'd be working that God-damn watch! When I found that out, I could have killed him."

The man who was lying beside Winters lifted his head. "What are you guys beefing about?" he asked. His voice was mild and inquisitive. "What now?"

"Carl," Winters said soberly.

The newcomer began groaning with vast contempt. "Oh, my God, my God, get something new. Won't you ever wear it out? A whole year now, and I haven't heard anything but crabbing about Carl. Here in the old days you used to crab

[87]

about everything, now all you do is crab about him. Jesus, show some imagination, get a new subject, give us a rest. Why don't you crab about Hagen here? He's behind it all, don't you know that? He's the guy that turned out the lights—he's in cahoots with the power company."

No one answered. The newcomer settled back again. "I get tired," he complained, "of the same old crap all the time."

Winters shifted away from him in annoyance. Someone from the crowd—the man who had asked Hagen what he was going to do—fumbled his way through the darkness and sat down beside the newcomer. "Hello, Jug!" He threw himself heavily on Jug while Jug was stretched out and snoring. Jug began screaming, "Oh! Oh! Oh! I'm boogered! I'm boogered!" and they began to thrash around on the pile of lumber. Winters could not hear what Hagen was saying, and after a moment he got down on the floor.

"I have to stay right here," Hagen was saying. "If I don't, he'll come back and say he had to spend half the night looking for me. He'll say it anyway. I don't give a damn, but I won't give him any excuse for it. Then look. He sent my kid up to tell Dwyer to watch the heat. What does he think Dwyer's here for? Dwyer's been watching them kilns four-five years now. He was watching the heat when Carl was still selling shoes. When he's asleep he knows more about the heat than Carl will ever know about anything. You think that makes any difference? Hell, Carl can't tell the difference when a man's doing his work and when he's going through the motions. If a man just sweats enough and runs around enough and blows off enough steam and get so God-damned rattled he don't know what he's going—then Carl thinks he's working."

Winters listened. How many of us now? He could name most of the voices, grading them roughly by their harshness: Sorenson and Prent Fisher and Bullett and Gil Ahab, the religious nut, the *Millions Now Living Will Never Die!* man. All over the factory and on the tideflat, some of them making some mild and general complaint and some of them furious as Hagen himself. He sat back silently, somewhat behind the others, his hand moving nervously over his face, peering through the darkness at one speaker after another. In how many groups are they talking like this? Hagen and Sorenson and Ahab—they hated Carl because he interfered with their work, because the factory could only run when they disregarded what he told them to do. But the rest of them hated him because he drove them, drove them endlessly and senselessly even when there was nothing to do—or most of all when there was nothing to do—drove them in a fever of activity to do something that would have to be done over again tomorrow, or drove them like mad on some insane job they would have to spend the rest of the week, at the same sweating pace, undoing. Oh, how bitterly they hated him! There were no words that could get down deep enough to say what they felt, and they fell back on savage monotonous curses, never describing him except in terms of filth, of excrement, as though his very name suggested only some nauseating mess.

I don't care, a voice said. *I can take anything. I've worked in some of the toughest jobs on this coast, and when I worked on the Milwaukee, putting it over the mountains, the section boss carried a gun and would rather shoot you than talk. I could stand it. But I won't work for a guy that's nuts.*

"You think Carl's crazy," Bullett said. "Hell, I'll tell you about a guy we used to have at Claiborne-Kelley out of Vancouver—what a nut! Oh, he was dizzy! He made Carl seem like a God-damned sage. But up he went. I remember I was working in the yard, and when I first went there he was nothing but a yard boss. Then they made him foreman of the graveyard. Jesus, he gave you the creeps. You'd look around, there the son of a bitch would be, peeking around a pile, grinning like a God-damned baboon. *Yowie!* What a guy! Finally son of a bitch went stark, raving mad. Same day they made him general superintendent." He paused for a proper

[89]

effect. "There he was," Bullett ended solemnly, "right in the middle of the street, waving it at the girls."

For a time no one said anything. Winters glanced toward Bullett; he was afraid that the conversation would veer off Carl and get lost in a welter of miscellaneous reminiscences. "What of it?" he asked.

"What of it? Nothing! I'm just telling you, what do you guys expect—I'm just trying to show you Carl ain't as bad as some of them."

"He's bad enough."

"Sure he is. But what the hell of it? What are you going to do about it?" Then Bullett poured a little salt into the wounds. "You guys make me sick, all you do is beef about that poor little sucker. Why don't you get a new subject? Jesus, I'm sick of hearing about him."

"I'm sick of seeing him," Winters said.

"Christ, go down the road! Nobody's keeping you. You don't have to see him, this is a free country."

Winters suddenly tightened up inside. "You just been telling us they're worse everywhere else," he said bitterly. "Free for what—to break my neck for some son of a bitch like Carl? No. We can get him out of here. Don't tell me we can't do it. Three hundred guys on this shift hate that sucker like poison. Why can't we get him out? What's to stop us?"

There was another silence, and the men stirred uncomfortably. Winters sat back and waited. His heart was pounding; he was afraid that now, because of the sense of discomfort that had settled over the men, the subject would be dropped, or the group would break up. But Bullett too backed down; he settled back with another loud groan of despair. "Jesus, you'd think *I* was keeping him here. I didn't hire him! When he first came here, I said somebody ought to drop one of them hundred-and-fifty-pound irons on his thick skull, but nobody backed me up—besides, it probably wouldn't have done any good, his head's so thick he wouldn't have felt it anyway."

[90]

Beside him Fisher spoke up with his whanging Southern voice. "You ought to do what we did with a fat old boy we had when I was working for the E. I. Pristley Sash and Door in St. Louis. We took that old boy out and we just beat the living Jesus out of him." As no one answered him, he turned to Bullett and began talking to him in a low voice.

"These guys make me sick," Bullett said wearily, "they crab their heads off, but they never do anything."

Presently Hagen said again, "I'll get that guy out of here. I'll get him out or I'll get out. I've taken enough off him. He gets in the road, he can't do a damn thing, he's got his finger up everything."

One of the old men said vaguely, "When he first came here, I remember there was some talk of getting up a petition. I don't know that anything ever came of it, but I remember there was a good deal of talk about it at the time. I never signed it; they never brought it around to me; but if they had brought it around, I'd have signed it."

Someone explained, "That was the shipping department. They were getting paid by the hour, and Carl put them on a straight weekly rate. They were working a lot of overtime—it was when all that stuff was going to Australia. So they kicked. But it was just in the shipping department. Nothing came of it. The shipping clerk took their petition in the office and that girl in there—Miss Hazen—she put it away in a drawer. She said it would make MacMahon sore if he saw it."

"What happened?"

"Well, I don't know—they kicked about it, and a couple guys quit, and finally after that big Australia order was finished Carl came around. He said he heard they was beefing about not getting any overtime, so they'd put them back on straight time. But then there wasn't any more overtime, and pretty soon the poor bastards only worked three-four days a week for about six months. They were sore as hell for a while, and four-five guys quit—they got a whole green crew out there now."

[91]

"You can't go by the shipping department," Bullett said. "Those poor bastards are nuts. They're all nuts. They wouldn't be out there if they wasn't nuts."

They were interrupted. Three girls were feeling their way through the darkness to the ladies' toliet. They were holding hands and crying out in little suppressed giggles whenever they bumped against some substantial portion of the darkness. Winters could hear them breathing and hear the rustle of their clothing as they approached. One of them whispered, *Oh, kid, be careful!* and another replied, *What do you think I'm being?* They passed behind him so close that their overalls brushed against his back. Someone asked, "Where you going, girls?" and they laughed vaguely in reply. Winters could hear them as they found the pile of lumber and turned to pass by it. One of the girls suddenly screamed. The others stopped and after a moment screamed with her. Hagen switched on the flashlight. They stared at it blindly, their eyes widening in happy alarm as they backed against the whitewashed wall and huddled together.

The screams had reached the other end of the factory. Someone shouted, *"Let her up! Can't you see she's tired!"* Bullett and Fisher began laughing raucously, and Hagen switched off the flashlight.

The girls started on again. Winters heard one of them say, "What did he do? Did he do anything?"

"I put out my hand. . . ."

Bullett and Fisher were rolling around on the pile of lumber, laughing over something the rest of them could not hear. The girls went on, the little suppressed giggles and warning plaints and whispers marking their progress. Winters stirred restlessly; he had a sick feeling that something was lost, that some gain that had been made was threatened. They're breaking up, he thought, hearing some of them stirring and moving out toward the tideflat. For a moment he thought of giving up too, drawn by the cooler air and the quiet voices and no interruptions of

[92]

outside. But then he remembered the way Hagen had turned on Carl, and the faked, hollow resolution when Carl said *I'm not pulling anybody's card!* and the way Carl had mumbled to himself, stumbling out of the factory, the way his own heart had suddenly lifted!

"Walk out," he said suddenly. "Who'll walk out?"

For a moment there was no answer. Someone who had started outside sat down again. He could feel the words going through them, the question sinking in, stopping them and holding them. He was nervous, and his nervousness surprised him, and he waited, his heart beating more rapidly, afraid that no one would answer or somebody would say, you're nuts, forget it.

"I'll walk out," Hagen said. "I won't work with that son of a bitch any longer."

Bullett said, "You can't make these wooden-heads walk out. You couldn't drive them out with a club."

He turned on Bullett. "Will you walk out?"

They waited.

"Me?" Bullett said.

"Yeah. Will you walk out?"

"For God's sake! Why not? But why chew the fat about it? They won't move. You couldn't blast them out. But why jump on me? If Carl ain't jumping on me one of you guys jumps on me.

"Jesus," Bullett said, after a moment, "I get sick of it."

"They're picking on you, Jug," Prentiss Fisher said. "That's all they're doing."

"You mush-mouthed bastard," Bullett said. Fisher suddenly yelled and began thrashing around in the dark, *Oh he's got me by the!* .... They began wrestling again. When they stopped Bullett said with an air of surprise, "You know this son of a gun ain't got good sense. He can't talk English. He says *whop*. '*Ef I fight ye,*' he says, '*All sure's hell whop ye.*' "

"I'll walk out," somebody said. "Any time you're ready."

"I'll walk out."

[93]

"They're talking strike at the Superior. They got a fifteen per cent cut."

"I'll walk out."

Somebody said in excitement, "I'll walk out! To hell with them!"

Hagen got up suddenly and walked toward the head end of the mill. The light went on. Somebody was calling him. He called out *What?* and turned back to the men, "Shut up you guys."

Prentiss Fisher said, "They coming back on?"

Bullett said, "Leave them off, Hagen! Give us a rest!"

"Shut up!" Hagen said again.

Someone was calling him.

Bring it here! Bring us the light! Sharp, a panic voice.

Hagen started off toward the head end of the mill. There was a rustle of movement in the group lined up against the wall and pile of lumber. Most of the men stood up. Winters walked over to see where Hagen was going. Sorenson and one of the sawyers followed him. Hagen was already hurrying down the corridor. The light sent back wavering reflections as he passed behind the machines; the shadows washed backwards, enlarged, dissolved into the darkness. Sorenson said, "What is it?" noncommittally, not expecting to be answered. Then Winters could hear the questions spreading out, *What happened? What happened?* the waves of questions spreading out as ripples spread when a rock is dropped into a pool. He started out after Hagen. The two men beside him hesitated a moment before they followed him. The light was already a long way ahead, and they could barely see the larger obstructions in their path. This part of the mill was unused. Some of the worn-out machines were stored there, and the floor was covered with small chunks of bark and the fine, powdered sawdust that was not drained off by the fans. The discarded machines were stored against the wall, gradually being pulled apart as one piece after another was used for replacing broken parts

[94]

of the machines that were running. At the entrance of the storeroom there were barrels of oil mounted on racks, and bulging sacks of waste looming up, transformed and unreal. As Hagen hurried on, the light leaped from the floor to the empty darkness ahead and then dropped swiftly back to the floor again. One of the men stumbled on a pile of discarded chains and sprockets that littered the corridor. Winters heard him stumble and heard him draw his breath sharply. "Damn," he said. "God-damn thing."

Some distance ahead of them Hagen met someone. The light touched him for a moment. "Jesus Christ!" a voice said. "Didn't you hear me!" There was a moment of talk before they both hurried on.

Sorenson said, "Somebody's hurt."

"How you know?"

"I can tell," Sorenson said. He was panting along beside Winters. The sawyer was following them. "Why don't they clean up this place?" the sawyer said. "God, I broke my leg."

The log deck opened out on a platform over the line of vats; the floor of the platform was almost on a level with the roof of the vats. Between the vats and the platform there was a canyon, twenty feet wide and ten feet deep, the track at the bottom of it. The logs were taken from the vats to the track and then hoisted to the platform. Hagen and his companion had already climbed down to the track when Winters reached the platform. The light from his flashlight streamed up over the platform; Winters could see the steam escaping around the doors of the vats and rising slowly from the log. When he looked over the edge of the platform he could see nothing at first, nothing but the scattered rays of light and the shadowy bulk of the log. Off at one side, leaning against the door of the nearest vat, a man was holding a torch, trying to get the dim flame started by holding the wood down and letting the flame lick up the side of the wood. Hagen had crawled under

[95]

the factory, directing the flashlight into the darkness under the log.

While Winters looked over the edge of the platform, Sorenson swung over the side and dropped down one of the posts. The sawyer asked senselessly, "Who's hurt? Who's hurt?" Winters shook his head and walked away. A sudden sickness and weakness almost paralyzed him. The log looked swollen and distended in the dim light; he could feel the heat of it when he leaned over the platform. For a moment he walked around blindly, all his senses tightening with revulsion. The sawyer too crawled over the side of the platform. For a time he held his head and shoulders above the floor, his weight resting on his elbows, his feet scraping for some support on the post. Winters glanced over the edge again. He did not know this end of the factory and he was trembling too violently to trust himself to drop over the edge. He walked back and forth across the platform, looking for a way down. Hagen moved the light a little, and Winters could see the supports that branched up from the posts. He let himself down slowly, his foot clamping and twisting in the crotch where the brace was fastened to the post, his hands scraping over the splinters in the floor. Then he crawled down the post, wrapping his legs and arms around it.

The man who was holding the torch suddenly dropped it and stamped on the flame. "It's no good," he said, almost apologetically. He ground the wood into the damp pulpy earth between the tracks. "It won't burn."

"Who is it?" Winters asked.

"The hoist man."

They looked at each other nervously. The man stamped again on the torch. "Log rolled," he said. His voice was hard, almost self-consciously calm. "It was about half up when the power went off. So it stayed there with all the pull on it sideways and finally it gave way and swung. While he was waiting." Winters nodded. He tried to remember who the hoist man was, or what he did, but he did not know him. He looked at the steamy bulk of the log. It was resting on the track and against the pilings that made up the foundation of the factory. The curve of the log was now a tunnel of light as Hagen was under the factory. The men were crowded around each end of the tunnel; it was impossible to get nearer.

Winters asked, "What can you do?"

"Nothing. We called the hospital. Broke in the office."

Winters could see other men wandering around helplessly in the canyon between the vats and the platform. It was quiet except for the muffled voices and heavy breathing of the men around the log. There was a steady hiss of steam escaping from the closed vats; an occasional rattle as the steam pipes trembled under the pressure. The man standing beside Winters suddenly said *Ah, poor bastard!* in a racked voice, *Ah, poor bastard!*

Winters ran his hand nervously over his face. The bark splinters from the floor of the platform had stayed in his hands; he felt them on his cheek with a kind of dazed awakening; he felt the dirt stay on his face and forehead. Unconsciously he walked to the log, standing on its dark side and listening to the muffled voices beneath the factory, the words tense and indistinguishable, broken by the heavy panting as the men worked in the cramped space beneath the factory. Someone had made a foolish attempt to free the log by tearing up part of the track. A peavey was stuck in one of the ties. Winters pulled it free and carried it out of the way with a kind of senseless, mechanical orderliness; he leaned it carefully against the door of one of the vats, thrusting it deep into the earth to hold it upright.

When he walked back there was a stir among the men grouped around the log. Someone crawled backwards from under the factory. As they broke away Winters got a glimpse into the narrow tunnel of light; he could see Hagen's face, red and sweaty, turned sideways in the narrow cramped space; he saw the hoist man lying on his side, his shoulder jammed up high against his cheek, almost over it. *"Hagen!"* someone said. *"You're too big! Let me under there!"*

Hagen crawled out awkwardly, his shoulders forced into a knot as he pushed himself free. He put his weight on the flashlight clasped in his hand, and it dug into the mud; the steam and the water draining from the log had soaked the ground. He held it up stiffly, shifting his weight to his other hand. *"Take it!"* he said. Then he crawled out, breaking free of the men clustered around the log. Someone else dove under the factory with the flashlight. Hagen grabbed one of the men by the arm. *"There's a pair of jacks in the fireroom. Take somebody with you."*

The two men started off down the track. Winters had crowded up to Hagen again, and Hagen saw him. *"Winters,"* Hagen said, *"get Carl's light. He's in the office."*

Winters climbed back up on the platform, suddenly released from the sense of helplessness that had paralyzed and sickened him; he felt his hands hard and firm on the post; he was conscious of his strength as he lifted himself up on the platform. He could hear them talking behind him as he felt his way swiftly along the wall. *"Get some blocks for the jack,"* Hagen was saying. *"Anything. Anything."* Then as he left them behind even the weak reflected light of the flashlight was lost, and he stumbled along with his hand touching the wall to guide him, lifting his feet high to clear the barriers in his path. He remembered the man holding the weak torch, standing by helpless and harassed, the flame barely creeping up the grimy wood—*Ah, poor bastard,* he thought, *poor bastard,* and broke into a run.

H

E was lost.

On one side of him there was a trap of some kind for the steam pipes that led to the kilns. He could feel their heat and hear them trembling under the throb of the pumps from the fireroom. The way ahead was blocked. When he put out his hand he touched the flat expanse of one of the presses, a solid piece of metal rising like a wall, and draining with the thick, gritty perspiration of its oil.

Now what? he thought.

Tell Frankie Carl said to watch the heat. Tell Frankie Carl said to watch the heat.

He remembered Carl yelling at him and his father's stern face. He made a feverish scurry around the barrier. No use. He was lost at the dead-end of a blank passage, lost in a dangerous tangle of creeping vines and poisonous wires, surrounded by lurking saber-toothed machinery. If he moved the other way he got burnt.

I wasn't cut out for this kind of work, he thought.

In the jungle heat. Someone opened an outside door and a breath of fresh air fluttered around the factory like a swallow, beating itself to death against the hot pipes.

How would you like it? he asked some invisible enemy. All right, if you think you know so much. *You dummy! Can't you hear?* And my foot asleep. He winced in a moment of anguish when he remembered the light full on him and Carl bawling him out in front of all the men. I should have told him: *I'll do it! Don't be in such a rush!* Something like that.

Or no. Look him straight in the eye: *Listen, pipe down, I'll take care of it.* Or no. Look him straight in the eye, grin, nodding slightly, *Rave on, rave on.* Yow! What a shock! His face dazed, his eyes popping out of his head, Carl gulped, looked around, stammering uneasily, "Now, see here. . . ." Yow! Baby!

All at once he remembered his father telling him sternly to take it easy, and the memory cooled him off like a bucket of cold water poured over him. *Tell Frankie to watch the heat!*

I'm a nut, he thought despondently. No wonder he thinks I'm a nut.

But immediately he jumped to his own defense again. Why not? he thought. I'm not cut out for this kind of work. It's too heavy for me. He thought of straightening up and bowing down behind the rattling machine, piling the endless pieces of wood on a truck, eight hours a night, every night for the rest of his life. The thought cut through him; it hurt him like a cramp; he could not think of anything else when he thought of it. Leaning over and straightening up, all night long, while his eyes burned and his back ached and the sweat ran down his face, every night for the rest of his life—his blood ran cold when he thought of it; his mind went blank; he had to think about something cheerful to drive it away. He sighed and put his hand against the press. Why was he always looking at the dark side of things? he wondered. Why couldn't he look at the bright side, just for a change? *Tell Frankie to watch the heat!*

Suddenly he heard voices on the far side of the press. They were quite near. He leaped to attention, alert, inquisitive, creeping to the edge of the press so he could hear better.

"He's a damn liar," a voice said dispassionately. "I never said that."

Johnny waited, but there was no answer. Presently he called out, "Do you know where Frankie is?"

"What?"

"Do you know where Frankie is?"

There was a pause, heavy with no answer, until after a time a second voice commented vaguely, "He wants to know where Frankie is."

While Johnny waited, he relaxed against the steel wall of the press. He relaxed from weariness, although he did not know it was weariness, for he had as yet found no name for the curious hunger to lie down which attacked him at this hour every night. His hand slipped on the mushy steel surface of the press. Then he wiped his hand against his trousers, thinking that in the darkness this huge piece of machinery felt as though it were made of mashed potatoes. Something he had read once about three blind men and an elephant crossed his mind. He thought about the blind man grabbing the elephant's trunk and saying that elephants were snakes—what a mistake! Suppose some poor blind man got in the factory, what would he think it was like?

"Maybe he's outside," the voice said. "There's a door over there."

Where? Johnny asked soundlessly. What door? He waded back through the darkness the way he had come, sneaking around until all at once he came to the secret door and a flight of steps leading down into the darkness. He stopped at the top of the steps. The fresh air tasted good. He breathed with a calisthenic regularity. Something was happening to the sky. While he watched, a red streak spurted over town and climbed toward the clouds, streaming up and up until it crashed suddenly against the far edge of nothing, crashed in a silent explosion and shattered, sending out wonderful bubbles of yellow and blue and red light that sank slowly and went out, leaving the sky as cloudy and as vacant as before. A moment later there was a distant rush of noise, a series of muffled explosions chattering together and chasing each other around the top side of the clouds.

He waited until he remembered that he was supposed to be

delivering a message. A man was leaning against the building directly below him. Johnny cleared his voice and asked, "Do you know where Frankie is?"

The man did not answer, but from the darkness beyond him another voice said, "Here I am. What do you want?"

"Carl said to tell you to watch the heat."

"All right."

That was all. Didn't anybody know how hard it was to get from one end of the factory to the other? Steaming and sweating and bumping into things and barking his shins? After all this, was Frankie only going to sit there without moving? Anybody could tell that it was too hot in the factory. But Frankie merely sat by the wall and continued to smoke a cigarette.

"The son of a bitch," Frankie said abruptly.

There was no response, and no more talking. Another rocket lifted over the town. As the globes of light fell the hills beyond came to life for an instant, the trees looking gray and mildewed. The boy dropped down the steps and found a place for himself, somewhat away from the others, on a pile of steel casks. The words kept swinging through his mind, *Tell Frankie to watch the heat,* like some nagging song he tried to forget and couldn't. All that, the bawling out, running through the factory, barking his shins, all for nothing! And now Frankie didn't move; he sat there like a bump on a log; and now Carl would think he hadn't delivered the message, and would probably fire him. Yes, and then there would be hell to pay! What's the use? he asked himself drearily; the workingman hasn't got a chance; he works like a dog, and what good does it do him? All right, let them fire me. All right, fire me, he thought, if you want to fire a man for trying to do his duty. But at the same time a cold uneasiness crept over him as he thought of what the folks would say if he got fired, of his mother sighing and apologizing for him, saying not to worry about it. . . . Then another rocket sailed over town, and the dark gloomy thoughts flapped away, scattering like crows frightened when a shot is fired.

Johnny looked about him carefully to see if anyone was near before he lit a cigarette. He shielded the flame of the match with his hand, a trick he had learned after hours of secret practice. He had bought a package of cigarettes after his first night at work, but he was still shy about smoking them for fear people would think he was showing off. Also, it was difficult for him to light a cigarette. He could get it lighted most of the time, but he could not keep it lighted after it was lit. If he smoked he was able to keep the cigarette burning, but this meant that his lungs would fill up with smoke, that he would cough and choke and feel generally despondent, and it did not seem worth the trouble it caused him.

He drew back behind the steel barrels and struck a match, jumping nervously because the light flared over a wide area and because he knew his features must be clearly outlined and visible even from the factory. In a momentary agitation, as he attempted to cover the flame, he burned the palm of his hand. He dropped the match at once and pressed his hand to his lips, sucking at the carbony residue of smoked flesh and rocking his head from side to side with the pain.

And now what? He hated to light another match. All the men sitting around, he thought, would know he had been unable to light his cigarette with one match. Even now, in his fancy, they were sitting back snickering and whispering to one another, "Look at that kid, he can't even light a cigarette." But then, he thought, if he didn't try to light it again, they would be chuckling harder than ever, knowing that he had given up because he didn't have nerve enough to try again.

For a moment, in a helpless and harrowing nervousness, he pretended that his cigarette was actually lighted all the time, and pretended to be smoking it, but this ruse was obviously unsuccessful, and the dead taste of the unburning tobacco hurt his throat. In the darkness he took the cigarette from his lips with a gesture indicating extreme surprise. What! he exclaimed soundlessly, not lighted after all! and gave way to silent astonishment while he searched through his pockets for another match. Then he climbed down behind the barrels and hid himself as much as he could while the light flared and the tip of his cigarette began to glow. With his desperate manner, as well as his appearance of secrecy, he gave an impression of attempting to set fire to the factory.

As he sat down again he heard someone scrambling across the barrels. He ditched his cigarette. "Say!" this newcomer asked unexpectedly, "ain't you Johnny Hagen?"

Johnny jumped. "Yes," he said. He was much surprised. "Why yes," he repeated. "That is, yes, sure."

"I thought so! I thought I recognized you! Maybe you know me—Connor's my name, Walt Connor."

Johnny jumped to his feet. This was something like it! "Hagen's mine," he responded warmly, clasping Walt's outstretched hand, "John Hagen. Glad to know you." This was more like it, he thought with pleasure, this was the way fellows introduced themselves to each other in college, or even in high school if they were smart and willing to get out in the world and learn how to meet people. So he shook hands warmly, pressing Walt's palm with great vigor because he had frequently heard that there was no surer sign of a weak character than a flabby handshake.

"Well," Walt said, "I never thought I'd see you here, Hagen. How long have you been working?"

"Well," Johnny replied, somewhat off at a tangent. "I never thought I'd see you here either."

"You just starting?"

"A week," Johnny said. "This is the end of my first week."

"Where you work?"

"I'm off-bearing behind the cut-off saw."

"Ah," Walt said. "That was the first job I had when I came here."

"Was it?"

"Yeah. I worked there about three months, then I got put

on the kiln and then I got put out in the stockroom and now I'm breaking down presses."

He could see Walt's large face and the expanse of his white shirt. A white shirt, he thought: How does he keep it from getting dirty? He remembered him as the president of the Student Council and the president of his class and getting two letters in football the year they never won a game. He flicked the ashes off his cigarette.

"Did you graduate this year?" Walt asked.

"Yeah."

"You going on?"

"Yeah. Well," Johnny said, "that is, I don't know. I want to go this fall, but my old man won't let me and I thought maybe I'd save enough money by the time school started, but now I was supposed to be getting three and a half a day to start—when I started I heard that was the lowest they paid—but now I found out tonight I only get two and a quarter. I was supposed to get two and a half the timekeeper told me, but then they gave everybody a ten per cent cut."

Walt nodded. "How much did you get?"

"Well, I only worked three days on last pay day, so my check was only five dollars and twenty-five cents because they took out a dollar for insurance and fifty cents for the doctor or something and then they took off a lot for other things."

Walt nodded again. "It don't look like you'll go to college this fall, does it?"

He drew back at a note of satisfaction in Walt's voice. Rubbing it in, he thought. "No," he said. "Are you going back?"

Walt sat down. "How the hell can I?" he said bitterly. "I've been working here almost a year. I haven't saved a cent. My old man can't give me any money—I have to give him money. If I don't we'll lose our house. What chance have I got?"

Chilled, Johnny said, "That's tough." He sat down beside Walt on one of the oil cases. What a life! He took a weak drag on his cigarette. Why look at the dark side of things? he thought. Why not look at the bright side once in a while?

"I'll go back," Walt said grimly, "some way or other; I won't stay here. If I do stay here I won't stay at this lousy job. I work like a dog now and I have to work harder all the time. The Polack I work with, he gives me the heavy end of every truck. He knows I'm new on that job and he shoves off everything on me. . . . Hell, at first here I had it soft; I was working with Winters and he was breaking me in, but now I work like a dog. You work with Winters?"

"Yeah."

"He's a good guy to work with. He's the only one here I like; he's the only one that don't try to make it hard for you if you're a new man. These God-damn Polacks, hell, they knife you every chance they get."

Johnny listened. He sat back and let his cigarette burn down and listened. Walt moved around restlessly, sometimes beating his fist impatiently against his open palm. "All they do is beef," he said. "Right now . . . I got a chance at a good job and they're making a lot of trouble. . . ."

Another skyrocket sailed over town.

"If I was back in school!" Walt said. "You don't know what you miss. Now I'd appreciate it. Now I'd know what to get out of it. Before, all I did was run around and blow in the old man's dough. After the football season I was drunk three nights every week. Girls used to come around begging for it."

Johnny sighed and tried to sit back more comfortably.

"I'm going to go," he said. "Sooner or later. If the old man can't send me I'll find some way."

Walt gave a skeptical grunt. He said nervously, "They all do it. Even Winters. They beef all the time. You can't depend on them. All these foreigners try to take advantage of you. If you don't stand up for your rights—Jesus, you're done for. Like this Polack I work with. He knows I'm a new man, so he thinks I can't tell when he's shoving off all the work on me. . . . It reminds me," Walt said, "of a story I read once in *The Saturday Evening Post*. It was in them lumber camps up in the Canadian woods; a college man went up there, and the French Canadians, tough bastards, tried to raise hell with him. Put icicles in his bed, and stole his shoes and did every Goddamn thing. You know, they tried to break him; if he was yellow, they'd beat the hell out of him. Finally he beat some of them up, and they saw they couldn't walk over him."

"I think I read that story," Johnny said. "There was a big fight in the end where they jumped on each other with their calked shoes and tried to gouge each other's eyes out, wasn't there?"

Walt nodded. With his head tipped back, looking out across the tideflat, he seemed preoccupied and determined; Johnny felt sort of sorry for the Polack. He wondered vaguely if they were trying to put anything over on him because he was a new man; but the only person who could be doing it was Winters, or maybe Carl. "Gee," he said, "it certainly seems funny—I never thought—what I mean is, everybody here! Sort of hard to get along with!"

"Yes," Walt agreed. He lit a cigarette. Inhaling thoughtfully, with his head thrown back, he flicked the match out on the tideflat. "A bunch of Polacks," he said. "They're all Polacks. The squarehead I work with drives me nuts."

Here Johnny felt a little chill. After all, his father worked in the factory, and he worked in it too, so it was hardly fair to go calling them all Polacks just because they worked in the factory. Walt corrected himself. "Oh, of course some of the fellows are all right," he said. "Winters is all right. But most of these guys are hopeless. The goofy Polack I work with now, he always gives me the heavy end of every truck. Some day I'm going to lam him one. He thinks he's putting it over on me and that I don't know what he's doing. Some day I'm not going to say a word, I'm just going to haul off and paste him one. I don't care if they fire me for it."

[107]

Somewhat impressed by this determination, Johnny did not say anything. The spasms of the rockets followed one another at periodic intervals, and once an underslung tugboat, with its mast and stack tilted so it could pass under the bridges, floated by close to shore. The men stretched out in their varied attitudes of repose, crabbing to each other in low voices, or stirring to rest more comfortably or to light their cigarettes. Listening to Walt, Johnny felt a confused stir of worry and longing. Suppose he couldn't go to college? For the last year, all during his senior year at high school, he had been worried about it; all his friends were going; everybody knew that ninety-nine per cent of the men in *Who's Who* were college graduates. But how could he go? He was beginning to see that unless somebody left him a lot of money, or he won a prize or something, he wouldn't have a chance; his father would never earn enough to send him; and now with all the family home. . . . As he listened to Walt he thought about something he had read, about dusk stealing over the campus and the late students hurrying from the ivy-covered buildings toward the lighted fraternity houses and the sound of young carefree voices rising from Fraternity Row. What could he do if he didn't go to college? Work in the factory all his life? The thought of it made his blood run cold. When Walt, after throwing away his cigarette, took out his square, blunt, English pipe and said he guessed he would stoke up, Johnny was thinking about college with such intensity that he was almost in despair. Suppose he could not get to college? Suppose he could not get enough money, ever? Suppose his father never earned any more than he did now? Suppose he had to work in the factory for the rest of his life?

Oh, he thought, why am I always looking on the dark side of things?

He sat back and listened to Walt, dreaming of the ivy-covered halls, the long slopes of green lawn, the beautiful coeds, each with her own sports roadster, giving herself so gaily and passionately with a true F. Scott Fitzgerald abandon; yes, and long canoe rides on the lake, with the water lapping the frail sides of the fragile craft, and long bull-fests, blue with tobacco smoke, before the open fire of the country-club fraternity house, and fellows smoking pipes sitting up all night chewing the fat about philosophy and sex! What a life! Yes, and real hard work too, cramming for exams in the spring, when the air was raw and the leaves off the trees, staying up all night drinking hot coffee and cramming for exams tomorrow morning. And the beautiful girls, each lovely coed with streamlined hips and dainty breasts barely perceptible under a clinging pull-over sweater, pinned down and yielding on the secret davenports of a dark sorority house. "The Dekes are a good house," Walt said. "We got some good men." Johnny decided that soon he too would buy a pipe.

A lot of questions began circling around in his mind. "I been wondering," he said hesitantly, "what I mean is, I read an editorial once, are fraternities a good thing? This editorial, I remember, it said they made for an un-American snobbishness among the students, sort of, like Greece and Rome."

"Hah!" Walt said. "What the hell. Some independent probably wrote it, some sorehead, son of a bitch, couldn't make a fraternity himself, so he's got a grudge against them. You run into that all the time."

"That's what I thought." They were silent for a time. "Then I was reading in *College Days*—there was an article—is too much emphasis placed on sport? You know, it said there was too much emphasis on sport, and the moral standard was low and there was a lot of drinking and orgies going on all the time."

"It makes me smile," Walt said, "to hear you refer to *College Days*."

"Why?"

"Well, for one thing, you never see a copy of that magazine within ten miles of the campus. Nobody at the house ever read it."

[109]

"I don't read it," Johnny said hastily. "I just happened to pick up a copy, and I saw this article, and I wondered."

Walt sat down, leaning forward with his elbows resting on his knees, his pipe cupped in the palm of his hand. From time to time, between his comments, his pipe gave off a choked, strangled, bubbling sound.

"A lot of people," he began, "think college students are always running around and raising hell."

Here he stopped, and Johnny waited breathlessly. Were college students always running around and raising hell? Walt did not answer him at once. He puffed thoughtfully at his pipe before he said anything, and tamped the tobacco down in the bowl with great care.

"As a matter of fact," he said, "I doubt if you could find a more serious-minded bunch of fellows anywhere than the fellows in the house."

At this point he stopped, waiting somewhat belligerently to be questioned. Johnny nodded. He had never doubted that the fellows in the house were among the most serious-minded you could find anywhere.

"I mean it!" Walt went on emphatically. "You don't believe me when I tell you some of the fellows in the house never go out. They just stay in all the time." He paused again, and Johnny made a noncommittal *uhm!* sound in his throat. "That's why it's such a laugh," Walt went on, after a moment, "when all these people say the fellows never do anything but run around. They haven't time! How can they! Why good God!" he cried with sudden vigor, "Some of these people who are always saying that college is a waste of time never saw the inside of a college! That's a fact! They don't know a damn thing about it!"

"That's right," Johnny said quickly, filled with contempt for all the people who gave snap judgments on things they knew nothing about.

Walt removed his pipe from his mouth and spoke with a

slow, deliberate intensity. "Listen, Hagen," he said. "Ninety per cent of the fellows at the university are working their way through school. Ninety per cent! I think it's ninety per cent. Think of that! I know a guy—Flynn his name is—his folks never gave him a cent. Every summer he had to go to work as a forest ranger. You think that makes any difference? *Ha!*" he exclaimed scornfully. "And then people say it's only a waste of time!"

They were silent while they considered the injustice of it.

"The dirty bastards," Walt said at last.

Nodding, Johnny acknowledged the truth of these remarks. Of course, he thought, naturally the people who didn't know the first thing about colleges would be the first to criticize them. If they knew the facts they wouldn't be so critical. He was filled with a growing anger against these people who were always saying that college was a waste of time. "The crazy boobs," he muttered.

"Can you imagine it?" Walt asked. "Can you imagine it?"

"Gosh," Johnny replied. Then, as this seemed inadequate as an expression of his contempt, he went on, "It's pretty terrible."

"Terrible!" Walt roared. "Terrible's no name for it!"

Johnny was thinking that it certainly wasn't true that fraternities made fellows snobbish! As a matter of fact, he had never believed this, because he thought that it must be a good thing for a lot of congenial fellows to be living together in the same house, sort of sharing each other's problems, besides the social advantages, such as learning how to meet people and making good contacts that would be useful in later life, for everybody knew that the friendships formed in college were among the most precious things in a man's life. And from the way Walt Connor, who you'd expect to be stuck on himself, was acting, coming up and introducing himself and shaking hands in the most natural way in the world, it certainly didn't look as if fraternities made fellows very snobbish!

[111]

Checking his mirth, Walt went on in an *oh-of-course-in-certain-instances* voice, "I won't say there aren't some fellows who don't go out of their way to raise general hell and give the school a rotten reputation. I won't say there aren't. There are. But what can you expect? You can't get any bunch of healthy young fellows together and expect them to just sit at home all the time."

At first Johnny was sobered to think that there were two sides to every question, but as soon as he saw what Walt was driving at he was reassured. Naturally there would always be some who would want to raise general hell because they were young, like himself; he wouldn't expect himself just to sit around all the time, so why expect others? When Walt was talking about how serious-minded everybody was at the house, Johnny had wondered uneasily if he would be serious-minded enough, but now he saw that there was a way out—you could be serious-minded and still run around and raise hell once in a while if you wanted to.

"Of course not," he replied. Then he took a savage blow at the people who were always criticizing colleges, and fraternity men in particular. "What do they expect?" he asked scornfully.

But Walt went even further. "I won't say," he said quietly, "that there aren't some fellows who aren't just looking for trouble and go to college for whatever they can get out of it. Some of them do. I admit it. In fact, I know of one case in particular . . . a fellow you may have heard of—fraternity man, too—you may know him. . . ."

Here his voice died away, and he sat back shaking his head while he tamped the tobacco down in his pipe, making quick jabs against the coals with his finger. Johnny waited to find out what the fellow had done. What could he have done? Steal? Cheat? Get some girl in trouble? Probably he was weak, Johnny thought, not vicious. But as the silence continued, he realized that Walt was not going to say any more. For a moment he was puzzled, and then he understood that

Walt was not going to repeat idle gossip or injure a fellow who was down. It was a real gentlemanly sporting attitude, and the first time Johnny had observed it at such close range. He was deeply stirred, and somewhat awed, but at the same time he racked his brains trying to figure out what the fellow could possibly have done.

Suddenly there was a loud scream from the factory. After a moment there was another. Johnny jumped to his feet. What had happened? He looked at Walt. Should they do anything? Run back inside? Was somebody hurt? But Walt was only listening. There were no more screams. In a moment there was a shout from inside, nor far beyond the nearest wall. *Let her up! Can't you see she's tired?*

"They're screwing in there," Walt said quietly.

Johnny said, "Ah," in an involuntary expression of disbelief, before he corrected himself with "Are they?" and added in confusion, "How do you know?"

"I know."

Johnny turned to stare at the factory again, seeing it dimly outlined against the sky, a huge and shapeless heap of darkness more intense than the darkness surrounding it. His heart began beating more rapidly at the thought that people were actually screwing inside, beyond the thin walls a few feet away, in the hot, oppressive silence. Where? Right there? He had suspected that the girls were all as hard as nails, but to think that right there, in the factory. . . . "Gosh," he said. It was too much for him. There was a long silence as they both stared at the lascivious manufacturing plant standing there in the lonely tideflat like a car parked in the bushes beside a country road.

Walt put his pipe away. He relaxed and drew a deep breath. "Bunch of chippies," he said. His voice was a little strained.

Johnny nodded. His heart was still pounding. How did Walt know? He glanced sideways at his friend, wondering if Walt too. Probably, he thought. Yes. "God," Johnny said.

His hands clenched and he walked a few steps from a restlessness that gripped him too suddenly for him to wonder whether it was right or not, whether it was what a fraternity man ought to do. *Let her up!* Were they? he wondered. Or was it merely? Another burst of fireworks spilled out across the sky in all directions, but he did not look up, scarcely aware of them for the inner excitement that held him. All of them? Or only a few? He tried feverishly to remember how the girls looked, but he could not visualize them personally or distinctly; in his memory they all seemed exactly alike.

Walt stood up and stretched. He was a good deal taller than Johnny. He put his hands over his head, clutching at the air and yawning. "I've got my car here," he announced.

"You have?"

"Yes."

A long silence fell while they stared at the dark building. Nothing else happened. There was no more shouting, no more screaming, only a passionate silence. Johnny felt weak. His legs were beginning to tremble.

"Jesus," Walt said, after a time, "I hated to come to work tonight. I tried every way I could to get out of it. There'll be a lot going on downtown even after work. I was thinking I might go home and change my clothes and go down to the Biltmore. It only ought to take me about half an hour to get a bath and slip into my tux and get back downtown. . . ." He yawned again, flexing his quarterback muscles. "What a life!" he said. "Without a wife!" He turned to Johnny abruptly. "By the way," he said. "Do you know the two girls—sisters—work on the table up at this end?"

"Where?"

"One's tall," Walt said. "Black hair. Sister's about your height. I've seen them around town." His voice was somewhat stiff. "Polacks. You know who I mean."

"Oh," Johnny said. "The Turner girls."

Now he understood. Putting two and two together, Walt's

[114]

car and the Turner girls, a cold chill went down his spine as he realized what Walt was suggesting. Now he understood why Walt made such a point of having his car at work. All his life he had known about the Turner girls. Their name was not really Turner. It was Dombroski, or something like that, but they had changed it to Turner when their mother married again. Even in grade school he had known about them. Once some big kids had put Johnny and some of the little kids up to asking the Turner girls if they would for a nail, on the supervised playground of the Benjamin Franklin school. Then in high school Marie Turner finally got expelled for doing it under the grandstand with the quarterback of Centralia's tricky eleven. Everybody knew they did it all the time, living as they did on the wrong side of the river and maintaining a low standard of living like all the foreigners because they sent all their money back home to their folks in the Old Country. When Johnny began to think of himself and the Turner girls in Walt's car, he thought only *I wonder* and *Suppose,* with his mind floundering downstream among the possibilities.

"You see I thought," Walt was saying, "I wondered if you. What I mean is this. If you want to take the little one home, I'll take her sister. You see? You know them better than I do. You ask."

Here a quick flash of resistance crossed Johnny's mind. Why me? he asked silently.

Then, a moment later, a dirty, disloyal thought, cynical and unworthy of him, set him to wondering if Walt had come to him with such complete fraternity-brother affability with this secret mission always at the back of his mind. No, he decided, depressed at his own pessimistic disloyalty in crediting such morbid cunning to his new-found friend.

"Me," he said blankly. "Why don't . . . I mean, why should I. . . ."

"It's my car," Walt replied.

[115]

At this an uncomfortable silence fell. There was no evading the truth of this remark, however depressing it might be.

"Besides," Walt went on, "you know them better than I do."

Here Johnny defended himself again. "I don't know them." He felt a twinge of resentment that Walt should think just because his father worked here he was friendly with the Turner girls, although at the same time he would have liked to pretend that he knew them very well.

"No, but you're . . . you're more in contact with them than I am."

Johnny remained silent.

"What the hell!" Walt said. "What is there to it? Just go ask them if they want a ride home—tell them your friend's got his car here, what's hard about that?"

"Yes," Johnny said. "But."

Walt walked away. "Of course if you don't want to. I just thought if you wanted to take the little one I'd take her sister. But if you don't want to, what the hell. It don't mean anything to me."

"No, it ain't that. . . ."

Walt sat back down again. "Never mind, never mind." They stared at the dissolute factory building. "Some of these Polacks," Walt said, "are damn good nooky."

Johnny did not reply.

"Come on, don't be yellow. What the hell. What's so hard about it? Just go ask them if they want to ride home; tell 'em your friend's got his car here, and he's perfectly willing to let them ride home—what the hell? Is that so hard?"

"Why don't you ask them?"

Walt made a gesture indicating extreme impatience. "I already asked Marie. She wouldn't. I just thought maybe if you was there to take her sister she would. I'd ask her again only I thought maybe you wanted to take the little one home, and you know them better than I do. Besides," Walt said, "these God-damn chippies, they sort of look down on a college

[116]

man. . . . But, Jesus, if you don't want to, forget it! It don't mean anything to me. I just thought maybe you wanted to take the little one home, so I'd be willing to take her sister."

He strolled off and pitched a few pebbles into the darkness. Johnny tried to think. What should he do? How begin? Should he be polite and say, "How do you do, Hagen's my name, I was wondering if you girls wanted to ride home tonight?" Or should he be breezy, informal and begin with a happy-go-lucky, carefree smile, "Listen, baby"? He thought and thought but he kept getting cold feet because he could not imagine what they would say in reply.

"Come on," Walt said. "Ask them. What the hell."

And suppose they did agree, then what? He tried to think of himself with Ellen Turner in the back seat of Walt's car, in the dark back seat with that little chippie—what should he do first? How begin? For although he hoped for the best, he could not imagine Ellen Turner, like all the this-side-of-paradise sweethearts he read about, placing her smooth white arms around his neck and murmuring, You can have me if you want me, darling. You can have me.

No.

"Come on," Walt said. "What are you afraid of?"

Listen, a voice said. *Just say the word and I'll walk out.*

6. ROSE

IN town too some of the houses were dark. Along the waterfront and in some of the residential districts there were great patches of shadow, lighted only by the headlights of the cars that passed through them, and from the hill in back of the city these areas were like those parts of maps marked unknown, standing out all the more clearly because the street lights were still burning in the areas around them. In one of the large houses on the hill, Rose MacMahon stood looking down at the tangle of light and dark, attracted by the feverish unreal beauty of the night and repelled by the quarrel that her parents had been having in the house, turning her back on them and trying to close her mind to what they were saying. Upstairs her father was moving around on some mysterious task. Below the MacMahon house the lawn sloped to the driveway where the car was parked. Beyond the driveway there were a few scattered houses and then the hill leveled off to the crowded streets of town, the first widely separated lights growing more dense and frequent until they merged in an indistinguishable glow at the main streets and the lighted tower of the Past Bay National Bank. Over the harbor beyond town the searchlights of the destroyers darted nervously, the beams solid and firm in the smoky air.

The girl looked down at all this, seeing its strangeness for the first time and unconsciously responding, still shaken and exposed after the fury of the quarrel her parents had had, still sick at heart at their crudeness, at the savagery with which

[118]

they had turned on each other. An hour before she had been composed and waiting; the house had been quiet. Her mother had been dressing, the girl had been finishing her work in the kitchen and the faint sounds of her movements, the rattle of the dishes and the sound of water being drawn and drained off, had been quiet and familiar and comfortable, and then the peace had been broken when her father came home and she had been drawn into a quarrel before she even knew what it was about. Anything could start it, a word spoken in the wrong tone of voice or a glance of contempt, and in an instant her parents would be at each other's throats and the abyss of hostility between them would be revealed. She had heard them when her father first came in, their voices gradually growing more bitter and more loud as the restraints dropped away, and the quarrel, like some untrustworthy animal, had got out of control. She heard the familiar warnings they wasted on each other and the insults and loud cries of anger, before they started accusing each other of extravagance and deceit. In the kitchen, she knew, the maid would be listening in excitement, and the next time they passed the girl would give her a poisoned, embarrassed, understanding glance, a kind of gloating hidden in the uncertain expression on her face.

She could not stand it. It was nothing new but she could not harden herself to expect it, and her shame for them and her fear of the ridicule or amusement she thought she saw in the eyes of her friends was too much for her. When she sensed the danger of these outbreaks she tried to get away and to see to it that none of her friends visited the house, for she could not trust her parents to control their anger even when other people were around. A long time ago when they had lived in another part of town she had learned how these quarrels grew, how they would begin with a single word or a glance, how that drew an answer and then another, until at last she thought of her parents as periodically being caught up in some huge mechanical device that carried them through the same cycle of screaming at each other, the same tense and broken cries of humiliation, the same slamming of doors, tears, her father leaving the house and her mother coming to her, holding her in her arms and sobbing her vindictive endearments. . . .

She knew all this by heart. Once in her childhood one of the girls she played with had said, "Your mother and father don't get along." Even then she had known that this was an echo of something someone else had said, and that if she heard this much, it meant there was a great deal that she did not hear. She learned to protect herself by being uncommunicative and not exposing herself to any mention of the common mystery of her family; then she learned to be casual and indifferent and to make fun of their squabbling. But even so her girlhood was marked in her memory by these gross landmarks: a period when her father had disappeared for a week and had come back morose and unyielding; a time when something had been delivered at the house and there was not enough money to pay for it and her mother, in a rage, had thrown the package out into the yard. She remembered the yellow grass, the box breaking open, and countless scenes of torment stretching back into her memory like ugly monuments, such as are put up after battles, to commemorate shameful happenings.

She looked down at the city, tasting the smoky air, still weak and shaken after flying at them both, hoping that the boy who was coming for her would get there before the brief peace was broken. She had not known why they fought, except that she was sure it was about money and about her father's drinking and some promise he had not kept, about something her mother had said and then about all their quarrels, one after another, to the beginning. She heard their voices growing more urgent and upset while she finished dressing, and she went downstairs, calmly at first, to call her boy and tell him that she would meet him somewhere else. They stopped while she phoned. Her mother had been saying mysteriously, "It will be a long time before you'll have a chance to humiliate me again!" and her father had been sitting on the davenport, his face flushed and coarse, when she came into the room. From the expression on her face, from some look of contempt, her mother had guessed that she was going to let them see how she felt; she had turned on Rose suspiciously and she had looked hurt when Rose answered her question by saying that she was going to call Roger and tell him she would meet him at his house. She had thought briefly of the girl listening in the kitchen, storing up the words she heard and carrying them to her friends to gloat over in secret.

They had been silenced for a moment, not too far gone to see the reproach in her phoning, until she called Roger and learned that he was out. Then she thought she saw a dull malicious triumph on their features, and when her mother said innocently, "I thought you said he was coming here," she slammed the receiver back on its hook.

"It doesn't matter," she replied. "I just thought I'd save him coming here."

She started out to the front of the house, and her father said for her benefit, after a period of silence, "I got the garage bill. It was a hundred and twenty dollars."

She knew why he had said it, for if her mother was triumphant about his thoughtlessness or unreliability, he could answer her by charging her with extravagance, so that when he lost and she had succeeded in making him feel his guilt he would try to force the argument back to grounds where he was sure of victory. But her mother saw it too and flared up, "And is that why you've kept me waiting!" Then as she went outside, to watch the first skyrockets bombarding the sky, she heard them beginning again as heatedly as if they had not been interrupted. It was his story that his debts and the money

[121]

they spent and his overwork excused whatever he did, and hers that he begrudged her the simplest necessities.

She heard him saying monotonously, "I don't know about that. But I do know we've got to cut down and we've got to retrench and we've got to stop throwing money right and left and I can't put out a hundred and twenty dollars every few weeks on that car. They're doing it at the mill and we've got to do it here." She was stirred at the dull conviction in his voice. She walked out into the yard where the lawn sprinkler was beating lightly on the grass and though she could no longer hear them she knew they were still going on in the quiet room, her mother moving heavily back and forth, the beads on her dress making a faint gravel sound when she moved, straightening a rug by moving it with her foot, pausing to move an ashtray back where there would be no danger of its falling, and her father watching her sternly, the flush on his cheeks emphasizing the gray decaying pouches under his eyes. She could no longer hear them but the knowledge that they were still fighting made her restless, and Roger's being late wore on her nerves. When she went back her mother said bitterly, "You've reminded me of it enough!" and she knew that they had reached the stage when they were going back over the old fights, digging up the sore points in them. She sat down quietly, paying no attention to either of them, sitting down and waiting nervously until her mother asked, "Isn't Roger coming for you?"

She said "Yes," and the three of them eyed one another, all on guard against hidden insults. The girl left, closing the back door softly, and walked down the lighted driveway, her head turned away from the house. Her father said abruptly, "And if you knew how things stood there wouldn't be any more talk of going to the mountains." They raged at each other for a few minutes, until she looked up and tried to make the distaste clear on her features:

"I can't blame him for not wanting to get here early."

[122]

He turned on her. "By God, Rose, I'm telling you the truth! I've got a letter from Digby right here!" He waved the piece of paper, conscious of the effect Digby's name had on them. "I mean what I say!" he cried. "I'm borrowed up on everything I own. The mill won't be running this winter if things don't pick up." Then he began reciting details to them, mentioning interest and stock he had put up with the bank and figures on orders, knowing the words were unfamiliar to them and knowing that it increased his stature in their eyes to rattle them off so fluently. "We're running on export orders now," he said. "And we lose on every foot of stock we ship. We've got to cut down and we got to begin doing it and I'm in earnest! I'm in earnest! If we shut down this winter and the bank calls in my loan I won't own a share of stock in that plant. Now you think that over."

She said impatiently, "I know it and have I said anything? Have I complained? But you don't have to tell the neighbors and you could at least wait till Roger and I leave."

"You keep out of this," he said.

"You just told me you wanted me to listen!"

"If I can't talk over business affairs with my own wife in my own house," he said, "without having to wait on some little college boy who hasn't two cents to his name. . . ."

Her mother said, "Charles, you've no reason to take that attitude."

He warned them, "I'm fed up with it."

"I'm fed up with it too."

She started to speak but he turned to her again. "You keep out of this. This doesn't concern you."

Her mother said sharply, "Charles! There's no excuse . . ."

"Ah, Christ," he said in disgust. He lit his cigar, his hand trembling with irritation. "If you only knew," he began, and she knew that he was going to say again if they only knew what he really thought.

"You've no right to talk to us that way," her mother said,

[123]

and she looked at her mother, at the large features now frozen into what her mother thought was calm dignity, the beaded dress that draped on her elegantly and made her look like a madame in a whore house. . . .

"Let him alone," she said impatiently. "You know when he's like this. . . ." Now I've said it, she thought.

"Rose, I've given you everything you ever asked for," he said.

The skyrockets began to rise toward the smoke, one after the other, mounting from some hidden pit behind a rise on the hill and climbing toward the sky in a rush of fire. The hills turned gray and green and the unearthly light revealed the roofs of the houses. There was a faint *hush!* prolonged after the silent explosion, and then the noise of the explosion. I shouldn't have said that, she thought, remembering her outraged fury when he said *I've given you everything you ever asked for,* and the discomfort and guilt she felt as she did not reply. Oh, have you? she had thought, bitter and remorseful, thinking, Everything but what I wanted, while he spoke of ingratitude and having his own daughter ashamed of him, sometimes whining with pity for himself and sometimes lifting his voice in anger against her. Then he had gone upstairs, but there was no end to it, for when she had gone outside to get away from them her mother had waited sorrowfully in the front room, large, poised, noble, never conscious of how ridiculous her pose of noble suffering made her seem.

She waited. Roger was half an hour late but there was not enough life left in her to be angry; she listened to the rustle of the water from the sprinkler on the grass and watched the stray skyrockets dart like huge, lighted insects across the sky, her eyes dilated from crying. When they first began, when the first colored bubbles had begun to float down to earth, she had called to her mother to come watch them, mostly to show that she was sorry for the way she had acted and now wanted to make up. But her mother had moved around with her intolerable sweet-suffering dignity, getting up slowly from the heavy chair and crossing the room while the beads on her dress made a faint gravel sound as she moved. Large, silent and poised, she had stood in the doorway for a few moments, smiling mistily at the broad darkness below the hill, until Rose had thought, Be a companion to your daughter, and her mother had said, with a quiet, sharing-my-little-girl's-enthusiasm inflection in her voice, "Have they started?" Was it any wonder?

The wonderful ginger-ale bubbles had risen and faded; the hills had mildewed green, disappeared, and she had suffered with her mother's affectations. "Isn't it pretty?" her mother had said, and she had answered silently, Isn't it? Out on the harbor the searchlights from the destroyers crossed the sky, focused on the yellow clouds of smoke. Another rocket lifted; another, another. She looked at her mother, wanting to make up, but her mother looked so sad and so spiritual she could not say it. I'll never learn, she had thought. I always fall for it; I try to be nice and cheer her up, and look.

"Beautiful," her mother had said softly.

Was it any wonder? She bared her teeth at the darkness. "Has he shut up?" she had asked. She remembered her mother stiffening at her tone, glancing at her reproachfully, deciding not to speak, while her features melted slowly to suffering womanhood.

"No," she had confessed, and the beads on her dress had jingled musically as she sighed.

He had yelled down from upstairs, *"I said I didn't know! I told you before I didn't know!"* the words floating off into the windless dark.

"Oh, dear," her mother had murmured, and touched her hand lightly to her forehead. Slowly she turned toward the interior of the house and stepped inside with heavy grace.

"Charles?" she called gently.

A slobber of questions trickled downstairs from behind the closed doors.

Patient womanhood, her mother called back, "Did you call me, Charles?"

Oh, God, she had said to the darkness. Oh, God, I can't stand this. She heard the dim rumble of his words and saw her mother, self-sacrificing patience, standing in the middle of the room under the light, her head tipped sideways to catch his words, her hand pressing over her heart, the sparkles glinting from her long black beaded dress and her face almost as round, almost as bright, almost as expressionless as an electric-light bulb.

"*If I'd known I would have told you!*" he had shouted. "*I simply didn't know!*"

"All right, Charles" her mother had said wearily, "let's don't say any more about it."

"*What?*"

"Let's don't say any more about it."

"*I didn't say anything about it! That's a lie.*" She had winced at his voice, rasping like a file on her nerves. "*I didn't say anything about it and I don't intend to say anything about it. I told you I didn't know I had to go!*"

Her mother had cried out, "*I said, let's don't say any more about it!*" In the front room her mother had smiled mournfully and nervously and put her hand with an aspirin gesture to her forehead, saying, "Very well, Charles, very well," and then she could not stand it any more.

"Let him alone," she had cried. "Can't you see? Haven't you any sense?" Her mother had looked at her blindly and turned on her *you-too!* expression, mouth twisting at life's bitter irony, until she had stammered, "You don't have to look so stepped-on." Then she had wanted to say, *I'm sorry, I'm sorry, I'm sorry I said it, you don't have to tell me,* but her mother had looked at her with her eyes hurt. "I think I've been humiliated enough, Rose," she had said, "without you joining in," and she had tried to say, *I'm sorry,* but no words came. Then they heard him stamping around upstairs, and all at once her mother was no longer affected and annoying, but only a fat and ugly old

[126]

woman, bewildered and disappointed and lost, and she had cried out without knowing what she was saying, "Oh, you make me sick! You mope and yell at each other and I sit here and think I'll go crazy and you go on and on and on and on and I can't *stand* it! Nobody can stand it! I don't see why I have to listen—why you can't let up on it—why you can't." She had felt the tears begin pumping up through her and her mother's figure suddenly began dissolving, rain on chalk, and the room ran together in the candlelight. "Now, Rose," her mother had said in her my-poor-little-girl, my-poor-little-darling voice and the fat arm went around her and she could see the tears beginning to drip silently from the electric-light bulb face. *"Rose!"* her father had called. *"See what your mother wants!"* and "There," her mother had said. "My poor baby." She had pulled herself free and stepped back out on the porch, composing herself in the semi-darkness. She had heard her mother coming after her and had gone down the steps to the lawn. The sprinkler was still turned on and she had heard the needle streams and the wash of water on the grass. "Rose!" her mother had said anxiously, and controlling her tears she had thought, Tell the neighbors.

Then he had yelled down again and her mother had started upstairs. Now she'll tell him, she had thought. Now she'll give him hell.

It was a few moments before Roger came up the walk, his white shirt front shining in the reflected light, his flat straw hat thrust far back on his head. At the far edge of the light he stooped down and brushed his trouser leg, ran his hand lightly over his fly to see if his pants were buttoned, pulled down his coat smartly, touched his hat, and stepped up on the sidewalk.

"Here I am," she said.

He turned quickly, a smile on his face, and walked across the lawn toward her, removing his hat and transferring it from his right hand to his left as he came near. "Well, sweetheart!" he said lightly. "What are you doing out here?"

"If you want to know," she said, "I was moving the sprinkler."

"Ha, ha!" he said. "Moving the sprinkler!"

"Well, I was."

He threw back his head and laughed. "You moving the sprinkler!" he cried. She stared at him.

"You have to," she said. "If it stays in one place it washes up the grass."

"No!" he cried playfully. "You don't mean it washes up the grass!" What a surprise! What a joke! His head went back, the dental smile spread, the straw hat waved.

"Well," she said, after a moment, "you broke your neck to get here."

"What a mob!" he replied obliquely. "You ought to see it. All over the streets. And the sailors."

"What are you trying to do?" she asked. "Teach me a lesson?"

"What do you mean? I'm not late. You didn't say."

"Oh, didn't I? I'm sorry," she said. "I thought I did."

"Well, you didn't."

You liar, she said silently.

They looked toward the house. The orange light from the front windows spread out over the lawn. She could see the shadow as her mother moved inside, and she thought wearily: Now I hope they stay quiet. Now if they'll only stay quiet. The broad smile stayed on his face. Habit, she thought. It must be. He was worried; he swung his straw hat in a nervous embarrassed manner, the smile staying on his face like something left over from some other mood, and ran his free hand over the shining lapels of his dinner jacket.

"Well?" he asked.

She looked away, hiding the expression on her face by looking hard at the lighted tower of the Past Bay National, where your money works for you.

[128]

"Well, what?"

"Well," he said, "did you?"

"No."

The smile stayed on his face. Like a scar. The life went out of it and it stayed on the front of his face.

She pulled off a piece of the cedar hedge and chewed on it. "No," she repeated. "But why'd you ask?"

"Nothing," he smiled. "Just neighborly."

"It's nice of you," she said. "Nice of you to show so much interest."

"Listen, Kit, don't worry. You'll be all right."

The dumb smile never moved.

Over town, the skyrockets. She watched his face while he followed one in its rise.

"No," she said. Then she added, "Worry's the worst thing you could do."

He winced. The smile began to sag a little. I'll get it, she said to the hedge. She could feel her lip drawing back from her teeth. "The very worst," she repeated in a my-goodness voice.

"Did you talk to Madge?"

"Yes."

"What did she say?"

"She said not to worry."

"Ah, Kit," he said. "Listen."

A car came up the drive. They watched it swing around the hairpin curve and slide past with a low steady hum on the far side of the hedge. He looked at her helplessly and she weakened, but then she could see him beginning to build up the defenses again, trying to hide behind his nice teeth and his dumb smile and No, she thought, I won't help you.

"I'm listening," she said.

"Why you sore? Because I'm late? I didn't think. You didn't say. I thought it was all right. When you phoned. It just makes it worse when you act like this."

He stood before her, begging for peace of mind, a word of relief, a crumb of comfort. Helpless without his smile. He must love it, she thought, and she thought of his smile as a toy she had taken away from him, and he would cry until he got it back.

"You *knew* so much," she murmured. "You *knew* so much. And then you said Madge knew so much. I even know more than she does. I at least know what ergot is."

"What did she say?"

She felt a rising disgust. "She was tickled to death," she said. "It'll be all over town by now."

He said, miserably, "No. What did she really say?"

"She was. I could see. She couldn't wait. She asked me and asked me and asked me. Then I drove her on home and she said she'd find out this woman's name and ask Madie and try to think what that girl who was staying with the Murphys did."

He sighed again.

"What about Harry?" he asked. "What'd she say?"

The smile was all gone now and he was not asking for it back. He stood looking miserably at the house, at the water from the sprinkler glinting faintly, his face humble and relaxed.

"She said Harry took care of it." Then she weakened and moved over toward him. "You know something," she said. "They must not do very much because when I said, when I asked her what they did she looked so dumb. I thought for a minute she was pretending to be dumb because she didn't want to tell me what they did, but I asked her and she really is dumb. So I said, Well does he? and she looked so bewildered I knew she never heard of it and her eyes popped out of her head. What can they do?"

He looked absorbed and puzzled, glancing at her with a faint awakening interest crowding out his worry. "She did?" Then he said, "That's funny."

"How could he?"

He grinned. "I guess you could, if you had lots of self-control."

She thought about it for a few moments, thinking what he did and wondering how anybody. "Golly," she said. "I don't see how that could be very much fun."

"Neither do I."

She took his arm and pressed it. "Something else she said," she began.

He said in a low voice, "Jesus, you know something? That must be hard as hell on him. No wonder he looks so all in."

"Would it be?"

"It'd kill me."

She was awed. "Because when you," she said.

"Yeah."

They walked slowly toward the graveled driveway. She held his arm and watched the grass to keep her slippers out of any place where the water from the sprinkler had drained. She laughed abruptly and squeezed his arm. "You know something?" she whispered. "I've been thinking all afternoon. What will he think when she asks him? Because I know she will. And what will he tell her? Because he'll feel like a perfect fool unless he's as dumb as she is."

They stepped into the light from the porch. His eyes glistened; there was an amused superior smile on his lips; he held himself proudly conscious of her hand on his arm. "Hah!" he exclaimed.

She motioned toward the house. "Let's go. They're at it again and they'll be down."

"Mad?"

"No." She whispered hurriedly, "He was supposed to take mother some place for dinner and he didn't come and didn't come and she got hysterical and then he came home drunk— he said he had to go out with the officers from the destroyers— he's on a welcoming committee and then they started to fight and I'm a fool, I got mixed up in it."

He kissed her. "I love you," she said. "It's wrong for you to make me stay here when you know it's such hell." He kissed her again and caressed her for a few moments before he replied. "I didn't know. You didn't tell me when I phoned."

They stepped into the shadows at the edge of the driveway and he kissed her more ardently. She heard the faint rustle of the lawn sprinkler and when she opened her eyes she saw a star suddenly burst overhead, swell into a blue globe as large as the moon and then shatter, and all her nerves felt alive and hot as she closed her eyes while the blue and yellow lights floated softly through the air. She pushed his hand away.

"Come on," she said briskly. "Let's go."

Her father came out on the porch. "Rose," he said. "Rose."

"What?"

"Rose."

His large figure blocked the doorway, sending out a wide and wavering shadow over the lawn. His evening clothes looked wrinkled.

"What is it, papa?"

"Have you gone?"

"No, we're still here."

He peered nearsightedly into the shadow below the porch.

"I wanted to tell you," he began.

They moved into the light. Oh, Lord, she thought. Now all this over again.

"Oh, hello, Claude!" he said.

"This is Roger, Papa."

"Oh, yes! Excuse me, Roger. I thought for a minute you were Claude."

Roger stepped forward cheerfully. "How are you, Mr. Mac-Mahon?" His dental smile was fast asleep on his face. "Fine weather, isn't it?"

"I'm fine, thank you, Roger. As well as I can expect, I guess." His voice was sad; now he's going to be sorry, she thought unhappily, and looked at him; he had been crying; the pouches under his eyes were gray-colored and decayed.

"Don't let me keep you. I just wanted to say. . . ."

She said coldly, "We were just leaving. We're late now." He heard the coldness in her voice and glanced toward her, a fixed, glassy, appealing smile on his face. *I'm sorry,* his body said. *Can't you see that?* He swayed slightly in the doorway, and once his large body gave a sudden jerk as he belched inaudibly. There were huge beads of sweat on his forehead.

"Kitten, I've got to take the car for a few minutes. I'll just be a few minutes."

"Where are you going?"

"Well, I've got to run down to the plant for a while, they're having a little trouble down there. I've got to run down and see what's wrong. I don't expect I'll be gone more than a minute; they called me up a few minutes ago; the lights went off and they're having trouble generally, so I thought I'd better take a run down there and see if I can't get things straightened out."

There was another silence. Her father made no move to leave. "You promised me the car," she said.

"Well, I know, Kitty, and you can have it the minute I get back. I won't be but half an hour, I don't imagine, if that long—probably not that long, certainly no longer. And the minute I get back you can have it, I'll be through with it for the night."

"You promised," Rose repeated bitterly.

"But Kitten," he said. He stomped over to her and put his hand on her head. "How could I know this was coming up? Now how could I?" He smiled at her and then glanced up and smiled at Roger, shaking his head as if they had some secret understanding between them. Roger smiled.

"Oh, I don't suppose it matters," she said. "Nothing I want to do matters. If it wasn't this it would be something else."

He looked appealingly at Roger. "Now, Rose. I told you

[133]

you could have the car when I got back. Can't you take a cab if you're in a hurry? I'll be back in a few minutes."

"Why do you have to go? You never have to go. Can't somebody else go?"

"There's nobody in town, Kitten. Walker's on his vacation and everybody else is away. I'll only be a minute."

"Well, can't we just drive you down and leave you?"

"How would I get back?"

"Couldn't one of the men bring you back?"

"They're busy. They wouldn't be working at all tonight if they weren't busy."

Her mother came out on the porch. "What is it, dear?" she asked before she reached the door, moving with loud and stately poise as her beaded dress rattled when she walked. "Is something the matter? Oh, hello, Roger! How are you?"

"Fine, Mrs. MacMahon, thank you. I'm fine!" he replied, the smile spreading like a bruise. He leaned forward with a salesman's joviality when she held out her hand.

"Sit down!" her mother cried. "Why are we all standing here? Sit down! Isn't it lovely?" she asked Roger.

"Isn't it!" he cried in turn.

"Oh, *lovely!* I've never seen anything so lovely! I've been watching them all evening!"

"Have you?" he cried in delight.

"Oh, I love them," her mother said. "I've always loved fireworks. I've always been crazy about them. When Mr. Mac-Mahon and I were in San Francisco one Chinese New Year."

She heard it, watching to see if they were going to be nice, afraid of something happening. She said, "We'll go down and wait for you. There's no need to wait here."

Her mother looked at her.

"Come on, Roger."

"Where are you going, Rose?"

"We've got to take papa to the mill."

"I thought you were going to wait till he gets back."

[134]

"No, maybe he'll be a long time and if he finds out he'll be a long time we'll leave him and come back for him."

"Oh, very well." Alone again. Sad and sweet.

"Good-night, Mrs. MacMahon! Good-night!"

"Good-night, Roger." So sweet!

She walked ahead of them to the car. Her father's heavy steps on the walk. Hell, she said silently, hell. I never get to do what I want. She jerked the door open viciously, hearing him. *I suppose you run into trouble like this all the time.*

Well, yes, in a way, yes. In another way, no. I will say in the main we've got a smooth organization, seldom any trouble. Even tonight it only happens that Walker, my superintendent, he's away, or I wouldn't be bothered.

Oh, God, she thought. How can he keep it up?

She drove up beside the office and switched off the lights. Two men approached them from the shadows. In the weak, indirect lighting of the dash she saw one of them looking like a detective, carrying a flashlight in his hand. The other moved about uneasily in the background.

"Well, Carl," MacMahon began. "Been having trouble?"

Carl came up and leaned on the door of the car. "Nothing very serious, Charlie," he said. "The lights went out, and I thought I better let you know about it. I would have called Walker, but I remembered he was out of town, so I figured I better call you. . . . It's nothing very serious, but what I was wondering is, I wondered if it wouldn't be better to blow the whistle and send them home. You see, somebody broke in the office—I haven't found anything was taken, but they been raising hell in there ever since the lights went out, running around and yelling, you know. They didn't want to work to-night, so they been raising the devil."

There was a glow of red light from one building, barely visible, but the huge factory itself was dark and silent. The hot smell reached even here. She could see the huge blower perched precariously on the roof, looking as if it were balanced there; a network of tubes and pipes rising above one end of the factory; vague plumes of steam.

"How long have they been off?"

"Ten, fifteen minutes—just before I called you."

"You found out what's wrong?"

"Well, yes," Carl said. "That is, in a way. I'll tell you what I did—I had Hagen check through the factory, to see where the trouble was, and it ain't in the factory. Of that we're sure. Then you see I had to send somebody to watch the heat—I had to take care of that, too, so the sprinklers wouldn't blow. That's all taken care of."

She moved restlessly. "Oh, excuse me!" MacMahon said. "You know my daughter, Carl. Rose, this is Mr. Belcher."

She smiled at him.

"And this is Mr. Hanson; Mr. Belcher, Mr. Hanson."

Carl thrust his hand in front of MacMahon. "Glad to know you, Hanson!" he said cordially.

As they shook hands, Roger murmured, "Schwartz."

"What was that?"

"I say Schwartz."

Carl nodded, looking somewhat puzzled. "Yes," he said. There was a slight, embarrassed silence.

"Well, let's get down to business!" MacMahon said. "They been out now, fifteen, twenty minutes, you say? Is that right? You don't know what the trouble is."

"No. We know it ain't in the factory."

"Did you call the power house?"

"Well, yes, in a way, that is. I had Morley call the power house; you see, I had to hurry around in there before I found a light, and I nearly broke my leg—I tripped over some stuff in there and cut a terrible gash in my leg, right below my knee, and I had to tend to that. I was going to call the power house as a matter of fact when I found they had broken into the office, so I thought I better call you."

[136]

"Did they take anything?"

"Well, no, not so far as I could tell. I only had this one flashlight and I had to get some iodine for my leg. I was afraid it would fester."

"Hum," her father said, "what do you know about that."

"I thought you ought to know."

"That's the limit."

"They're worked up about the cut. I hear them complain."

"Hum," her father said, "that's the limit."

"I thought I ought to tell you before I decided."

They waited. She stared at the dashboard, thinking over the disappointments that had piled up uncontrollably and the slow steady drain of everything she ever looked forward to, and looked up to see Carl watching her father with a curious tense expression of impotence on his pear-shaped face, and really saw him for the first time, stocky and stupid-looking, a kind of brutality marked on his heavy jaws and a kind of animal cunning in his eyes. She was quickened with a moment of vague fear, remembering what her father had said earlier in the night and other warnings he had made before, remembering all the excitement when Carl had first come to the factory and remembering that he came from the Eastern office where Digby sent out his orders. Roger sat back, bored and polite, and her father looked troubled, as though he were making an effort to remember something. The little man moved in and out of the shadow. Beyond them the dormant factory sent out its waves of heat and she looked up at it, trying to read through the technical phrases they used.

"There was that export to finish," Carl said softly. "You said to get it out if we worked all night."

She heard the antagonism in his voice, and knew that her father did not.

"Oh, yes," he said vaguely. Then he sighed. "More trouble. You never know when it's going to get you, do you, Carl?"

"No, you sure don't, Charlie, not in this business you don't," his voice smooth and friendly.

She said, "Hurry, papa. We don't want to be here all night."

"Now, just a minute, Kitten. Just a minute." He turned to Carl again. "You don't know how long they'll be off?"

"No, we don't."

"Hum, I suppose the thing to do is send them home. But I hate to send them home, and then have the lights come on five minutes later."

"That's what I thought."

"Yes, I hate to do that. . . . You're sure it's not in the factory?"

"No." She could see the contempt he felt, and knew her father had asked that question before. As though conscious of his sharpness, Carl went on, "We checked it through—I told Hagen to check it through. You can't depend on him but it's all I could do."

Her father eased himself out of the car. "I guess I better look things over before I decide," he said. "I'll only be gone a minute." As he walked away with Carl and Morley she slumped back in the seat. Beside her Roger stared after them with a childlike inquisitiveness, impressed, she could see, with the way they had consulted her father. She too felt a little pride, but she only said, "They bore me stiff when they get started that way. They never stop." They lit cigarettes and looked out over the town where things were happening, where people were dancing in the hotels and where the drunken sailors would be staggering through the streets, the firecrackers clattering and the skyrockets rushing toward the clouds. "We'll be here all night," she murmured sadly. "Jabber, jabber, jabber, it's all they do."

He nodded, running his finger gently under his stiff collar where it pressed against the tender flesh of his neck.

7. Carl

IT happened almost as soon as they went into the factory, and it was over in an instant; there was a moment of confusion, a brief struggle, and then someone hit him and then he was standing alone in the singing darkness wondering what had happened and who had hit him. He had been telling Mac-Mahon about having Frankie Dwyer watch the sprinklers, and Morley had been tagging along behind, when all at once he heard them shouting, *There he is! There he is!* and from all parts of the darkness they bore down on him. "My God," he heard MacMahon say, and then there was a wild stirring in the darkness and before he could lift the light a man came running up to him, almost colliding with them before he stopped. In a moment, as the light caught him, he could see the man's face; he could see the sweat and dirt on his cheeks, his eyes wide open and almost protruding from their sockets. He was panting so hard that the words broke from him between gasps for breath. Carl backed away in alarm and the man crowded up to him. "Hurt!" the man shouted. "We need the light!" He backed away, holding his arm up to ward the man off—*Wait!* he said, *wait!* "The hoist man!" the man said. "He's hurt!" Then he shouted rapidly and the men crowded around. "What's the trouble here," MacMahon said, "what's the trouble?" But the man grabbed the flashlight and Carl pulled it free. *Let go of that!* There was a brief, confused struggle. Carl turned sideways and the man tugged at his arm. "He's hurt," the man said. Carl pulled away, swinging his elbow back into the madman's stomach. There was a sharp expulsion of breath. The man dropped back. Then he grabbed the light again. They stood rigid, the light directed against the floor, a round yellow pool covering their shoes and making a little circle around them. Then it began to waver across the floor, darting like a fish under water. Carl felt the flashlight slipping from his hands. He cut back again with his elbow. Then he got up slowly and watched the light go bouncing across the factory. It bounced like a tennis ball, touching the floor and then the piles of doors, leaping up to the roof and dropping back to the floor again. Then it disappeared.

His mouth was bleeding. He could taste the blood and feel it drying on the back of his hand. He groped through his pockets for a handkerchief, pressing it softly against his tender mouth. His mouth felt swollen. Standing there with the darkness singing around him, he wanted to wash his face. He could think of the clean white enamel basin with the cold water dropping silently from the tap; he could imagine dipping a wash rag into the water and pressing it against his mouth. He could think of all the details of filling the basin, down to turning the tap and putting the stopper in place, and hearing the changing sounds the water made as it grew deeper. In a dim incredulity he heard Morley asking, "What did you want me to do?"

What?

"You said for me to do something."

He took the handkerchief away from his mouth and shook his head. His head was clearing. He found the pile of doors behind him, and sagged against it. The muscles in his back relaxed. "Yes," he said. He felt Morley's hand tugging at his upper arm.

"I guess you're right," MacMahon was saying. "Things seem to be upset. I suppose you better let them go home."

The darkness was intense. He could hear Morley's breathing and MacMahon's vague mumbling a short distance away.

A voice asked, "How do you feel now? Do you feel better?" Yes, he said silently. I feel all right.

"Yes," MacMahon was saying. "I imagine it's the only sensible thing to do. Send them home. No use making a lot of trouble."

His head was clearing. He tried to think over what had happened. This fellow had come running up to him. Give me that flashlight. Why? Never mind why. Then the man swung on him. Grabbed the flashlight and hit him in the face with it. Before he had a chance.

He asked Morley, "Who was that?"

"What?"

"That fellow," Carl said. "Fellow I gave the light to. Was here a minute ago."

He was surprised to find that he spoke in a low mumble and that his mouth hurt when he talked. Morley replied surprisingly. "He said the hoist man," Morley said. "He said the hoist man was hurt."

MacMahon began puffing audibly as he felt his way along the alley between the piles of doors. He cleared his throat, making a *hack, hack* sound, several times in succession.

"Warm in here," MacMahon announced.

Leaning against a pile of doors, Carl felt that his head was clearing. I made a pass at him, he said silently. If it had connected. Then this other fellow came up behind me. Grabbed me from behind. I made a quick swing.

"About ten-thirty," Morley said. "That is, I can't say exactly, but I judge it must be about ten-thirty. Maybe not that late. Maybe a little later."

I didn't have a chance, he said silently. No sooner had I swung. Then he brought the flashlight down. Hit below the belt. I ducked. Wonder it didn't kill me.

MacMahon moved over closer to him. "What was that?"

Carl said painfully, "I say he outweighed me."

There was a long silence. The stockroom was very quiet.

Morley was still tugging at Carl's shoulder; he released it when Carl straightened up.

"Well," MacMahon said, "everything seems to be settled down. You might as well blow the whistle and send them home, I expect. . . . No use having a lot of trouble."

No one answered him.

"Well," MacMahon said, "I guess I'll be running along, everything seems to be settling down now. I've got my daughter out in the car out there, and I hate to keep her; she's going somewhere, due there now, I expect. I guess you can take care of it all right now, Carl—everything seems to be straightened out, and you blow the whistle and send them home and I don't expect you'll have any more trouble."

"Blow the whistle," Carl said.

"Yes, it's the sensible thing to do, I imagine. Everybody seems to be sort of upset, might as well send them on home."

MacMahon made a few cautious movements along the pile of doors. "About that fellow," he began. "You ought to look into that. If anybody's hurt. Morley, you better come with me. I can't remember how we came in."

Carl said heavily, "I was thinking it might be better for Morley to go tell Mike to blow the whistle."

"Yes," MacMahon replied. "Come on, Morley."

They moved a little. His head cleared. "Wait," he said. "I might just as well go with you. No use separating. I probably can't find him anyway."

There was another silence. MacMahon was edging slowly away. "We can get out all right, Carl," MacMahon said.

"Well, wait, Mac," Carl said. "Wait. Listen."

"What good does that do?"

"Wait. Listen."

MacMahon was getting accustomed to moving through the darkness. He spoke in a low voice, but from some distance away. "All right, all right! I can find my way! Everything seems to be straightened out now! You two ought to be able to take care of it!"

"Mac," Carl said.

They listened while MacMahon shuffled down the alley. They could hear him panting and blowing as he edged along the pile of doors. Carl ran his fingers over his bruised face. You son of a bitch, he kept thinking. You God-damned yellow bastard. As he touched his swollen lip a hot rise of anger curdled through him, but at the same time he felt a kind of uneasiness that was all mixed up with the thought of himself lying on the floor and watching the light go bouncing across the factory. "You might at least have seen who it was," he whispered bitterly. "I can't do everything."

"He wanted you to blow the whistle," Morley suggested.

"A lot of good it did, getting him down here. What good did it do? Send them home."

The stockroom was very quiet; they could no longer hear MacMahon. "If I was running this place," Carl said thickly, "things would be different. . . . I'm going back to the office," he said painfully. "I got to call the power house. I should have called them before. Go around and tell them to punch out. Tell Mike to blow the whistle."

Morley moved about indecisively. "Tell Mike," he said. "Tell them to punch out."

"You heard him, didn't you? You heard what he said, didn't you? Can't you hear?"

Morley said hastily, "Oh, yes, yes," but Carl's outburst died away immediately.

"Made us come out tonight," he said bitterly. "Then look. He didn't know what we were working on."

He thought with a sort of weary pleasure of getting back to the office and of going to the washroom to wash his face.

"All right," he said shortly. "Get after them." His brusque, executive voice pleased him a little, and did something to restore him. He began shuffling down the alley between the piles of doors. He could feel them on both sides of him, and held his hands out before him like a sleepwalker so he would not run into them. Almost immediately Morley disappeared. He had a dim feeling that Morley was glad to get away.

Then he stopped shuffling his feet, hearing a little commotion near him. Someone chattered away restlessly. "Oh, what a sock! Oh, what a blow, what a blow! Jesus, you should have seen him. He swung like an old woman. Then *sock! Sock! Sock! Sock!*"

Someone else said, "Shut up. The Old Man's here."

"I don't give a damn. What the hell. I didn't do it."

"No, shut up. The old man's sneaking around. Vincent run smack into him. Scared the — out of the poor old bastard."

There was a brief silence. Then someone jumped up and began dancing around in the darkness, singing with a kind of whispered exultation:

"Oh, what a sock, what a sock, what a sock!
Oh, what a sock, what a sock, what a sock!"

Someone started to laugh. "Come on, Nuts," a voice said. "Let him alone, he's nuts."

Another voice said sharply, "Shut up! You want to get booted out of here? Your card will be gone if you ain't careful."

They quieted down and he could no longer hear what they were saying. For a moment he had a wild idea of calling to them. But even while he listened he felt tired and almost sick; when he put his hand on his face he was surprised to find that his lip was thrust out so far from the rest of his face. He thought of calling to them and telling them to punch out, but he thought that in a moment the whistle would blow and there would be no need to tell them. Besides, he wanted to get to the office where he could rest and be alone for a while.

He shuffled away silently. By this time, he felt, MacMahon must have left, and there was no chance of running into him. He reached out for the pile of doors, intending to lean against

[144]

it and get his breath, when he discovered that it had disappeared. He moved slowly toward the place where it should be, but it continued to evade him, and when he turned around, to find the pile on the opposite side, he discovered that this pile had moved too. He gave a sigh of exasperation. For a time he stood motionless, attempting to get his bearings, trying to think back over the way he had come, but there was nothing anywhere that would help him to locate himself.

Presently his foot touched a heap of refuse. He sat down, sinking heavily into the feather-bed pile of sawdust and small pieces of wood. He sighed with relief. He was very tired; when he sat down his legs began to tremble in a sort of independent dance that did not disturb the rest of his body at all. It was getting hotter in the stockroom; the sweat was again streaming down his forehead. Then he became conscious of the extreme stillness; there was no more shouting and laughing; everyone must have gone outside. It was so quiet that he could hear the faint hiss of the steam pipes far across the stockroom in the factory.

After he had rested for a while he got up slowly and painfully and continued on his way. He kept sliding his feet and waving his arms before him in circular, side-stroke fashion, partly to avoid running headlong into the piles of doors, or into the posts that held up the roof, and partly because he did not want to miss the wall that would guide him to an outside door. He discovered that walking had grown extremely painful. His head was aching. In the intense darkness every step sent up its colors like visible manifestations of the pain he felt.

He was moving slowly ahead, waving his arms, when the floor abruptly opened and he dropped, landing on his feet and pitching forward on his knees, five feet below where he had been.

For a few moments he was stunned. His hands felt the coarse grains of sawdust and the hard scraps of wood. When he pushed his feet backward they encountered a steel surface. The wind was knocked out of him, and breathing hurt him for a time. One of his arms was skinned—he could feel the stinging pain crawling slowly up to his elbow, as if someone were moving a lighted match up his arm.

I must have fallen, he thought.

At least he knew where he was. The conveyor ran diagonally under the factory, picking up the scraps from the saws and finishing machines. The scraps were carried to the hog, which ground them into the small chips that were used as fuel. Instead of going out of the stockroom toward the office, he had got turned around and had gone back into the factory. It explained why the piles of doors had disappeared. It also explained why he had thought the stockroom was getting hotter.

He realized this immediately after he fell, while he was still gasping for breath.

As his head cleared, he checked over his bruises. He was still too badly shaken to feel much pain, or to attach much importance to it. He felt of his arms and legs methodically, as though he were someone else who had fallen. Aside from the place where the skin was scraped off his arms, and a shattered feeling that he was badly hurt, he felt no acute pain. But he had grown very tired, and he could imagine no greater comfort than to lie quietly in the rubbish until the light came on again.

The refuse conveyor sloped upward, and was quite deep where he had fallen, so that it would still be beneath the level of the floor at the far end of the factory. Walking up the conveyor, he could have climbed over the side without difficulty at some point where it was only two or three feet beneath the floor. But this would have put him back in the very heart of the factory, and he did not want to go back. He had a dull conviction that if he ever got lost in the middle of the factory he would never get out.

He was still lying on his stomach, with his head resting on his good arm. He raised himself stiffly and looked around.

He had fallen quite near the lower end of the conveyor. He could see a faint glaze of light that he knew must come from under the factory. The factory was built on wooden pilings that supported it several feet above the ground, and the light from the tideflat was reflected under the factory. He got to his feet, feeling sick and dizzy, supporting himself by leaning against the steel wall on the conveyor. A steel shield had been put on the conveyor here, for when the pieces of wood were thrown into the conveyor the walls became torn and rough and the wood caught in them and piled up.

He began to move cautiously toward the dim glaze of light. He had a confused feeling that if he could get under the factory he could reach the tideflat and so walk smoothly to the office. He had never been under the factory, but the thought of walking carelessly over the broad tideflat, being able to see all around him and not having to shuffle his feet or risk running into anything, was almost overpowering. He lowered himself cautiously over the drum at the end of the conveyor, lying flat on his stomach with his hands clutching the conveyor chain.

It was still pitch-dark under the factory. He was still holding to the wooden supports of the conveyor, smelling the salt, moist air, so different from the dry heat in the factory, when he felt a curious tickling sensation in his shoes; it took him a long time to realize that he was standing in water that reached almost to his knees.

He moved away as quickly as he could. The heavy, seaweed grass pulled at his feet, and he had to walk with his legs far apart, balancing himself by swinging his arms widely. It was like trying to run through soft sand. He bumped against a piling and held to it for a moment in relief. Then he moved to drier ground and rested, for wading through the grass had winded him again.

It was quiet under the factory except for the splash of water that drained from the kiln. There were complex smells, raw and heavy, like the smells in a swamp: the smell of the heavy grass, and the hot water on the mud, the acid smell of the chemicals that had spilled from the place where the doors were glued together. But it was cooler under the factory, and an occasional breath of fresh air came in from the tideflat, washing the smells away.

There was a sudden tremendously loud splashing in the darkness. Startled, Carl made an involuntary run away from it. He thought that something had fallen. But the splashing went on; there was a powerful thrashing around in the grass; an irregular grunting and puffing; then another loud splash before the silence settled.

A voice said in disgust, "Son of a bitch."

Carl did not move. He could hear the man grunting and muttering to himself as he moved about. He breathed loudly; there was a little wheezing sound when he breathed. A few muttered exclamations broke from him, scraps and syllables of words that seemed to be forced out by his exertions.

"Who is it?" Carl asked.

His own voice made him jump.

The splashing and wheezing stopped. "How do you get out of here?" the voice asked. "This God-damned muck."

"Mac?" Carl said. "Is it you?"

"Yes. Carl?"

"Yes."

"How do I get out of here? I nearly broke my neck. I must have fell twenty feet. I'm soaked through. In that crap. Did you fall?"

For a moment Carl hesitated. Then he said, "I walked down the conveyor. I wanted to get back to the office and I didn't want to go back through the factory."

"Where are you?" MacMahon called.

"Here."

"Where? Where is that?"

"Here," Carl repeated. "This way."

"Is it dry there? I'm in water up to my knes. God-damn

[148]

filthy stinking stuff it is . . . I been trying to get out of here for an hour. I fell through back over there—hit right on my side—I think I broke a rib—I yelled, nobody heard me." His voice lifted suddenly, almost in a panic. "Where are you?"

"Here," Carl said.

MacMahon splashed along more rapidly. "Well, wait," he said irritably. "Wait a minute." He saved his breath, only grunting and muttering as he worked his way through the water and the weeds. Carl waited, too surprised to say anything and too bewildered to try to help MacMahon through the darkness.

"Son of a bitch," MacMahon gasped. "Dirty, filthy, stinking water. Got it all over my clothes."

"Did you fall?" Carl asked.

"Fall? I fell twenty feet. Nearly killed myself . . . I yelled, nobody heard me, I been under here since I left you. Couldn't get out, I bumped into things, fell down, son of a bitch, I went around that way, hit a wall, came back around this way, got in water up to my neck, what the hell, why don't you close up those places in the floor? I laid there—wonder I didn't drown, somebody get killed some day, God-damned carelessness. Wonder I didn't get killed myself, son of a bitch, I was over there, over there, back and forth, half a dozen times."

His voice died away in a sigh of weariness and relief. He was now quite close to Carl; Carl could hear him grasping for one of the pilings.

"Wait a minute," MacMahon said. "Let me get my breath."

He was still dazed, but to hear MacMahon stumbling and panting made him feel less helpless and more composed than he had felt before.

MacMahon breathed more easily. He asked, in a subdued voice, "Have they quieted down?"

Carl did not understand him.

"Upstairs," MacMahon repeated. "Have they quieted down?"

Carl said painfully, "We got them quiet, yes, they quieted down."

"Somebody pushed me. Just after I left you. . . . Didn't hurt me any."

They became silent again, listening for some stir in the factory. But there was nothing unusual, and they could hear nothing but the dim splash of the water draining from the kiln.

"Getting serious," MacMahon said, "when they act like that."

Carl replied vaguely, "Hagen. He's back of it. He's got it in for me. Tried to make trouble before."

"Hagen?"

"He's made trouble before."

"Hagen," MacMahon repeated. "Good God." Presently he sighed, "I can't believe it."

Carl did not answer him. He remembered Hagen screaming at him, *pull my card, if you want to,* hysterical, his fat face getting tense, his eyes wild. *If you don't like the way I work, go pull my card.* He remembered Hagen screaming at him, hysterical as a woman, in front of the whole crew. It had made Carl nervous; when he had any trouble he liked to talk things over quietly; it was no use getting excited, yelling, making a lot of trouble. "Hagen never liked me," he said slowly. "When I first came here he tried to make trouble. I don't know why. I did everything I could. He knows more than he lets on. . . . God knows I tried to make up with him. Used to go talk to him in his shop every night. Wouldn't talk to me."

"Yes," MacMahon said mysteriously. "You're probably upset." Then he went on, "Let's get out of here; I'm wet to the skin. How do we get out of here?"

"We may have trouble. I came this way because I thought it was easier than going back through the factory. If we once get to the tideflat, it's easy."

MacMahon accepted the warning humbly. They started off through the grass and the water. Now and then Carl stumbled in one of the shallow drainage ditches that scarred the ground.

[150]

After he had stumbled, and thrashed about for a time, he would warn MacMahon of the ditch, and a few moments later Mac-Mahon would stumble in it in turn. The air grew increasingly foul as they approached the place where chemicals had spilled from beneath the glue room. The glue had drained through the floor and down the foundations, covering the ground in a moist and rotting heap. As the stench grew stronger, Carl became agitated for fear that he was heading back under the center of the factory, for the glue room was approximately in the center of the building. Now and then he thought he could catch a faint gleam of light vaguely ahead of him, but it appeared and disappeared so unsteadily he could not tell whether it was light or merely his eyes deceiving him.

His arm had begun to sting, and his leg was still bothering him. Behind him MacMahon puffed and groaned, occasionally grunting some brief question, such as, "How far is it?" or "Why don't you have this drained under here?" Sometimes they fell or got tangled in some complex network of the pilings where they were close together to support a heavier piece of machinery. Their arms swinging out before them got tangled in the weeds and sunken crossbeams. But Carl did not hesitate. He did not want MacMahon to think that he did not know where he was going, or to lose confidence in him. When they rested he would say, "At least it's easier than going through the factory."

Brushing aside the damp growth and plowing through the mud and weeds, MacMahon was beginning to have his doubts.

"Wait a minute," MacMahon said. "Let me get my wind."

They stopped. Abruptly Carl discovered that he was standing on dry land. At the same time he thought that the darkness had grown less intense; he could see patches of darkness alternating with lighter spaces; he could see the dim outlines of heavy objects near him.

He said, "We're almost out. I'm on dry land."

MacMahon floundered through the weeds to join him.

[151]

"Son of a bitch," MacMahon said. "I'll never get under here again."

They went into a thick tangle of heavy brush. As the branches slapped back in MacMahon's face, Carl said, "Must be almost out. The brush only grows around the outside."

MacMahon put his arms over his face, took a deep breath and plunged into the brush. There was a loud crashing and stamping. Carl drew back and let him pass. Evidently MacMahon believed that he could make a final charge and come out in the open. But the crashing became less and less violent, and MacMahon's breathing became louder, until at last he sank down in exhaustion. "I'm played out," he gasped, almost in relief. "I can't go any farther."

Carl worked his way forward more cautiously. When he reached MacMahon he too sank down in a kind of relief. The ground was dry and almost warn. There were a few small trees, alders or willows, in the brush, but they were trapped principally by some kind of spreading bush that grew into a tangle almost as tight as a wire net. The leaves had a bitter, acid smell. The cobwebs struck their faces and felt like the annoying brush of insects.

Carl was lying on his side. Suddenly the leaves of a bush a few inches away from his eyes turned a dull gray color. He could see it quite clearly. The leaf seemed to come out of the darkness, shine with a gray light until its outlines were plain, and then disappear.

"It's getting lighter," MacMahon observed.

Presently another soft and mysterious glow spread over the bush. While it lasted Carl could see MacMahon lying beside him.

"Fireworks," Carl said.

"What?"

"Fireworks."

Carl got to his feet. When he started to walk the water pumped up out of his shoes. MacMahon did not move.

"You better come on, Charlie," Carl said unsteadily. "We must be about out now, I guess."

MacMahon mumbled inaudibly in reply.

"Come on, Mac. You'll only catch cold laying here on the ground."

"To hell with it," MacMahon replied. "I'm all in."

Carl pushed on by himself. "I'll see how far it is," he said. "You come on when you get rested." MacMahon did not reply, as he could not hear Carl very well and could not make out what he was saying.

Carl moved forward slowly. He saved his energy by trying to find the spaces in the brush that gave way most easily. He could not tell exactly when the darkness grew less intense and clear spaces began to show; he became conscious of fresher air and discovered that it was easier to move forward. When the bushes lighted up he looked overhead and saw that the sky had grown light; he could even see the interlaced branches over him; he realized that they had come out from underneath the factory and were lost in the tangle of brush that grew to the edge of the harbor.

A moment later he pushed aside a screen of vines and got a glimpse of the water, seeing a single channel light a long way from shore. When he stopped breaking through the brush he could hear the faint wash of the waves against the driftwood that was piled up all along the edges of the bay. He was completely bewildered. He stood for a long time watching the channel light in a curious and baffled hope that he was mistaken, and that it would move or turn out to be the headlight of an automobile coming toward the factory. Then he tried to figure out how they could have got so far from the factory, and tried to remember where the brush grew so high around the foundations. But when he looked back he could see nothing at all; and when he let the screen of brush drop, the channel light disappeared.

Behind him MacMahon began thrashing around and cursing.

Carl could not hear what he was saying, as the brush crackled too loudly.

When he grew quiet Carl called to him.

"Mosquitoes," MacMahon said in reply. "Oh, God damn it," he said.

Carl felt his way back slowly, hunting for the easiest way through the brush. A dreary bewilderment pulled at the muscles in his legs. When a bush slapped him, or a cobweb got in his mouth, he was too disheartened to curse about it. He merely crept back and sank down near MacMahon.

"I'm all turned around," he confessed. "I should judge the factory ought to be over in that direction."

"What direction?"

"That way. I got all turned around somehow. I don't know . . . I can't see, I can't figure out which way we came."

MacMahon had pulled his coat up over his head to protect himself from the insects. His voice was indistinct. "We ought to have some sort of an emergency light system," he murmured. "Be here all night."

Carl did not reply. He was too weary and too confused to do anything but stretch out beside MacMahon and listen to the ringing in his ears. It went on and on, steadier than the shrill scream of the insects that swarmed through the brush. He watched for the occasional skyrockets that lighted the sky to a dull and fading gray. When they flared up the brush became watery and translucent. All at once Carl felt relaxed and almost tranquil. He did not want to start breaking through the brush again. As long as he was lying down he did not have to think about it, and as he rested he closed his mind to the thought that eventually he would have to try again. Stray worries tried to break through this momentary peace like the insects that tried to reach him, but he brushed them off and they flew back as the insects swarmed away when he moved his hand over his face. The whole evening dissolved into a kind of nightmare unreality, with only the sprains and bruises to remind him that it had really happened. He thought of falling over the pile of scrap iron, of trying to put life into the electrician's son, of pounding some sense into the foreigner, of Hagen screaming at him like a hysterical woman, of watching the light go bouncing like a tennis ball across the factory— he thought of everything that had happened in a kind of awe at all he had had to do, and with a sort of surprise that he could endure so much. How many men could do it? He had been through so much he felt free to lie back and take it easy.

"You know that fleet," MacMahon said suddenly. "That's a wonderful organization." His voice was startlingly loud. His words were so far from Carl's train of thought that Carl merely repeated, "Fleet."

"A wonderful organization."

MacMahon rolled over on his back and put his arms under his head.

"I was thinking about it tonight," he went on dreamily. "It's a wonderful organization. Those fellows, now, they've got things down to a system."

Carl propped himself up on his elbow to listen, and brushed the twigs off his face with his free hand. "I had dinner with Captain Nichols," MacMahon said dreamily. "He was telling me about what they do. Like Captain Nichols, now, he has a launch all to himself and those fellows—that run it, I mean— they wait right there till he gets back, if they have to wait till daylight. As soon as they see him, they salute."

"A fine bunch of men," Carl observed.

"A splendid body of men. Finest body of men in the world. . . ." MacMahon suddenly began churning around and slapping at a mosquito that was bothering him. The bushes crackled when he moved. When he grew quiet he went on, "They pay those fellows a dollar a day. Never a murmur. If they kick, they lock them up."

"System."

"Wonderful organization. Nothing like it." MacMahon's

[155]

voice lifted with enthusiasm. "When you stop to think, there's a thousand men in the harbor right this minute. Like Captain Nichols said, if they wanted them, those thousand men would be in their places in half an hour's time. No excuses. . . . That's the way things ought to be. You say, 'Do this,' and by Jesus Christ, they do it."

"No questions," Carl said.

"No talking back, no quitting, not a God-damned thing."

Carl sensed that MacMahon was criticizing him indirectly and that he was comparing the way the men had been acting in the factory and the way they saluted and jumped briskly to their duties in the fleet. This awakened a dormant antagonism in him, for at the very mention of the fleet he had a picture of all the excitement going on in town while he had been tied down in the factory, and when he thought of MacMahon having dinner with the captain he thought again how unfair it was that MacMahon could take things easy while he was breaking his neck running around in the darkness. He stretched out again and looked up through the screen of bushes at the less intense darkness of the sky. Now he could barely see the gaps where the leaves were less thick, and beyond them the faint discolorations of the low clouds.

"A dollar a day," MacMahon was murmuring tranquilly. "Less than that, now, I guess. And they like it. Come ashore, the girls hang around, they get a piece of tail and then they're satisfied to go back to sea again. . . . Like that salute, now. They show their officers they respect them. Whenever they see them, they salute."

"My wife's brother was in the Navy," Carl said. "He was on one of them destroyers in that wreck in California. You know, there was a dozen of them run into a big rock at Honda Point five-six years ago."

"Was he in the wreck?"

"He was drowned."

MacMahon was silent. Presently he sighed, "Accidents happen. Nobody's perfect. You have to take the good with the bad. . . . Anyway, it was seven."

"I thought it was twelve."

"Seven."

"Jesus," Carl said. "My wife . . . her brother."

MacMahon was lifted out of his tranquillity. "I don't give a good God damn about your brother! I was talking to Captain Nichols tonight—he ought to know! Or maybe you think he don't know. Maybe you think you know more than he does."

Carl backed down. "I don't know. I just thought. . . . It seemed to me I remember reading. . . ."

"Seven," MacMahon repeated stubbornly.

"Well, seven, then, it don't make any difference to me. Only like I told my wife at the time, I said, one thing it shows, you have to give them credit, they followed orders. When the first ship went ashore then every God-damned one of them stuck right in line and piled up one on top of the other one. Like I told Grace: it's an awful tragedy, I said, it's a real tragedy such as the world has never before seen, but if that isn't proof of wonderful discipline . . . you got to give them credit. Like one of my wife's brother's friends from the same town she's from, he said they were going so fast when they began piling up, them destroyers looked like they were trying to screw each other. Like he told me, I remember, afterwards, he said if only the Old Man had run into the coast a few miles north, the way everybody hoped, there wouldn't have been any drowning, they would have come up on dry land; they were going so fast, he said, they would have climbed half way up the Sierra Nevada Mountains."

"The way I look at it," MacMahon said, "nobody's perfect."

He flattened out and moved his bruised legs in an effort to find a more comfortable place.

"I guess you're right," Carl replied.

The taller bushes made a sort of screen that blotted out the dull sky. When MacMahon moved, then Carl noted that more light was let down into the tangle in which they were trapped. The fireworks had become less and less frequent. When the rockets exploded a hazy shimmer appeared on the leaves and some of the stalks over them seemed almost phosphorescent. As Carl listened to MacMahon's regular breathing the last weak promptings of his worry disappeared. If he doesn't care, he thought, why should I? This was connected in his mind with the picture of MacMahon having dinner with the officers of the fleet while he was bumping into things in the dark factory. He wondered why Morley had not blown the whistle and how he was going to find out who had hit him; he wondered what was going on in the factory, and if Morley was having any more trouble. But all of these questions were far away, like things he read about in the papers, and they seemed so difficult that he only wanted to free his mind of them.

He could hear MacMahon preparing to say something. Before MacMahon opened his mouth he shifted his position slightly, straightened his legs, moved his large belly and cleared his throat, and the sounds, usually unnoticeable, now seemed loud and significant in the silence of the brush.

"You know," MacMahon said at last, "we never used to have any trouble like this."

Carl did not reply.

"I can't remember," MacMahon went on, "when we ever had as much trouble as we do now."

Presently Carl said stiffly, "You can't depend on that light company."

MacMahon twitched and tossed about as his words rose to the surface.

"What I was thinking about was that fellah pushed me. Fellah broke in the office. We can't have that. Wonder I didn't get killed. Hit right on my side. Gets started, you can't tell when it will stop."

"You always have that," Carl replied, "whenever you got a monply."

"What?"

"A monply."

There was another silence. MacMahon asked suspiciously, "What about a monply?"

"The light company. They got a monply."

"What's that got to do with it?"

"It's a monoply," Carl explained. "They got you. So they don't give a damn whether your lights go off or not. Like a monoply, they don't co-operate."

MacMahon brushed it aside. "I don't care about that. . . . What I was thinking was this fellah. Run right into me. You ought to get people like that out of here."

"I was thinking," Carl explained painfully, "if they'd turned on the lights we wouldn't have had any trouble. But they never give you any satisfaction. I remember last year I had to call them. I couldn't get any satisfaction. Maybe if there was competition, maybe they'd want your business."

All at once MacMahon lurched up on his elbow. He thrashed about unsteadily. Then he cried out in a terrible voice. "*What ruined the railroads?*"

"What?" Carl said in surprise. "What. What."

"What ruined the oil business? What ruined the railroads? What ruined the lumber business? All right! What!"

"Well," Carl began.

"Man," MacMahon said, "you're crazy."

"Jesus Christ. I . . ."

"*I happen to know!*" MacMahon cried. "God Almighty! Don't you think I know! Do you think the National City Bank is crazy?"

Carl began in a slightly aggrieved voice, "Jesus, all I said was—"

But MacMahon interrupted him, "Wait. Don't say anything. Wait a minute now."

He waited obediently. He heard MacMahon draw a deep breath. A twig worked its way through his clothes and

[159]

scratched his thigh. He moved his toes nervously, feeling the water pumping around inside his shoes.

MacMahon asked in a soft voice, almost a whisper, *"Do you think the National City Bank is crazy? Do you think J. P. Morgan's crazy?"*

"No," Carl replied honestly.

"Ha! All right! I happen to know the National City has had a man out here since 1924. What do you think he's here for? All right, what for? *I'll* tell you what he's here for!" Here MacMahon pounded on the damp soil with his fist. *"He's here because them sons of bitches will not get together!* That's what he's here for! Every time Bassett and Monahan, Superior and John Grigsby Manufacturing, every time they get together what happens? *I'll* tell you what happens! Some little son of a bitch like the Peabody cuts their throat, or that Jew son of a bitch what's his name—South River L. and S. All right. Now what do you say?"

Carl thought for a time. Then he said, "I don't see. . . ."

MacMahon broke out in disgust, "You don't know the first God-damned thing about economics. What ruined the railroads?"

"The way I look at it," Carl replied, "the buses ruined the railroads."

"Ha! Now we're getting some place! All right! The buses ruined the railroads. Listen." Here MacMahon's voice dropped again, and he became intent and earnest, *"What ruined the oil business?"* He did not give Carl an opportunity to reply. The independents, Carl said silently, but MacMahon talked so rapidly he did not have a chance to say it aloud. "I know," MacMahon was saying. "I was talking to Phipps just the other day. Then there was a piece in the paper. Then some people want that God-damn municipal light and power! Like I said to Charlie Harris. Who pays the taxes? He didn't know what to say. Cheaper power! I said. What in the name of Jesus Christ are you talking about! You *want* higher taxes? you

God-damn fool, I said; look, I said, you *want* a bunch of thieving politicians, I said, can't even clean the streets?"

Carl could not quite follow this and it made him a little uncomfortable. But he was impressed by the names MacMahon mentioned. "What did he say?" he asked politely.

"Say? What could he say? He didn't know what to say." MacMahon seemed to savor the memory of this triumph for some time. He gave a few guttural chuckles and muttered a few indistinguishable words of contempt, even of pity, for his beaten antagonist. But the memory of this triumph led him to speak of other successes and to go into detail about other arguments he had won, and he forgot about his argument with Carl. He began by remembering some of the things he had said to people during the elections, and as he lived back over the ready replies he had made to the stupid questions that had been asked him, his voice grew rich and warm, and his good humor led him to interrupt himself frequently with outbursts of hearty laughter. He relaxed; he lay on his side again in as comfortable a position as he could find, and when he laughed the shaking of his body made the leaves around him tremble.

Carl, meanwhile, lay very quiet, but a rising and confused bitterness prevented his enjoying MacMahon's reminiscences.

MacMahon rumbled on with his warm good humor: "All right, I said. You're so God-damned broad-minded. How would you like to have your sister marry a nigger? His face got as red as a God-damned beet. You're dragging in the race issue, he said. Screw the race issue, I said, I asked you a question. Finally I said, Man, I said, you're crazy. You God-damned fool, I said, if there wasn't a tariff on shingles, I said, there wouldn't be a shingle mill in this state. They can make shingles in British Columbia for less than you pay for your logs. Shingle weavers here have got the industry right by the balls, I said; they got rates jacked up so high the American manufacturer hasn't got the chance of a snowball in hell. Like them Hindus in British Columbia, I said, what do they get, five-six dollars a week, less than you put out for—what is it now a thousand?—five-six hours' work. Look at it this way, I said. Supposing you got a store where you sell your goods for twice as much as you have to pay for them. All right. That's a favorable balance of trade. Now wait, I said. Supposing you keep on buying and you don't sell a damn thing. Think it over, I said. Where the hell would you be? The worst thing that could have happened to this country, I said, was when Coolidge decided not to run, and anybody with any sense can see it. But be that as it may, I said, it's no use crying over spilt milk, I said; no good can come out of choosing as his successor a man committed to I know not what reckless policy of government interference in private business."

MacMahon's voice trailed away gently, and there were long mumbling sentences that Carl could not hear. Only once in a while MacMahon would give brief cries of amazement or scorn at some argument his adversary had advanced, and these interjections lifted high and clear over the peaceful rumble of his report. *What?* he would cry in exaggerated surprise. *My God, man, think what you're saying!* Then the drone of his words would begin again, a familiar and dozing sound, with these notes of excitement growing less and less frequent. Carl listened. He lay flat on his back with his hands under his head. The sweat had dried on his face and the twigs in his hair made his head itch. Occasionally he touched the tips of his fingers very gently to his swollen lip, but the real pain of it had gone away, and now it was not so much pain that he felt as humiliation that his lip stuck out so far from the rest of his face. The brush had a rank, bitter, seaweed smell, cleaner and purer than the smell under the factory, and moist and cool compared with the dust he had breathed inside. Only his wet feet and the water that was still draining from his trouser legs made him feel sloppy and uncomfortable, and even that was not so bad as it had been when he first decided to rest.

He relaxed. His eyes closed. He heard MacMahon muttering dreamily. "What this country needs is men with vision. Like nobody wants to go into politics; we don't pay our politicians enough to attract the big men away from business; like who wants to give up a good income, a good job, to work like a dog, no thanks, nothing but trouble? Like I read a piece the other day—'We Kill Our Presidents' was the name of it—this fellah showed how they have to shake hands, you know, talk to Boy Scouts. Take Harding. When I first met him was when we drove through Marion in 1920; there he was; healthiest looking man; public life. When I saw him again it was when he went to Alaska, just before; there he was, no better 'n a shadow, you might say, of his former self. Digby knew him well, I met him through Digby, I remember, and Digby told me, I remember, he said he knew of no man who took more seriously his obligations to the public. Like it said in this piece, I remember, a few days before the illness which proved to be fatal, Harding had to get out, even though he was feeling like the morning after the night before, sort of, poor son of a bitch, and greet a delegation of Eskimos came down from Alaska to welcome him to Alaska. Any other man in those circumstances would have said, Screw the Eskimos, but Harding felt it was his duty and nothing could deter him, even if he was shaking so he could hardly stand on his own two feet. Inside a month, he was dead."

Here MacMahon's voice died away entirely. Carl was now breathing rhythmically, and MacMahon was merely talking as he exhaled, and the long snoring sentences did not disturb either of them as they lay in the quiet of the dark thicket. The insects buzzing around them were almost as loud as MacMahon's voice. The tide had come in, and the sound of the water washing against the driftwood reached them clearly. Now and then a twig snapped, or the dry leaves hissed under an imperceptible breeze.

"Dead!" MacMahon repeated in a mournful voice. "Poor fellah, he never knew what hit him. There he was, still a

[163]

young man, in the prime of his life, you might say, just getting to the point where he could take things easy, it makes a man wonder. Fellah works hard all his life, tries to make both ends meet, gets a little ahead, where does it get him? Like I told my wife, I said, man's only got one life to live here on earth, I said, what good does it do him if all he does is work and worry? No rest, no chance to take things easy, always something; like I told her, I said, man's only got one life to live; what's the use? Sometimes I wonder. Like I read a piece the other day—'We Kill Our Presidents'—fellah said in there. Then I remember once when I was in Chicago some years back there was a fellah. I remember once when my wife and I was in Hot Springs, fellah jumped out the window. Like I remember not long ago there was a piece in the paper; I remember young girl; came out not long ago; seventeen years old, said in the paper. Like I told her at the time, nobody knows. Nobody knows what we're here for and we're here for only a brief span, and puff we go out like a rotten candle and nobody knows where we go. I remember once years ago, I remember. Once I remember fellah came in the office; he was a Shriner. Who knows? Then there was this woman, leaned out the window to see if it was raining; fell forty-five stories to her death. Tiny particle of steel no bigger than your fingernail. When I was a boy there was a woman living not far from where we lived on South Nickleby Street and I remember all that time once when I was a boy—that whole winter—there was a man came running up this woman all that time my father came running up I remember, sort of. Tiny particle of steel no bigger. Ah God! I said, like I told her, what's the use? What good does it do the first thing you know, like I told her, I said, what the hell? What are we here for? What does it get us? There was that fellah in Hot Springs, there he was, jumped. Insurance salesman married man nobody knows why. Nobody knows, we were there, several years back I remember there was this fellah came over to us there he was there was this place he was dead."

Carl opened his eyes. He heard MacMahon sigh, and then all at once what seemed like a morning light began to spread through the tangle of brush; the darkness became a pattern of light spaces crossed with intricate planes and nets of darkness; and directly before his eyes leaves and stalks came to life, still shadowed and wavering, but real and substantial, hard firm outlines, things that could be seen! When he turned his head he could see MacMahon's large ghostly face not more than a foot from his own. For a few moments MacMahon did not move. *What do you suppose?* he murmured, *what do you suppose?* Then his whole body gave a startled jerk. He mumbled something indistinguishable and turned to stare at Carl. They both got to their feet, Carl moving more rapidly than Mac-Mahon. MacMahon lost his balance and went down again, thrashing about wildly before he fell, and breaking a great area of the brush as he tried to grab something substantial.

"Ah, God!" MacMahon cried aloud. *"How I hate this God-damn brush!"*

Looking over the tops of the bushes, Carl could see the outlines of the factory. It was a long way off. They were almost on the far side of the tideflat away from it. All the time they had been pushing through the brush they had been going in the wrong direction, and now the factory seemed to have jumped all the way across the tideflat. The light streamed out through the ventilators and doors and the small windows under the roof. It looked strange and unfamiliar; it looked like a ship lighted up and moving along close to shore. But Carl put his hand to his bruised face and let the waves of sickness and despair rush over him; he thought of what MacMahon was going to say, of sneaking back to the factory through the brush, of explaining, apologizing, covering up. . . . Even while he was going down he grabbed wildly at excuses: *I got turned around,* he kept thinking, *I must have got turned around.* He

[165]

drew himself up, almost shrinking from what MacMahon was going to say, waiting for it as he might have waited for a blow on the back of his skull, or a knife between his shoulder blades.

But a long time passed before MacMahon caught on. He looked at the factory in a dull and shrunken surprise. "Look," he said. "Look." Carl did not answer him; his mind was still trapped and darting; he did not know what to say.

8. Winters

H E tossed the light down to someone standing on the track. Around him the men began dropping off the deck down into the narrow canyon between the vats and the log deck. The man who received the light darted under the factory. The log had not been moved. It rested in a pit between the foundations of the deck and the track, the side toward the factory brightly lighted now with the two flashlights and the other side shadowed and steaming.

Here, someone said. *Give it here.*

He could see where they had tried to build up a support for the jacks to be set against, and where the supports had given way. Timbers had been set against the pilings but they were crushed and the head of the jack had buried itself in the soft bark and the wood. Now they were building up another support against the pilings under the factory. Loose timbers were being passed underneath and arranged in place.

He heard the men call to one another in sharp, absorbed cries.

Give me a hand, someone said. *Here.*

He dropped to the track. Gil Ahab passed him, carrying one end of a weather-beaten timber. The light from under the factory caught Gil Ahab for an instant and he could see his face twisted with the weight he was carrying and the effort he made to keep his balance. The timber was dropped and moved under the factory. There was a cramped stirring about as the men adjusted it in place.

[167]

The group around the log suddenly split, and Hagen crawled out of the cramped space under the factory.

He could see the hoist man still lying pressed into the ground in the narrow tunnel of light, lying on his side with his shoulder jammed up hard against his cheek, precisely as he had been before Winters ran for the light. Someone pushed him violently. *Get out of the way!* Another timber slid under the factory.

He stepped back. Gil Ahab stopped beside him, breathing heavily, watching the timber being slid under the factory by the men kneeling beside the foundations. When it disappeared he called out, "How many more?"

Someone close to the log crowded forward. "How many more?"

The answer from under the factory was strained and muffled. "Five—six more."

He started off after the men who were carrying the timbers. Passing along the doors of the vats, he felt the heat that escaped around the doors and smelled the hot wood inside, a kind of medicinal smell that came from the steaming bark and sap. When they were out of the light he staggered over the rough track. He could hardly see his companions, but he could hear the rustle of their clothes and their heavy breathing. He glanced back. The kneeling figures around the log were screened by the steam that escaped from around the doors of the vats.

The timbers were being taken from a pile of refuse at the end of the row of vats. Here the darkness was complete, and as Winters felt over the pile of rubbish, searching for a piece that was substantial and that could be taken away, he heard the other men stumbling over the pile, tugging at some timber that seemed the right size, or moving the heavier pieces to free one that was caught. There was no talking. Now and then someone cursed briefly when he hurt himself or wasted his strength tugging on some piece that could not be worked free.

He groped forward unsteadily until his hands touched a timber that seemed suitable. He felt along it to find out if it was too long to go under the factory. One end was buried in a pile of heavier timbers. For a few moments he pulled at it senselessly, until a kind of red glow spread over the darkness and his hands burned from the splinters in the wood. He gave up, and leaned against the wall of the vat to get his breath. Someone said, "Here's one. Give me a hand." He started toward the voice, but someone else said, "I got it," and he heard the men cautioning each other as they carried it away. *Easy now,* they said. *Easy. All right. Watch out.*

Someone shouted, *Don't bring any more! Hagen! Don't monkey with that! Get twenty-thirty men and lift one end and block it up. Then roll it back.*

He heard Frankie Dwyer yelling, *Use your heads! Some of you guys go look in them cars and see if you can dig up another light!*

They ran around the head end of the mill toward the office and the parking space. In the intense dark he stumbled and fell. He could hear the others running through the tall grass and the stray curses as they stumbled. The ground was cut with drainage ditches and was still damp with the seepage from the factory. As soon as he got away from the buildings he could see more clearly; the ditches and the heaps of scrap metal became great pits of shadow. A car was drawn up before the office. As he approached and his footsteps sounded on the driveway there was a stir of movement in the car; two figures separated with a violent, explosive movement.

He called out, "Have you people got a flashlight?"

There was no answer. The lights went on. In the indirect light of the dash he saw a girl sitting behind the steering wheel, looking ruffled and indignant, her head lifted up and her large chin thrust forward. On the opposite side of the seat a boy was watching him, looking scared and uncertain.

"A man's hurt," he said. "We need a flashlight."

They looked at each other. The girl made a little convulsive movement and smoothed her dress around her legs. Her dress

[169]

had been pulled up around her waist. He repeated that a man was hurt, but they only stared at him blankly. The boy's light hair was ruffled and his face was flushed.

"Come on!" he said sharply. "A man's hurt. You hear? We need a light."

The girl straightened up obediently and the boy lifted the seat cushion. They searched among the tools and in the pockets on the doors, silently but hurriedly, occasionally glancing up to see if he was watching them. They were afraid of him. The knowledge of it surprised him. Then he saw some of the men looking into the other cars, and called to them.

"Never mind! It'll take too long! We'll drive this one up and use the headlights!" They came back, gathering around the car. The ambulance was coming up the road; some of the men ran out to hail it. It drew up in the parking space and two men, their white uniforms conspicuous in the dark, stepped out on the gravel.

Here! someone said. *This way!*

He said to the girl, "Drive on around the office. I'll show you where to go. If you get stuck we'll lift you out."

She looked at him, her large face empty and dazed. The boy said, "See here."

"Come on!" he said impatiently. "We'll use your headlights. See? We'll push you out if you get stuck."

She looked at him and then at the men crowding around the car.

"We haven't got a flashlight," she said.

He stepped on the running-board and held the side of the car. She drew back, looking in bewilderment at the mud on his hands.

"All right," he said. "We're set. Go ahead."

Walt Connor pushed his way through the men. "What's wrong? What's wrong, Winters? What's the trouble?"

The girl said, *"Walt! What's the matter? Who's hurt?"*

[170]

Walt pulled at his shoulder. "Come on, Winters, what the hell's the matter with you?"

He tried to explain. "We'll push you out if you get stuck. You won't have to go far. Just so your headlights reach them." He turned to Walt. "Let go! They got to have light, you dumb bastard."

"The ambulance is here!"

"That don't give them any light!"

"They got two flashlights up there now."

"*Who's hurt?*" the girl said. "*Walt! Who is it?*"

"Look here," the boy said weakly. "Listen."

"For Christ's sake!" Winters opened the door and pushed the girl over on the seat. The headlights spread over the waste of bunch grass. "Push me if I get stuck," he said. The car lurched off the gravel and into the first shallow ditch. The rear wheels spun in the mud for an instant. Then they went out into open ground, and as he shifted into second he saw the men running beside the car. The boy was gripping the side of the car with both hands. His dinner jacket was pulled awkwardly around him, his high collar sank into the soft flesh under his chin. Except when he glanced at Winters, he watched the ground that opened up under the headlights, his mouth sagging open, his features frozen into an expression of alarm. He had a high forehead and a great mass of light curly hair. Whenever they approached a deeper gash in the field tense lines of anticipation crossed his forehead, his lips drew back from his teeth and his hands tightened on the side of the car. Winters thought: they're afraid I'll wreck it. They don't believe I can handle it. He whipped the car around a heap of scrap iron, feeling a little thrill of pleasure that the car responded so easily, everything tight and tuned up, the control perfect, a light touch on the wheel moving at once through the whole machine. To reassure them he said, out of the side of his mouth, "I won't hurt it. We got to have light."

[171]

His words made them jump. They think I'm crazy, he thought, and grinned as he bore down on the gas.

The girl too was extremely nervous. She sat far forward in the seat, awkwardly, bracing herself with her hand against the dashboard when the car lurched. As the front wheels approached a drop her whole body rose and a grimace of pain and fright, almost of anguish, shot convulsively over her round features; her eyes tightened shut. When they got around the corner of the building the lights opened up a cleared space to the head end of the factory. The lights were reflected, dimly, against the log vats. When the car dropped into one of the ditches the lights danced up to the roof or toward the sky or straight at the tangled grass. A drainage ditch opened up at the far reach of the light and he stepped on it, bearing down on the gas while the girl began to scream. The drop almost threw him out of the car. The car hung suspended, weaving back and forth, the rear wheels singing against the grass and mud, until the men crowded around it, heaving until it pulled free. When he could see the men working in the space between the vats and the log deck, he stopped and switched off the motor.

"Leave it here," he said.

He got out and sprinted toward the vats. The light was still too far away but the track and the log were clearer; the men were standing back to let the light fall full on the log. They were jacking it up slowly when he got there, thrusting the blocks under the log to save each grudging inch that it lifted. Frankie Dwyer heaved at the jack and as the head of the jack pressed against the log the sap squirted out and ran down the threaded metal.

The men were silent. Winters could hear the doors of the vats tremble under the pressure of the steam inside, the scrape of the jack, the heavy breathing of the men. The headlights did some good. It was not enough, but it was better.

Under the factory one of the men from the ambulance said, "Easy. Don't try to pull on him."

[172]

The log lifted slowly. The crew stood by, jamming the timbers under it to save the lift if the jack gave way.

Dwyer stood up suddenly. "That's all," he said. "That's all the higher it will go."

They crowded around. "Heave on it," somebody said. They stood packed close together, each with one hand on the log. "All set?" Dwyer asked. There was an answering murmur from under the factory. *"Heave!"* he said. *"Heave!"* The log lifted slightly. Winters could feel the man beside him tremble. The damp ground sank under his feet; the soft bark of the log cut his hand. He could feel the flesh on his face tighten and draw away from his mouth and eyes before the red light began to spread and blot out the uncertain light of the flashlights and the reflected light from the car.

"All right," a voice said. "Let it drop."

They stepped back. The hoist man was lying on the stretcher and they were moving him out from under the factory. Both his legs were crushed and covered with mud where they had been buried under the log. *Easy,* the men said. *Easy.* They brought him out; the men from the ambulance straightened and lifted the stretcher; someone grabbed a flashlight and held it on the ground before them. Then they went off toward the ambulance, the crowd moving slowly behind them.

Hagen said wearily, "Somebody help me put away these jacks."

Winters watched the stretcher until it disappeared around the building. All at once he let down, crumpling up inside with the weight of misery he was carrying; only the effort he had been making had held him up. Unconsciously he moved toward the vats and leaned against them for support. He was sick. He breathed through his clenched teeth and the breath seemed to reach only the top part of his lungs, not to get down to the depths where the pressure was aching and intense. A hundred men were crowded into the narrow space between the vats and the platform. A dull murmur arose from them as

[173]

the hoist man was carried away. The brutal images forced themselves on Winters' memory as he waited, the full abyss of his plight opened up; in anguish he thought of them all sitting in the factory, complaining about Carl, while the hoist man had lain crushed and broken under the log, the bones of his legs slowly emerging from their sheath of flesh. In anguish he knew what was going to happen, and as surely as he knew that there was no hope for the hoist man he knew that Ann was dying, and understood what it was going to mean to him, and saw that he could not lie to himself any more. He saw her again lying in the hopeless room of the hospital, her hands clenching as the spasms of pain twisted her. No, he said, I can't think about that; but now his memory would give him nothing but images of misery and terror, until it seemed he had lived all his life on the scene of some vast wreck that had strewn the world with its victims; now he remembered the "accidents" in the logging camps and in the mills where he had worked, the ruined bodies of cripples, the loggers whose intestines were ruptured and torn from the weights they pulled and the mad pace of their labors, the old men who had worked in the mills and now had no hands on their arms or no fingers on their hands; he remembered the times in his childhood when, in the little lumber camp in the mountains, the heart of the town stopped beating while the accident siren screamed at the mill.

From the time of his childhood these memories had been mounting up within him, but he had never been so conscious of their weight before; he had never gotten so close to the edge of horror. He could not endure it; the strength went out of him. Around him the men murmured dully and bitterly, blaming themselves for not having moved more swiftly, complaining because men had to do work that was so hazardous and could so easily be made safe. Some of them were moving back into the dark factory, silent, sickened at the accident and exhausted by the strain they had been under, by the minutes of helplessness before they could get the hoist man free. Suddenly Hagen said, in answer to some inaudible question, "I've seen twenty men killed since I've been here," and at the sound of his voice Winters pulled himself together; he tried to grope his way back to life. I'm finished, he thought; this is my last night here, wondering dully why Carl had not already found him and told him to get his time. He tried to make himself think of leaving, of looking for a new job, of going from one place to another while Ann was dying—how would they treat her if he could not pay anything on the hospital bills? But there were no answers to those questions. As he waked up he saw that some of the men had gathered around him and in a dim way he thought they were waiting for him to tell them something, to answer the questions they had not learned to ask, but he was too sick and disheartened to speak. They waited patiently and silently and when he did not say anything they were not conscious of any disappointment; they were sorry that he would be fired; they wanted to know what to do.

Someone asked, "Who's got a cigarette?"

Dwyer handed them around, and they smoked, standing in the steaming dark and waiting.

"I heard you konked him," Dwyer said.

"Yeah."

"What was the matter?"

"He wouldn't give me the flashlight."

"Did he see who you were?"

"Yeah." He hesitated. "MacMahon too. He was there too."

"What do you figure on doing?"

"I don't know. I'm going to try to get a job on that road crew working in the mountains. If I can't connect there I don't know what I'll do."

A voice said, "They're hiring men up there. They fire two and hire one."

[175]

"You konked him," Dwyer said. "Jesus."

"Yeah."

"Come on," Hagen said. "Somebody give me a hand with this stuff."

They moved reluctantly. Dwyer stepped on his cigarette. "I wish I'd seen it. I only wish I'd seen it."

They picked up the jacks and started to carry them back to the fireroom. "Somebody bring the peavey," Hagen said. "It won't be here if you don't."

Somebody asked suddenly, "Who was that guy?"

"Who?"

"The guy who was hurt."

"The hoist man."

"Yeah, but what was his name?"

"I don't know. . . . Frankie," Hagen called, "what's the hoist man's name?"

"I don't know. All I know is they called him Little Rock because he was born in Little Rock."

"Little Rock," Hagen said to the man who asked him. "Little Rock."

9. CARL

IT WAS shadowed where he came out of the brush, and no one could see him. He took a deep breath in relief. Then he saw a group of men standing about twenty feet away from him. He did not hesitate. He hurried toward them and slapped his hands briskly. "All right, men!" he called out. As they turned toward him he said cheerfully, "We've got them back on! Let's get back inside now!"

For a moment they did not move. They gaped at him. One of the men was sitting down, and he got to his feet slowly, watching Carl as he did so. "The whistle hasn't blown!" Carl reminded them. The man nearest him gave a sickly smile and the group stirred; in the dim light he saw one of the men in back looking over his companion's shoulder, his mouth hanging open in an idiot surprise. But Carl felt no rancor. He only wanted to get something accomplished. "We've had a long rest!" he reminded them. "Whistle hasn't blown!"

The tideflat was littered with them. There were hundreds of them in the cleared space between the office and the head end of the mill. They were clustered in small groups and he hurried from one group to another, holding his arms extended and herding them back into the factory.

"All right, men!" he kept crying. "Back inside! They're back on now! Let's get back inside!"

He was dimly aware that they were watching him, that they moved slowly, that they stopped after they had moved a few feet. He did not care. He was glad to be busy again. He smiled as he hurried from one group to another. He came up to one young fellow standing off by himself, staring toward the office, and slapped him amiably on the shoulder. "All right, Jack!" he said. "Let's hit the ball!"

The boy turned around and started. He gaped at Carl. Then he stepped back awkwardly and fell down. A grotesque spasm of panic crossed his features as he fell. Carl grinned as he watched him scramble to his feet again.

"That's the stuff!" he called heartily, and hurried on to meet another group. But someone began tugging on his arm.

"I wanted to ask you," Morley said abruptly. "I called the power house."

Carl turned around. Morley was standing behind him, holding a sheaf of papers in his hand.

"Morley!" Carl cried. "Where have you been?"

"I called the power house," Morley replied nervously. "They said they'd be on in a minute. So I didn't want to have Mike blow the whistle until I asked you."

Carl nodded. But he felt tired, all at once; his enthusiasm for sending the men back into the factory drained away. "Fine," he said, with a mechanical cheerfulness. "Fine, Morley."

Morley ruffled the papers nervously and stared at his feet. "I didn't want to have to blow the whistle," he explained, "until I saw you, after I found out they were coming back on."

"That's right!" Carl cried. "That was right!"

"I figured you didn't know they were coming right back on. So I thought I better wait till I asked you before I told him to blow the whistle."

Carl nodded.

They were silent for a few moments.

"Mr. MacMahon wants to see you," Morley said. "He told me if I saw you to tell you that he wants to see you."

Carl sighed, "What does he want?"

"I don't know. He asked me where you were, and I said I

[178]

didn't know so he told me to go find you and tell you he wanted to see you."

A crowd had gathered around them. Carl waved his arms. "Back inside!" he said. "All inside! All right, men!"

No one moved. They gawked at him.

He turned to Morley. "Listen, Morley," he whispered. "What's the matter?"

Morley whispered back, "Somebody was hurt. I guess that's what's the matter."

"Hurt?"

"Yes. A man was hurt."

"Who?"

"I don't know. They took him away in an ambulance."

"Tonight?"

"Yes."

"My God," he said. "Hurt. Who was it?"

"I don't know."

"You sure?"

"Yes. The ambulance came and took him away."

"Ambulance."

"Yes."

"My God," Carl said. "Poor fellah," he said blankly. When he put his hand to his face he felt his bruised lip and the sweat and dirt on his face. "I hate to have that happen. How did that happen? Who was it?"

"I don't know," Morley said. "You see, I had to call the power house and then when I found they would be on any minute I wanted to ask you if you still wanted Mike to blow the whistle so I had to look for you and I never had a chance to find out."

"How was he hurt? Bad? Was it bad?"

Morley ruffled his papers and half turned in embarrassment. "I don't know, I. . . ."

Carl gave a great sigh of despair. "Ah, God," he said sadly. "To think. . . ." He put his hand over his eyes.

[179]

Morley was surprised at this turn of affairs. He had been working too hard trying to find Carl to think very much about the man who was hurt. Also, he thought he had been very daring in calling the power house instead of telling Mike to blow the whistle, and he had been excited and stimulated with wonder about how Carl would react to it. Since Carl had told MacMahon that Morley had called the power house, and since he had not done it, he was afraid he might be blamed if the lights remained off. First, making a decision cost him a great deal of nervous energy, and afterwards, feeling his way through the dark and dodging the men as he looked for Carl gave him no time to think of anything else.

He also felt a stricken shame at Carl's emotion because he had felt so little. He had not realized how tender-hearted Carl was. He felt guilty and shallow that he had not been similarly moved. Now a sad look came on his face. His mouth drooped and he shook his head in a melancholy fashion.

"Poor fellow," he said.

Carl pulled himself together. He threw back his shoulders and looked the whole world in the face. But there was a sad expression around his mouth. "It's hard," he said simply. "That's the way it goes." He spoke to Morley, and although he looked directly at Morley there was a far-away look in his eyes, as if he were seeing something beyond.

"Too bad," Morley replied. "Certainly is too bad, all right."

"Why do such things have to happen?" Carl asked the uncaring night, repeating man's age-old question as he reached down and scratched a mosquito bite on his leg. "No matter what you do. . . . It gets you in the end. Never know."

Morley said haltingly. "It certainly seems like a shame, all right."

Carl sighed again. He pulled himself together once more and looked around. Not all of the crowd had followed the stretcher. Some of the men were watching him. They were clustered together about twenty feet away, gaping at him and whispering among themselves. Carl was somewhat confused. He did not know what to do. It seemed somewhat out of keeping to order them briskly to get back inside. He had a vague desire to let them see that he was profoundly stirred by the accident. So he said to Morley, but in a slightly louder voice, "One of my own men . . . I don't know. . . . It's hard."

After a decent pause, Morley replied, "Mr. MacMahon wants to see you."

"Tell him I'll see him in a minute. I've got to see if everything's all right."

"Tell him—" Morley began.

"Tell him I'll be busy for a while," Carl said soberly. "Explain. A man's hurt. He's got to be taken care of."

"Then you'll come up?"

Carl nodded.

Morley hesitated for a moment.

"He's up there," he said, waving his arm toward the shadows.

"Up there?"

"Yes."

Carl nodded thoughtfully. "I'll come up as soon as I finish."

He walked over to one of the workers. "Is everything all right," he asked gravely.

"What?"

The man gawked at him.

"Is everything all right? Is he taken care of?"

Carl noted that the man, as well as others who gathered behind him, were staring at his legs. He looked down. His overalls were covered with the white pulpy chemicals from his wading under the factory. One trouser leg was torn to ribbons. Large gobs of mud were plastered on his clothes. He looked up at the man again, this time sternly.

"Well," he said, "what about it?" His voice was a little sharp. The cat got your tongue? he asked silently. "Is it all settled?"

The worker said, "Yeah. I guess so."

From the crowd a voice said distinctly, "Son of a bitch is drunk."

Carl flashed a dirty look in the direction of the voice. The faces that he could see were expressionless. It surprised him to note how few individuals were required to make a crowd. A hundred workers seemed to cover the whole tideflat. Carl's sad feelings had disappeared. The man he had questioned was looking up toward the clouds and absently caressing his neck. Carl watched him for a moment with intense hostility. "All right," he said. "Let's get back to work then." He spoke in a low voice. He intended to speak loudly but somehow he got started wrong, the words thinned out in his throat, and no one could hear him except the people near by. No one moved. Carl hesitated and then turned and walked back in the direction in which Morley had disappeared. He walked with a self-conscious dignity, frowning at the rubbish and at the clumps of weeds he could barely see. He could hear the men following him at a distance. For a moment he thought of turning and ordering them back into the factory. But then he decided it would be useless just to send in a few at a time; they wouldn't be able to do anything; it would be better to round up the whole crew and send them in together. Yes, he decided, that was more sensible, and immediately he felt relieved and glad that he had thought of such a sensible plan so he wouldn't have to turn around and tell them to go back to work.

He walked slowly, with his head slightly bowed. A large crowd followed him. "He's all right," he mumbled, while he was still some distance away.

He did not want to give MacMahon a chance to say anything to him about the time they had spent in the brush. As he came near the car he decided he would start to talk before MacMahon had a chance. In order to accomplish this, he wished to give an impression of great business; he wanted to bark out orders, hurry the men back into the factory, and get started on all the things he had to do.

"Who?" MacMahon asked suspiciously.

"Fellah was hurt. We got him in the ambulance."

"Hurt?"

"Yes."

"Who was hurt?"

"A fellah. . . . We got him in an ambulance—sent him to the hospital. Only thing to do." Here Carl sighed and shook his head. He was standing quite near the car, and he looked at MacMahon somberly, his eyes dark and shadowed, his bruised lips pressed shut.

"Who? Who was it? Was it bad?"

"Bad, pretty bad. Had to go to the hospital," Carl sighed again. "Carelessness, carelessness," he murmured.

MacMahon stared rather helplessly at the crowd drawn up around the car. He looked as if he were awakening in some strange place, and could not determine where he was, or as if he were unable to decide whether or not some involved practical joke was being played upon him. The crowd gathered, silent and inquisitive. The faces were dimly revealed by the lights from the factory and from the car.

Now Carl shook off his despondency in the way that a man takes off his coat before plunging into a fight. After he had murmured, "Carelessness, carelessness," he stared at the ground for a moment in a silent tribute to the injured man. Hail and farewell! He filled his lungs and exhaled audibly. Then he leaped into action. First he shook his head violently as a swimmer does when he rises above the water after a long dive. Next he gave a swift, searching, disapproving glance at the crowd gathered around. *"Morley!"* he said. Morley started. "Get them back to work," Carl said, speaking loudly so that the men would hear him. A few of them edged a short way back into the shadows. Most of them continued to watch Carl and MacMahon with a fascinated incredulity.

Carl saw Hagen walking back toward the head end of the mill. He called to him in the same sharp voice, "Hagen! Come

[183]

here a minute." Hagen looked up, and as he did so Carl called again, adding, "Come here a minute, will you?" a little more gently, thinking perhaps his first order had sounded somewhat too abrupt. Hagen responded with a sort of sluggish patience.

"Well, Hagen," Carl said briskly. "Have you got them fixed? Are they on for good?"

Hagen realized that this was for MacMahon's benefit. He nodded. But he could not keep from smiling at Carl's appearance, and at MacMahon's dirty tuxedo. He looked at the glue on their pants and at the mud smeared over them, and wondered dimly what they had been doing under the factory.

"All right then," Carl went on. "Let's get back to work. No use hanging around here."

Hagen nodded again. He thought of explaining that he wanted to get a small crew to clean up at the head end of the mill, but it was too much trouble; he knew that Carl would not be able to understand what he wanted to do; that he would show off because MacMahon was standing beside him; that he would ask a lot of fool questions; and that he would believe that Hagen was merely stalling. Hagen felt too tired to go through all the explanations that Carl would require; it would be easier to scrape up a crew somehow and get it done with no talking.

When Carl saw the faint grin on Hagen's face he was conscious of a tense rise of excitement. He took it for granted that Hagen was grinning because of the tricks that had been played on him. He watched Hagen's expression while he put his fingers to his bruised lips, and when Hagen looked away with a kind of forced indifference, Carl's suspicions became stronger.

"What was the trouble?" he asked ominously.

"What?"

"Did you find out what the trouble was?"

"What trouble?"

"The lights! I thought you were going to find out what happened. What was it?"

Hagen glanced at MacMahon, who was listening to this conversation with a deaf expression, as though hoping to be able to understand something later on. Now MacMahon looked at Hagen with an obvious accusation on his features. Hagen expected this sort of underhanded evasion of responsibility from Carl; nevertheless he was always indignant when it happened and when Carl hinted that he was to blame for whatever went wrong. "Nothing was wrong here," he said. "Whatever happened was at the power house. I thought you were going to call them. I been working with the hoist man. I haven't had any time."

Now MacMahon, who began, after a few moments, to comprehend the general drift of the conversation, said, "Look here, Hagen; I want to ask you a question."

"What?"

"I want to ask you a question, Hagen," MacMahon repeated. "Look here a minute. I want to ask you. What was the trouble?" He waved his arm toward the factory. "What made all that trouble now, what made the lights go out? We can't have that all the time."

"It wasn't here," Hagen replied. "It was at the power house."

"Power house?"

"Yes, the power house. Something happened at the power house. The power went off. So the lights went out."

"Then we ought to get after them. The minute it happened. Can't have things like that . . . I nearly killed myself in there. Fell right on my side." MacMahon prodded his side gently. "Wonder I wasn't hurt worse."

Hagen said nothing for a moment while he watched MacMahon probe at his bruises. Then he said, "Another guy was hurt, too."

"Yes. You see? We can't have things like that, Hagen. No excuse for it. You want to watch that."

[185]

Meanwhile Morley was urging the men back into the factory. He walked about, murmuring apologetically and almost inaudibly, "All right, men. Might as well get back inside now, I guess." Most of the men paid no attention to him. Some of them pretended that they did not hear, and a few moved a short distance and stopped; Morley hurried through the crowd because he did not want to pause long enough to see whether his orders were being obeyed. One man said, "No use, Molly. There ain't any steam. Mike pulled his fires," but this created so many disturbing thoughts that Morley rushed on without waiting to find out if it was true.

Carl finally said, "No use crying over spilt milk, I guess. We better get back to work." He gave MacMahon what he felt was a meaning look. Then he shouted impatiently, "All right, fellows! No use hanging around here! Get on inside! The whistle hasn't blown!" The men began to break up, starting back toward the factory, but too slowly to satisfy Carl. "We haven't got all night!" he shouted. "Let's get a move on!"

He saw a man lagging behind, watching him steadily. The man barely moved. He shuffled along, making a pretense of walking, just beyond the circle of light from the car. Carl did not hesitate. He took a few steps toward the man. "*You!*" he snapped. "Can't you hear?"

Winters was waiting for Hagen. He thought at first that Carl recognized him.

"Yes."

"Then what are you hanging around for? I said get on inside." Carl drew a deep breath and raised his voice so it could reach MacMahon. "God dammit, the minute anything happens here you guys think it gives you an excuse to take it easy—you've had an hour to take it easy, now what are you fellows hanging around for?"

"I haven't been taking it easy," Winters said.

Carl saw Winters clearly for the first time, and he felt a weak clutch of memory and recognition. Something, he did not know

what, made him remember the man who had knocked him
down; he remembered lying on the floor and watching the light
go dancing off across the factory, and Morley tugging at his
arm; he remembered himself holding his mouth and listening
to Morley, and thinking of washing his face, the whole experience mixed up into a confused and humiliating and miserable
sequence of thoughts and events. When he looked questioningly at Winters, expecting some support for his memory, or
some sign as to why it reoccurred, he saw Winters merely waiting impassively, his dark features expressionless, but with a general attitude of distaste and impatience suggested by the way in
which he waited. Now Carl looked doubtful, and turned
mechanically to appeal to Morley, but Morley was nowhere in
sight.

On his part, Winters saw the half-recognition that was reflected on Carl's face. As soon as Carl turned away he became
excited; his indifference disappeared; he started at once to in-
crease Carl's doubt. "I been working up there," he said, "helping get the hoist man loose. I surer than hell haven't been loafing. I told Hagen I'd help him pick up some stuff—them jacks
and some stuff."

Winters said this somewhat sharply, with a faint desire to
lead Carl off the subject and to make him forget that he had
been knocked down. But Carl was irritated by his tone. "Are
you working for him now?"

Winters flushed. He said, "Hell, I just wanted to find out
where the stuff belonged."

"Well, get a move on. *Get a move on!* The minute the lights
go out you fellows think. . . . It don't do any good to tell you."

Winters flared up a little. He spread his hands before Carl
indignantly. "Look at that," he said. "You think I been
loafing?"

Carl did not hear him. He was merely aware that Winters
was arguing with him, and he was depressed with his memory
of being knocked down in the factory; he saw that the crowd

was gathering again, drawn by the argument, and he lost his temper. But this time his anger did not explode in accusations or insults; he looked at Winters tranquilly, noting the dark flush on his features, his air of resentment and uncertainty. He said, without passion, with a kind of surprise that he said it, "Go punch your card."

Carl had fired a great many men in his life. Most of them he never saw, for they merely found their notices when they came to get their pay. There were only a few ways in which those who were fired on the job responded. Usually they shrugged with an affectation of indifference and walked away. Sometimes they became angry and tried to argue, and on these occasions it was Carl who shrugged and walked away. Sometimes, though less frequently, a man who was fired tried to explain or apologize, and on a few occasions Carl had got into fights when he fired someone. He was prepared to have Winters follow any of these courses. His own emotions were not disturbed. On the contrary, he felt relieved and at peace as soon as he told Winters to punch his card; it was like getting over some painful operation, and as soon as it was past there was no further reason for worry.

Winters too shrugged his shoulders and glanced around with a slightly uncertain and embarrassed smile. "All right," he said. He was surprised to see the crowd that had gathered around. As he walked away Sorenson grabbed him by the arm and spoke to him in a low voice.

"What happened?"

"I got the can."

"What for?"

"Nothing. . . . Son of a bitch is off his nut."

Winters looked back at Carl. He saw the crowd gathering, the men looking at him questioningly. He felt slightly embarrassed, even through his anger, at being in the center of the crowd.

Sorenson said under his breath, *"The little bastard."* Then he lifted his voice in a querulous protest, "Hey, Carl! What's the sense of firing the kid? He wasn't doing anything. What the hell?"

Someone else said, "Jesus, what do you pick on him for?"

Carl was undisturbed by these voices. "Never mind," he said. "Let's get back to work."

Hagen pushed his way through the crowd.

"I asked him," he said hotly. "It ain't his fault. I asked him to give me a hand with that junk. Jesus Christ. For a thing like that."

They were standing about fifty feet away from the car. The light here was ragged and dim, and Carl could barely see Hagen's large, pulpy face, thick and fat and streaked with sweat and grease, before a wave of physical loathing blinded him. He could not say anything for a moment; the words kept going through him—*Butting in, butting in*—until it seemed to him that he had said them aloud. He lifted his hands in a curious interrupted gesture, holding his hands clenched as he brought them up beside his waist. *"Then why don't he do it? Why don't he do it?"* His voice sounded mad and almost exultant in its fury; some of the workers automatically stepped away from him. He turned to Winters. *"Go on!"* he shouted. *"Go punch your card!"*

Hagen said, "If you fire him you can pull my card too. It ain't his fault."

This time Carl did not hesitate. His voice was trembling with excitement. He said, "Go punch your card, then," and waved his arm in a jerky, interrupted gesture toward the factory. "Punch it, get out of here, stop butting in—*God, stop making trouble!*"

He walked toward the factory for a little way, stumbling in the rough ground, before he turned and headed back to the car. The men stepped aside as he approached. He walked with his head down and his features were distorted with an expression of impotence; he looked suddenly helpless and blind.

Hagen did not lose control of himself. He watched Carl contemptuously, with relief that he could express his contempt. He said to the men, "Are you going to stand for it?"

Winters had grown extremely excited. He rushed up beside Hagen and began talking incoherently to the men. "Let him fire me. I don't give a damn. But are you going to let him get away with it? What for? So he can shoot off his mouth—for nothing—so he can go punch your card—a little tin god. Are you going to let him get away with it?" Carl had stopped and lifted his head to stare at Winters. "Why jump on me?" Winters asked him. "What was I doing? I been doing my work. I been doing what I was supposed to do. You know God-damn well I have. You got no reason to fire me. You only want to shoot off your mouth. You only want to raise hell with somebody."

Sorenson pushed his way between Winters and Carl. "Wait," he kept saying. "Wait a minute. Don't fly off the handle." He turned to Carl, "What's the idea?" he asked. "Why jump on the kid? Everybody else. Why jump on him? Why jump on Hagen?" He began to argue, keeping his face close to Carl's and starting when Carl tried to interrupt him. "You can't settle everything in a minute. Listen to reason—it just makes trouble; listen, Carl, listen. Now wait. What was he doing?" From time to time Sorenson would turn to warn Winters and the men around him. "Pipe down," he would say. "Take it easy."

Winters said, "I don't give a damn. Let him fire me. But you guys. You going to let him get away with it? It don't mean anything to me. I'm out of here. But you ought to kick—he can pull anything he wants if you don't kick—he can do anything he wants to."

Five or six men began talking at once. Some of them pressed in, asking what had happened, and some of them joined in with Sorenson as he questioned Carl. Carl looked around uncertainly. The voices were loud and confused, some of them angry and most of them only excited, but they wore on his nerves like the sound of files on steel. Still his uncertainty increased his anger, for as he glanced at the faces around him, and drew back from the repeated cries, the sharp *Wait a second. Listen, wait a second,* he held to his anger in the way that a man holds to a rope that prevents him from drowning. He tried to brush Sorenson aside. *"Morley!"* he shouted.

Morley said, "Yes?" and appeared mysteriously beside him.

"I told you to get them inside! What the hell's the matter with you?"

Morley nodded apologetically, but before he could answer Sorenson pushed him away. "No sense sending them inside, Carl. There ain't any steam—Mike pulled his fires. Listen." Then he turned hotly toward the men. *"Let me finish, will you?"*

Carl grabbed Morley by the arm. "Go tell Mike to blow the whistle. And do it. You hear." He stared at Morley with a hatred so shameless and abandoned that Morley instinctively drew back. Then Carl pushed him slightly, a weak, contemptuous shove. "I told you," he said, "an hour ago." The crowd gave way around them, and the men became silent. Only a few could hear what Carl said, but they saw Morley move away a few feet and turn back on Carl with a bruised and shocked resentment, and they saw the fury on Carl's face. When the blur of voices stopped the air seemed thin, the silence was like the sudden deafness that comes as one drops down in an elevator. Morley had grown pale; his eyes darted indecisively around the circle of men. But Carl had turned on him too suddenly and too brutally for him to accept it; and the number of men watching him, and the sudden silence, prevented him from leaving. He began to protest and explain, his indignation becoming clearer as he spoke, his sense of injury and humiliation making his voice tremble. He said that he had intended to tell Mike to blow the whistle when he found out that the lights were coming back on, and that afterwards he had looked for

Carl and had not been able to find him. Then Carl had told him that he had been right in not having Mike blow the whistle, and since the lights had come on he had been too busy to do it. After he started to talk he could not stop, for every time he paused he became conscious of the crowd again, and stricken with the novelty of talking back to Carl; he had to lose himself in his indignation by going on. But in the half darkness he looked wizened and afraid, like some small trapped animal turning in its flight and facing its pursuer with a desperate and gasping bravery. The men were silent, as they were always silent before an outburst of emotion. "What could I do?" Morley kept saying. "I looked for you. I went all over. I went out in the stockroom. I went back to the office—I thought maybe you were hurt. I told them to get inside; what else could I do?"

Carl glanced at Morley. "All right," he said. "Go tell him now." Then he said to the men, "Get on inside," his voice cold and dead, and nodded to Winters and Hagen, "Go on," he said, "get out of here."

Winters grinned. "Go to hell," he said. "Will you?"

10. WALT

HE had no quarrel with Winters; he only thought it was senseless to drive the car over the tideflat and that Winters was making a fool of himself ordering Rose around, and he had tried to stop him, to bring him back to earth. It was senseless because anyone could see there was no help for the man who was hurt. He had been up there. The talk with Hagen's boy had left him with a dull self-disgust that was partly a fear that he had put himself too much in Johnny's hands or that the girls would make fun of him, and partly revulsion at talking down to Johnny. He had walked around the tideflat until he found the accident; it sickened him, and there seemed to be nothing he could do to help, so he wandered away again until he saw MacMahon's car and saw Winters, evidently out of his head, yelling madly and finally getting in and driving across the tideflat.

He ran over the uneven ground after the car, conscious of the growing crowd around the head end of the mill in the distance. I told Carl to send them home, he kept thinking. He can't say I didn't tell him. When he caught up, he found Rose pressed back against the corner of the seat, her eyes darting at the men who ran past toward the head end of the mill, her mouth twitching nervously, and he felt sorry for her, suddenly, thinking how strange and bewildering it all must seem to her. Her features lighted up with relief when she saw him.

"Walt," she asked, "who is it?"

He had known her in school, but then she had been only a quiet girl with few friends and he had paid no attention to her, and now the thought of all that had happened since then crossed his mind with a memory of how ordinary she had seemed then and how indifferent he had felt toward her.

"I don't know."

"Was it?"

"No. It was one of the men."

She smiled shakily and sighed. The people were still coming across the tideflat. Someone stood midway between the car and the vats shouting, *"Keep out of the light!"* whenever any-one passed in front of the car. He was stirred again to think how much she must have been worried about her father. . . . "What do you suppose happened to him?" she whispered. "He's been gone an awful long time."

"He's probably trying to get that poor devil free," he said. "A log rolled on him." She looked up toward the men moving rapidly around the vats, her eyes widening. She had changed since he had seen her, he decided, the sullenness had gone out of her face and she looked older. The long white evening dress made her look slim and cool. He did not know the boy sit-ting beside her, and after he had glanced up and seen the boy staring at him inquisitively he ignored him, suddenly aware of his working clothes, his dirty hands and the grease and dirt he knew must mark his face.

She was still frightened. The boy was frightened too. He saw it and responded, feeling himself at ease in this place that was lost and strange to them, cursing Winters for making a fool of himself and being sure to get in trouble now.

"I wish he'd come," Rose said helplessly. "I've never been so nervous."

"He'll be all right."

She whispered, "Walt, who was that man?"

"Oh. . . ." He hesitated briefly before he answered, "One of the men from the stockroom. I never heard his name."

"He nearly wrecked us."

The boy kept watching him, occasionally turning around to stare into the darkness when someone passed by the car.

"I know." He felt a dull oppression at the memory of Winters' turning on him. "He," he said, and then stopped; he did not want to get Winters in trouble. "You have to make allowances," he said painfully. "Probably some friend of his was hurt. You see? His nerves are all shot. His wife is sick, maybe, or something like that."

Rose looked at him questioningly.

"You understand?" he asked. "You can't just say. . . . His nerves are all shot."

She did not understand him, and he felt a rise of irritation with Winters for exposing himself to trouble; I can't protect him, he thought, when she said, "I don't see what difference. . . ."

"No, I know it don't," he said gloomily. "He's getting the big head; he thinks he owns the place."

They were silent. Presently he smiled, "Well, Rose, how have you been?"

She smiled back. "Fine. And you?"

"How does it look?"

"You look fine," she smiled. "Why don't you ever come to see me?"

"Well, for one thing your father never gives me a chance. When I'm not here I'm in bed getting strength enough to come back."

"He told me you were working here."

"Tell him I think he must have it in for me."

"Why? Do you really have to work hard?"

"Hard? Good God," he said. "Look at my hands. I do ten men's work."

She smiled, "Poor you." She turned to the boy beside her. "This is Roger Schwartz, Walt," she said. "This is Walt Connor, Roger."

They shook hands.

"Glad to know you, Schwartz," he said.

"Glad to know you."

He felt uncomfortably that the people who passed were watching them, and he hesitated when she asked him to sit down, moving over in the seat to make room for him. For a moment he thought of saying that he had to go up with the others, but the boy with her was watching him with a cautious unfriendliness, taking him for some workman Rose happened to know and wondering at their intimacy, and he got in the car abruptly out of an involved desire to show him who he was. They were still busy at the far end of the mill; the figures appeared and disappeared in the weak light, but the factory seemed deserted and most of the people had crossed the tideflat. Roger looked straight ahead after they shook hands, an odd set expression on his empty features, his hands pressing against his waistcoat as if he nursed some pain deep in his abdomen. Rose tried to make up for his unfriendliness, chattering steadily, partly, he thought, to smother her own worry. "What do you suppose happened to papa? I've never seen so much excitement. And how am I going to get back out of here?"

He nodded, grateful for her friendliness.

"What's the trouble, Walt?"

"The lights went out."

She smiled at him with a cheerful affectation. "Well, for goodness sakes," she exclaimed. "Do you *always* have so much trouble when the lights go out?" He felt a twinge of embarrassment and annoyance, recognizing this bewildered impractical womanhood, terrified and bewildered by the complex world of machinery; he felt a dull shame for her for having adopted this pose.

"It's tough," he said.

They were silent for a time. "Poor me," Rose sighed. "It's all over my head!" Someone passing the car overheard and gave a startled glance toward them. He flushed. When he looked at her she was smiling at him with her head half tipped to one side and a friendly, affected smile on her face, and for the first time he saw the rich folds of flesh on her neck and her large chin—She'll look like hell in a few years, he thought, and then he thought nervously, Why'd I think that?

The boy with her looked off toward the factory, a blank indifference settling on his features.

Walt looked at him with a sudden fury, conscious of his overalls and his sweaty face, trying to tell himself that the boy's clothes didn't fit him, that something spoiled the bored superior air. He said suddenly, "I'm going to try to get back to school next year, Rose. I may go back. Some of the fellows from the house were down last week. . . ." He paused, aware of how strange the words sounded, "If I do go back I'll be in fine condition. That's one reason why I wanted to work. I wanted to keep in condition, in case I decided to go back next fall."

Rose nodded and the boy glanced at him.

"So you see it's not so bad," he said nervously.

"I see," Rose said. "If you do go back you'll be in fine condition."

Why'd I start that? he asked silently, and answered himself, trying to let him know. He felt a twinge of disgust, but something uncontrollable had seized him and he plunged on desperately, "I don't care much. I figure the first two years are all a man really needs. After that. . . ."

The boy interrupted him. "Say," he said. "How long do you suppose we'll have to stay here?"

Rose looked at her boy and then gave Walt a glance of understanding and apology.

He got out of the car as MacMahon approached, shocked at the old man's appearance, at his feeble walk and sagging features, his clothes torn and smeared with mud and some white pulpy chemical; twigs, dried leaves and other débris clinging

[197]

to his shirt and hair. As he staggered up to the car Walt stepped forward to help him, but the old man waved him aside.

"Papa," Rose said in a watery voice.

MacMahon grasped the door of the car.

"Don't papa me," he said.

Suddenly he shook the door of the car as though trying to tear it off.

"Don't try to papa me!" he cried

Rose backed away from him. "What's the matter? Papa! What's the matter?"

"Driving up here," he said sadly. "Of all the fool tricks. You know better, Rose. It's not as if you were a ten-year-old child."

"Papa," Rose begged.

"I'm ashamed of you," MacMahon said.

They stared at each other.

"It would be different if you didn't know better," MacMahon said.

Rose cried desperately, "Papa, I *had* to! I didn't *want* to! I *had* to. A man *made* me!"

MacMahon replied in a voice which was both aggrieved and accusing, but one in which the note of anger had grown a little uncertain. "You think I'm made out of automobiles," he said.

"I had to, papa! A man was hurt!"

For a moment MacMahon looked lost and stricken. He turned his head rapidly to stare into the shadows.

"You," he said in confusion. "What?"

Rose noted his bewilderment and took advantage of it at once. She said, "A man came down and said we had to drive up here, a man was hurt, he said they didn't have any light, first they wanted a flashlight but we couldn't find it so what could I do? I didn't want to. Didn't he, Walt?"

"Yes, Mr. MacMahon. A man was hurt up in the head end. A log rolled on him."

"Hurt?"

"Yes."

"Who was it?"

"One of the men."

"Tonight?" MacMahon asked. "You mean tonight?"

"Yes. When the lights were off."

"Where is he?"

"The ambulance took him to the hospital."

"Ambulance," MacMahon said.

The crowd was gathering. He looked around nervously, ashamed for MacMahon, trying to keep him from making a fool of himself, feeling sorry for the old man's bewilderment. He's too old, he kept thinking, it's too hard for him.

MacMahon got in the car. "It don't make any difference," he mumbled. "She always drives too reckless."

Carl came into the light. His face was swollen and there were streaks of dried blood on his chin.

"He's all right," he said.

MacMahon looked up. "Who?"

"Fellah was hurt. We got him in the ambulance."

"Hurt?"

"Yes."

"Who was hurt?"

"A fellah. . . . We got him in an ambulance—sent him to the hospital. Only thing to do." Carl sighed wearily, his features expressing only despondency and regret, his eyes somber.

"Who? Who was it? Was it bad?"

Carl nodded. "Pretty bad." He waited a moment, moving his hand over his forehead. Then he said quietly, "Morley. Get them back to work."

He looked directly at Walt and Walt nodded, starting back toward the factory. The wan light from the buildings spread over the pitted ground. Somebody ought to drive that car back, he thought. Somebody ought to help. He thought of going back to help but then he thought, No, Rose would think he was trying to get himself noticed, remembering the snotty blond kid and his dumb superiority. He ran into one of the sawyers standing alone on the tideflat, looking back toward the car.

"What's the matter?" the sawyer asked.

"Nothing. They sent us back in."

The sawyer started back toward the car. Walt looked around. Some kind of quarrel was going on; he could see the men pressing together and hear the excited voices. He raced back to the car. The men were standing in a tight knot a few feet away from the car; he could see Hagen's head above the crowd and hear Carl's strained and bitter voice. MacMahon had got out of the car. There were a few men standing near him.

"You, Connor!" MacMahon said. "Come here."

He went to the car. He glanced back at the crowd, hearing the broken and passionate cries and seeing the circle of men tightening around Carl and Hagen. Sometimes there was a solid ring of backs and then the crowd would shift and break as the men pressed closer. He could see the dark figures hurrying back across the tideflat, appearing and disappearing in the dim light from the factory.

"Who is that?" MacMahon asked. "Making all the trouble?"

"Hagen."

MacMahon had changed. The weariness and bewilderment had disappeared. He shook his head impatiently. "No. The other one."

Someone edged up beside him. "Winters," Jug Bullett said.

"Tell him to quiet down. Tell him I said if he's got any complaint let him come see me in the morning."

Someone said, "We won't be working tomorrow. You won't be here in the morning."

"Saturday, then. Tell him to come see me Saturday."

Walt asked uncertainly, "What do you want us to do?"

MacMahon frowned. "Bullett," he said, "go tell him." He gestured toward the rest of the men. "You fellows go along.

This is no place for that. If they want to fight they can do it somewhere else."

Walt raced up to Winters. "Listen," he said. "MacMahon said to pipe down. He's sore as hell."

"Tell him to go screw himself."

"No, listen, you'll get in trouble. I'm telling you."

Winters said to the men, "He won't do anything. But you ought to kick."

He saw Carl standing a short distance away, watching one of the men who was jabbering to him excitedly.

"Good God! Do you want to make trouble?"

Winters looked around at him in perplexity. "What's eating you, Walt? I don't give a damn what he said. I ain't working here any more."

Bullett came up. "It's what he said. Come see him Saturday if you got a kick."

"To hell with him."

Walt grabbed Winters again. *"I'm telling you, let up on it. He'll smooth it over. You can get back on."*

"Let go, Walt. Do you swallow that stuff?"

He felt himself go cold, drawing back from Winters' distorted face.

"All right," he said. "Cut your own throat."

Winters looked at him steadily, in surprise, seeing him for the first time, the bitterness in Walt's voice breaking through his excitement. Walt had been irritated at Winters' unreasonableness; now he was angry with himself for pleading with Winters, for plucking at his sleeve and begging him to quiet down while the men were watching. He could sense them putting up with him; he knew they were waiting impatiently, and he felt young and uncertain as the flush mounted on his cheeks. But even through his embarrassment, as he saw Winters looking at him appraisingly, a deeper and more confused emotion stirred in him, a memory of the times when he first came into the factory, when he had not

[201]

known what to do or how much was expected of him, and the Indian had helped him, patiently, even holding up his own work to make it easy for him and taking the blame when Carl kicked. Now, when Winters asked, "Who are you trying to help?" he felt a puzzled, probing note in Winters' voice; he thought that Winters was ashamed of him, and for the first time he saw the coldness and arrogance in Winters' manner. Beyond Winters he could see MacMahon standing beside his car. Rose was half-standing, trying to see what was going on, supporting herself by holding the windshield. A group had gathered around Carl; he could hear their rushed voices.

"I'm trying to tell you," Walt began, but then he strangled on the words. Winters tried to quiet him. He knew it. He could tell by the patient way Winters nodded before he spoke, by the way he gently touched Walt's shoulder. Me, he thought incredulously, you conceited bastard. "Listen, Walt," Winters began gravely, but Walt pushed his arm away. "You damn fool," he said. "You God-damned half-breed."

Someone pushed him. Someone said, "You're nuts. Lay off."

Winters held his arms. "Cut it out," Winters said. "I won't fight with you." He began harping on the same thing again; nothing could get him off that subject. He said to the men, "I'm out of here. It don't mean anything to me any more. But don't let him get away with it. Don't take it. You've got to get that guy out of here. This is only the start. He hasn't been here a year. We've had three cuts since he's been here. Fifty-sixty men have been dropped. *And this is only the start!* You got to drive that guy out of here. You can't *work* as long as he's here. You got to fight him off."

Someone pushed between them. Walt was shoved aside as the men moved down toward MacMahon's car. Someone bumped him and he lost his balance; they passed him as he stumbled in the uneven ground. When he caught up with them they were

[202]

already around the car. Someone was talking to MacMahon, trying to smooth things over.

MacMahon smiled with a ghastly forced movement of his lips. "I don't like to interfere in these things," he said. "It's up to you fellows to settle this among yourselves."

"But I just told you! How can we settle it if they both been canned? What good does it do to settle it if they ain't working here any more?"

"Well, I don't like to interfere."

The men looked at one another. MacMahon saw them hesitate, a rising impatience and irritation on the faces close to the car. "Come talk to me Saturday," he said. "We're all tired now. No use trying to settle anything now."

There was a long silence. "Well," Sorenson said hesitantly, "do they come back to work or not?"

"We're all tired now," MacMahon replied obliquely.

Again there was a long silence. Rose glanced at the faces surrounding the car and then studied the dashboard; she felt silly and conspicuous in her white dress; she tried to make herself little as she shrank down in the seat. Hagen pushed his way through the crowd. "Well, am I working here or not?" he asked harshly. "I don't give a damn. But I want to know."

MacMahon gave a final look of appeal to Carl before he gave in. "All right, all right, come on back to work, then! Come on back to work! I can't bother about all these things! I can't stay here all night."

Hagen gestured toward Winters. "Is he working here?"

"Yes, yes, let it go, forget about it! Now let's forget about this, fellows, let's forget about it, everybody's tired, everybody's upset. . . ."

You see? Walt thought bitterly. I told you he'd give you a chance.

The whistle blew, a weak, steam-saving blast. The crowd broke up. The young guys raced for the clock. The old

[203]

hands lagged behind, talking it over. They were proud; they were excited; some of the kids began yelling as they ran toward the factory. They had their first sure knowledge of their strength.

PART TWO

The Education of a Worker

PART TWO: THE EDUCATION OF A WORKER

1. JOHNNY

HE ran out to the car where Walt was waiting.
"Will they?" Walt asked.
"Yes. . . . They can only ride as far as the bus line. Somebody's going to meet them."
"Who?"
"I don't know."
"Oh, hell," Walt said. He was standing beside the car and he gave the door a sudden hard slam. He walked a little way nervously and came back. "Why didn't you—" he began bitterly, but then he stopped.

A car pulled out of the parking space and headed for town. "Tell them to come on," Walt said. "We might as well. 'It's what I get."

He went back to where Marie and Ellen were standing in the shadow of the loading platform. The crew was coming out of the factory, down the low steps, the voices rising steadily and coming back scattered as the men headed across the tide-flat or started down the road. He came up to Ellen, trembling inside with eagerness, and saw her watching him as he approached, looking small and frail beside Marie.

"It's over here," he said politely.

She nodded and started beside him, glancing up at him occasionally. He was conscious of them beside him, of her neat little figure in her tight overalls and white shirt and of the sister walking on the far side of Ellen, silent, dim, stepping with care over the rough ground; he thought the crew coming down

[207]

from the time clock looked after them. "Do you know who was hurt?" Ellen asked. He was warmed by her friendly voice and he could tell that she was only making conversation.

"No, I didn't hear."

"Even Old Man MacMahon came down," she said.

"I saw him. He had some trouble, I guess."

She glanced at him. "I heard he fired your old man. . . . I heard he fired Winters and your old man and then took them back again."

He was conscious of her light walk and the rustle of her clothing. In the light from the cars and from the factory he could see the outline of her breasts under the shirt she wore. Beyond her Marie, larger and more richly built, walked carefully, paying no attention to them or to what they were saying. "Yes," Ellen said, "I've known your old man ever since I came to work. The first day I came here I was so scared, I remember, I was working so hard and he came up and watched me—'You trying to do it all?' he said. 'You think nobody else works here?' I felt like a little fool."

Walt was already in his car.

"Here we are!" Johnny said brightly. Then as he saw them looking at Walt he added, "We're here because we're here."

"Hello, girls," Walt said with composure. "How's every little thing?"

They hesitated. "This is Walt Connor," he began nervously. "Maybe you heard of him. This is Ellen and Marie Turner." He saw them glance at each other and wondered if he had it wrong, the girl's name first, or the boy's? He opened the door. The car was an old Maxwell four-leaf clover; the front seat folded down and to get in the back seat, the front seat had to be held out of the way. Ellen got in back and Johnny sat beside her. As Marie sat down beside Walt, Ellen explained, "We can only go as far as the highway."

"Now why?"

"Somebody's going to meet us there."

[208]

"Who?"

"Somebody we know."

Walt turned around.

"Oh, yeah!" he said brightly. "Oh, yeah!" He put his hand on Marie's knee. "That's what *you* think!" he yelled. Marie drew away and pushed his hand off her knee, "Hi yah! Hi yah!" Walt yelled. "Let's go!"

Johnny glanced at Ellen. Her face was impassive. He felt that he ought to enter into the spirit of the occasion. "Ha, ha!" he yelled back.

Encouraged, Walt gave a great scream. "Wowie!" They passed some of the workers walking beside the road. As they stepped off the gravel when the car passed, Walt stuck his head out the door. *"Whoopee!"* he said to them.

Marie sat in the corner of the seat, staring straight ahead. Ellen was watching Walt; Johnny could see that she was frowning at him distrustfully. The ribbon tied around her head gave her a high forehead, and somehow made her seem severe; Johnny tried to think of her the way he had when they had waited on the tideflat, but he could not do it. He felt chilled and ill at ease, and he wished that he could holler and yell cheerfully the way Walt did.

But now Walt became conscious of the lack of response in the car. He reached over and grabbed Marie around the shoulder, pulled her to him violently and kissed her. He pulled her so hard that her feet flew up and she nearly fell off the seat. "Come on, sweetheart!" Walt said. "What are you so gloomy about?"

Marie pushed at his face. He had to straighten up to get the car back on the road. Marie continued to push him away, with her hands under his chin. He pulled her forcibly to him.

"You like that?" he asked.

But Ellen sat up in the seat and leaned forward. "Let her alone," she said.

"Pipe down in the back seat!" Walt struggled with Marie for

a moment. "What's the matter, Johnny? Can't you keep her busy?"

Marie braced herself and gave Walt a terrible shove. His head snapped back. He said, "Oh!" and put his hand to his neck. For a moment, he seemed about to hit her. Then he controlled himself. "Come on," he said. "Don't get so hot." Marie seemed exhausted after she freed herself. She sank back in the far corner of the seat.

"Let her alone, you God-damn clown," Ellen said distinctly.

"Take care of your girl, Hagen!" Walt said. "Do I have to take care of them both?"

They were silent as they rode on toward the highway. Johnny and Ellen were sitting close to each other in the narrow back seat. Their legs were touching. Ellen seemed to be satisfied that Walt was leaving Marie alone; she sank back in the seat, and when she did so her shoulder also pressed against Johnny's. Now Johnny wanted to start a conversation, but he did not know how to begin. He tried to think of something dirty to say, so he could get the conversation started on the right track, but he could not think of anything that seemed fitting. Besides, when he had winked at her and said that some people had a good time when the lights went out, she had not paid much attention and had not even replied.

Presently he asked, "How do you like working?"

"What?"

"I said . . . how do you like working out there?"

Ellen looked at him "It's wonderful," she said. "Good God. How do you?"

Johnny felt that she was making fun of him, but he was glad to be talking anyway, "Oh, it ain't so bad. It gets tiresome sometimes . . . I don't mind."

He wondered if he ought to feel her up. If it had been some girl he had gone out with in high school he would have known how to act, but Ellen seemed so hard-boiled he hesitated; he was afraid she would laugh at him. They rode the rest of the

[210]

way to the main highway in silence. In the front seat Walt whispered to Marie and made a few ineffectual passes at her. She pushed him aside wearily, and did not answer his whisperings except to say, "This is where we get out. Let us out here."

Walt stopped the car and began to argue.

"Come on, why wait here, I'll take you on home, what's the idea?"

"We're going to meet somebody here," Ellen said. She was already crowding forward past Johnny.

"Who?"

"Her boy friend."

"Where is he? He ain't here. He won't show up. . . . Come on."

"He's working—he don't get off till twelve."

Ellen reached past Marie and opened the door. But before Marie could get out, Walt grabbed her again and pulled her to him. He started to whisper something to her, but she pushed herself away and Ellen pulled at Walt's shoulder, saying, "Let her alone—haven't you got any sense? Grow up, will you?"

"Lay off, will you?" Walt turned on Ellen. "Whose party is this? Lay off before I smack you one." Nevertheless he released Marie, and she climbed out of the car.

As she did so she said to Ellen, "I can take care of myself."

Ellen got out. She slammed the door. "Thanks, Fathead," she said. The two girls walked off toward the highway. Another car from the factory drew up to a stop at the edge of the pavement, hesitated while the driver looked to see what was coming, and moved out on the pavement. As Walt followed it, Johnny got a glimpse of the two girls standing beside the road, swinging their lunch pails while they waited, staring toward town for the lights of a car. Then Walt swung out on the pavement. He jammed the gear-shift lever hard as he shifted into second; the scrape of the gears seemed to give him some satisfaction. "Little bitch," he said forcibly. Johnny climbed into the front seat. "You," Walt said. "Why didn't you do something?"

"Me?"

"Oh, you're nuts. Why didn't you do something. You didn't do a damn thing. You just set there . . . I'd been all right. If your girl had kept her mouth shut."

"I don't see," Johnny replied.

"You don't know how to handle these chippies. You got to grab them. You see how I did? That's the way you got to handle them." Then Walt forgot about blaming Johnny; he stared straight at the road, frowning restlessly, his large face twisted with disappointment. "Bitches," he burst out. "Bitches, bitches!" Suddenly he stopped the car at the side of the road.

"Nothing passed us," he said.

Johnny did not understand. He was too humiliated by Walt's criticism to keep up with what he said. He had been accusing himself for not having grabbed Ellen and done it to her right there in the back seat, and trying to make himself believe that the next time he would know what to do.

"That was a stall," Walt said. "Nobody's coming for them. They just wanted to get out. Smart," he said. "They're smart."

Johnny still did not understand, except that he gathered that the girls had put something over on them.

"Bitches," Walt said. "Nothing's coming. Look." He pointed down the road. There were no headlights approaching them. "Let's go back. But listen, Hagen. You got to do your part. Make a play for her. She's hot for it. Anybody can see that. She's burning up. All you have to do is get her started. She'll come across. You see? Use both hands. Like my girl . . . she just as good as told me she would if it wasn't for her sister."

Johnny sighed.

"What do you say?"

Johnny tried to picture himself grabbing Ellen and getting her worked up. He did not believe there was any sense in going back. If the girls had wanted to ride with them, he figured,

[212]

they wouldn't have got out in the first place. But he was afraid of Walt's scorn if he did not show some enthusiasm.

"It's all right with me," he said.

Walt was determined. He swung the car around in the road and stepped on it going back. "Now do something this time," he kept saying. "Let me do the talking. Watch me. And do something."

The girls were still waiting where the road from the factory joined the highway. Most of the workers walked home across the tideflat to the poor sections near the waterfront, and only those who had cars drove to the highway. Walt slowed down so that the headlights focused on the girls for a few moments. They looked into the light; it was obvious that they were expecting the car; they moved a little toward the pavement. All at once, while he watched her from the darkness of the car, Johnny thought what a good-looking girl Ellen was; he had never realized it before. The band tied around her hair made her forehead look high and smooth, and her features were small and delicate; she was frowning a little at the headlights, and her lips were partly opened as she tried to see who was in the car. Her dark blue overalls were fitted tightly around her waist and the upper part of her legs, flaring out at the cuffs to conceal her shoes. She wore a red sash around her waist, and a white shirt open at the throat. The shirt fitted her loosely; a slight breeze ruffled the cloth over her breasts. As Walt swung the car around, and the light moved away from the girls, Johnny felt himself tremble with a different kind of excitement from that he had felt before; he felt uneasy and troubled, and when he breathed there was an empty feeling in his chest, as though he could not breathe deeply enough.

"*Let me do the talking,*" Walt whispered.

He stopped the car. The girls came over to it, unfriendly and distrustful, trying to see who was behind the windshield. "We thought we'd see if he'd showed up," Walt said loudly.

[213]

Neither of them replied; they stopped and looked disappointed.

"Maybe he broke down," Walt said. "Come on, we'll take you on home."

"We'll wait," Ellen said. "Thanks."

"Come on! Don't be sore. I was only playing . . . haven't you got a sense of humor?"

"No."

Walt opened the door. "Get out," he whispered. "Talk her into it." Johnny walked uneasily over to Ellen. He could see her watching him as he approached with a frank suspicion and contempt, and a slight tremor of pain passed through him; he wanted to tell her that he was really friendly; he did not ever want her to look like that when she saw him.

"What do *you* want?" Ellen said.

"Nothing!. . . I just wanted to say . . . you know, if you want to ride home, maybe his car broke down, you can't tell, you don't want to wait here all night, do you?"

"We won't have to. We'll take a chance."

Johnny agreed at once. "All right, all right! I just wanted to say—you know—if you wanted. . . ." His voice trailed off until he was only mumbling to himself.

He was vaguely aware that Walt had eased the car slowly down the pavement, and that he was talking to the other girl. Now all at once Ellen's face became distorted and she shouted something wildly. Johnny looked around. The other girl had been standing beside the car, and Walt had dragged her across the front seat. Now she was lying sprawled out on the front seat, with one knee on the floor of the car and one foot on the running-board. Then her feet kicked in the air as Walt dragged her on inside. The car started to move. Ellen ran after it. The door remained open; Johnny could see Marie's feet sticking out over the running-board as it went out of sight. A crazy thought kept going through his mind; he thought that Marie's feet looked surprised. Then, a long time afterwards, he heard the door of the car slam. In a few moments the red tail light was out of sight around a curve in the road.

Ellen was standing in the middle of the road. "You bastard," she kept saying. "Oh, you bastard, you bastard." She turned on Johnny furiously as he approached. "Leave me alone. I'll kill you, you hear? I'll kill you."

Johnny backed away. He tried to reassure himself by thinking that Walt would drive back to pick them up in a few minutes. But the darkness seemed intense as soon as the headlights of the car disappeared. There were no houses or lights along the road. The brush of the tideflat grew in a solid mass on both sides of the highway, and the new pavement shone with a greenish light. There were no cars coming from either direction, and there was no sound except a faint stirring from the brush.

"I didn't do anything," he stammered. "I swear . . . I didn't have anything to do with it."

He tried to think that Walt would not leave him out in the middle of the tideflat like this, that he would soon be back for them, that it was only a trick. . . . But he was deeply shocked; he felt sick to think of what Ellen must think of him; and he was ashamed for Walt, in a curious way; he wanted Walt to do something to make it seem less bad. "I didn't!" he repeated. "I swear to God I didn't!"

Ellen seemed to believe him. She calmed down and came back to the edge of the road. "I'll kill him," she whispered. "Fred will kill him." She spoke with such venom that Johnny could imagine a knife going slowly into Walt's heart. "Oh, God!" Ellen said. "Then why do you hang around a guy like that?"

She picked up her lunch pail. She had thrown it down when she ran after the car. Very slowly Johnny realized that she was crying. The lunch pail had opened when it was dropped, and as Ellen looked for the spoon and for the cup that she carried fruit in, she kept drawing her free hand across her eyes and

[215]

face. Johnny listened to her crying and watched her in a tightening spasm of misery. Didn't Walt have any sense? he wondered. Doing a thing like that? How could he do a thing like that? He struck a match and tried to help her. "I'll help you," he said, and crawled on his hands and knees holding the match close to the ground.

She said brokenly, "You don't have to." Her voice was so bitter that Johnny closed his ears; he was shaken and thoroughly miserable. Then he found the missing parts of her lunch bucket. There was a small jar with a lid, and as Johnny picked it up he noted automatically that Ellen had had raspberries for her lunch—there were a few left in the jar

"Here," he said. "Is there anything else?"

"No. That's all."

She put the things back in her lunch bucket. She was still crying, though not so hard as she had been before; only at times she would draw in a deep and trembling breath, and at other times Johnny could see her whole body draw up in a brief spasm of nervousness and fatigue. Her hands were trembling so much it was hard for her to fasten her lunch bucket.

"They ought to shoot people like that," she said at last.

Johnny was relieved that she had controlled herself. "The damn fool," he said. He was surprised at the anger in his own voice. They were silent for a long time. Ellen sat down, and after hesitating, wondering whether or not he should, Johnny sat down beside her.

The dark mass of brush towered over the road. The faint, dry, summer crackling came from it as the twigs snapped and the leaves stirred. Ellen leaned forward and put her hands over her eyes and forehead. He did not dare sit very close to her, and he could not see her very clearly, he could see only the white blur of her shirt and of her arms and face. But he was moved because she seemed so distressed, and he tried to think of something to say to comfort her. He watched the road, hoping to see the headlights of Walt's car and Walt coming back. The stream of pavement disappeared a short way ahead. He could see it for a little way, before the brush made a wall of shadow, and beyond it he could only see the tops of the taller bushes outlined against the sky. He shivered. It was hard to believe that town was only a few miles beyond the wall of brush.

Ellen straightened up.

"You want a sandwich?" she asked.

"What?"

"You want a sandwich?" After a moment, she explained, in a tired voice, "I got one left over from my lunch. I don't want it. You can have it if you want it."

Johnny hesitated. He did not know what to say, but he was touched that she should offer him a sandwich. It was true that she had offered it indifferently, in a voice that was worn out by her crying. "Don't you want it?" he asked.

"No. I'm not hungry. . . . If you want it. Otherwise I'll throw it away."

"Then I'll eat it."

She watched him mournfully while he unwrapped the sandwich and bit into it. "How far do you live?"

"On the other side of the flat. About four miles, I guess." Then he thought. "But it's only about two miles to the car line."

"They won't be running now." She sighed. "Something must have happened to Fred. But you never can depend on him. I don't see why Marie runs around with him. He never does do what he says he will. He goes out and gets drunk and then he tells Marie he couldn't get his car started. And she believes him."

"How far do you live?"

"Way on the other side of town."

They relaxed into another silence. It was growing a little cold. Johnny awakened to the fact that no cars had passed and that they had a long walk ahead of them into town, unless

Walt came back, and he was beginning to believe that Walt was not coming back. Even if he did . . . .

Ellen stood up. "We might as well get started."

They walked slowly down the deserted road. Now Johnny felt let-down and tired; every time his feet came down on the pavement he felt it all the way up his spine. He tried not to think of the dirty trick Walt had played on them. All sorts of confused memories kept crowding into his mind; it seemed that days had passed since he had gone running through the factory, and days since Walt had come up to him and greeted him like a fraternity brother—a fine fraternity brother he turned out to be!—and the girl in the white dress and the boy in evening clothes had nestled down in the big car while they watched the accident, and his father had been in some sort of fuss. It was too much; Johnny could not grasp it all. No cars passed them. The great banks of brush on both sides of the road rustled in the darkness, and when they spoke their voices sounded loud and unearthly. Johnny felt a tugging despondency the longer they walked—how could anybody do such a thing? How could anybody be so mean?

"If he hurts her," Ellen said, "I'll kill him."

She was stumbling a little. Her white shirt and her white face were misty blurs in the darkness. "She's sick," she went on. "She just got out of the hospital."

"Oh!" Johnny said.

"Yes."

Hospital, he repeated silently.

"Nobody could ever treat me the way Fred treats her. He says he'll come after her and then half the time he don't show up. He's always got some good excuse. . . . If anybody ever did to me," she said threateningly, "what he did to her, I'd kill him."

The threat in her voice was so live and real that he thought it was intended for him.

"What did he do to her?"

"First he knocked her up," Ellen said. "Then after he raised fifty dollars for an abortion he lost thirty-five dollars on a punch board trying to win a twenty-dollar gold piece so he'd have the rest of it. So she had to raise the money from a guy she used to work for and then she had to come back to work before she was supposed to because she was afraid Carl would fire her if she didn't. That's why I despise him," Ellen said. "Do you blame me?"

"No."

"If you ever tell anybody," she said abruptly, "if you ever tell anybody I told you, I'll kill you.'

"I won't tell anybody."

"If you ever do."

They walked along in silence.

"God Almighty!" Johnny cried.

"Now what do you think?"

"God."

"Now," Ellen said, "why do you hang around a rat like that?"

"I don't know."

The lights of a car opened in the road ahead of them. She stepped out into the light. The car stopped; he heard the voices and the sliding brakes. The car turned around heavily, backing across the wide pavement, starting and stopping before it headed the way they were going and drew up beside them. It was a high old-fashioned touring car, a seven-passenger Chandler, and the motor knocked so loudly that Ellen had to shout to be heard. Great waves of brown smoke poured out of the hood when it stopped.

"Where's Marie?" a voice called down.

"You!" Ellen shouted back. "What happened to you!"

"I couldn't get it started! Where's Marie?"

"Get on in back," Ellen told him.

Ellen got in the front seat. Two young fellows sitting in back moved over to make room for him. He could feel them watching him inquisitively. There were two more in the front seat, a tall fellow sitting behind the steering wheel, and a boy who stood up so Ellen could slide in between them. He heard Ellen explaining what had happened. The tall driver began to curse. He turned around and spoke to the two in the back.

"You hear that?" he demanded incredulously. "Some son of a bitch ran off with Marie. Pulled her in his car. . . . Who was it?"

Ellen asked Johnny, "What's his name?"

"Walt Connor."

One of the voices said, "I know him. I know who he is. Football player. Remember?"

There was a moment of silence. The driver said, almost in awe, "I'll kill the son of a bitch. I'll murder him." He turned to Johnny again. "Who the hell is that?"

"Nobody. He came out with me."

"What's he doing here?"

"You want him to walk home? It ain't his fault. It's your fault. It's your fault. If your car won't run you ought to start earlier."

"Which way did he go?"

"Toward town."

They started out, the car lurching heavily and the gears grinding as they got under way. He sank back against the torn upholstery. One of the men in the back seat leaned forward and shouted to the driver. "There's a side road down here a ways! Maybe he turned in there!" He sat back beside Johnny. "What a rat," he said. "What a rat that guy must be. You want a drink?"

"What?"

The man handed him a flask. He took a small sip out of it and handed it back. The man leaned over and tapped Ellen on the shoulder.

"What?"

"Here's a drink."

Ellen took the bottle and threw it out into the brush. It broke. "Why you why you," the man said. "You little devil."

The car turned off the pavement and dove into a dirt road. The brush slapped against the side of the car. "Fred!" the man shouted. "She threw away my bottle."

"I haven't got any time to pay attention to you," the driver shouted back. "I'm looking for the guy that run off with Marie and when I catch him I'm going to beat the Jesus out of him."

From the far side of the car a voice said, "Where's Marie?"

"A guy run off with her."

"Run off with her?"

"Yeah."

"Where are we?" the voice said.

"I haven't got any time to monkey with any bottle," the driver called back. "I'm going to find the son of a bitch that run off with my girl and beat him up."

"This is a private road," somebody said. "I saw a sign back there."

The man beside Johnny sank back in the seat. "Did you see that?" he asked. "That little devil threw out that whole big bottle."

The car bounced over the private road. "When I catch him," the driver called back, "I'll tear off his arms and beat him with the bloody stumps."

"*Oh, shut up!*" Ellen cried. "*You crazy bastards!*"

"Well, why'd you throw away my bottle?"

They stopped. The road ended. In a cleared space they saw a house brightly lighted and a crowd of people dressed in evening clothes on the lawn. There was a little group standing together some distance from the front porch, and as they stopped the group scattered, the people ran back toward the house and there was a loud shouting. Sparks began to fly at the place where they had been. They heard a loud *whish* like a sound of a safety valve popping off; a broad stream of fire climbed into the sky, mounted straight up, dropped and exploded and great globes of colored light dotted the air.

"I told you this was a private road," a voice said. "I read it on a sign back there."

"Turn around," Ellen said dully. "Go on home and wait there. He'll have to take her home. Anyway."

2. Walt

HE bore down as hard as he could on the gas, feeling the car spring ahead while he drew her up on the seat. He reached over her and pulled the door shut, sensing the car edging off the road, jerking it back wildly with one hand while he closed the door against the wind. The steering wheel was firm and responsive and as the car gained speed he whipped it back and forth for no reason, only to feel it under his control. The girl pushed at him. He heard her saying, "What do you think you are?" in a dull weak voice. He put his arm around her and pressed her so tightly that she could not speak. His hand went under her arm and closed over her full breast. He was conscious of her kicking awkwardly at his feet and pulling at his hand on her breast with her free hand.

This is a good old car, he thought feverishly. This is a good old car. "You know how fast we're going?" he asked her. Her mouth was pressed against his shoulder. She tried to bite him; she tried to free her head. The pavement opened up ahead, wide and free and safe. At the turns he swung it around lightly, proud of the feeling of power as the car responded with his one hand on the wheel.

She stopped struggling but her body was still tense and watchful. "You're not fooling me," he said. He felt himself grinning at the pavement that opened up before the headlights. They're not fooling me, he told the pavement. They're not putting anything over on me. Under his hand her breast was soft and pliant and he molded it tenderly. Her legs were awkwardly spread, and he glanced down, smiling at their funny position, one knee clamped around the gear shift and the emergency brake and one leg half drawn up on the seat; he could see the firm lines of flesh under her overalls and see the flesh move when she tried to free herself and her hips swelled against where the cloth pressed tightly. Don't worry, he thought tenderly. I'll work you up. I wouldn't hurt you.

The road branched and he turned up toward the hills. In a moment he was sorry. If I have to shift, I'll have to let her go. Now she was lying tense and flexible, ready to free herself if his hold weakened. You aren't fooling me, he said silently. Don't think you are. He said to Winters and all the men, you're not putting anything over on me, and, to the goofy Polack, I know what you're up to. The car climbed the first hills and shot out on the level ground of the first suburbs. There were lights in some of the houses and there were a few scattered street lights, so he turned still higher, giving it all it would take, skidding in the loose gravel so he would not have to shift.

Here.

He turned off the road and switched off the motor and the lights. His hands were sweaty.

For a moment he sat motionless while the motor creaked into silence. She made an ineffectual struggle.

"I won't hurt you," he whispered.

He moved his hand cautiously to her breast again. Still pressing her firmly against his shoulder he bent his head over hers, smelling her rich hair, barely moving his lips as he whispered, "I've been watching you for a long time. Ever since I came to work. Don't be afraid of me. I wouldn't hurt you. I wouldn't hurt you for anything." She made a brief convulsive struggle. He began to caress her gently, gently, barely letting his hand move over her breast and her thigh while he murmured, "I didn't mean to be rough. But I didn't want those kids along. And I didn't want to argue. Do you understand?

[224]

Can you hear me?" She relaxed; he could feel her growing lax and waiting under his hand and his murmuring voice, and he tried to move slightly toward her while his hand fumbled with the belt of her overalls.

"You're a God-damn fool," she said distinctly.

He tried to kiss her. Her lips were tense and closed and no matter how hard he pressed her they stayed clamped shut and she pulled her head away. Her feet kicked at his legs and her free hand beat on his side, tried to reach his face unless he warded it off with his upper arm.

"I'm sorry I was rough," he said. "I didn't mean to hurt you. You understand? I wouldn't hurt you for anything. Do you think I would? Why should I?"

She gasped, "Well let me breathe then. Let me get my breath. You're choking me."

He released her. She breathed deeply and put her hand on her mouth. "You nut," she said shakily. "Of all the nuts."

"I'm sorry, Marie. I didn't mean to hurt you. But I didn't."

"What's the matter with you? What do you want, anyway?"

He put his arm around her again and tried to draw her to him. She did not struggle but she kept saying, "Oh, of all the nuts, of all the nuts." He kissed her unyielding mouth but when he put his hand on her she began to scream, over and over, while he tried to kiss her to stop her and she kept on screaming, the crazy sound splitting his ears. *I'll stop!* he yelled, *I'll stop!* She kept on screaming and he looked around in terror at the dark road and started the car to drown out the sound. Then he drove away, imagining the people running from the scattered houses on the hill, shouting *I've stopped! I'll leave you alone!* until at last she stopped screaming and began to cry, rocking back and forth on the seat with her hands over her face. He drove up and down the hills for a long time until she calmed down. Then she sat back in the corner of the seat with her eyes closed and her face pale and exhausted.

Gradually he calmed down. Now he could feel the sweat on his face and hear his own shaken breathing. "I'm sorry," he said at last. "I didn't think."

She did not open her eyes. "Take me home," she said. "I'm sick."

"Where do you live?"

"On Hume. At the corner of Nestle."

He turned back obediently.

"I'm sorry," he repeated desperately. "You hear me? I didn't mean. But I get sick of it. I been there a year now. I don't know a soul. If they get it in for you . . . and they never give me a chance. They never give me a chance. I been there a year now and I don't know a soul. I've seen you there ever since I been there and I thought. I didn't mean. I didn't want to hurt you."

"Yes," she said. She looked at him. "You got a hard life," she said. All the life had gone out of him; he felt her watching him and he turned the car toward town.

3. JOHNNY

THEY drove through the main streets to the shadowed district near the waterfront. There were still the remnants of the crowds downtown, left like the burnt-out firecrackers that littered the streets; there were a few groups clustered before the all-night restaurants and in front of the hotels; there were a few drunks sitting on the curb tossing firecrackers out into the street, and an irregular crackling came from all parts of town. There was a strong smell of burnt explosives in the air. A few cars darted through the empty streets. They looked small and lost, like insects racing across a tile floor. Out in the dark neighborhood where Ellen lived there were bands of sailors scattered along the sidewalks, and when the car stopped, out of the light of a street lamp on the corner, Johnny could see the whore houses on the waterfront lighted up and hear the occasional racket from them.

This was where Ellen lived. The house was set back from the street, between a store building on the corner and a whore house on the other side. The windows of the store were boarded over and there were large advertisements for cigarettes pasted on the boards. Behind the Turner house the gas tanks were outlined against the reflected light from the main part of town.

Most of the time they waited in silence. Occasionally one of the men stirred to light a cigarette. The car creaked mysteriously from time to time as the engine cooled. Johnny could see Ellen's head outlined against the street lamp. The others

[227]

were lying back relaxed and waiting, but she sat stiffly upright, watching for the lights of a car to appear on the darkened street. Johnny came to life again, and felt excited and alert. Whenever a car passed the house his heart began to pound and he found himself hoping feverishly that Walt would have sense enough to drive right away. . . . People passed on the sidewalk beside the car, so close that he could reach out and touch them if he wanted to, without looking at the car and without knowing that there were people sitting in it who could hear every word they said. A man dressed in a bright pink suit, with green trimmings on the sleeves and green stripes down the trousers, stopped under the street light and looked all around, trying to get his bearings. He carried a large fat horn coiled around his arm like a snake, and when he stopped he took off his hat—it was a tall fuzzy hat shaped like a watermelon—and ran a handkerchief over his bald head. Then he sighed and walked unsteadily toward the center of town.

"He's taking his time," the driver said.

No one answered him.

"Let me take care of him," the driver said. "I'll take care of him. Only watch he don't try to swing a jack or anything. I'll handle him."

"You'll do wonders," Ellen said.

"You think I won't?"

"Well don't brag so much. You brag too much. If you'd come out and got us there wouldn't be any trouble."

"I told you I couldn't get it started."

"You never can get it started. . . . Why don't you start trying earlier if you know it won't start?"

"Shut up," someone said.

A car approached. Johnny waited, in an almost unbearable tension; he could imagine the men rushing for Walt, pulling him out of the car and pounding his face in; he could imagine Walt struggling as the four of them jumped on him. And maybe Walt had just turned around and gone back and was

[228]

still looking for them. . . . The car passed. The men sank back, and Johnny drew a deep breath of relief. Then he saw another car, coming in close behind the first, hidden behind it, stop before the house.

Before he knew it he was out of the car and racing down the street. *"Don't stop!"* he yelled. *"Don't stop!"* He jumped on the running-board of Walt's car; he saw Walt stare at him with his face stiff with surprise; and then, as the others began to climb out of the car and to run down the street toward them, Walt's car lurched ahead, speeded up in second, and sailed over the uneven pavement. He fumbled at the door and climbed inside. Walt was looking back to see what was coming. He looked frightened and bewildered; he kept looking from the road ahead, to Johnny, and then back through the rear window. Marie was slouched down in the front seat between them. Johnny had to push her over to make room for himself.

"What is it?" Walt said.

"Four of them . . . they'll beat you up. They been waiting for you."

Johnny could not get his breath to explain any more. He leaned back, breathing hard and trembling. Walt bore down on the accelerator and the car jerked ahead. Then Marie raised herself up from the seat.

"Let me out," she said.

Walt did not answer her. Looking back, Johnny could see the dim, flickering headlights of the car. He felt reassured. It could never catch them. He felt a thrill of pride that Walt's car could make such time.

"They came a little while after you left," he said, breathlessly. "They been waiting."

"How many of them?"

"Four of them."

Marie pushed weakly at Johnny. "I'm sick," she said. "Let me out."

"Are they in sight?"

Johnny looked back. He could still see the headlights, but now they were dim, and looked like only one light. "Just barely in sight," he said.

Walt swung the car to miss a hole in the pavement. "They'll never catch us!" he shouted. "This old hack can make time!"

"Let me out," Marie said.

She was half standing and trying to reach the door handle, leaning against Johnny and reaching over him. Walt slowed down and glanced back. Then he swung the car to the side of the road. They were beside a mill yard; there was a high board fence running beside the road for two blocks. Walt said sharply, "All right. Let her out." He stopped the car. Johnny fumbled nervously with the door handle. His hand slipped from it as he pressed on it. *"Pull up! you God-damn fool!"* Walt shoved him viciously and opened the door. Johnny tried to stand on the running-board as Marie got out, but she fell forward and he stepped down to grab her. He saw Walt looking back through the rear window as he stepped down. Then all at once, as he held Marie, the light disappeared and Walt's car went sailing down the road.

He started to run after it. He ran a hundred feet before he heard the door slam shut and understood that Walt was leaving him there. He had a dazed feeling that it had happened before. He thought of running away from the road, but the darkness tripped him and he fell down as soon as he left the pavement. In an agony of fear he tried to hide in the brush beside the road, but he could feel that the bushes were not high enough to conceal him. For a few moments he scrambled through the brush, sometimes half running and sometimes crawling on his hands and knees. Then his head cleared. He got back on the pavement and walked back to Marie. She was sick; he could see her vaguely against the wall and hear the terrible gasping sounds as she vomited. The car bore down on them. He waited for them to jump on him. He saw them climbing out of the car, and saw Ellen brush past him to run to Marie. He heard their confused shouts, and thought of how much noise the car made; it shook all over as the motor idled, and the smoke and steam floated up around the hood. One of them grabbed him by the shoulder. "Where'd he go?" somebody shouted at him. "Where'd he go." He was conscious of pointing down the road and of thinking what a foolish question. Then, somehow, he was back in the car, and it was racing down the road again.

For a long time no one said anything. The wind beating on his face revived him. As his heart slowed down he leaned forward, his hands clenched and his feet bearing down hard against the floor boards, trying to make the car go faster. He thought of what he would do when they caught Walt. He pictured Walt lying on the ground and himself running at him and jumping on him with both feet. In the darkness one of the men slapped him hard across the face. Johnny swung back blindly. "You little bastard!" the man said. "What'd you do it for? Why'd you tell him?" His voice sounded baffled and disapproving, as though he were disappointed in Johnny and could not clearly understand what Johnny had done.

Another voice said, "Left you there! What a rat!"

Johnny was too choked to answer. He felt impotent because the car moved so slowly. It shook and rattled; the top flopped in the wind, and it made a lot of noise, but gradually he realized that it was not going very fast. "We'll never catch him!" he shouted. The words burst from him. He was almost crying. "We'll never catch him! We'll never catch him!"

The car stopped. The driver turned back to Johnny.

"Where does he live?"

Ellen and Marie were in the front seat. Ellen said, "Take her home. You can find him afterwards."

"Where does he live?"

"I don't know."

"Fred," Ellen said, "use some sense. Take her home. She has to go home."

[231]

"Don't lie. You do know. I'll knock your can off."

"You think I wouldn't tell you if I knew! You think I wouldn't tell you! I wish to God I *did* know. I wish to God I *could* get ahold of him."

"*Shut up!*" Ellen said. "Take us home! You hear me!"

"*Well, why did you tell him then? We would have had him if you hadn't told him!*"

"I," Johnny said. But he could not defend himself. "I'll never do that again. The bastard."

"You shouldn't have done it the first time."

Ellen said, "Fred." She jerked at his arm. "You listen to me. You hear? Take us home. Who are you thinking about? She's got to get home! You can take care of him! Some other time!"

They drove back to the house. When they got there Fred turned on Johnny again. He got out of the car and stood beside Johnny. "I ought to paste you one," he said. "Anyway."

But Ellen said wearily, "Oh, let him alone. He's harmless. He's just dumb!"

Johnny stood uncertainly on the sidewalk, watching Marie get out of the car. Fred and Ellen walked with her as they went on toward the house. One of the men came over beside him and lit a cigarette. "You better beat it, kid," he said. "He's liable to beat the Jesus out of you if he has to see you much longer." Johnny nodded dully and started off in the general direction of home.

All sorts of dizzy ideas flashed through his mind. He was tired; he was almost trembling with his weariness. Ellen's indifferent defense of him. *Let him alone. He's harmless. He's just dumb!* Oh, how bitterly it shamed him! He could not rest, he could not put it out of his mind, he could not forget it any more than he could forget the aching muscles of his legs. And he could not dismiss it, for whenever he thought to console himself, *She's just a little chippy, she's just a little Polack,* he remembered her crying by the roadside and the way she looked under the light of the car, and he remembered Walt driving away like a bat out of hell and the blindness of his own terror and bewilderment. When he thought of his betrayal it was not hatred for Walt that moved him, but revulsion, a deep and sickened shame for mankind, an emotion more powerful than any he had ever known. Some day I'll tell him, he thought. Some day I'll pay him back, and he stumbled on home through the littered streets.

They let me off easy, he thought. They should have beat me up.

He awakened painfully, hearing voices inside the house and the fitful cries of the children in the yard, his body heavy with sleep and his head thick with the dreams that had tormented him all night. The shade on the window was drawn except for a few inches at the bottom; the window was up and the light came in hot and unsparing, lighting up the torn and spotted wall paper, the door frame that did not fit tightly into the wall, the little cloudy balls of dust under the other bed. He opened his eyes and brooded on these marks that lay like the wounds of poverty on the room, turning his eyes slowly from the sagging ceiling to the disordered covers on the other bed, where his younger brother slept; he closed his eyes again and tried to go back to sleep. He could feel the glaze of sweat on his cheeks. Noon. Outside he heard the sunlight drying the world, the sounds weighed down in the heat and going only a little way in the thick and windless air.

One of the children cried out in the house. There was a fervent hushing sound, and he could imagine his mother or his sister whispering fiercely, *"Be quiet! Johnny's asleep!"* and the children drawing in their breaths in exaggerated alarm and tiptoeing out with elaborate caution and covering their shame at having spoken loudly by warning the others as they crept outside.

Misery. The house was crowded. For a month his sister

and her husband and their two children had been there, doubling up the beds in the small rooms, his brother coming into his room, the two children upstairs, his sister and her husband sleeping on the cot in the front room. There were always beds that had not been made and somebody was always sleeping in the house. When he came in at night he had to creep past the bed where his sister and her husband slept. Sometimes they were awake and spoke to him, and he answered them briefly, in embarrassment, as he sidled quickly to his door and closed it behind him. When they were not awake when he got in from work he also felt uncomfortable at going through their room, seeing the two figures beneath the covers, feeling that he had intruded on them while they slept; sometimes, before he went to sleep, he would hear them whispering beyond the door, hear one of them getting up and moving secretly through the dark house and returning, more passionate whispers and a dim stirring in the darkness before the silence settled again.

For a time he kept thinking it was Sunday because of the stillness, and then he remembered that it was the Fourth, remembering the rockets swarming through the sky last night, the memory bringing all the nightmare rushing back upon him. He turned toward the wall and closed his eyes, trying to make it dark, whispering to himself, *It's night, it's dark outside,* and trying to make himself sleep. Down the street, somewhere, a few firecrackers rattled, somebody setting off the last of a package, and he pictured the kids gathering in little groups all through the district, hoarding each cracker, their hearts sinking at the ones that didn't explode, saving each one that didn't explode to break it and make a sizzler out of it later on when all the good ones were gone. In the kitchen his mother moved around; there was a rattle of dishes, the sound of her voice when she spoke to his sister. Mildred was always washing the kids' clothes, usually on the back porch, or going out into the back yard to hang them on the network of lines, pinning the damp garments up with strong sure movements, calling out, "Johnny, help me carry this!" when there was a tub to be emptied, or "Johnny, will you see what's the matter with Little Mildred?" when she was busy and the children were complaining. He listened; he could hear the steady mechanical sounds as she bore down on the clothes, the pauses when she dipped them into the soapy water, the casual words she called out to her mother or her husband in the house. Sometimes he heard his father's heavy voice and the smooth salesman's voice of his brother-in-law, the rustle of newspapers, the sound of heavier footsteps inside. Once in a while a car passed the house. For an instant he thought of being at the beach or in the mountains, stretched out taking it easy, listening to the hum of the waves, in the sand at the beach or lying out in some cool place in the mountains—I wish we had a car, he thought, and he tried to make himself think of all the places he wanted to go.

It was no use. His arms and legs were stiff and tired. Even if he did not move a dull ache spread over his shoulders. The flies moved heavily around his head; he could hear them drawing near, lighting somewhere on the bedclothes, waiting to light on his face and hands, flying away when he stirred or breathed deeply. When he opened his eyes he saw one on the pillow only a few inches from his face, drawing itself together ready to fly if frightened. It moved in little spasmodic jerks across the pillow, hesitating before lighting on his open palm, and he whispered silently, You haven't got nerve enough, while it paused, turned around and around, and leaped into the air.

Get away.

He remembered Walt slamming the door of the car and driving off, and twisted in sudden anguish.

Do you know what I'd do if I had a car? he asked himself.

He tried to think of all the good places he could remember, the stretch of wide beach just this side of Point No Point, the widest and smoothest beach in the world where at low tide the wet sand was harder than pavement and you could hold a car wide open for an hour without having to steer it, the opening in the mountains near the Indian reservation where the river came out black and silent, and all the good places up near the headwaters of the Humptulips and the resorts in the mountains where the neat little houses were built right down to the water with the rowboats and canoes tied to their front porches. But it was no use, and more and more he remembered what had happened, until at last he was wide awake, thinking back over the whole night, remembering all the things he shouldn't have said and shouldn't have done without covering anything up or lying to himself or trying to make excuses. He remembered from the beginning when the lights went out until the time he stumbled across town home, bruised and shamed and sick as a dog over the way it had turned out. And what would they think of him? What would Ellen think of him? He remembered her standing under the lights of the car when they drove back, just before Walt drove off with Marie; he remembered the waiting, questioning look on her face and the disappointment when she saw who it was, and then her voice when she said *Let him alone. He's harmless. He's just dumb.* Now he would have to go back to work and see them all again, and he tried to think of how they would act, how Walt would face him and what he would say. He imagined himself going into the factory, listening silently while Walt tried to explain, listening with a scorn too deep for words, and that was nice to think about, but then he remembered himself running down the road and falling into the weeds after Walt drove off, running around in circles as blindly and madly as he might have run if someone had thrown acid into his eyes. Ah, how could anybody? *They ought to shoot people like that,* Ellen had said. *They shouldn't let them live.* Now he thought of the shock he had got when he first talked to Ellen and had seen, without thinking about it, that she was tired, and worried as much as his mother or Mildred or any-

[236]

body else he knew, and in all that he had heard about Ellen and Marie he had never thought about their being tired or worried or anything like it; he had only thought about their running around all over hell and getting drunk all the time and being screwed by everybody and his brother. Let him alone, he's just dumb—that's what she meant, he thought, and she's right.

Suddenly his brother-in-law's voice came clearly from beyond the door, "It's the richest community in America," he said.

"Johnny's still asleep."

"What?"

He heard them murmuring. "I'm awake," he called. His voice was thick; his tongue felt dry and swollen.

His sister opened the door and looked at him. "What happened to you?" she asked. Her hair was pushed back from her forehead and her face was flushed because she had been working; she looked at him, friendly and malicious, hesitating about saying anything about the time he came in. He could see that she was going to tease him about it, as she sometimes teased him, amused at his discomfort, when he came home and they were still awake; she would lie beside her husband and ask him one stupid question after another, merely to keep him in the room when she knew he was embarrassed and wanted to get away. One of these times, after he had escaped, he heard her giggling to Gerald, "He's so funny. He must think we do it all the time," and Gerald had said, "Let him alone." Now some look on his face, some look of expectancy or shame stopped her. She looked ill at ease, suddenly, as she said, "You'd better get up if you want anything to eat."

The voices rose stronger in the other room now that they knew he was awake. He dressed and went out into the kitchen for his breakfast, stupid with having slept in the hot room, waiting for them to torment him. At the window in the corner his father sat staring intently at the bills grouped on the table before him. His spectacles and his stiff Sunday clothes made

[237]

him look unfamiliar, like a postmaster or a druggist, and as he read he tipped his head back and looked out through the bottom of his glasses. Gerald, sitting in the open window, cool and shaved, nodded to him brightly when he came in. He could see them waiting to ask him what had happened and where he had been, why he had got home so late, and his heart sank, but after the first moment passed and no one said anything he saw that they were going to leave him alone. Mildred was out on the back porch again. When he came out of the bathroom his mother had put out his breakfast, two pieces of toast and his coffee, glancing at him apologetically when he sat down. Still they had said nothing and he had not spoken to them.

"As I was saying," Gerald said to his father, "You got no conception of the wealth of Santa Barbara. You have to see it to realize it. A million dollars there don't mean a thing. I forget who it was said lately there were more multimillionaires to the square mile in Santa Barbara than for any similiar area on the face of the globe. Arthur Brisbane, I expect."

Gerald leaned over and ran his finger around the edge of his oxford. His golf socks sagged somewhat around his legs and the creases bulged out above his shoes. He tugged at his golf socks and the creases disappeared, and then he straightened up in the window, leaning back while he pulled at the socks until the checks were even and the lines were straight on his legs. His legs in the bright checked socks looked funny; they bulged oddly at the calves and looked like tenpins set upside down.

Mildred stopped at the door. "Pop looks funny in his glasses," she said. He looked up. "You look funny in your glasses," she told him.

In reply he waved the light bill. "Two-eighty," he said. "You know we use a hell of a lot of light around here."

Johnny picked up a folder that came with the light bill. It was a large pamphlet, printed in three colors on smooth paper,

[238]

and was filled with pictures and a story of the history of light. "Primitive man," he read, "lighted his cave with the fitful glow from an open fire." There was a picture of a group of cave men gathered around a fire. He turned past the candles and torches and whale-oil lamps and kerosene and gas lights until he came to modern lighting, feeling a little rise of satisfaction that everything had turned out all right, and people no longer had the trouble lighting their houses that primitive man had.

Inside the pamphlet was another folder that opened out like a map, and inside it were printed cards reading *Don't strain your eyes! Use more light!* He read them carefully. *Are your children cross and fretful? Do you suffer from headaches?* One picture showed a group of puny, undersized children trying to read in a dark room, their foreheads wrinkled with eyestrain and looks of anguish on their features. *Mumsie, my head hurts so!* In the next picture the room was well lighted and the children were smiling happily. They had put on weight, too, and their clothes were better.

Use more light, he read. *It pays in the long run.*

That's true, he thought. People shouldn't try to read if they haven't got enough light.

Gerald was going on, undisturbed at being interrupted, "That's why it's such a good place for a decent agency. All the swell dress shops from Paris and London and New York—they've all got branches there. We got inside information about two months ago. All the old buildings are going out. The real-estate men got their own council now and there's going to be standardized specifications, minimum requirements for residences and shops or commercial buildings and uniform, California-Spanish style architecture that's going to make it the most beautiful city in the world—there won't be a place that can come up to it as far as ordinary beauty is concerned. The earthquake is the best thing that could have happened to Santa Barbara," Gerald said earnestly.

Hagen nodded politely, looking at Gerald and then at his

son before he turned back to the bills. Gerald was absorbed in his thoughts, staring at the floor and frowning as he thought of the wealth in Santa Barbara. "Two-eighty," his father repeated. "Whew." His mother was standing by the stove, and he saw her frown at his father, moving her head toward the porch where Mildred was with a swift, warning gesture, a look that had become familiar in the past month—he understood that she was warning his father not to complain about the bills because it made Mildred feel bad when he did. He drank his coffee, trying to turn his mind away from their troubles, away from all the hurt feelings and the memory of the times when Mildred and Gerald quarreled, when Mildred said he could get work if he only would. His mother always moved in swiftly, seeing some unpleasantness coming up before anyone else sensed it, warning anyone who spoke carelessly of the discomforts of being all cramped together, trying to keep Gerald and Mildred from feeling unwelcome. He looked at the folders again, at the stupefied faces of the people in the last picture, when they finally had enough light, but he could not free his mind of family troubles, for his memories of the times when Mildred had cried or stormed at Gerald were too painful and too powerful.

"Well, at that," his father said loudly, "it's less than it was last month."

"We certainly don't waste it," his mother said.

"I don't see how they get it," Hagen said. "They've got them college kids reading meters and I don't think they can even read."

Gerald waited until they had finished. "When I think of everything opening up there I think maybe I was foolish not to stay on on a commission basis," he said. "Erickson wanted me to. I may be a damn fool, I told him, but I'm not that kind of a fool. I know what happens when a man tries to play that game." He paused and looked at them defiantly. "What happens? Well, a man gets over-anxious and he drives a client away; he starts economizing on little things, you know, he wears a shirt another day, he don't keep his shoes shined, he don't give away cigars and he begins to figure he can't spare the money for lunch so he gets out of touch with the other men. . . ." A look of pain crossed his smooth face. Johnny listened, moved by the decay that Gerald pictured, wondering dully at the sad figure of the man who went down and down, economizing more and more, his shoes growing less polished, his shirts dirtier and his suits more ragged, until at last the very thought of him trying to sell real estate was a horrible mockery. And Gerald too was moved as he spoke, his voice rising faintly with the pain his words gave him; "I know that game!" he cried, "I know how a man feels! He gets so he don't want to take a prospect out to some property he's sure the prospect don't want, and the prospect thinks he's trying to put something over on him and he gets suspicious and then it's the same old story all over again! Don't tell me!" he cried out passionately. "I told him, I said, I'm too good a salesman myself to take that old gold brick off your hands!"

But then in a moment he had quieted again, and shook his head doubtfully, making a nervous salesman motion when he talked. "What did I stand to lose? When a man's starting out it's different. But when so much is opening up, why take a chance? Erickson knows it. He knows there's nobody in California knows that Santa Barbara real-estate field the way I know it. And I told him: By fall, I said, you'll see the biggest building program Santa Barbara's ever known. You'll see five buyers for every vacant lot. You'll see real-estate values surpassing your wildest dreams within two blocks of this office. I'll stake my life on it. If I had ten thousand dollars I'd grab every lease I could lay my hands on. It would pay you to hold every inch of space you could carry if you didn't collect a penny of rent for a year."

Johnny looked up, stirred and impressed at the passionate voice and the surge of conviction behind it. Gerald waved his hand in an abrupt gesture at the close of every sentence. He clamped his lips shut and frowned. Suddenly he got up and walked out on the back porch and down into the yard.

His mother watched him, a little apprehensively, as he walked out. She said to his father, "You ought to listen to him."

"I do."

"No. . . . You ought to listen."

"By God," his father said. "You know a light bill of two-eighty. . . . A dollar for water."

"He'll be here tomorrow."

"Who?"

"The light man."

"How much did we pay in June?"

"A dollar. It was two-ten and I paid a dollar."

"Three-ninety," his father said. "Practically four dollars." He looked at Johnny. "That's a hell of a lot of money to pay for lights." He looked at Johnny sharply from behind his glasses, and as Johnny looked away, after his first fear that something was going to be said about his getting in so late, he understood that in some dim way his father was bringing up the quarrel with Carl the night before, trying to see if he understood how serious it was and how close he was to not having a job. The thought tightened him. He glanced back at his father, seeing the heavy, expressionless features, the round head under the thinning fringe of hair, the eyes hard and questioning behind the thick glasses. Almost to his own surprise he asked softly, "How is that man? The one who was hurt?" not understanding that he wanted to let his father know what was in his mind until his father answered him quietly, saying that he had not heard. He drank the rest of his coffee, his mouth puckering from its bitter, warmed-over taste, his mind going back to all that had happened the night before, paying no attention as they talked over the bills and the little money to pay them. He heard his mother's plaintive voice, and answered her, No, when she asked if he was still hungry, but the emotions that had begun to stir in him were too powerful to let him think about their troubles and he wanted to get out of the house where he could think about his own. Now he was afraid of his father's questioning him any more, however indirectly, about his fight with Carl and the danger of his being fired, for he did not know how to answer and the thought was too troubling to be faced. At one moment he felt a cold resentment at his father for getting into trouble when they were so hard up, and he felt hard and contemptuous because his father could not provide for them after all this time he had worked, but at the next moment he was stirred because his father talked back to Carl no matter how many people depended on him or how many bills they had, and at these moments he felt in on something intense and adult and mysterious, ready for anything for the few moments before his excitement cooled. These were the moments when he thought of getting back at Walt in some way, doing something, making Walt see how much he despised him, yes, and maybe Ellen somewhere around seeing it—the thought made him glow inside, until he checked himself: *You're dumb, you'll never do anything,* and the misery held him again.

He would not have gone outside, or downtown under the pretext of watching the parade, if the kids had not come running through the house and interrupted him whenever he tried to think back on what had happened and to decide what he ought to do. He would have stayed in the house, in spite of the heat, in spite of his heavy head, if they had only left him alone, if Mildred and Gerald had not started quarreling, if Mildred had not started tormenting him, for he did not know which way to turn in the outside world that had grown inexplicable and dangerous. But they gave him no peace. Little Mildred came running into the room, screaming *"Make him stop! Make him stop!"* and Mildred answered from upstairs, *"Little Gerald! Stop teasing Little Mildred!"* though Little Gerald was not even around. He sat back, holding a paper out in front of him, watching his niece with intense hostility while she shouted to her mother upstairs and then to her brother in the yard. Mildred had dressed her daughter in a stiff dress that stuck out all around her like a bell, and had fixed her hair in artificial-looking curls so that everybody said she looked like a little doll, and now, as she called to her mother in her piercing voice, whirling around and around as she pretended to be hurt, he watched her with a smothered loathing and told himself that little kids were vicious. She knew that he hated her; she knew that she got on his nerves; and after she had called out she would look at him slyly and triumphantly and prepare to scream again. When Gerald and Mildred first moved into the house she had pestered him once until he put her out of the room. That was the first sign of what it would mean to have them there. When he closed the door she had dropped over backwards and screamed that he had pushed her, lying on the floor and kicking and screaming until his mother and Mildred both bore down on him in fury. Now Little Gerald came in, shouting over and over, *"I wasn't teasing her! Mama! I wasn't!"*

"Well, stop it!"

He went out on the back porch. The air was dull with smoke from the fires. He stayed on the porch for a while, but there too there was no escape, for in the kitchen Mildred turned on Gerald while he was talking, saying, "Give Santa Barbara a rest."

"What did I say?"

"Well, we heard all that."

For a moment there was a silence. Then Gerald said bitterly, "I can't even carry on a conversation."

"I don't care. But you don't have to keep harping on it. You know you couldn't make a living there."

"I made a good living there for seven years."

"But you can't now! You can't any more! So why won't you admit it?"

He waited uncomfortably, sorry for Gerald and thinking that Mildred ought to leave him alone. But Gerald said abruptly, "The Jews ruined Santa Barbara. It takes a Jew to beat a Jew. If I was a Jew I'd be making a good living now."

"Why?"

"Because I would. Because they stick up for each other. . . . Did you ever see a poor Jew?"

"Yes."

"Where?"

"Oh, Lord," Mildred said. "You don't know what you're talking about."

"I know the Jews ruined Santa Barbara."

"How?"

"Because they did!" Gerald cried. "They came in and they grabbed off all the high-income property and nobody else can close a lease! Do you think I've got eyes? They got control of all the banks and they got control of all the newspapers and I hope you won't tell me they haven't got control of all the movies! You won't deny that, will you? You won't deny they got control of all the movies, will you?" His voice rose passionately. "You can't beat them! They've got their fingers in everything! I know! I've done business with them! To me there's nothing lower than a Jew unless it's a Filipino or a Jap or a nigger, and I've done business with all of them!"

"You don't have to yell!"

"You'd yell if you knew what I know about the Jews."

"Oh, Mother of God," she said. "Between you and Little Mildred."

"What did Father Condon say?"

"That old faker," she said.

"He's a Catholic priest!"

"I don't care if he is! He's crazy and everybody knows it!"

Gerald said in disgust, "It's no use arguing with you."

He heard Gerald starting for the porch, and slipped down around the corner of the house. Now he did not know where to go. In front of the house the kids were planting their fire-crackers in the dust, their shouts of excitement rising more loudly than the small explosions, and as he watched them he tried to think of somebody he could talk to, somebody to whom he could tell everything that had happened without leaving out the important things and without being asked a lot of questions, but as he went over the names of everybody he knew, checking them off one after another, he knew there was nobody, nobody he could trust. Already he had found that the kids he went to school with did not respond when he tried to tell them about working, or about how much skill his job demanded at that critical moment when the trucks were changed, and he told himself that they were all growing different and getting dumb; it was no fun running around with them any more. One after another he checked off their names in his mind, leaning against the shady side of the house and treasuring the little moment of privacy there. He tried to imagine himself telling them, "Do you remember Walt Connor? You know what he did?" In his heart he knew they would not believe him, or they would think that Walt was smart and he was a damn fool for getting out of the car and not making Ellen come across too. . . . Then all at once he heard Mildred's irritable voice, right at his elbow, *"Mamma, make Johnny do something! He moons around here; he gives me the creeps!"*

He turned on her, startled and offended. She was standing behind him on the porch, appealing to his mother in the house.

His mother replied, "What is it?"

"Come look at him."

His mother stepped behind Mildred, peering over her shoulder, her round face a little troubled and impatient, as though she resented this interruption in her work. She gave him a swift scrutiny, concentrating the way she did when she thought one of the children was sick.

He cried out indignantly, "What's the matter with me?"

"What's the matter, son?"

"Nothing! She just snoops around. . . . What does she have to pick on me for? Let her mind her own business!"

"Look at him, Mamma! He looks so dopey! Mamma, he didn't get in last night till three o'clock. I heard him and I looked to see what time it was. It was *after* three! Look at his eyes."

For a moment he was too outraged to answer. Then he said bitterly, "You sneak around. . . . You have to sneak around."

"Now Johnny," his mother said. "Now Mildred."

Mildred was alarmed at the bitterness she had aroused in him. Her voice softened. "No, Johnny. But you have to take care of yourself. Don't he, Mamma? And you look like the devil. Have you got a headache?" She began to win him back, speaking softly and good-naturedly, until at last he was calmed.

"I've got a kind of a headache," he admitted.

"Why don't you go for a walk?"

"I guess I will."

His mother went back inside, after saying, "Now, don't torment him, Mildred." Mildred stirred about on the porch, always working tensely, as if only a few moments were left before she had to catch a train or get the children to bed. As he thought about it he decided uneasily that he did have a headache and probably he did look sick, no wonder, while she worked back around to the questions she wanted to ask him.

"Where'd you go, Johnny?"

"Just downtown."

"What girl?"

"What?"

"Which one was it?"

"What? . . . Oh."

"Was she pretty?"

"Sort of . . . She works at the factory."

"What was her name?"

He looked at her with a sudden suspicion. "What do you want to know for?"

"Come on, tell me. I won't tell anybody."

"Peggy."

"Peggy what?"

"I don't know her last name."

He could sense her studying him and he felt a little secret pleasure at deceiving her. She continued to move briskly around the porch, but now he knew that she was not thinking of what she was doing, only trying to cover up her interest in where he had been and what he had been doing. She was separating the colored clothes from the white among the things that were to be washed, dividing them swiftly into the two piles, sometimes throwing a stocking or a dress that would fade among the sheets and pillow cases and recapturing it without changing the rushed pace of her movements.

"Did you like her?"

Did I like her, he thought. Why didn't she say *do* you like her?

"Oh . . . she's all right, I guess."

She looked up at him. Their eyes met. He could see her trying to see into his mind, her eyes candidly inquisitive and searching. "Where'd you go?"

"I just took her home. . . . I guess I'll go for a walk," he said. He did not turn his eyes away from her until she looked down. "I've got a kind of a headache. I guess I'll go downtown." As he walked out to the street, past the open windows of the front room, he heard Gerald talking in his nervous salesman voice.

"The French can't fly," Gerald said. "Take the *Yellow Bird*."

She's trying to find out if I did anything, he thought wisely. Let her worry. Inside him the thought was warm and pleasing. Let her worry, he repeated. That's one thing she'll never find out.

[248]

The houses were all alike. The district where the people from the mills lived was larger than all the rest of town put together, acres of close packed wooden dwellings crowded between the hills and the waterfront. It was quiet now; a few children were playing in the dusty streets and here and there a few firecrackers snapped, but most of the people had gone to town or out on the harbor where it was cool. He walked down the narrow sidewalk, sick of the smoky air and the heat and the racket at home, disturbed at Mildred's questioning and wondering why she turned on him, until his mind began to go back once more to his dim plans for getting out of there, buying an old car, maybe, and heading for the mountains, finding some old deserted shack, maybe, and living off by himself some place in the middle of the woods, or getting a bunch of money together and starting to college before he was too old to enjoy it—no, to hell with that, he thought, thinking of Walt coming up to him like a fraternity brother, saying *All right, Shake on it,* when he finally promised to try to get Ellen and Marie to go home with them. The bastard.

The air was thick and dead. Sometimes the heavy flakes of ash floated down in the still air, wavering, settling like leaves. The sight of them made him think of the men out fighting the fire in this heat, and he whispered to himself, *Poor devils,* his brief pity an echo of thousands of comments he heard at home, the first natural response of people whose lives were so bound up with working that they could scarcely see a train without being conscious of the men who ran it, and whose first thought when they watched an exhibition of fireworks was of the rushed and feverish toil of the men who prepared the rockets and set them off. So a bit of ash or a sudden taste of burning fir called up to him a picture of the men burned sweatless in the woods, starting their back fires and driving themselves to clear a space too wide for the fire to leap. Someone called to him and he answered. The sound of the bands in town reached him faintly, and with a little rise of amusement he remembered the forlorn man who had stopped under the street lamp the night before, the huge horn coiled around him, the odd colors of his uniform. But then he began thinking about Ellen again, tormenting himself with the picture of himself that he thought must be built up in her eyes. . . .

Too much! There was too much to think about, too many mysteries, too many worries and surprises! You could not tell what people were going to do. You could not depend on anybody because a man might come up and shake hands with you and the next minute desert you in a moment of danger, the son of a bitch, or sacrifice you like something tossed to the wolves to worry and delay them for a while. I'm going to get out of this town, he thought. I'll be damned if I'll live in a crazy place like this. He remembered with a rise of pain the warm excitement that had held him as he sat beside Ellen in the back seat of Walt's car, remembering her serious little face and the neat fit of her overalls and her shirt unbuttoned way down her neck; he remembered sitting beside her while they waited on the road, her troubled voice, soft and controlled even when she was mad. . . .

Beside him a voice said quietly, "Watch out you don't knock her up."

Frankie Dwyer leaned over the fence in front of his house. When Johnny turned to him Frankie looked at him steadily, his expression unchanging, his eyes narrow and cryptic. His eyes were always narrowed because of the heat where he worked and his face was so burned that his eyebrows looked white. Now he said in quiet delight, "I can always see it! I can always recognize that old tail light. . . . Where's your Old Man?"

He replied swiftly, hiding behind the words, "I don't know. I think he's still home. He was going down to Winters'."

Frankie Dwyer came out into the street. "I want to see him. I just heard something. Carl's going to fire your old man anyway. I was going down to your place when I seen you coming. . . . You don't want to walk that way when you don't look where you're going. Somebody's liable to trip you. Down where I was raised, down west Texas, a man couldn't walk ten feet thataway 'thowt some son of a bitch tripping him. That's a fact! It's the God-damnedest country for tripping you ever saw. . . . "

He asked in a low voice, "How'd you know. . . . How'd you hear?"

"Oh. My cousin told me. Some of his wife's people—niece, I guess—she takes care of the Addisons' kids and the Addisons live right next door to the Belchers. . . . I wouldn't pay no attention. Carl's just talking. He'd a fired your Old Man last year if he could have."

Johnny was not reassured, and he did not believe Dwyer intended him to be. He looked at the wooden sidewalk as the pulse began to pound behind his ears. He saw the torn planks that were marked with a thousand little dents, like worm holes, from the corked shoes of the loggers, his eyes searching for something substantial and motionless. The sidewalk sagged in places and some of the planks were broken; at the edges the thistles and other weeds grew high as his knees over the level of the walk, their green hidden under the coating of powdered dust. He forced himself to look hard at the ground until his anxiety subsided. "I don't take much stock in that kind of talk," Dwyer said. "There's always a lot of it going around."

They turned in at Winters' house and walked to the back yard where Winters was working on his car. It was a battered old Chevrolet, and Winters spent most of his spare time working on it. He had taken off the hood and the engine head and now he was getting ready to grind the valves, smearing the compound on and setting the grinder in place.

He nodded briefly as they came in. Dwyer asked, "How's Ann?"

"Better. She's a good deal better."

They were silent for a few minutes. The formalities were over. Winters worked on the valve. His fingers darted with

[251]

feverish adroitness, grasping the tools and holding them with no waste motions or loss of purpose. There was a faint shine of sweat on his dark Indian features.

"I don't know why I'm doing this," he said. "I guess it's because I haven't got anything else to do."

Dwyer had sat down and drawn a few aimless marks in the ground beside his feet. "The hoist man died," he announced abruptly.

"I heard."

"Poor son of a bitch."

"He never came to."

"Good thing." Dwyer looked hard at Johnny. He began to speak in an unvaried voice. "Made me think of something happened once when I was working up at Maloney's Camp Number Twelve, way hell-and-gone up in the Olympics. That God-damned National City outfit, the worst highball camp I ever worked in—they kill a man up there every week."

"Bassett kills a man every week," Winters said.

"For that matter so does the Oberstaller Logging Corporation. So do them Chase camps. But this was different. These guys made a science of it. We logged with the equipment Oberstaller threw away. Once I seen the head rig come down and when the main block hit the cold deck them logs—big bastards; it was fine timber—shot sixty feet in the air. The guy lines whipped around like snakes. That same morning the engineer wouldn't go to work—said the whole rigging was coming down. But this was different. There was a kid working on the loading crew, just a kid, see, eighteen or nineteen years old—they couldn't get old hands up into that slaughter-house. Well, they was highballing it so hard they had the whole train always waiting and the minute they pulled the last hook off the last log they pulled out—twelve miles to the main line and they raced their God-damn shay back and forth so fast they finally burnt it up. Anyway, before the kid got out of the way they pulled out and he slipped—it was raining, it was getting dark—and he went right in under the wheels, got both his legs right here." He drew his hand swiftly across his thighs.

He paused and Johnny looked away, sickened at the picture his words called up, turning to look at Winters who continued to work on his car without seeming to hear what Dwyer was saying.

"The train went on. No way to stop it. We had to wait till it got back. Nobody wanted to go down where the kid was. The guys all stood around out of the way. Finally I went down. Both legs were practically off. But the funny thing was that the weight of them logs sort of clamped the flesh together and he wasn't losing much blood. And he was conscious. Some goofy bastard yelled to me. 'Is it bad? What'll we do?' I was down by the kid, I wasn't sure if he could hear me, but I said, 'One leg is mashed, not so bad, only stop that God-damn shay!' It was getting dark; it was raining like hell; I didn't think he could tell. But he said [here Dwyer's voice grew heavy with contempt] *'You're a God-damned liar!'* Jesus, I didn't know what to say. I stood there. The guys were all standing back about twenty-thirty feet—it was a green crew; they couldn't get old hands up there with a gun—and that kid yelled back at them: *'He's a God-damned liar. They're both off, right at the ass'.*"

Johnny drew a deep breath. Dwyer ground his cigarette into the damp ground. At the house next door the woman stepped out on the porch and shook out a tablecloth, glancing at them briefly before she went inside. "Ah," Johnny said.

"Tough kid," Winters said.

"Yeah," Dwyer replied. "He was tough."

But Johnny drew up inside, racked at the brutal picture and the hard words, trying to put them out of his mind and hoping something better happened. . . . "What happened?" he managed to ask.

"What?"

"What happened to him?"

"Nothing. He died. You think a man lives when he's cut in two?"

In the oppressive silence his father came into the yard. He greeted them briefly and sat down on the wooden walk that led to the shed in the rear. Presently he asked Dwyer, "What'd you hear?"

"The same thing. He's going to can you anyway."

"The Perkins girl?"

"Yeah."

Johnny looked up in surprise, recognizing the reference to the way they got their news and wondering that they took it for granted.

Hagen asked, "What'd she say?"

"Nothing. She just heard him beefing. He said you'd spent your last night there." Dwyer grinned slightly. "When I think about it," he said, "it's a wonder to me you fellows didn't get the can last night."

Hagen nodded and asked Winters about his wife. "Better," Winters said. He put down the valve grinder. "I don't know why I go on working on this old bastard," he said. "Sometimes I think it ain't worth the trouble it causes me. . . . Did she hear him say anything about me?"

"She didn't say."

"I figure I might just as well be looking for a job. Ever since I popped him."

"He don't know you popped him."

"Somebody'll tell him."

Hagen disagreed cautiously. "You can't tell. A man don't like to go around asking people who it was smacked him one. Besides, a lot of people are glad you popped him. More'n you'd think."

Sorenson came into the yard. "I figured I'd find you men here," he said. "I just had an idea. I had to take my kids down to see the parade, and when I got home the thought just came to me—it's two to one they'll be over at Winters'. I figured

[254]

they wouldn't be at your place," he said to Hagen, "because of all your people being there. So that left only Dwyer and Winters, and I could see there was nobody at Frank's place. There's going to be trouble tomorrow," he announced. Johnny thought he heard a slight note of satisfaction, a rubbing-it-in tone, in Sorenson's voice. "Carl's been all over the district. He was down at Bullett's place by ten o'clock and as soon as he left, Bullett went and got Prent Fisher and they waited till Carl got back. Then Carl drove up on the hill to the Old Man's house and got Morley and him and Morley went out to the plant."

"How you know?"

"My wife seen him go into Bullett's and Molly told Gil Ahab about going up to MacMahon's. Old Mike seen them out in the factory."

"Son of a bitch gets around," Dwyer said. "I never saw a fat man get around the way he does."

"He works hard at his job. You got to give him credit," Sorenson said. "He never rests. Mac will run out to Chicago or go off shooting bears some place, but Belcher, he never lets up. You have to give a man like that credit."

They sat back and waited again, hovering uncertainly before saying the questions that were in their minds, waiting for someone else to start talking. Winters continued to work on his car. They watched him as intently as if he were carrying on some unique experiment or as if he were performing a major operation and they were a group of students studying his methods.

"The way I look at it," Sorenson announced abruptly, "There's a good chance he'll fire all of us."

"I was just thinking. . . ."

"What do you figure on doing?"

Winters put down his tools. "Figure it out," he said. "Why do we have to take it? How many we got? How many we sure of? Sooner or later he's going after you guys because you

stuck up for Hagen. Sure as hell he'll clean out every God-
damn one of you. Now, how many can you count on to walk
out when he fires Hagen?"

"We got the whole head end of the mill," Dwyer said.

One of the sawyers and a helper came into the yard. They
saluted vaguely, lifting their arms in indifferent greetings,
maintaining an air of aimlessness until it seemed they had
merely been passing the house and stopped because they saw
the men in the yard. Dwyer and Winters glanced at each other.
The sawyer worked with Winters and was a new man, one of
the men who had come in after Carl finished his first clean-up
of the factory, so his presence meant more than that of the
the others. He said nothing at all. He stared dully at the
ground under his feet, looking dense and patient, all the expression long since driven out of his heavy worker's features.
The helper's face too was expressionless, only his eyes alert and
questioning behind the habitual protective blankness of his
face.

"We been figuring what we ought to do," Hagen explained.
"We got word Belcher's going to give some of us our time. We
been going over the men we can count on. We got most of the
head end. Some in the glue crew."

"Five-six in the saw crew," the sawyer said.

The helper nodded.

"Who?"

"Me and him," the sawyer said. "Winters and the kid here."
He nodded toward Johnny. He named the others, hesitating
over some names, trying to bring in everybody he could, while
they tried to identify the men he named, testing them in their
own minds and trying to decide how they would act.

"Not more than thirty-five or forty," Dwyer said. "Even if
you get all of them."

But Winters said quickly, "Think where they are. The
whole head end. The electrician and the drier crew and

[256]

enough sawyers so the saws can't run. They won't be able to run."

"Old Mike," Hagen said.

"The fireman."

"Gil Ahab."

"Yeah."

Waino and Vin Garl came into the yard. Waino stopped uncertainly beside the back porch while Vin Garl called cheerfully to Winters. "Waino told me you had some trouble last night," Vin Garl explained.

"He fired me and Hagen," Winters explained. "Frank and the Dutchman here raised such a stink they had to take us back."

"Who was hurt?"

"The hoist man. A new man. He died this morning."

The two Finns found places for themselves and sat down. Vin Garl looked over the men with a faint appraising air, hiding his interest by questioning them carefully about the accident and talking about the man who had been burned at the power house. Waino sat down beside Johnny, nodding to him with a faint uneasiness, unsure of Johnny's response. But Johnny was too disturbed to notice, preoccupied with the accidents, the man killed at the factory and the man burned to death at the power house, the deaths connecting up with the story Dwyer had told him until it seemed to him that everywhere, all the time, men were being crippled and killed until death did not mean very much to anyone. And they always spoke as if the killings were deliberate and not accidents. "They killed a man in the woods yesterday," his father would say, or "They killed another logger up by Goose Creek," as though "they" were out with guns hunting them down. . . . The Finnish boy relapsed into silence, thinking Johnny did not want to talk to him, Johnny's manner connecting up in his mind with a thousand rebuffs he had received outside the Finnish part of town, in high school, everywhere except among his own countrymen

[257]

or at work, and sometimes at work too. Slowly the conversation got back to what they were going to do, but now Johnny had lost interest in it for it seemed to him they were no longer trying to work out ways of keeping his father from losing his job, but arguing back and forth and not getting anywhere. Before Vin Garl came they had been talking easily, but afterwards there were more questions and more explaining, and the Finn, cold and skeptical, seemed to think he knew more than anybody else.

At last he asked Winters what he intended to do. For some reason the question seemed to disturb Winters; he hesitated and looked at the others before he replied. "I don't know. . . . We just figured we'd get fifty-sixty men signed up and we'd all walk out if they did anything."

"Don't do that," Vin Garl said.

Waino backed him up. "No."

"Why not?"

"We did that . . . we did it two years ago over at Saint Augustine's Manufacturing. They were going to can the edgerman and we heard about it, so thirty-forty of us agreed to walk out if they fired one of us. But they heard of it and they didn't fire the edgerman—not then—they waited till one guy showed up drunk one night and they canned him, and some of the guys wanted to walk out and some kicked about walking out because a guy got canned when he came to work drunk, so we started scrapping back and forth and finally about a dozen of us got canned."

"What do you say to do?"

"Why don't you call a strike? The whole damn shift. The day shift too. We should have struck when they gave us a cut. If we had any sense we would have struck when they first slapped it on."

He spoke with assurance, the authority of experience behind his words, but they hesitated; he was a single man; he had not been in the factory long; the word had gone around somehow that he was a trouble-maker. But he worked on the day shift and they were surprised at anyone from the day shift hunting them out and speaking as if he thought the day shift would walk out too. They thought it over, trying to remember the things they had heard that indicated the day shift might go out with them if they walked out.

"It'd be harder," Sorenson said at last.

"Yeah, but it would work. And this other way you'd just get ———. And besides if you tried to get the cut back everybody would walk out."

"Yeah."

Winters said, "I'd hate like hell to have anybody lose his job just because I was getting canned."

"They got that export order to finish," Hagen said. "It's way overdue. That's the first big export order we've had lately. They won't want to have any trouble till they finish it."

Sorenson shook his head. "It don't make any difference to them. Don't you know there's a clause in these orders terminating them in case of fire, earthquake, strikes or acts of God? If there's a strike, the company ain't responsible for its commitments."

"You God-damned lawyer."

"That's the truth!"

"You're dumb," Vin Garl said. "What the hell difference does that make? There ain't a mill on the harbor that ain't running on export orders. They're fighting like hell for them. We get a hell of a big Australia order. How you think they got that? They got it by cutting the price. Then they made up the difference by slapping the cut off on us—made it up and a hell of a lot more. Now suppose they get half the order out and the rest of it tied up. You think them guys in Australia will give them another order, no matter what price they quote? You're nuts if you do."

"They'll fill it at one of the other mills."

"And what'll that cost them? Besides, where will they fill

it? There ain't a door factory in the Northwest that some of us ain't worked in. I know guys who've left the factory since I been working there, and they're up in the Puget Sound outfit's mills now or at Kitsap Bay—you think them guys would cut a scab order if they knew it?"

"Yeah," Sorenson said.

"Would you do it?"

"No. But they don't know what they're working on. They get an order with a number on it or a bunch of letters like that Fishba order we had—we cut on it for a year and nobody could figure out what it was for until finally somebody saw it was Fisher Bodies. How the hell would they know?—all they'd know was it was an export order."

"We could tell them, couldn't we?"

"Aw," Sorenson said. "Get back to earth."

"I am! I am down to earth! Now listen to me a minute. What have we been running on for the past year? What? We been running on export. We had that big German order for them big ships they're building. Then we got that big English order for that hellishing big ship they never finished. Then we got that Italian order for them big liners they're building. They got to get out and fight like hell for them orders, they got to keep knocking down the price all the time, or them orders'll go some place else. Last year there was a special amendment to the Sherman anti-trust law permitting corporations to make combinations for export trade. You're such a hell of a good lawyer, you ought to know about that. Now look. All the companies here in the Northwest signed an agreement setting export prices—all except us. *Digby never went into it.* Why not? Because he can undersell the whole damn bunch of them and he can do it because he pays lower wages. And even if he *did* go into it, it wouldn't make any difference, because if they jacked up the prices the orders would go to the Japs or Canada—them Japs are getting logs right here now and shipping them across and cutting them up and shipping the lumber back here. . . . You think Digby just decided all at once he'd slap a cut on us? Hell, he's *always* trying to cut wages. The difference is when the orders are coming in he tries to keep wages from going up, and when they ain't coming in he begins working harder, *driving* wages down. . . . Don't be a damn fool," Vin Garl said gently. "You can see that. He wouldn't be where he is if he wasn't always trying to beat wages down. He wouldn't be where he is any more than a guy who thought the world was flat would be sailing one of them lumber schooners down in the harbor to Japan."

Sorenson grinned slyly at the others, saying "Listen to this. This is good. So it's the Japs," he said scornfully to Vin Garl. "So the Japs are in back of it, are they?"

"No. But you said they could cancel their order if we struck. And I'm just showing you they'll do *anything* to keep from canceling that order."

The boom man came into the yard. He grinned cheerfully at Winters, "I heard you konked that little son of a bitch," he said.

"Me?" Winters replied. "I never konked anybody."

"You God-damn Indian. You got a lot of nerve. Hitting a poor old fat man like that."

"I'd be afraid to konk him," Winters explained. "I'd be afraid I'd lose my job if I did."

"You know something?" the boom man asked. "I'd have konked him myself only I was afraid I'd lose my job if I did."

He climbed into Winters' car and sat down in the back seat. "Well, men," he said. He looked at them inquiringly.

Hagen said, "We got to figure."

Johnny looked around the yard. There were ten of them there. He understood that they had come in because his father had fought with Carl, because they knew Mildred and Gerald had moved in with them and Ruth and Bill were coming and so his father could not afford to be fired. And other men from the factory were coming in all the time. "The

[261]

whole yard will be filled up pretty soon!" he said to Waino; and then felt foolish when Waino, who had been listening to the arguments, looked at him in surprise.

Vin Garl said restlessly, "You can't do anything with a little bunch like this. The thing to do is get all the guys together you can. Go around, get fifty-sixty men. They can come here, come down to my place—it don't make any difference. Get a bunch from the day shift. It don't pay to go off half-cocked."

"When?" Winters asked. "I got to go to the hospital. I probably won't get back till about eight."

"Seven. Eight. It don't make any difference."

Sorenson added, "Look at me. I told my kids I'd take 'em on the hill and let them watch the fireworks."

"Come afterwards," Vin Garl said. "It don't make any difference about you. You know all about it anyway. We want to get the guys from the day shift that haven't heard about it."

The boom man looked at Vin Garl with a sudden interest. "You a union man?" he asked.

"Me? What union is there for a man working where I work?"

"Wobbly?"

"I used to carry a red card during the War. I had a red card when a red card would let you ride on damn near any railroad this side of the Rockies and I had a red card when it was worth your life to get caught with one. I was in that fighting in Everett and after Centralia it got so hot for me I had to beat it to Canada. . . . But there's nothing left of them now."

Johnny looked around at the men gathered in the yard. The harshness of the Finn's voice repelled him and he searched the faces of the men, trying to see some approval or disagreement in their responses to his words. The boom man, large, red faced, was lying back in the seat of Winters' car, staring off at the smoky sky. Winters was cleaning the grease from his hands, frowning as he probed with the waste around his fingernails. "They didn't die out," Vin Garl said abruptly. "They were wiped out." He said "wiped out" with a curious intensity, his mouth closing over the words as though he were biting into them.

Sorenson said cautiously, "We don't want to get everybody thinking we're a bunch of Reds. We'll all get canned if they think we're a bunch of Reds."

Vin Garl started to answer him. Then he nodded.

The boom man said awkwardly, "Reason I ask. There's been a lot of talk about the A. F. L. organizing the lumber workers."

Vin Garl said *hah!* in bitter disgust.

Frankie Dwyer roused himself. "I won't have anything to do with the A. F. L.," he announced. "My brother's a printer."

They began to argue again. Johnny pulled himself up and began to edge out of the yard. Arguing got on his nerves. Besides, he thought, they were so far off the subject they would never get back. Waino looked at him as he started to leave, hesitated for an instant, and then, as Johnny stared at him, lifted his hand. Johnny waved in reply, merely lifting an arm and letting it fall, but as he went on out he thought, Why did you have to butt in? and thought about foreigners sticking together and living on the wrong side of the river instead of living ordinary decent lives like ordinary American citizens. But then he remembered Ellen and Marie and the pain tightened in him again. A part of his mind kept repeating, *I'm going to get out of here. Too much is happening.* Sometimes he thought about the folks crowding together, his father getting fired, Walt running off and leaving him, and it was too much; he did not know what to do. He walked along with his head down until he remembered what Dwyer had told him about getting tripped if he walked that way, and then, thinking of Dwyer, he remembered the story Dwyer had told him, the boy no older than he was who had said, *you're a damn liar* when his legs were cut off.

"He told me that on purpose," he thought suddenly.

How could anybody? How could anybody do a stunt like that and then leave a man standing in the road with a bunch of thugs after him, after he'd taken such a chance? How? What would he say to himself? What would he think of himself and how would he make himself think he was a good guy afterwards and how would he act the next time he saw the person he ran off and left to his fate? *Let him alone. He's harmless. He's just dumb.* And what would she think the next time she saw him? What would she say? But how could anybody do it and how could anybody with a girl just out of the hospital? *They ought to shoot people like that. They shouldn't let them live.* He tried to remember back over from the very beginning when Walt came up to him on the tideflat, when Carl bawled him out, remembering little things that shamed him or that he kept forgetting, trying to remember what people said and how they looked, how he felt and what he should have done. Ah, how could anybody? How could a man run off like a cowardly skunk and yellow cur leaving a friend to his fate right after the friend had been risking his neck and trying to save him from being beat up? How could anybody? He went back to the very first, remembering lighting a cigarette and how he felt when Walt came up to him. *If you don't want to don't do it. Some of these Polacks are damn good nooky.* From the very first, he thought. He planned it from the very first.

Then he went around the factory where the man was hurt, and there was MacMahon's girl and the boy in the tuxedo sitting in the big car, and he remembered the girl said *I thought we'd never get out,* and *Poor me!* The words strange and senseless. Then Walt got in the car, looking like some rich kid who had just pulled on a pair of old overalls because he wanted to go to work on his motorboat, and the three of them sat there, the girl cool and comfortable in her white dress and the boy in his tuxedo all connected in his mind with a thousand carefree images: advertisements that showed a beautiful shiny car parked in front of a smart country club with a lovely girl smiling at the men holding rackets and golf clubs and right under the wheels the magic words *Now you too can own one!* and thousands of scenes from movies and thousands of rotogravure sections, crowds at tennis tournaments and races, great hotels and ships and stray tender sentences, golf all year round, Hawaii calls you, yours for the asking. What a life! Somebody was hurt and the people came running past.

How could anybody? He remembered Ellen standing in the road when they came back, hoping it was somebody not them; he remembered her high smooth forehead, the band tied around her hair, the way she frowned at the headlights, her mouth partly opening as she tried to see who was in the car. *Let him alone. He's harmless.* Ah, how could anybody?

The air was bitter and smoky with a burnt firecracker smell in the streets. Some little kids called him, but he said, "I'm going downtown," and when they told him somebody wanted him to go out to the ball park he repeated that he had to go downtown, he had to see somebody, brushing them aside without even hearing what they called to him. Downtown the parade was moving slowly through the dusty street. The cops came first, three blocks of cops, looking sullen and hot as they marched, murmuring to each other when the parade was held up, taking off their caps to dry their foreheads. Behind them the Legion Fife and Drum Corps, the trumpets screaming the few raucous notes over and over, the sound repeating like a phonograph when the needle gets caught in one groove of the record. On the sidewalks the people stared. The Drum Corps passed, the beautiful pink and yellow uniforms sticky and hot, and in the brown afternoon light the faces of the marchers looked swollen and ill. Their feet sank into the soft tar at the cracks in the pavement. The sound stopped; there was a moment of silence like a sudden cooling breeze; then a whistle blew and the trumpets were lifted and the drums gave a dull preliminary rattle.

[265]

He watched. A truck passed, the huge pasteboard Statue of Liberty trembling as the truck started and stopped and lurched forward unsteadily in low gear. In the cabin of the truck the driver leaned sadly over the wheel, his eyes fixed on the back of the drummer a few feet ahead of him. Smoke from the exhaust poured up through the floor boards and filled the cabin and floated back over the Statue of Liberty.

The sailors followed, marching in ranks, looking bored and tired and dissipated.

He remembered the sailors they passed while they were looking for Walt and the poor guy with the big horn lost under the street lamp, wandering around at that time of the night in that kind of uniform, carrying a big heavy horn and trying to get his bearings.

Ah, how could anybody? How could people be so mean. *Let him alone,* he remembered. *He's harmless.* Oh, am I, he said to the crowded street. Wait and see. In the sweat and dust the Elks band played "The Stars and Stripes Forever." From their swollen and miserable faces the sound poured out into the crowd, echoed between the packed buildings, pounding like blows on the eardrums. The people waited patiently, drawing back a little from the rush of sound, and the children started to cry. A big Rock of Gibraltar passed on a truck, a sign underneath it reading The Past Bay National, As Safe As the Rock of Gibraltar. Then a tank rattled blindly over the car tracks. The smoke from its exhaust almost concealed it. Through one of the open flaps of the turret he saw a soldier standing beside a machine-gun. He looked hot and uncomfortable as his body trembled with the vibrations of the tank.

There was a gap in the parade and the people hurried across the street.

The Boy Scouts were coming.

He went off the main streets and into the poor section near the river. Here was the store with the boarded windows and the cigarette advertisements pasted on the boards. Here was her house. The shades were drawn. He walked back and forth across the street from it before he could make up his mind to enter.

She came to the door at once. She looked different in a dress, younger, less sure of herself, like a little girl surprised at someone's coming to see her. "Hello," she said. It sounded as if she meant, what do you want?

"I wondered how your sister was. I was down this way so I thought I'd stop in and see."

Her face was still unfriendly. "She's all right."

"Thanks," he said hurriedly. "I just wondered. I just thought. I happened to be down this way. So I thought why not?"

She nodded.

"Well, so long!" he said. But she stopped him. Someone in the house called to her. She turned back and spoke in some foreign language to someone in the shaded interior.

"Won't you come in?" she asked.

"No, I hadn't better. I got a lot to do, sort of."

She smiled, opened the door wider, and he went inside. A woman came out of the half-darkness, gray-haired, large, kindly faced, nodding to him hospitably before Ellen introduced him. He sat down, noting that the house was about like their own, only smaller and more dilapidated, the wallpaper stained with large brown marks. "Marie's still asleep," Ellen explained. "I just got up a little while ago. It was so hot I didn't want to stay in bed any longer."

"The work is too hard for her," Mrs. Turner said gently. "She isn't strong enough." He realized that this referred to Marie, and wondered if her mother really knew what was the matter. Then he wondered what ever happened to Mr. Turner and why they were so hard up if both the girls were working.

"It's pretty hard all right."

Mrs. Turner said, "Yes. It's too hard for a young girl."

Ellen sat down at the small table and ran her finger absently

[267]

over the oilcloth covering. "Did you get home all right?" she asked abruptly.

"Yes."

"How long did it take you."

"Oh, about three o'clock. . . . I walked slow."

"Gosh." She turned to her mother. "He walked from here all the way across the tideflat."

"You must be tired out."

"Well, I was sort of tired."

He relaxed a little. Ellen was wearing an apron that was cut very short; it barely reached her knees and when she crossed her legs he glanced away quickly, not wishing to be looking at her legs while her mother was around. But she seemed to pay no attention, and her mother, if she saw him look at Ellen's legs and look away again, gave no sign that she had.

"It's hard," Mrs. Turner said earnestly, "when young people have to work so hard."

Ellen asked him, "How much do you make?"

"Two and a quarter."

"We make one-eighty. We only made two dollars before the cut."

"Gosh."

"Believe me we work. I'm so tired when I come home I can't even sleep. Ask mom. I just lie in bed till three and four in the morning before I can get to sleep."

Mrs. Turner nodded. They shook their heads thinking of it. It was cooler in the shaded room, and he sat back more easily, his muscles relaxing and the nervousness and tension going away. Mrs. Turner said something more about working but he did not hear her; he was looking at Ellen's rich mouth, noting a little habit she had of turning her under lip out when she seemed to be thinking deeply. "It's cool in here," he said abruptly, just as Mrs. Turner said, "We're poor people," and Ellen announced, "Marie's going to quit."

"What?"

"Yeah. We're not going to let her work any more. She can't stand it."

"It's too hard for her," Mrs. Turner said indignantly. "She isn't strong. They shouldn't make a girl like that do such hard work. It isn't right. There ought to be easier work than what she does."

"It's hard to get work." He began to understand what it would mean to them to have only Ellen working. "I looked all summer," he said. "My folks are hard up—my brother-in-law lost his job so they're staying with us now; that makes it hard."

"Oh, it's hard," Mrs. Turner said. "It's always hard for the poor man. . . ."

She got up heavily and moved toward the kitchen. "Get some water, Ellen, and I'll make some tea. . . . We have to carry water," she said. Ellen went into the kitchen and came back with a bucket.

"Do you want to come with me? . . . Something happened to the water pipes last winter and they never got fixed. So we have to borrow water."

They went out into the sunlight again. They walked in silence for a few moments, past one empty house after another, stopping at last before one exactly like the Turner house except that some children were playing in the narrow yard. "Who was that nut?" Ellen asked suddenly. "What do you run around with him for?" He tried to tell her who Walt was, but it seemed impossible.

"I don't know him very well," he said. "I don't want to either."

They went around back and drew the pailful of water from a faucet on the porch. He carried it back to the house, conscious of her walking beside him in her short apron, unhappy at being reminded of what a nut he was last night, worried for fear she would think it was the way he was all the time.

"You look different when you're dressed up," she said.

"So do you."

"I'm not dressed up."

"No, but I mean when you're wearing a dress."

"I feel different. . . . I get tired of wearing overalls."

He said bravely, "You look good in overalls."

"Do I? What do you mean?"

"You know. You look good. Some of the girls don't."

That was the first audible tender speech he ever made. Always before, when he thought up graceful speeches and tried to say them aloud, something happened; he lost his balance, or tripped, or somebody bumped into him, or he merely saw something that attracted his attention at the critical moment and kept him from finishing what he had started to say. So he waited to see how his words took, trying to read some expression, some pleased expression, in her expressionless face, to decide whether the little smile was one of gratification or amusement and, at the same time, to keep from spilling the water in the bucket he carried.

"You shouldn't hang around with a rat like that," she replied unexpectedly. "You run around with those college kids, that's the way people get in trouble."

As first he took this humbly. Then he became angry. The transition took place swiftly. He was not even conscious of it. He thought that he had apologized enough for getting mixed up with Walt and causing so much trouble. He had said that he was sorry, and he had come down today to see how Marie was—what did she expect? In the same way his sister insisted on reminding him of things, of little things, things he had done when he was only a kid, that he wanted desperately to forget and anybody who loved him could see he needed to forget them for awhile. "I said I was sorry," he announced stiffly. "I told you three times."

But she did not back down. She looked at him, her eyes hard, her will tightening. "Believe me if I was. . . ." she began. "If I had anything to say. . . . Nobody like that would ever get in my house."

[270]

4. WALT

IT WAS a good thing, he told himself. Probably she had a dose. He sank back in the tub and told himself quietly that he could have made her if he had wanted to.

It was late; it was quiet in the house. The radio murmured in the front room. He felt relaxed and gradually at peace; the disgust and shame that had hurt him when he woke up and remembered was slowly driven down. I didn't really do anything, he told himself gently. I would have stayed and fought it out with them if they hadn't outnumbered me. And those fellows always stick together. If you lick one you have to lick them all.

Lying in the half-warm water, soaking quietly, thinking things over, he decided that he would always be able to take care of himself. If they showed any fight, if they came after him, he'd be ready. They would gang up on him. He could count on that. Four at once. He picked out the leader. He swung out hard and knocked the leader down. That left them bewildered, leaderless. They drew back. But then somebody pulled a knife. *Watch out!* He ducked the gleaming blade. Then he let them have it. That was the last straw. Now he was really sore. They went down, one after another, while the sparks flew from his fists.

Pleased with his victory, he got out of the tub.

A man got dirty working in the factory. Sawdust got in his hair. The grime on his work clothes rubbed into his skin. Oil soaked into his hands and nothing could get it out. If you wore gloves, the gloves become oil-soaked. And the grease and muck on the floor soaked through your shoes and socks and left marks like welts where you sweated.

It was different if you weren't brought up to notice it. The hands of some of the men were cracked and misshapen; the skin pebbled like alligator hide. And all the fingers missing. Almost every sawyer had a few fingers off. Carelessness, he thought. He remembered reading an article about Russia, telling of all the accidents they had; they had bought a lot of machinery and since they were primarily an agricultural nation they didn't know how to run it and were always getting their arms cut off and the Five-year Plan was a failure. He looked at his own hand, wondering how it would look if he lost a few fingers. To find out he bent down one finger after another. When he held up only his thumb and little finger the crippled hand fascinated him. He tried to pick up the soap to find out how hard it would be if he lost some of his fingers. It was hard. Some night the Polack might drop a load of doors before he was ready and then it wouldn't be a question of fingers. His whole hand would be gone.

"If you ever do," he muttered, clenching his good fist and preparing to drive it into the Polack's dumb mug.

Then a strange thing happened. For no reason he thought of Marie's friends ganging up on him. They rushed him, he knocked the first one down, and then somebody pulled a knife on him. But this time he was too late and the knife sank into his ribs. He saw it, in stunned amazement, while the blood pumped out of his heart.

For a moment he was paralyzed at this unexpected development in his imagination. Then he dressed hastily, moving with athletic gestures around the bathroom, in an effort to dispel the terrible vision.

When he came out of the bathroom his sister said, "You took your time."

She was sitting in her kimona in the dining-room, not reading or anything, merely sitting there smoking a cigarette. Her face was a bleached gray color, with the circles under her eyes like stains.

"God, you're beautiful," he said. His heart was still pounding.

She got up stiffly and walked into the bathroom. She puts out, he thought darkly; but that thought could no longer arouse his anger.

In the front room the radio said softly, "That gallant band of patriots whose achievements will never be forgot, whose words are writ imperishably in letters of fire in the heart of every American, whose high purpose shall never be diverted by self-seeking men or selfish interests, to them we owe this duty."

He listened.

Growing more urgent, the radio said, "Let every man and woman and child listening here today but think, if for a moment only, on the magnitude of *their* sacrifice, let him but think, if for a moment only, on the high ideals for which *they* laid down their fortunes and their lives so gallantly and so self-sacrificingly, and we may be certain that no menace to our liberty can long survive."

He stood still, trying to draw the dagger out of his heart.

His parents were listening. His mother looked at the radio scornfully, with an expression like that she adopted when somebody tried to sell her something, but his father smiled, tapping his foot rhythmetically, pretending he could hear the music. His father would not admit that he was deaf. Sometimes, when there was a play on the radio, or an advertiser's announcement, his father would take off his glasses, hold them up before him like a baton, and pretend to beat time with the orchestra he imagined he heard. Now his mother suddenly leaned forward and began to shout. "No one could tell me how I was going to spend my own money!" she cried passionately. "If you think more of your brother's family than you do of your own, all right! You've made your bed. Sleep in it."

His father nodded.

"To whom do we owe this fealty?" the radio asked. "Today we are rich in material things. Rich beyond the dreams of the wildest prophets of that day and era! But let us beware lest, in our pursuit of material wealth we do not neglect that fine fidelity to freedom, that steadfast devotion to liberty, that unshakable allegiance to spiritual values to which the founders of our country pledged their lives when they signed the Declaration of Independence a hundred and fifty-three years ago today."

It's the Fourth of July, Walt thought.

His father stopped keeping time with his foot. "It's six of one," his father remarked, "and half dozen of the other."

He walked past them and outside. The crazy thought still hovered in his mind. He was afraid to think about last night for fear that it would overpower him again. But now he could not keep his mind off the other uneasinesses that had troubled him, his argument with Winters and the way Winters had acted when he tried to smooth things over, Rose and her boy friend who had mistaken him for an ordinary worker and had not believed him when he tried to talk about school. No wonder Carl was always so nervous and keyed-up, he thought; no wonder MacMahon looked like a nervous wreck. The thick, smoky air filled him with distaste; the thought of going down town in the heat, getting caught in traffic and being held up at every intersection made him jumpy if he merely pictured it. The sight of his car, sagging in an unsightly heap in the driveway, increased his irritation with the world. The dust had piled on it so thickly its color had changed. The tires were nearly gone and needed air. When he glanced inside, noting the rubbish on the floor, the tools he had used and forgotten to put away, the hot smell of grease and upholstery, he slammed the door shut and walked back to the front of the house just so he would not have to think about it. If he gassed it up and started to the beach he would have to change the oil as well, check the tires and have the spare fixed, and even then, he told himself savagely, it probably would not take him there.

Rose drove up before the house. The car slid lightly up to the curb; she tapped the horn gently. She was leaning back negligently when he came out, looking cool and composed in spite of the heat. The car had been shined up. He could see the reflection of his white trousers and sport shoes as he walked toward it. "Mamma sent me down to see if you want to go to the beach," she said indifferently. "We were all going, but Papa didn't feel well this morning."

He was at the point of betraying his delight. He drew back in time, and showed concern about her father. She made a brief grimace, whether of evasion or impatience he could not tell, and answered, "He's tired out. Besides, he hurt his side some way last night." She began to caress the steering wheel gently. "I wish he would leave things to other people. He's too old to work as hard as he does. But he takes things so seriously . . ."

"I thought some of going out," Walt said, "I didn't have a definite date, but I had a sort of understanding. . . Only it's so hot now."

"It probably won't be much better. I didn't really want to go, there'll be such a mob there, but I promised the folks . . . Roger wanted me to go out on some boat party, but I decided I'd stay with the folks, and now Papa . . ."

"Where shall I meet you?"

"Oh . . . I can't say yet, because Mamma isn't sure yet if she wants to go and leave Papa here—anyway, I'll have the car. I'll come by for you." She began to talk quickly of other things, of how glad she was she had seen him last night, of how worried she had been about all the excitement, while he studied her legs, her breasts, her air of self-possession, and finally reached his conviction: She puts out, he told himself. And she was not bad-looking if you looked closely; it was dumb of the guys to call her Horseteeth. He had to check himself to keep from showing too much satisfaction about going out with her; in a dim way it was a triumph over the snotty kid who had been with her the night before. But after she drove off he began to wonder and have his doubts again. Maybe her boy had stood her up; maybe he was letting her drop. That worried him. He did not want to think he was taking what nobody else wanted, and by the time Carl came he was uncertain and restless again, wondering why she hadn't made it more definite, why she had come down at all, what she had up her sleeve.

Carl was alone. He looked bad, pale and tired, his eyes swollen and his bruised lip discolored by some antiseptic. Still he moved swiftly across the yard, slamming the door of his car before the sound of the engine had stopped. For a fat man, he was light on his feet.

"I've only got a minute," he announced. "I've got to go back up to Mac's, I've got to run on home, I've got to get out to the factory and put through a call to Digby. I've been all over town already this morning. This is hot weather for running around. But that's the way it goes."

"Hello, Carl," Walt replied.

"Hello, Walt. I've only got a minute. I've got to phone Digby. That God damned export order . . . Mac's sick. I don't think he's going to be able to come to work. I'm trying to tell him he ought to take it easy for a few weeks. Mac is getting old. He can't stand up under it any more. Times have changed. He's too easy-going. Like last night," Carl ended mysteriously.

"A nice Fourth you're having."

"Yeah. That's the way it goes. I'm as all in as Mac is. The difference is I don't let myself go. If I let myself go, I'd be in bed too." Here Carl shook his head in wonder at his own endurance. His face was covered with little blisters of sweat. "They raised hell proper last night," he said abruptly. "In a

[276]

way that's why I'm so busy. We can't have that. I've made up my mind. Mac's been too easy. They don't respect him. You give them an inch and they'll take a mile. And they'll turn around, the first chance they get, and knife you in the back. Look how I've put up with Hagen! And the first time I needed him, the minute the lights went out, he tried to leave me in a hole. Well," Carl said, "that ended Hagen with me."

After a period of silence Carl went on, "It taught me a lesson. I'm not going to let myself get in that fix again. No, by God . . . I figure—what I've been thinking is, I'm afraid I've got to get rid of Morley. He's no help to me. I need some young guy. Somebody with initiative. I can't make you any promises. But that's a pretty good job. It'll pay you twice what you're making now. And it'll open up a lot of opportunities."

Walt nodded.

"There's going to be a shakeup," Carl murmured. He looked at Walt searchingly. Walt tried to think of the best thing to say. He started to say that Morley was too soft for that job. Then he decided that it would sound as if he were too anxious for it himself if he began running down Morley.

"As long as you got soreheads like Hagen and them dumb Polacks in there," he observed, "that's bound to be a tough job."

It was a wise thing to say. Carl looked gratified. He nodded his appreciation of Walt's understanding. "Don't tell me," he sighed. Then he drew back again. "You think it over," he said, rather coldly. "Let me know what you decide . . . I only got a minute now. I got to phone Digby. I'm afraid Mac won't be any good for a long time, and that's going to put the whole weight on my shoulders."

Walt raced back into the house. When his sister asked, "What's the matter with you?" he said exultantly, "I think I got a new job." He went into the bathroom and looked at his face in the mirror. It was a good face for an executive, he decided. It was firm. He practiced narrowing his eyes and

[277]

looking displeased. It was easy. It was easy; his mouth narrowed naturally, a hard look came into his eyes, wrinkles of responsibility creased his forehead.

"All right, you bastards," he murmured. "Get the lead out."

The gang of Marie's friends approached him again. It was night; they waylaid him on his way home from work and ganged up on him. But this time he caught the first one right on the point of his jaw. Down he went. Somebody pulled a knife. He laughed. The blade gleamed. He ducked (and now a thrill of fear held him tense) and it missed him, missed him, and he swung hard and caught the guy who handled it right on the point of the chin. He smiled at the square stern face that smiled back from the mirror.

Winters walked slowly on his way to the hospital. He was early. He dreaded his visit, the hours in the hopeless room, never learning to wait but sitting back and watching in a dull hope that she might see him and recognize him or want him, unable to make himself believe that it was over, that she would never need him for anything again. He knew that he was building up this last memory of her and that it would drive all the others out of his mind; he knew that he would think of the strained and caved-in face, the wire muscles of her throat and the lips drawn back from her teeth, the fan churning the dead air. But now his panic was over. He knew. If he thought of her dying he was driven and wracked by his pain, but when he thought of her fighting, sure to lose, he could go with her and remember the way she had fought all her life. And now all the vast machinery for saving her or helping her, the nurse waiting beside her, the doctors who sometimes seemed so keen and so sure and sometimes so careless and indifferent, the instruments and devices for easing her pain or charting her death —all this he could study at work, his heart sinking when he sensed its weakness and filling with an obscure pride at signs of its strength.

[278]

The men in the yard returned to his thoughts. In the down-town district he watched the police and the sailors and Elks in their demonstration, studying the sullen features of the sailors, the patriotic, self-righteous look on the faces of the Boy Scouts, the fatigue and boredom marked so plainly on the business men who had turned out only from a sense of duty. Around him the people watched, forever disappointed, looking for something they did not see. But as he waited, killing time, he remembered what Sorenson had said about Carl, that Carl was always working, speculating on all that Carl had done that morning. It was true. He had not thought of it before. He had thought of Carl as having got a soft job for himself, but now he saw that Carl worked as hard as the rest of them, in his own way; that even all the trouble he caused must be a lot of work, must take a lot of thinking. How else could he cause so much trouble? He's been all over town, he thought, and here we've barely got started.

The demonstration passed. He got across the street.

He walked through the business district, wondering where he should begin. Somebody had to get the men together. We've got to get him out of there, he repeated to himself; it was the one thing they could agree on. He remembered Hagen saying bitterly, "We can't work as long as he's here." It was true. He was tearing it down, he was wrecking the whole factory, letting the machines go to pieces and demoralizing the crew so that no one could get anything done. It had been bad in the old days, it had always been bad, but there had been moments, at least, when it had run smoothly, when the whole factory hummed like a single, intricate machine, smooth and beautiful, perfectly coördinated, perfectly timed. Then for a few moments, even for an hour, they would all be refreshed with pride at the way they worked, each man in his place, each tiny act fitting in perfect time with the swing and drive of the factory. Now he saw what Carl was doing, now he under-stood why they could not endure having him in the road. He

[279]

was wrecking something that had been built up out of years of practice and labor, and even though they were not conscious of it they sensed what he was doing and they were horrified and outraged as they would have been at any wanton destruction, responding as they would if they should see food being destroyed while people were starving, or clothing being burnt while people needed it.

He hurried through the streets, grateful for a task that could pull his thoughts away from Ann, rehearsing what he intended to say to the men he saw. It's what they're doing, he thought. They're wrecking this town. But then he thought no, they're wrecking this country; they're tearing it to pieces! He ran into the demonstration again, this time a lost group of Shriners in purple uniforms wheeling and dancing like strange foreign animals in the street, forming in intricate marches and maneuvers, now gathering in a starshaped cluster and wheeling around and around with little mincing steps, now backing away, marching off in the wrong direction, turning at the sound of a whistle and forming into a hollow square. In the brown smoky light they looked troubled and unhappy, their faces caked with sweat and their purple uniforms padded and hot. On each face he could see absorbed concentration, the deadly fear of making one misstep or doing something wrong. The people watched in bewilderment. He started to cross the street, but a cop pushed him back. Winters got angry; he only had an hour and he wanted to see a dozen people in that time, but then he backed down, afraid of getting in trouble, and went back to where the parade had passed.

Walt opened the door for him, looking at him in surprise. He took in Walt's white trousers, his sport shoes, changing his mind about what he was going to say to him.

"I'm on my way to the hospital," he began. "I just wanted to explain about last night."

"It's all right," Walt said uneasily. "I was just trying to tell you what MacMahon told me to."

[280]

"Yeah."

"That was all."

"Carl had already fired me. I was fired when you told me. So it sounded foolish."

They waited, in embarrassment, thinking back over the brief struggle before the whistle blew. Walt was sorry he had called Winters a half-breed. He wanted to find some way to apologize, for he thought that was why Winters had come to him. But Winters attached little importance to having been called a half-breed; he had been called that before; besides, he was one. He merely thought Walt had lost his head because Carl and MacMahon were there, that he did not know how to act while the bosses were watching him. Now he was puzzled at Walt's manner.

"I want to get along with the men," Walt said unexpectedly, "I don't want to have any quarrel with them."

"They're easy to get along with. You make it hard. They're the easiest bunch in the world to get along with if you understand them."

Walt nodded. "I'll meet them half-way," he replied. His eyes narrowed. "You can't expect," he began, but drew back.

Winters made a last attempt. "Listen, Walt," he said. "I worked with you. I'm not sore. Everybody flies off the handle . . . Why don't you come up to my place? They're going to raise hell with us now, after last night; some of the men are going to talk things over."

Walt was stirred. A curious look of bewilderment and pleasure crossed his face, a kind of vain satisfaction that Winters had come to him. "I've got a date," he said. "I can't make it tonight." Winters saw it; he was sorry he had come there, sorry he had said it to Walt, and in the moment of silence, before Winters left, Walt's self-satisfaction dwindled; he was drawn to Winters; he was troubled in a way that he could not understand. When he went back into the house his mother was looking out, watching Winters as he walked down the street.

[281]

"Who was that?"

"One of the fellows from the plant."

She said, "He looks as if he had Indian blood in him."

They're beginning to come to me, he thought secretly. They see I'm going to amount to something. But he was not sure, and when he thought of the guys calling Rose Horseteeth, of her boy looking down on him, he was sorry she had not picked out a better day to come down, a better day to ask him.

THE car stopped before the house. Hagen saw the luggage tied to the running-boards and the canvas pouch bulging out in the back before he saw the Texas license.

Here they are, he thought.

He started to walk toward the front of the house. He stepped back and called into the kitchen, "They're here!" There was a confused racket as they ran toward the front door; sharp, excited cries and the sound of their moving rapidly through the rooms. Before he got around the house Mildred and Johnny were out at the car, the children were dancing in excitement on the sidewalk, Mary was coming out on the porch, and they were climbing out stiffly, disentangling themselves from the luggage and stretching as they got down to the ground.

For a few moments there was only a great noise of greeting as they embraced one another and called out in excitement, *Well, here we are! Well, it's good to see you!* before they climbed down and a mild embarrassment seized them. The two children stood by, tired and dirty and confused by all the excitement, looking uneasily at their parents and back at the car and then at the strangers who greeted them so affectionately. Hagen picked up the youngest boy when he was momentarily free, "Well, Jackie," he said, "don't you know me?" But the child only gave him a polite, embarrassed smile and looked back doubtfully at his mother. Ruth came over to him again while he was standing a little distance away from the others.

"Well, pop," she said, "here we are."

[283]

"I'm glad you are."

"I'll bet. . . ." She smiled nervously and tiredly. "What's the matter, Jackie? Don't you know your grandpa?" He put the boy down. "I'll bet you are," Ruth said again.

"You've lost weight," he said.

"Not only that. . . ." She watched him with her nervous, weakening smile and his heart contracted with pain as he saw that she was in danger of crying. Around them he saw Mildred and Gerald talking to Bill, and Mary trying to make the children feel at home; *It stood up pretty well,*" he heard Bill saying. "*When you think it's five years old. I had a little trouble in Utah.*"

"You're welcome here," he said. "Did you ever think you wouldn't be?"

"No. . . . But that doesn't make it easier."

He asked in a low voice, "You've had a lot of trouble?"

"Nothing else."

"Well," he said.

"How is it here?"

"Well, it's so-so," he said. "It's so-so."

They were interrupted as Mildred ran over to Ruth and embraced her again. How much older their faces were! He could not get over the dull pain he felt at Ruth's pale nervousness and her tired voice; he walked over to where Bill was standing beside the car and tried to join in their casual talk about the trip. Bill looked tired. His heavy face was badly sunburned. "No," he was saying to Gerald, "we stayed at auto camps." He looked up as Hagen approached, a curious expression of defiance and shame on his features. "Well, we're here," he said.

"I'm glad you are."

"Well, I don't know. . . . I thought there might be something I could pick up here. I couldn't find anything there. I thought maybe if I had a few weeks to look around in. . . ." His voice trailed off indecisively.

"You'll find something. It hasn't hit here yet."

[284]

"You must be starved," Mary said.

Little Mildred ran across the yard and threw her arms around Gerald's knees. He lifted her up mechanically.

"Be quiet, Little Mildred," he said.

"Don't fix anything," Ruth called back. "The children shouldn't have anything. I fixed a lunch before we left."

"It would only take me a minute."

"No, don't."

"So things are bad in Texas," Gerald said.

"It's hell. . . . The poor people are starving."

They waited a moment. The children moved uncertainly around the yard, looking at each other and the house, getting used to the ground again. Up and down the street the women were looking out of their houses, trying to see what car it was and why it had stopped.

"We'll give you a hand unloading. . . . It's about time for Johnny and me to go to work."

"So Johnny's working," Ruth said.

"He just started. He's doing all right."

Bill was pulling the luggage from the car. He looked around quickly. "It can't be so bad here . . . No kid just out of school could get a job down home. No experienced man, even . . ." He began untying the clothes-line that had held the canvas bags on the car. "You hear that, Ruth?" he asked. She nodded, her smile a little forced; and Hagen suddenly guessed how many arguments had gone by before they nerved themselves to start out, how many scenes of hopelessness and hysteria and fear. His grandchildren were already exploring the house and the yard, Mildred's children staring indecisively at the newcomers and Ruth's wandering carefully until they could get accustomed to the new place, beginning by finding out what was under the porch. Bill was dropping things from the car as though he intended to start out looking at once, just as soon as he got unpacked and washed up. "By

[285]

God," he said, "That's the first piece of good news I've heard since I went to Texas."

Hagen said, "I don't know if it's so good." Then he felt uneasy; he did not want to discourage Bill or to make it seem that they were unwelcome. He looked helplessly at Mary, but she was with the children; she was happy; she was glad they were all together; he could not depend on her to say something to change the subject. Uneasiness settled on them again. Ruth had heard him. Even while she was talking with Mildred she had heard him; he saw her dark head lift and the tired relief of being able to talk to her own people give way to a rising alarm. She's sharp, he thought, and even then he was proud of her sharpness; nothing ever got past her.

"What do you mean?"

He hesitated again. "It's like this. A kid like Johnny might get a job . . ." Then he thought, no, if I don't tell them they'll think it will be easy and they'll be disappointed. "Down at the factory they've been letting the old hands go and hiring kids and new men at half the wages. The work is jammed up all the time. It's got so bad you don't know what to do. They're letting everything go to pieces. Breakdowns all the time. They won't buy a thing. . . I didn't want John to take the job. It's too heavy for him . . ."

Bill piled the luggage on the sidewalk. The ropes dangled from the dusty car. He began untying the knots absently, hiding his disappointment in the task. Suddenly he burst out, "What the hell has happened to everything? You read in the paper things have never been so good; there's never been so much prosperity; the God-damned stock market is booming; and then you find out you can't get work, everybody's losing his job, or their wages are being cut—Christ, there are thousands of people on the roads, thousands, men looking for work —sometimes whole families—all up and down the country— thousands! You see the poor devils hiking along the highways, even down in the desert, even up in them God-awful mountains in California, miles from nowhere, way out in the woods—everywhere you go. When you ask them where they're going they say they're looking for work. Things are better here, they say, or things are better in the Middle West."

"In Santa Barbara," Gerald began. Mary came up quickly; she had heard those words so often and they always made so much trouble that she tried to head them off.

"I'm going to fix just a little something," Mary said.

"No, please, mamma. I don't want the children to have it. They're upset now. I don't want them to be more upset."

"Fix something, Mary," Hagen called. "Don't listen to her." Johnny came up to him. "He's here again," he said. "Who?"

"The light man. . . . I told him to wait out in back."

Bill started untying the ropes that had held the luggage to the car.

"I'll see him," Hagen said.

Johnny walked part around the house and stood where he could watch them unloading and see anybody who was coming, with a feeling that he was standing guard. "I can't give you anything now," he heard his father say. "I can't give you anything till the middle of the month."

"Well, I haven't any choice in the matter, Mr. Hagen," the light man replied. "We have a record here that a notification that your service would be discontinued after the first of the month if the May bill was not paid was mailed to you from our office the fifteenth of June. Here it is the fifth," the light man said severely, "and we haven't received any word from you about it."

They came around the house out of sight of the kitchen. The light man was holding a black book of some kind in one hand and peering through his heavy glasses at a bill he had taken from his folder. He studied it in the way a doctor studies a chart that shows the patient is in danger. He shook his long head in a barely perceptible, disapproving movement as he stared at the bill.

"Our records show," he said.

His father replied, "I told the last fellow that was here, I can't give you anything till the fifteenth."

He watched Little Mildred jiggling around. She was listening to his father while she made hopscotch jumps around the back yard, making one jump and spraddling her feet out wide, and then jumping and closing them together again. Between times she looked at his father and at the light man to see if they were paying any attention to her. She would do anything for attention. She would sidle up to any group with an affected shyness, rolling her eyes and letting her head sag unhinged to her shoulder. If anyone looked at her she would lift herself on one foot and spin around and around, or she would give out strange cries and hide her head in her arm.

"It isn't my choice," the light man said. "But I have my orders to discontinue the service in the event that payment isn't forthcoming."

His father looked angry. "You'll get your money," he said. "What's the rush?"

Little Mildred stopped jumping and began edging toward them.

"Little Mildred," he said.

"What?"

"Your mama's calling you."

She looked at him distrustfully, glancing toward the house and back at him again.

"You better go see what she wants."

She did not believe him, but she could not see why he should be lying to her, and she watched him with a vacant, expectant stare, searching his face for an explanation.

"You better hurry, Little Mildred," he said

The light man fussed with his papers. "Well, Mr. Hagen,"

he said, "When do you think you'll be able to pay something on the account? Could you have something tomorrow?"

"I told you the fifteenth. I won't have any money till then. I don't get paid till then. . . ." His voice rose. "By God, I don't see what's the matter with you people. I paid my light bill every month for twenty years to your people. It don't amount to four dollars."

"Three-ninety, all told. . . . Such a small item," the light man said, "I'd think you'd want it cleared up, Mr. Hagen."

He tried to close his ears to what they were saying. Arguments over the bills disturbed or embarrassed him, or left him with an oppressed conviction that the collectors would consider his parents stingy or cunning. But he heard his father complaining about the bill's being too high, and the light man explained in a rehearsed voice, "People tend to forget that the private company has a heavy burden of fixed charges that ultimately rebound to the benefit of the community in the form of wages and taxes. The Past Bay Light and Power Company in one year alone turned over blubl thousand two hundred and eighty dollars in the form of taxes, to the city in one year alone, just for taxes. Their rates are fixed by the Government—the company can't do anything about it, so if they seem to be high, in times like these, you forget how low they were in good times. The lighting equipment in this town alone represents an investment of seventy-five million dollars, including plants and structures, poles, wires, conduits and submarine cables and assessed valuation of the property. The company also employs more than four hundred people, including the street-car system, which has been losing money steadily for more than ten years, and the annual payroll is close to half a million dollars. Public ownership pretends to offer lower rates, but people tend to forget that the so-called publicly-owned plant cancels its gains through less efficient and consequently more expensive production and higher taxes," the light man said sadly.

There was a long silence after this speech. He looked up,

[289]

wondering at the light man's mournful voice and at the in-comprehensible words he spoke. "If you could just give me something on account," the light man suggested. "So I'd have it to take back to the office. Even if it was only a dollar."

"Man," his father said feelingly, "if I had any money I'd pay you."

"Well, just a dollar, say," the light man pleaded. "So I'll have something to take back to the office. Surely you can give me a dollar."

"I haven't got it. I won't have it till the fifteenth."

"Not even a dollar?"

"Not a cent."

The light man shook his head, "I have to have something to give them in the office," he explained. "I have to give them something or the service will be discontinued." He looked around distrustfully . . . . "It don't need to be much," he murmured. "A dollar, now . . ."

"I just haven't got it. If I had it I'd give it to you . . . ." Then his father seemed to feel a little sorry for the light man. "I got my daughters staying here with me now. My son-in-law hasn't had work for months. I'll just have to run behind a little."

"Times are bad," the light man said. "This is going to be a hard winter . . . ."

"Yes," his father said. "I think it is."

"Maybe as hard a winter," the light man said, "as we've seen for a long time."

He looked at the light man, moved by the ominous words and the dead helpless voice. A hard winter, he thought, a hard winter, the words stirred him with the memory of old men's talk and with the memory of his mother's countless reminis-cences: *Ah, yes, that was a hard winter,* speaking of past times when things were different from what they were now.

"I can generally tell by the way I made my collections."

"I suppose you can."

"Yes, I can generally tell . . . ." He began putting his bills back in the case. "I heard this morning they're laying off two shifts at Superior. I wouldn't be surprised if they didn't shut down altogether." Then his voice became official again, and he made a notation in his notebook. "I'll put you down for something on the fifteenth, Mr. Hagen," he said. "Is that right?" Their voices drifted off in the gray air.

In a moment his father came back, looked hard at him and then toward the car where Bill and Gerald were unpacking and moving the luggage on the sidewalk. "A hard winter," he said. "I've said that every year for twenty years and I've never been wrong yet."

6. Johnny

THERE was a crowd in front of the plant. Coming across the tideflat, he saw the men moving into a tight mass before the factory office. A slight wind was blowing inland with the rising tide and the line of smoke over the firehouse moved lazily, a dark flag over the tapering brick pole of the stack. Always thereafter he would remember what happened as beginning then, when they stepped off the road and on to the tideflat, going over the plank laid across the drainage ditch and seeing the men gathering in a black knot before the office. He would remember the curious look on his father's face and his even walk, as though he forced himself to walk slowly and to show no surprise, but years would pass before he would understand what it must have meant to his father, before he understood that this was the last time he could expect to walk over a path that had grown so familiar and so even. For how many—twenty?—years, Hagen had come to the factory every day, coming down by the same streets and turning off at the same place to the path through the brush, seeing the crew of the night or the day shift converging from all parts of town at the same time he arrived. Now he knew it was over. Even if they took him back the old way was over, and it would only be a question of time before they found a new way to get rid of him.

But that was later. Now the scene drove itself into his memory with excitement, and he was irritated with his father's deliberate walk. His father swung his lunch pail easily, but

Johnny packed his under his arm like a football, getting ready to run to find out what was happening. Before they reached the crowd a man broke away from it and ran out to them. "Your card's pulled!" he cried to Hagen. "They pulled about twenty of them!"

"Twenty?"

"Dwyer, Sorenson, old Mike . . . ."

"I'll be damned," his father said.

They went up to the crowd. About a hundred men had gathered in the parking space. The rest of the night shift stood about in smaller groups near the fireroom or around the few cars. The car-loaders on the loading platform had gathered at the green doors of the box cars. In the office the girls stood at the windows, looking down with remote inquisitive stares, like people watching a wreck in which no one was hurt. Winters came up to his father.

"He did it," he said. "Every God-damn one of us."

His father said, "They must have finished the export order."

"He's got nerve," Winters said. "Fifteen men at once."

"Did they finish the export?"

"I don't know . . . . How could they?" Winters looked at the men. "Who knows if they finished the export order today?" No one answered. "Go ask the shipping clerk," he said to Johnny. "Don't tell him why you want to know."

"Hurry up," his father said. "Find out before the whistle."

He went into the stockroom. Someone pointed out the shipping clerk to him, a rushed, worried-looking man who leaned over an improvised desk at the entrance to the loading platform. When Johnny asked if the export order was finished he looked down in annoyance.

"Who wants to know?"

He flushed. "I wondered if we would have to work on it tonight."

"You work on what they give you," the shipping clerk said.

"They'll give you enough so you won't have to worry about what order you're working on."

He turned back to his desk and Johnny stopped indecisively. Then he walked off through the stockroom until he came to some of the men pushing on truckloads of doors down the alley. He called to them. "Who would know if they finished that export order today?"

"The shipping clerk."

"He's busy. Who else?"

"Go ask the tally man. A little guy with glasses down by the graders. But they couldn't finish it."

The tally man looked at him suspiciously, "What do you want to know for?"

He said nervously, "Molly sent me to ask you. He said Carl . . . ."

The tally man pulled a ruled sheet out of his book and handed it to him. "They didn't get started," he said. "Tell Molly if he'd do something on the night shift besides walk around with his finger up maybe we'd finish that God-damn order."

He ran back out to the office. The crowd had grown. The cars were coming up to the parking strip and the watchman came up to the crowd, saying, "All right, fellows. Let's break it up. Let the cars park," but no one moved. Someone said to the watchman, "Lay off, lay off," and he grinned uncomfortably and stopped pushing. The newcomers were crowding in, trying to find out what was happening, but Johnny ducked past them and got to the center of the crowd where his father and Winters and Sorenson were talking earnestly and looking toward the office.

"Go see MacMahon!" somebody yelled. "Don't monkey with Carl!"

"He ain't here!"

He handed the tally sheet to Winters. "I got it," he said.

For a moment Winters looked in surprise at the ruled paper. He pushed the men back so he could lift it up to read it.

"Hell," he said. "They didn't do anything. They didn't do as much as we did last night."

Sorenson said, "Why monkey with that? They can buy enough to fill out the order. That won't stop 'em."

"No, but they don't want any delay on it . . . . Look. It ain't half out."

The crowd split. Frankie Dwyer pushed up to them, waving his dismissal notice in his hand. His eyes were always narrowed because of the heat where he worked, but now they were almost closed and his lips were drawn back from his uneven teeth. He asked in a strangled voice, "Where's that little pot-bellied bastard?" pushing Johnny back into the crowd as he shoved his face up to Winters. "You seen him? Is he here?"

"What are you going to do?"

"I'm going to shove this," Dwyer said. He waved the dismissal notice. "This is to notify you," he said. "I'll notify the son of a bitch. I'll notify him." He moved on to the entrance of the office. The crowd broke and some of the men stopped at the steps. Dwyer went on inside. At the railing that separated the entrance from the desks of the girls he stopped and one of the girls came up to him timidly, her eyes wide with fright, faltering as she asked him what he wanted. Behind her the other girls sat paralyzed at their desks. He snapped at her, *"Where's Carl?"*

She replied automatically. "Mr. Belcher is busy just now . . . . If you care to wait . . . he'll be free."

Dwyer looked at the row of closed doors across the office. Behind him the men crowded up into the entrance. "Where is he?" he repeated. "Is he in there?" But she looked at the crowd behind him, at his large hands clamped on the railing, and suddenly turned on him with contempt.

[295]

"If you want to see Mr. Belcher you'll have to wait until he's free. . . . Is that clear? You can't see him now."

"Where is he?"

Winters and Sorenson pulled Dwyer back. "Hell, you'll have the law on us," Sorenson said.

The girl looked past them at the men crowding into the office. "Have you men any business here?"

They stared at her.

"Do you want to see someone? You can't stay in here unless you have business here. You can't loiter in here."

"I got business here," Dwyer said.

"Then sit down and wait . . . . You can't disturb the office like this." Then she called out, the disgust hot in her voice. "All of you men who haven't any business here, get out! Get out!"

The five-minute whistle blew its brief warning blast. The men stepped back out on the parking space. "I'll wait," Dwyer said. He sat down on one of the benches. The girl turned her back to him and returned to her desk. She picked up a notebook and stared at it sightlessly for a few moments, breathing deeply, her features rigid and controlled. Now some of the other girls began typing again, the hesitant clatter bringing the office back to normal. Johnny moved out with the others, getting a last glimpse of Dwyer staring at the floor, the dismissal notice trembling in his hand. Outside the night crew had stopped at the factory entrance. The day foreman and some of his helpers, the shipping clerk, the tally man, the order clerks, came out on the loading platform to look down at the crowd, and in a few moments some of the men from the day shift began to move through it asking, "What's up? What's the trouble? What are you waiting for?" but no one paid any attention to them, and no one went inside to stand by his machine. Then from inside the factory there was an odd, dwindling sound as the machines began stopping before the

[296]

whistle had blown. The saws stopped first, and when their high whine had quieted the deeper throb of the transfer chains and the rolls sounded louder, like the bass in an orchestra growing strong as the trumpets ceased. They waited, they listened; unable to believe what they heard until they saw the first of the day crew coming out of the factory five minutes before quitting time. Now the rolls began stopping as the men went through the factory and pressed the switches or called to the men still at work, and finally the main conveyor rumbled in the quiet factory before someone thought to press the switch that stopped it. The men on the night shift began yelling as they came out the main entrance of the plant, and then in a moment they were dropping down on all sides, off the loading platform and out through the side doors, the shouts rising as the two shifts came together. Johnny was caught up in the crowd that began moving steadily around the office, shouting to the girls who crowded at the windows inside. On the second floor a group of men stared down thoughtfully. He could see them turn to speak to one another. Beside him a little girl danced along in excitement, waving her lunch bucket to the girls who stood at the office windows. She was only fifteen or sixteen years old and she was too excited to march with the others—she danced, moving along sideways and letting her feet snap together and swinging her arms. One of the old women pressed up to him. "What is it?" she asked. "What's the matter?" but before he could explain, the voices rose again and they moved forward more rapidly; she shouted with the others and raised her hand when the rest did to call to the girls in the office. Then he was swept off his feet. He began to shout, *"Come on out! Come on out!"* and all around him they took it up, calling in time as they marched around the office, *"Come on out!"* The sound rose irregularly. After they had shouted, the words would come back to them like an echo from some other part of the crowd. *"Come on*

[297]

out!" How did it sound inside? The girls looked out sight-lessly; the deaf men on the second floor turned and spoke to one another as the cries broke in waves against the glass. When he broke free they were still shouting. *"Come on out!"* He looked at the moving crowd packing the space between the factory and the office. So many of us, he thought, feeling sorry for the bewildered girls on the other side and for the few forlorn figures in the factory. *"Come on out!"* they cried. *"Come on out!"*

That was the beginning. Nothing else ever gave him the same strange feeling of excitement and strength, and all during the next week he treasured the memory, calling on it like some powerful charm to help him in the moments of despair. At home he used it most, making himself remember when the wrangling in the house got too bitter and when the disorder and the lack of any quiet wore on his nerves, but he used it every day on the picket line when the waiting got tiresome or when someone got caught and was hauled off by the cops; he called on it when Sorenson and Dwyer had a fight and when, after the third day, a part of the factory began to run with scabs who came from nowhere. In a week it had lost its strength for him, for in the bitterness of defeat and in all the misery he lived through nothing, for a while, could give him any hope. But then that feeling died too, and years later he could call up the memory of the afternoon when the machines began stop-ping, when the day shift raced out to join them, when the girl danced along beside him as they went around and around the office.

At home he thought of it after the first meeting, when he came in still burdened with all that had happened and found them waiting distrustfully, badgering him with questions he did not know how to answer. As he came in the door his sister said, "I suppose you're one of them!" and he was dumbfounded that they already knew more about it than he did. His father was still with Winters and Dwyer and the rest of them. When he tried to explain what had happened Mildred interrupted him in a voice that seemed to have grown more shrill and nervous: "Well, why did they have to beat up the poor man! No wonder he wanted to fire them!" Then in a few moments he learned how the newspapers were run. There it was, the whole story, with everything just a little bit wrong.

STRIKERS STORM OFFICE: THREATEN GIRLS

A mob which threatened for a time to get out of hand today stormed the office of the Past Bay Manufacturing Company's plant in the industrial development district, called for the foreman of the factory and threatened the girls employed in the office until quelled by the quick action of one of the employees, it was asserted by officials of the company late this afternoon. The action, which came as a climax to labor trouble which had been brewing in the factory for some time, came after the discharge of fifteen men who, company officials claim, were involved in an assault on Carl Belcher, an industrial consultant now serving as night foreman in the factory, late Thursday night, when the lights were temporarily extinguished.

He read it again and again, and after the argument was over and he gave up trying to explain, he found the paper and studied the article until he knew it by heart, trying to figure out how anybody could get anything so twisted. It was all there: the strike and the marching around the office; even Frankie Dwyer's going into the office and Sorenson's saying,

"You'll have the law on us," but it was all mixed up and no one could understand it. Instead of stopping work the day shift broke into disorder and forcibly shut off the motors, and instead of marching around the office calling *"Come on out!"* they all, he now learned, milled steadily around the building, calling threats and were with difficulty induced to disband.

"It looks funny," Mildred said, "You don't even know what was going on. You didn't even know they beat up a man. Does pop know?"

"They didn't!" he cried. "I tell you I know what they did, don't I? I was there, wasn't I? I was down there and saw it, wasn't I?"

"Well, there it is. You can read, can't you?"

Troubled, he replied. "They made a mistake."

Gerald said impatiently, "He wouldn't know. It's always a little bunch of trouble-makers do all the damage." He was gloomy. "I'm afraid they've got your Old Man in hot water," he said, "they've put something over on him."

They kept it up all week, and even after his father was shot Gerald said, "They put something over on him. He got mixed up with that bunch and they used him." After a few days Johnny had to force himself to go to the house, only returning to it to sleep and occasionally to eat and to prevent his mother from worrying about him. She never doubted that what had happened was as he told it and as his father told it, but she was lost because she tried to keep peace in the family and to keep the girls from feeling that the little they and their children ate was begrudged them. Then Bill and Gerald got into arguments and Bill went down to the picket line while Gerald nagged at Mildred and spoke mysteriously of letters and telegrams he was getting secretly from the South.

Johnny hugged the memory of that first sweet hour when they danced out of the factory; it was a lamp that would keep him warm. Lying in bed at night he polished it until it shone.

He remembered tiny details, the look on someone's face; the friendliness of people he had never seen before. Some day it would happen again. Some day all the people would come out of the factories, singing in the streets . . . . He slept now on a cot in the front room with his younger brother sleeping beside him. Across the room was Gerald and Mildred's bed, and at night Gerald would go on with his talking, remembering all the little triumphs of his dealings in the past, the money he had made and the wealthy people with whom he did business. He would talk whether they listened or not, speculating on things he would like to be doing, and after they fell asleep he would stare wide-eyed into the darkness, sometimes murmuring some half-formed plan that came to his mind. From time to time he would rise up on his elbow and grope beside the bed for his cigarettes. The match would flare; the tip of his cigarette glow dully.

Each day Gerald dressed carefully, walked to town each morning after reading the paper, and talked to men he met in an insurance office and in the lobby of a hotel. Before he left the house he would warn them that he was expecting a telegram, and that if it came to send it back to the office, where he could stop for it . . . . Sometimes late at night Johnny would be awakened by their whispering; several times he heard Mildred crying, trying to muffle her sobbing so she would not awaken him.

The days passed in a rush. He learned to look through the paper for the new stories they made up. He read them, checking them with his own knowledge of what had happened, with a bitter amusement, only occasionally driven to fury by some cunning lie and spitting on the print or tearing the paper into bits. But now he had learned how to read them and he searched in the back pages for good news, and when he read of labor trouble at some other factory or of some mob threatening somewhere he could see between the lines and understand what had actually happened. Every morning, when his mother gave him his breakfast, she said, "I'll try to fix something better for you tomorrow," with a painful, apologetic smile. Then he went down to the picket line to take his place and march back and forth before the factory.

The line stretched for a hundred yards along the track. There was a steady blur of talk, almost as loud as the diminished sound from the factory. The men moved restlessly from one group to another, checking their own feelings, their ideas, with the others, driven by anxiety to move back and forth to find out the changes in the way people felt. Midway down the line the women were clustered in a small colorful group, some of the girls in their bright cheap dresses and some in the costumes they wore to work. When the mill was running and the young girls on the night shift came to work, they walked proudly through the streets, conscious of how their overalls fitted them and of how completely their costumes set them apart from the crowd. Some of them had learned how to decorate the men's shirts they wore with colorful neckties or a sash around the waist, and as they moved through the downtown crowds on their way to work these girls felt no shame or uneasiness at how they looked; they knew that if the well-dressed girls of their own age looked at them scornfully, and if the old women frowned at the way their clothing fitted them, no one else did.

The line was steady. The police trained it. On the second morning an invisible boundary was drawn at the edge of the company's property. No one could see it, but it was there, and sometimes fifty police were on hand to see that no one crossed it. It got to be something wonderful and mysterious, this invisible boundary of private property that the police would defend with their lives. They were told that anyone who stepped across this line was liable to arrest, and the picketing became something like a children's game, like dare-base, but perverted into something risky and mean. Some of the boys from the stockroom got into the forbidden territory and were taken off to the station while the crowd yelled and the boys waved back good-naturedly. As long as they were in sight the police handled them gently, but when the boys were released from jail after two days some of them were terribly beaten; one's wrist was broken and one had lost his teeth where a club smashed against his mouth. They waited. The boy who had been beaten came back to the line but left after Vin Garl searched him and took away a revolver he carried.

Each morning after Johnny had looked at the paper and eaten a small breakfast he joined the line without ever thinking that there might be something else he could do. The way it looked when he came on the tideflat made a difference to him. He left the house with the disorder there lingering like an unpleasant taste in his mind. A big crowd swept it away. If the crowd had thinned he suffered. Sometimes he went with Waino and Bill in his brother-in-law's car to call out the people who had decided to stay at home. He was bewildered that some of them preferred to sit in their houses or walk downtown—bewildered and indignant, and after they had been turned down he worried about it and used the refusal as a way of measuring people and deciding whether or not they were worth anything. Back on the tideflat he joined the pickets as they walked before the factory, watching the cops who lounged in the doorway or sat for hours in their cars; memorizing their faces and wondering what they were thinking and how they explained their actions to themselves. How out of place and awkward they looked! Their blue uniforms, padded and grotesque, their sullen and uncomprehending features, now reflecting contempt and the fear they felt at the strikers' number, and now reflecting only boredom and irritation at the interruption in their usual ways of life—there was not one of them who would have fitted into the life of the

[303]

factory or performed the tasks that it demanded. Always keeping at the very edge of the invisible line, the pickets walked back and forth, beating down the dirt of the tideflat, never letting the police rest for fear their line would be crossed or someone would rush them. Sometimes at the remote ends of the line the pickets and the police would begin talking, someone asking a cop if he wasn't sick of his work; or some of the girls would waylay an outpost and ask him if he didn't get tired scowling and making faces. Sometimes the police would call back, sometimes conversations would start, sometimes they would even tell the men what the company intended to do and how many scabs were working. But then their officers would move down the line, saying, "Break it up," or "Keep moving, there," frightening the pickets less than the few friendly men in their own ranks.

The first day he had seen Walt. When the crowd broke up around the factory Carl had left the office, and Walt had been riding in his car, sitting beside Carl and looking as important as Carl himself. They had sailed out around the few stragglers without glancing at them. He had a better reason for hating Walt, and when he heard that Walt had been given Morley's job he waked up; something he had not understood before became clear to him. Somehow he had thought that people worked and rose in the world. In one swift glance at Walt riding importantly in Carl's car the picture was reversed and now in the depth of his bitterness he saw Walt rising in the world, yes, but rising in the way that a corpse rises when it has lain for a long time under water, rising and rotting as it was pushed out by the strong cold currents at the bottom . . .

He saw all this and nothing could stop him from thinking about it. Slowly and painfully he learned that what happened did not depend only on how they acted here on the line. It was not only *this* strike, he learned, that determined what the police did; something else was in the air; there was a chance that there would be strikes in some of the other factories on the harbor and the cops were moving cautiously because of them. Sometimes when he stopped at Winters' house there would be men from the other mills there, the friends and relatives of the people on strike. Sometimes at night he sat in on the meetings because he did not want to go home, sitting back in a corner of the smoke-filled room and listening to the arguing that went on almost all night. Crowded around the table, their faces strained and sweating in the hot night, the men argued fiercely, trying to impose their wills on one another by the intensity with which they stated what ought to be done. The police, the unfinished orders, the price of logs, the way the men felt in the other mills, the length of time before an election, the newspapers—everything came into these talks. The dirty dishes piled up in Winters' house. The floors became covered with a powder of cigarette ash until the neighbor women came over every morning to clean it so it would not be in such a mess when Winters' wife got back. The doors were always unlocked and someone was always there. At times Winters or one of the other men would be asleep on the cot while the voices stormed all around him. Johnny would grow tired of their arguing and nervous as the sleep pulled at his eyelids, but he knew that if he went home Gerald would be there jabbering about what he intended to do, the two sisters would be making remarks on each other's children, his mother would be hovering uncertainly in the background, sparing herself from thinking by working madly around the house.

Oh, misery! He sat back in the corner of the smoky room, staring with heavy eyes at the faces of the men. Digby, he heard, and at the name of the man who owned the factory he felt a rise of interest, wondering what kind of man he was and how he felt about the strike in his plant. At first they talked about Carl and about MacMahon, but now Digby dominated their thoughts and they saw him everywhere, in the perverse stories that came out in the newspapers, in the strange and sinister men who, appearing among the spectators at the picket line, were talking gloomily about the sure failure or making friends with some of the men and buying them drinks at the speakeasies along the waterfront.

His father was there, with Winters and Dwyer, Vin Garl and Sorenson. The doors were open against the hot night and the insects swarmed around the naked hanging globe. His father had nothing to say. He looked toward the others; in the three days he had lost heart and his age seemed to give him no rest. "I've got four grandchildren," he would say unexpectedly. "I'm getting to be an old man." He began to confide in the spectators who came down on the picket line, the calm, inquisitive, well-dressed people who were attracted by the strange stories that appeared in the newspapers and who, believing these accounts in which people were shown as acting so abnormally, looked on the picket line as they might have looked upon some unknown submarine monster washed up on the tideflat. "I've worked in this factory twenty years," his father would explain earnestly. "I've always done my work," never seeing the looks they exchanged or the smiles they politely concealed. He was bewildered and shamed at his father's new humility. He had never seen it before. No, before he had sometimes been troubled because his father was too obstinate, too independent and too careless of what people thought. But now that he saw what the other extreme meant, he would never feel that way again. "I've worked here twenty years," his father would say, to people who did not understand, who did not care, and Johnny would listen, suffering, saying silently, *Don't apologize to them! Don't whine!* turning on his father the words his father had drilled into him.

"If we let them finish their export we might just as well leave the Northwest," Vin Garl said. He spoke to Sorenson.

[306]

"If we don't get back to work here we'll never get work anywhere they know about it. And you won't either. You might just as well get ready to move your family."

Sorenson said, "I've never been out of work so far when I couldn't get a job if I wanted it."

"You will be."

They were silent. The threats sank in. Sorenson looked at the Finn in contempt. "I'm not worried." He glanced at the others to see what support he was getting from them.

Vin Garl put his arms on the table. He stared at Sorenson while he spoke. "Listen, Sorenson. I been through all this. You want to get things settled, you want to get back to work and have it the way it was. You can't do it. They won't let you do it. You don't understand how sore they are or what they'll do. They'll jail us all, they'd shoot us down if they could. And they'll never forget it, they'll never forget it— we're all down as a bunch of trouble-makers and they'll never trust us again, they'll never hire us unless we make them."

Sorenson nodded. "So you want to make it worse," he said.

He pushed his chair back and stood up. Again he looked at the others, trying to make an opening in their argument, searching the faces to see which one was closest to him.

"I won't have nothing to do with beating up people," he said abruptly. "I said at the first . . . you're trying to get the whole God-damned town on us."

"I won't have anything to with it either," Vin Garl said. "But if the men go out after the sons of bitches stealing their jobs, I'm not going to try to stop them."

"You don't have to stop them. All you have to do is tell them what it'll do to us! It'll get the whole town on us. And it'll drive away our own people."

"Some of them," Vin Garl said evenly. "Not the best of them."

He got it; he saw Sorenson flush. "Oh," Sorenson said, and

added in confused sarcasm, "You want to drive away all but the very best, huh?"

Winters said, "We can't do anything tonight. I got to get some sleep. Let it go."

"Yeah," Hagen said.

"No, by God! I won't get mixed up in it! I won't let that guy get us in more trouble!" He pointed at Vin Garl. "Christ, they got a third of a crew there now! In another week they'll have a whole shift! He's just been telling us we won't be able to get work in this country. Now he's going to fix it so we *can't* get back, so we *can't* settle!"

The expression on Vin Garl's face did not change. Sorenson began walking around nervously, speaking in sentences that were broken and unfinished, ending them with abrupt motions of his hand.

"What good will it do? A few guys beat up . . . . The police on our necks . . . . Maybe a fight and somebody killed . . . . They stop us from picketing. All right. I got a wife and family."

"Yeah," Dwyer said. "The rest of us only got dogs."

Sorenson turned on him. "You . . . . Right at the first you got us in a jam. Right at the first! You raised hell in the office and it's only luck they didn't throw you in the can for threat. You got the whole damn town down on us. You got everybody in town thinking you ran in and smacked one of the girls . . . ."

"We need an organizer," Vin Garl said wearily. "You shouldn't have said that, Frank."

"Why does he always crab?"

Johnny slipped out quietly, shaken and afraid, and went down the quiet street to home. He went into the house and undressed without turning on the light, remembering his father's sleep-heavy eyes, Winters and Vin Garl springing up to quiet the two men. He tried to call up the memory of them coming out of the factory, but it was no good now and he lay sleepless in spite of the weariness that held him. After a long time Gerald stirred in his bed, a match flared and the tip of his cigarette glowed in the hot room . . . .

Sometimes he saw Ellen on the picket line, but after the first day he did not see Walt and after a little while that memory was crowded out of his mind. At first he spoke to Ellen whenever he saw her, driven by his shame at the picture of himself he thought she had formed, and though she seemed casual and friendly he thought there was something appraising in her interest, as though she asked herself, What does he want now? whenever he stopped beside her. He was conscious of it; he kept thinking, I'm different from what you think, and tried to figure out some way to recapture the little moment of ease when he was at her house. When the line broke up at the end of the shift he waited near the girls, hoping she would free herself of them so he could walk back across the tideflat with her. Sometimes he thought she saw him and stayed with her friends on purpose. Then he would pretend to be looking for someone, hurrying through the crowd and calling out, "Has anybody seen Dwyer?" or "Has anybody seen Winters?" until he could work his way out of there.

Once he asked, "How's Marie?" stopping in embarrassment when he met her away from the picket line.

"I don't know."

"What?"

"She beat it," Ellen said. "She took some of her clothes and left."

He could not understand; he could not picture anyone just dropping out of sight, nor could he see how it could be spoken of so calmly. "What are you going to do?"

"Nothing. What can we do?"

He thought she was lying to him, that she did not want him

prying into her affairs and was trying to tell him so. He murmured that it was too bad, adding painfully, "I just wondered . . . I've been wondering."

Ellen explained coldly, "She couldn't work and she didn't want to be an expense so she just beat it."

She was looking off toward the girls; perhaps she did not want to be seen talking to him.

Suddenly he said, "About the other night. I didn't know that guy. I didn't know what he was going to do . . . . When I ran and got in the car I was just thinking, you know, there was four or five guys there; I didn't want to have any trouble. So I just thought he could go a little ways and let her out. But I don't know him and if I ever catch him, I mean, if I ever have a chance . . . ."

She would not help him. She waited patiently for him to finish talking so she could go back to the girls.

"I don't want you to think," he said. "I'd know better now. Actually, I don't do that. I'm different, see? I wouldn't have anything to do with that guy. I'm sorry about your sister . . . ."

He strangled on the words, helpless without some faint encouragement from her. She did not look at him and she paid no attention to his discomfort. Only when his voice died away entirely she glanced at him to see if he had finished. Then she walked back to the girls. He got out of there, his humiliation gradually turning into anger . . . . I'll never do that again, he told himself. I'll never apologize again. I'll never eat dirt again. When he passed her afterwards he walked by sightlessly, his anger with himself giving him strength, and when he thought of rebuilding himself in her eyes, of doing something that would make her change her mind about him, he could drive out the thought in a moment by remembering this scene. It's bad enough to apologize, he thought, but when you don't get anything for it . . . . He went out with the cars to round up the pickets; he pushed his way scornfully through the townspeople who had come down to see what was going on; he went out with the crew that brought in the sandwiches for lunch. Sometimes he drove Bill's car into the district to carry a message or bring someone back to the line. He wanted to go with the crews that drove down to Kelley and Goose Creek, where the scabs were coming from, but no one would take him. As long as he was at the factory or at Winters' he could keep his mind off what had happened —it was only when he was at home or when he had nothing to do that he worried about everything and thought miserably of all the dumb and shameful things he had done.

Late in the week Ellen asked him when a car would be going to town; she wanted to go with it.

"I don't know," he said.

"You don't have to snap my head off."

"I didn't snap your head off. I told you I didn't know."

"Jesus," she said. "You're getting as bad as your friend."

She walked away. The words stayed in his mind. He would have worried about them, but too much happened all at once and he had no time. Before the day was over the storm broke, and after it had passed he was through with worrying about what people thought of him.

The rain began suddenly, the first large drops splashing like pebbles in the dust of the road. He looked up anxiously, knowing the violence of some of the summer storms and knowing that one could drive them back to shelter in a moment. Up and down the line the faces were turned toward the sky that was steadily growing darker. The black clouds were massed above the tan rolls of smoke; there was a solid blue line, a foot above the horizon, clear and shining in the afternoon sun of the Pacific. There was no wind. The smoke from the stack mounted straight up and billowed against the lighter smoke from the forest fires.

They stopped moving along the line and stared at one another as the first drops splashed in the road. He was standing with Waino and Frankie Dwyer and a group of men from the day shift. "I can stand a little rain," Waino said. "As long as it's only rain we don't have to worry." They listened without comment. He looked at Waino; he thought that Waino considered himself experienced because he had been in a strike once before. He was always bragging about it, and now he was sure Waino was going to tell them about the time the police ran them into a storage shed and the firemen turned their hoses on them for half an hour. Waino told them, his face flushed and eager, trying to strengthen himself and then by telling them that this was nothing to what he had been through before. But all the time it was growing darker and the narrow band of blue light on the horizon was growing thin, and though the rain was still falling irregularly and the puffs of dust continued to rise from the road with each drop, it was plain that the rain would be heavy and that it would reach its full strength before the shift was over. Over at the entrance of the plant the cops moved toward their cars or under the shelter of the loading platform. The car-loaders began pulling their trucks back from the edges of the shed.

"When a full, straight beam hit you," Waino was saying, "you never knew what hit you. I remember one guy tried to run out and *whang!* they caught him right on the butt and he rode that old stream of water fifty feet the way you ride a bicycle."

He stood in the center of the thin crowd, his face flushed and good-natured, little spots of red on the high Finnish cheek bones, his blond hair rumpled straight up over his forehead. When he spoke of what they had done and how bitterly they had been beaten—some of them had had their ribs cracked and all of them had been half drowned—when he spoke of this, an odd sort of amused surprise crept into his voice, even a kind

[312]

of pride, as though thinking back over all he had been through left him amazed at his own power of endurance. But now Johnny knew him; the world continually filled him with an immigrant's wonder. Sometimes when they walked the line he would talk about something perfectly commonplace and simple that he had seen or that had happened to him, and when he told it his eyes would widen as though he had stumbled upon something that no one had ever thought of before.

But now no one answered him. They watched the sky and the scattered drops, hoping the rain would hold off till the shift was over. In the office, across the tracks, one of the girls was washing up beside the plate-glass window, she looked out at them, and disappeared. During the first days the girls had spent all their time at the windows, looking down in the way that people crowd around an excavation, to watch a steam shovel at work. They could see the girls speak to each other, their lips move, see them laugh silently when someone said something funny. Now they had become accustomed to the picket line, and though they always looked out when they passed the windows it was an aimless interest; like fish in an aquarium they would brush up against the glass, linger there for a moment, and drift away again.

Someone said half-heartedly, "Anyway, it'll help the fires."

The shift was nearly over. There was only a faint running hum from the plant and, listening, they could tell the machines that were going, studying the rise and fall of the sound to guess at how much was being cut. In half an hour the whistle would blow, weakly, compared with the deep blast it gave when they were all at work, and then the scabs would sneak out into the cars drawn up at the entrance, the police would gather close and look as menacing as they could, and slowly the procession would get under way, the cars bunched close together, the police leading and following with their guns drawn, the motorcycle cops racing back and forth along the convoy. Then Johnny would stand at the side of the road with the others and shout his curses after the scabs, cursing them from the depths of his bitterness, while they tried to hide themselves in the dark interiors of the cars.

Someone from the day shift said abruptly, "Let's go."

The men looked uncomfortable. No one wanted to go. If the rain held off a little longer, or if it only rained lightly for a while, they would be there when the shift was over, and they had waited too long to give up the only thing they were there for. Now it was habit; they were afraid that if they left a crew would start the night shift too. "I don't mind a little rain," Waino said again, as the drops became heavier and fell a little more rapidly.

Johnny looked at the cops sitting comfortably in their cars or sitting under the shelter of the loading platform, the dry girls in the office, and scabs taking it easy in the factory. He could see them through the open doors of the main entrance and through all the openings from the stockroom to the loading platform. There was a full loading crew. Someone had said that Carl believed the sight of the cars being loaded and taken away would dispirit them and make them believe the factory was running full blast. He felt a moment of wonder at their childish cunning. Even he could tell that the scabs were loafing and he had already worked long enough to guess roughly from the sound which machines were being run.

Midway down the line the girls made for the few cars parked near by. The old women stayed in line. There were about fifty of them: a few grandmothers and the wives of some of the men. They came down every morning and spent the days talking of their debts and what they had to do, airing their endless grievances, confused and resentful at the sudden interruption in the way they spent their time, knowing more clearly than anyone else how far the loss of a week's pay had already put them all behind.

Waino said a little more cheerfully, "It's only half an hour. We can stand it."

The man from the day shift said again, "Let's go. It's going to rain holy hell."

"We're here now, we might as well wait."

The man from the day shift nodded sadly; he had a naturally sad face and now that he was newly worried the heavy lines around his mouth and under his eyes gave him a sort of grieving authority.

"I don't see any sense in getting wet," he said.

The big drops were cold. The dust of the road was now pitted where they had struck, and while Johnny watched he saw the fresh drops coming faster, breaking their holes in the rutted dust. The sky was dark above the rolls of smoke, and out at sea the steel line had closed at the horizon. Now the smoke from the stack was wavering and soon would be stretching out flat toward the town.

Someone jumped up and said passionately, "Hell, rain," and walked down the track.

"Come on," the man from the day shift said, "let's go."

Waino began talking nervously, all his eagerness marked on his red face. But the man from the day shift was saying what they were afraid of; they listened to him, and Waino knew it; he rattled on and on, seeming so young and foolish and eager in the circle of silent men that Johnny felt ashamed for him and wished that he would stop. The large drops of rain spotted his blue work shirt; the fixed grin on his face made him look embarrassed. Johnny looked away, wondering why Waino kept harping on it when nobody backed him up.

The groups were still scattered; there was still no telling how long a heavy rain would hold off. I hope it rains, he said to himself, somehow believing that if he wanted it to rain it would not. He wanted to be there when they stopped work. It ended the day when they had a chance to curse them and gloat over their terror and shame, and it drew them to the factory every day—that and the hope that something might happen, that some of the cars would break down or that one of the

[315]

motorcycle cops would take a spill and break his neck. They would not give it up unless they had to. That was why Waino's talk sounded so foolish, for he spoke as if everybody wanted to leave except him, or as if everybody else only intended to use the rain as an excuse to get away.

The man from the day shift grumbled, "It's bad enough coming down here. It was your fight in the first place. Now you want us to get soaked."

Waino too was nervous, and now he accused himself for shooting off his mouth before the men. "Nobody asked you to come out," he said stupidly.

"Nobody asked me," the sad man said. "And two weeks ago the whole night shift was down on its knees begging the day shift to come out."

"Not me!" Waino cried furiously. "I said if they want to come out, let them come out! If they don't let them rot. If they want to eat dirt, let them!"

"Oh, pipe down," Dwyer said. "Pipe down."

The man from the day shift went on stubbornly, "What quarrel was it of mine? Why should I lose my job because they fired Winters and Hagen and Sorenson and some of the rest of you?"

"And me," Dwyer said.

"Yes," the sad man said, looking straight at Dwyer. "Why should I lose my job because they fired you?"

The expression on Dwyer's face did not change. "Why should you?" he asked.

Somebody said, "If you still think that, you sure as hell shouldn't be here."

Waino rushed in again, "Didn't you take a cut? Or did they leave you out, maybe?"

"Yes, and I've already lost more than it would cost me for two months. A week, that's twenty-one dollars I lost and that's thirty-five cents a day for sixty days."

Somebody called out, "You ought to have been a bookkeeper, Happy. You're making a mistake working here."

"Laugh!" the sad man said. "They turned off my lights yesterday. They turned off my lights and now they're going to turn out the gas and when my wife goes down to buy anything she has to beg them for credit. She has to get down and beg for credit for another week." He said *beg* with a dull revulsion, as if the word was shameful and filled him with a morbid satisfaction.

They roared at him. "For Christ's sake! You think they give you *more* credit when you go on strike! What the hell you think we're doing here! You think they give the rest of us credit because we're on strike?"

The man from the day shift did not think it was funny. He looked at them for a moment before he said "Piss on the strike, piss on it," and walked away toward the cars. Johnny watched him, shocked at the dead weight of despair behind his voice. The rain was beginning in earnest; he could see the groups drawing together, the men trying to decide what to do. "He must have wanted to go home," Dwyer said, staring at the man from the day shift.

His father broke out of the picket line and came up to Dwyer. The rain began falling steadily, blowing a little with the intermittent wind from the harbor; the first large drops were beginning to drain off the roof of the factory. They were still waiting, but all up and down the line they were looking toward Hagen, waiting to make a break for home. His father stared uncomfortably at the factory, trying to guess how long it would be before the full strength of the storm hit.

"Hagen, it's raining," somebody complained. "Don't you know it?"

"I can't stop it," he said.

"Let's go."

"How long is it?"

"Fifteen, twenty minutes."

"It might do them good," Hagen said, "if they saw us here no matter how hard it was raining. It might make them think."

"Who?"

"All of them. The scabs, MacMahon too. Even them bastards." He nodded toward the cops.

Johnny felt a rise of pride. He thought vaguely that perhaps his father was getting over it, getting over the first bewilderment when he was only conscious of how old he felt and tried to explain how it had happened to strangers. "Here comes the wet blanket," he called out, seeing Sorenson hurrying through the rain toward them.

"We're going to stay, Sorenson!" his father said. "Maybe it'll make them think."

"Make them think we're crazy," Sorenson said. "Getting pneumonia. What the hell good does that do?"

"I'll stay," Waino said again.

"It's up to you," Hagen said. "I'll do what you say. Some of you kids go find out what the rest of them want."

But Sorenson cried, "Hell, they'll only ask the guys that want to stay!"

"Well, go with them! Go see!"

Winters came up and motioned back toward the line. "They're still here," he said. "They'd have left by now if they wanted to go."

The car loading had stopped. The loaders had drawn back from the platform and were waiting inside the stockroom.

"Let's get under the shed," somebody said. "Hell, they can't keep us out here in the rain."

"The hell they can't."

"That's a good idea."

"Go ask them."

"Let's all go."

All at once they had to bend against the wind. The smoke from the stack suddenly washed downward, swirled around the fireroom and swept across the tideflat close to the ground. The line broke; there was a little rush as a few more crowded into the shelter behind the cars.

"*No, wait!*" Winters called. He ran out, across the line, so everyone could see him. "Just a couple go! They'll get scared if we all go!"

The wind whipped the words out of his mouth. They could not hear him beyond a few feet down the line but they saw him wave and waited to see what was going to happen. The cops were looking up suspiciously, trying to understand what they were going to do. Hagen and Winters walked across the cleared space toward the captain's car, sometimes turning sideways under the brief hard blasts. The captain got out as they approached. Some of his men crowded around to listen. Johnny could see them talking, gesturing toward the line and then toward the factory, waving their arms and shouting to make themselves heard. Then the full force of the storm bore down. The rain blew horizontally with the level ground; the air was filled with the twigs and splinters that lifted under the wind. He could scarcely see. He was vaguely aware of the movement in the men around him; then he understood, and a moment later they were scrambling into the box cars and up on the loading platform into the stockroom.

In half a minute they were all off the tideflat. The storm rushed past. The low brush beyond the tracks bent flat, lifted, and was blotted out in another downpour. He shook himself, shivered, conscious of his wet clothes before he realized what had happened. Someone rolled shut the heavy doors to the loading platform. He could still hear the wash of rain on the roof and the irregular pull of the wind, but the great roar of the storm diminished; the wind stopped in the stockroom and the lights ceased to sway. Through one of the openings in the wall he could see one of the cars on the parking space tremble in the wind, the side curtains tearing loose and flapping like clothes on a line. A cop was wrestling with the side curtains on one of the police cars, trying to buckle it down while the coat of his uniform billowed like a sail.

The doors were being closed and the strikers were closing them. The stockroom became quiet.

The scabs had moved back through the alleys of doors, circling around hastily to get behind the police. There were about twenty cops huddled together around the time clock, dividing their attention between the strikers and their own scattered comrades still blowing around the tideflat or locked out on the loading platform. There was a group of workers closing the heavy sliding door of the main entrance, and the rest of the strikers swarmed in between the piles of doors in the first alleys of the stockroom.

The machines were still running in the main part of the factory. He heard the steady whine of the saws and the thudding of the conveyor chains.

The cops were watching, holding their guns ready to fire. Some of the men were out of sight of the police; he could see them shuttling between the piles of doors. When the scabs came up to the police they turned their guns on them nervously, not recognizing them or distinguishing between them and the strikers. *"Stay where you are!"* a cop cried. *"You men stay where you are!"* The scabs halted, collected in a still and frightened group.

One of the cops walked boldly into the group at the door, his revolver drawn, gesturing with it as he advanced. "Over here," he said. He pushed at the men, forcing them into the first aisle of the stockroom. They moved back obediently and then the other cops took courage and moved out from the wall, pushing, waving their guns while the men edged back in terror and excitement. But some of the men were already deep in the stockroom and at the far end of the line there was a steady shuffling as the crowd wavered and some of them ducked behind the piles of doors. One of the cops walked up to the scabs and forced them into the ranks of the strikers. Gradually they were all packed against the outside wall of the first aisle. A cop came up to Johnny and pushed him into the mass, saying, "Get on back, get on back," with a habitual and unimaginative roughness they are trained to employ, and as he fell back the man behind him asked, "What are you going to do, shoot us?" The police hurried back and forth, never getting far apart, occasionally giving their hoarse, automatic cries, "Nevuh mind about that," "Doan git smart," like the grunting of speechless animals, their coarse faces excited and afraid. Some of the men razzed them, asked if they were going to drive them back out in the rain. When the strikers near the time clock had been rounded up the police ranged themselves in front, guarding and menacing them with gestures and dark looks until everyone was packed in a fan-shaped mass against the wall. Then the police stopped the movement at the far end of the line.

The men became silent and motionless. The scabs worked their way to the front, edged out because the others drew away from them. Some of them tried to speak to the cops, but the cops had no time for them. In the silence Johnny heard the rain and wind again. Then he heard a sound that the police did not recognize: the motors stopping inside the main part of the factory. Some of the cops drew back and talked; one of them opened the small door that was cut in the large sliding door of the main entrance and went outside. The saws were still running and the transfer chains, but Johnny heard and recognized the gradual loss of sound, the others heard it too, and knew that their own men were moving through the plant, cutting off the motors.

The police captain entered, drenched to the skin, calling out angrily, "Where's your leaders? You men! Where's your leaders?"

Packed in the tight mass they passed the word along,

"Where's Hagen? Where's Winters? Where's Dwyer?"
Presently Sorenson moved out of the crowd. Someone started
to go with him but the cops pushed him back. Sorenson
began talking before he reached the captain, explaining and
apologizing, proud of his ability to talk and of his infinite
guile; "You can't blame us!" Johnny heard him say. "We
thought you said it was all right till the rain stopped!" But
the captain kept repeating, "You'll have to get out of here.
You'll have to get out of here. I don't want any trouble,"
without paying any attention to what Sorenson said.

The motors were stopping. He could imagine the scabs
running from the machines. One of the cops suddenly yelled,
"Get out of there!" All the way across the stockroom two men
were looking at them from one of the piles of doors. When the
cop yelled they ducked out of sight. The cop, who had seen
them, moved a little way in that direction, but as soon as he
moved the line bulged out where he had been and when
another cop ran up to drive it back the men spread out into
the alley. For a moment there was confusion and shouting,
and Johnny drew back in terror, expecting the police to shoot,
but they were afraid—they did not know how many were
in the factory and they wanted to break up the mass before
they started a fight. Before, the strikers had been crammed
against the very wall, packed so tightly they could scarcely
breathe. Now they filled almost the entire alley. And the
police had not shot when the line gave way.

The captain tried to brush Sorenson aside. "Open that
door!" he yelled. No one moved. Two of the cops standing
near the door leaned against it but could not push it back.
Until this moment the cut-off saws had been running. Johnny
could hear the high piercing swing as each panel entered the
saw, mounting to a shrill scream that died out just as the next
panel hit. Now he heard the funny dying groan that rose
when a saw stopped while it was still in the wood. He knew

[322]

what it meant. They all knew that someone had pressed the switch that stopped the motor and that the saw, the power cut, had turned over once or twice before the teeth stuck in the wood. But the cops looked around in alarm. Suddenly he realized how far off their native grounds they were, how uneasy they felt, the way he felt in the lobby of a big hotel, and suddenly saw what a lot of fear they concealed behind their loud voices and blustering air. The captain sent two men into the factory. The others tried to drive the strikers together, to attract their attention and frighten them, but the men were not afraid of them now.

He heard the dying groan of the cut-off saws and watched the two cops hurrying into the mill. The scabs were being pushed away from the strikers, forced forward as the men drew away from them and at the same time pressing ahead and trying to set themselves apart from the strikers, frantic to get on the other side of the guns of the police. But the cops could not tell the scabs from the strikers, and when they saw the scabs pressing forward they watched them more suspiciously and nervously than they watched the others. He saw it. He heard the cops who were struggling with the heavy door cry out, "Give us some help!" and saw the scabs leap forward to respond. A dozen of them pressed to the door. The two cops waved their guns to drive them back. There was a confused shouting; the door opened a few feet and the scabs in front rushed out. The other cops ran down toward the door. He heard a shot and saw the scab go down off the loading platform.

The crowd broke. The men began scattering through the stockroom. Someone turned out the lights. Even as he raced away in a panic he thought that it must have been his father who turned off the lights—no one else could have reached the switchboard so quickly. The gray light hovered near the roof of the stockroom, where the windows were larger, but down between the piles of doors and in the main part of the factory it was almost dark. There were a few more shots on the tideflat and then one somewhere in the building. As the echoes died he could hear the wind and rain again. Some of the men stopped in the stockroom, pushing the truckloads of doors to block the alleys behind them. Ahead of him, in the gloom, he saw a crowd gathering, and raced up to it. Three of the men were holding one of the cops, pinning his arms behind him. They had taken his gun away from him, unbuttoning his coat to get at it, and now his coat was bunched awkwardly under his arms. The men searched him swiftly, and he stopped struggling, looking dazed and frightened as the crowd around him grew.

The man who had taken his gun ran back to the stockroom.

"What are we going to do with him?" someone asked. "You want them to come looking for him?"

The man holding him said, "Never mind. We'll figure out what to do with him."

Waino grabbed Johnny's arm. "Follow me," he said. He dropped down into the conveyor and raced down it to the darkness under the factory. They could feel the storm cutting the weeds that grew up between the pilings. "I'm going to pull down their telephone in the office," he said. "You want to come?"

"What are we going to do? Stay here?"

"Why not?" He dropped over the drum at the end of the conveyor. "Watch it," he whispered. "It's wet here." Johnny followed him, splashing through the slime and groping for the pilings when he slipped.

"They won't let us."

Waino said, "They ain't got a hell of a lot to say about it."

"Suppose they start shooting?"

"We can always get out over the head end. We can always get out in the brush."

[324]

They came out under the box cars lined up beside the loading platform. Most of the cops were gathered in a group before the entrance of the factory, lined up around the man who had been shot. They saw the cops pull their coats around them against the wind and the rain, ducking when a sharper gust beat in from the harbor. The smoke from the stack still swooped down as the wind caught it; the rain drove along level with the ground. "It's a good thing," Waino whispered. "They'll think it's the storm."

"How you going to do it?" Johnny asked. "How you going to get there? How you going to know which wire it is?"

"That's what I'm trying to figure out."

They could see where the telephone wire entered the office. All of the strikers who had got into the cars were still crowded in them, so if they got across the parking space to the cars they were safe, and if they got to the cars they could get in back of the office where there was not much chance of their being seen. While they watched a car darted off toward town.

"I think it's a goofy idea," Johnny said. It was cold lying under the car and his wet pants stuck to his skin.

"I guess it is," Waino said.

"What good would it do?"

"I don't know. I was just thinking."

"Who told you to do it?"

"Nobody. I just thought it might be a good idea."

"Come on, let's get back."

They sneaked back under the factory. As they splashed through the brush Waino said cheerfully, "It would have been a good thing if we could have done it. . . . What a break! When the police start shooting scabs. . . ."

When they climbed out of the conveyor they saw the men crowded in a cleared space before the drier. From there it was open to the head end of the mill and to a dozen doorways that would let them out into the brush on the tideflat. When they came out someone said, "Now what are we going to do?"

[325]

THE light moved up and down on the road leading to the factory. He stopped the car. The flashlight was shoved up against the glass. He cranked down the window and the wind and rain swept in. As he ducked his head the cop asked, "Where are you going?"

Carl called out from the back seat, "It's all right, officer!" The cop turned the light into the car.

"Oh, hello, Mr. Belcher. Sorry. Go right ahead."

There were a dozen police cars in the parking space. The spotlights were turned on the main entrance of the factory, lifting it out brightly from the intense darkness of the storm.

They got out and ran for the protection of the office. A few cops stood inside, some of them shaking the rain water from their clothes. There was a mysterious movement outside; the shadowy figures shuttled behind the headlights and in the lulls of the wind he could hear the motors of the cars idling. A car turned around and raced toward town.

The captain came up to Carl from behind the railing. "Well," he said, "I think we got them right where we want them. There hasn't been a sound out of them. . . . He's over here; I suppose you want to see him."

Carl said, "There won't be a motor in there any good after tonight. There won't be a drive that won't be full of emery dust."

"Well, I don't know about that. I know you got them now where you can put your hand on them."

[326]

"A lot of good it does. There won't be a machine. . . ."

The cop looked at him steadily. His face was bloodless; the skin was drawn tight around his mouth. "You want to go in and see?" he suggested. "I'll take you in if you want to talk to them."

Carl murmured, "I'd have to speak to Digby about that."

"You want to phone him?" The captain nodded toward the telephone on the desk.

"I'm going up to see him in a few minutes. The damage is done. . . . I don't see yet how they got in."

"I don't know yet how many men are there," the captain replied obliquely. "I think between three and four hundred. They gave me twenty men. There was nobody in *there*," he jerked his head toward the factory, "to steer my men around. They couldn't find their way around in there. Now if we had some of your people working with us. . . ."

One of the cops stepped inside and waved his cap to drain the water from it. The water splashed on the floor and walls of the entrance.

One of them said, "Watch what you're doing! What the hell you think this is?"

The other cop said mournfully, "Jesus, I'm drowned."

"They could have picked a drier night to raise hell on."

Carl said to him, "You ever see a drive that's been choked with emery dust, Walt?"

"No, I never did."

Carl shook his head, implying that he could not describe it. The cop waited. For a time Carl stared at the floor, responsibility creasing his forehead. "God," he said at last. "I hate to have this happen."

"He's over here," the cop said. "If you want to look at him."

Carl nodded. He began pacing back and forth in the space between the desks. "Let's see, now," he said. He clenched his fist and drove it against his open palm. Beside him Morley looked at his shoes and frowned. The muscles in his cheek began to dance.

"Emery dust!" Morley murmured.

The cops were staring at them curiously. Presently Carl sighed. "On top of everything else," he said. Then the air of despondency left him. Suddenly he took control of the situation. Suddenly he leaped into action. His features grew stern. "Morley!" he snapped in a brisk, military voice.

Morley shuddered spasmodically.

"Yes?"

"Did you get hold of Jug Bullett?"

"What?"

"Can't you hear? Did you get hold of Jug Bullett?"

"I—" Morley said.

"God damn it!" Carl cried. "I told you to have him come down here!"

Morley looked stricken and lost. He grinned apologetically, his eyes widening and his head sinking in between his shoulders. When he looked up he saw them all watching him.

"I—" he said.

The cop said, "What is it? Maybe they wouldn't let him by. You want one of my men to go after him?"

"Never mind. It's no use now." Carl shook his head in resignation. "I run into this all the time. The thing to do," he said, "is look at the body."

They walked around the desks to where the man lay stretched out on a piece of wet canvas. Walt walked uneasily behind Carl and Morley, hearing the faint snickering of the cops in the entrance. His heart began to pound sickeningly when the cop pulled back the canvas. It was no one he knew. The dead man lay on his back, his head dangling sideways. The bullet had gone into the back of his neck and his neck was broken.

The cop looked at them. "You know him?"

[328]

"Not at the moment, no," Carl replied. "Who is it, Morley?"

Morley stammered, "It's one of the new crew. . . . It ain't one of the old hands." He gagged suddenly.

"What's his name?"

"You'll have to see the time sheet to get that," Carl said.

"Well, where's the time sheet? Who was in charge in there, anyway?"

"Well," Carl explained, "I was in charge. But lately I haven't been able to come down here much. Digby's in town now, and I've been spending a good deal of time with him. As a matter of fact, I've got to run up to see him when I leave here. I got to leave here in a few minutes and I'm going right on up the hill to see him—he's staying at MacMahon's."

"Well, how am I going to find out who this baby is? I rounded up about thirty of them squareheads that didn't get inside and brought them in here and they said they never seen him before."

He offered indecisively, "He's probably from Goose Creek."

"Well, I'll be damned if I'm going down to Goose Creek to find out who he is." He tossed the canvas over the body. "Christ, the trouble you run into."

"You got the one who did it," Carl said.

"He's in there." He nodded toward the factory.

"He can get out of there."

"But not off the tideflat. We can pick him up in the morning."

There was a dead silence.

"You got him identified," Carl suggested.

"All my men know him. He's been running up and down here all week."

"A heavy-set man," Carl said.

The cop looked at Carl and then at Morley, finally turning toward him and studying his face for some time before he spoke.

[329]

"A heavy-set man," he repeated blankly.

"I thought. . . ."

"No. A little dark fellah. Skinny, Italian, I guess. Maybe a half-breed. My men all saw him. . . . He took a gun off one of my men."

"Oh," Carl murmured. "Winters."

"That's the one."

In the dead silence Walt saw Carl's hand trembling. He walked back to a desk and sat down. When the wind hit the office it rocked unsteadily. There was a pencil sharpener on the desk and when he leaned on the desk the glass part that held the shavings fell open and spilled the shavings out on the polished wood. He heaped them into a nice pile, noticing that they looked like coffee grounds, and that his hand was steady as he piled them up. He smeared them out over the desk and began piling them carefully again. Without looking up he could see one of the cops staring at him. He wonders why I'm doing this, he thought with cunning, and without looking up he began piling up the coffee grounds, letting them sift through his fingers. When they went outside he saw that the tide had come up to the porch of the office and in a dim way he wondered what the tide was doing way up there, until he stepped down and found it was not water under his feet but the reflection of the lights of the cars. Beside him Carl and the cop yelled back and forth.

A HEAVY-SET MAN! Carl cried, and the cop shouted back:

WHAT?

I SAID A HEAVY-SET MAN!

Morley had got in the back seat. Walt sat behind the wheel, staring at the door of the factory that seemed to hang suspended in the darkness. He thought of the men inside working silently in the darkness, standing beside the machines that ran silently and moving the invisible doors through the

[330]

factory. The Polack would be working silently, breaking down the presses that he could not see; the saws bit soundlessly into the empty dark, and everywhere the ghostly figures moved and hurried—"Christ," he said. "I'm nuts."

Carl got into the car. "Well," he said, "the thing to do is go see Digby."

8. ROSE

THE candles looked wan and bendy, their little light struggling with the stormy gray light outside the windows. They ate silently and stubbornly, only Mr. Digby and her mother trying to carry on a conversation, speaking in low voices as if someone were critically ill in the next room. She bent over her plate, thinking that the candles looked cheap and affected, conscious that her mother was looking uneasily toward the kitchen, fearful that something would go wrong.

She suffered as she always suffered at her mother's attempts at elegance, thinking of her mother reading books and magazine articles that told her how she should dress, how she should act and what she should think about, pitiful works that told how one should conduct oneself with servants and how one's table should be set. Before tonight her mother had been excited and agitated for days, from the moment she learned that Mr. Digby was coming, fearful of doing something wrong, something old-fashioned and provincial, of serving the wrong things or serving them the wrong way, and then, perhaps, with a refinement of anxiety, not even knowing about it afterwards.

There were times when she felt sick at heart as she observed her mother at her studies. No matter how hard her mother trained herself, or with what discipline she memorized the doctrines which were so emphatically set down, there was always something which was wrong in the judgment of her authorities. As she read in preparation for one affair, she discovered that she had done something wrong at the last one.

Since she was so conscious of these mistakes, she could not imagine anyone's being unconscious of them. In her imagination, her friends, anyone who was ever in her house, left it only to be amused because some detail had been neglected. She was exhausted, with intolerable worry and suffering, even if she felt that nothing had gone wrong, for then she assumed, from her habitual thought on these problems, that she had merely overlooked something which was conspicuous to everyone else.

Rose was not conscious of it in this way. She merely felt sick at heart at times as she recognized her mother's efforts. This feeling, partly discomfort, partly irritation and pain and a curious involved sense of shame, came to her as she observed her mother reading with an unyielding patience, when her mother made some remark about the care of her house or those of her friends, and when her mother betrayed her nervousness by some anxious glance or some anxious intonation of a commonplace phrase.

Now her mother made no attempt to conceal her absorption in the difficulties of serving the dinner, except to Mr. Digby. When she looked away from him toward the door to the kitchen, a candid appearance of concern crossed her features, as though she thought some terrible catastrophe might take place beyond the door—an accident, perhaps, or an explosion that might occur at any moment. When she turned back, however, her features composed themselves so swiftly as to give no hint of anxiety, or of anything but a gentle attentiveness and a somewhat incomprehending courtesy.

Yet Mr. Digby, as he talked to MacMahon, or listened with a poised, deaf expression, or buttered a piece of bread, seemed not at all attentive to possible disturbances in the organization of the meal, or potentially critical of them if they should occur. On the contrary, his large and bony features expressed such serenity as should calm any alarm. Indeed, they expressed nothing else. As she examined him, during the course of the meal, Rose noted the resemblance to her father. Both men were of approximately the same build and their features were roughly similar, but in comparison with Mr. Digby's polished ease, her father's fluctuating grimaces of intensity and relaxation—of nervousness—made him seem a cruel caricature of his distinguished employer. The difference was reflected in their contrasting methods of putting food in their mouths. MacMahon would cut a bit of meat with one motion, and put it in his mouth with a swift, jerky movement of his fork; while for Mr. Digby there was no sharp break in the process, as his movements, like his words, were smooth and unvaried, and the lifting of the fork to his mouth was but a part of a calm, methodical process which began as soon as he sat down at the table.

Her father suddenly pushed away his plate and said in a strangled voice, "I can't eat anything."

There was a moment of silence. His face was gray and ill.

"You ought to eat something, Charles," her mother said. "You ought to try."

He repeated it dully.

"I can't eat anything."

She stared at him anxiously, seeing for the first time the gray decaying pouches under his eyes and the age and weariness of his face.

"You don't know how I feel," he gasped. "If they were in my own house I wouldn't feel any different."

Mr. Digby said in a kind and dignified voice, "Don't let it get you upset, Charles."

He stood up. "You don't know how I feel." His voice trembled; his mouth worked nervously. Her mother half rose from her chair. She too moved back, her heart pounding with her fear for him and her embarrassment for Mr. Digby.

"Charles," her mother said. "Charles."

"He could at least phone!"

Mr. Digby said with his grave understanding, "Don't worry, Charlie. There's nothing we can do tonight."

He nodded slowly and heavily. "I can't eat anyway. I'm too nervous to eat."

Her mother said, "You ought to eat something. Try, Charles."

"No, mamma, let him lie down. Let him rest."

"You'll excuse me," her father said. He moved awkwardly toward the door. They sat in silence for a few moments, glancing at each other and at the littered plates before them. Her father closed the door to his study. In the silence the girl came in and carried off their plates. Mr. Digby's face was expressionless, and for want of something better to do he rolled a crumb of bread between his fingers, flattened it, and set it carefully out of sight behind his glass.

"It's very disturbing," he said at last.

"Charles hasn't been well."

The girl moved in quietly, glancing in fear at her mother before she touched anything on the table.

"Very disturbing," Mr. Digby sighed.

Then her mother too got up. "You'll excuse me," she said, as she left the room to follow MacMahon.

Deserted, she looked at Mr. Digby. He looked grave, reserved and yet at the same time kind and understanding, and she suppressed a disloyal thought about how much nicer it would be to have him for a father than her father. She tried to think of something to say.

But what could she say? Did you have a nice trip? I said that, she thought. Isn't this weather terrible? That too.

"Your father's getting old, Rose," Mr. Digby said. "This is a shock for him."

"Yes. . . ."

"Too bad. . . ."

She roused herself.

"Have you been doing any hunting?" she asked.

"A little. . . . I went up in Maine last fall and early this spring I did a little shooting in New Mexico."

"Oh," she said. "That must have been thrilling."

"Well yes, in a way, yes." The girl brought them their dessert, looking shocked at the two empty places at the table.

"Mamma will be back in a moment, Clara," she said, feeling very carry-on and mother's little helper as she said it. "Papa doesn't feel well."

The girl nodded mysteriously.

"Fair, I would say rather than good," Mr. Digby judged, in his resonant voice. "Fair. I was with Able Massinger of the Massinger Rolling Mills of Toledo and Jerry Todd of the Todd Elevator Corporation of Duluth. We had some good shooting."

Her mother came back, sat down, smiled.

"He feels much better now," she murmured. "He's overwrought."

"I was just telling Rose about a trip I took early this year with Able Massinger and Jerry Todd," Mr. Digby said.

"Oh?"

"Shooting," he explained. "In New Mexico."

A talented raconteur, he launched at once into his lively reminiscences, and as she listened recognizing that he was speaking so only out of a gallant desire to lift them out of the depressed mood in which they were, she could not forbear thinking how much more interesting his hunting trips were than those her father took and later talked about, and as he mentioned the different parts of the woods in which they had hunted, and the amount and variety of game they bagged, and the cunning, dangerous or merely unusual behavior of the beasts they shot, the details of the trip were so vivid to her that she almost felt she had been on it herself, and had had a wonderful time. Yet when her father spoke of his hunting she always felt miserable, for every deer that Mr. Digby or one of his friends shot reminded him of a deer that he had shot or that some one of his acquaintance had shot. He was too insensitive to see that the different animals he had killed had not acted nearly so interestingly as those Mr. Digby had killed, or that the places in which he had hunted had not been so strange and remote, nor his companions so wealthy. Some deadly commonplaceness spoiled his adventures. His shots, although he described in detail their unique characteristics, as well as the make of the gun and the size of its bore, seemed easy in comparison with those which Mr. Digby described. If he had killed a lion as it was preparing to leap upon him he would have made it seem, in telling about it, as shabby an adventure as chopping down a kitten with an ax. Moreover, she had heard his stories before. Thus when he began, "I was in Alaska in nineteen-twenty-six, in the early spring . . ." she knew at once what he was going to say, even down to such fine points as the precise arrangement of the rocks on which he stood, the configuration of brush which obscured his vision as well as concealed him from his victim, and the unexpected behavior of the bear when the shot struck. In an instant, then, she thought through an episode which her father could not relate in less than five minutes. Her father adopted a curious voice in telling his stories. It was the voice of a person who is habitually not listened to, and who has come to insist upon matters about which there is no argument. He was too eager to be interesting to make any nice distinction between a real or an affected interest, like a merchant too anxious to make a sale to care whether he is paid in real or counterfeit money. He seemed to be making a speech to which no one would listen and which everyone hoped would be short, and when he began his anecdotes he seemed to be continually clearing his throat, continually facing his audience, and continually prefacing his remarks with a slight, unechoed chuckle.

[337]

He came back before Mr. Digby's stories were over. He had washed his face with cold water and it seemed less gray and swollen. "I'll have coffee with you," he said. "I feel a good deal better."

"Do you feel better?"

"Yes, I feel somewhat better."

Rose was disappointed that he had come back. When he began to talk she thought, *I wish you'd shut up. Can't you hear me, shut up,* until she had to turn away because she was afraid they would see what she was thinking.

"I talked to Carl," he said heavily. "He'll be up after a while."

"Is there anything new?"

"No. . . . They're still there. They shot a policeman."

"They did? Bad?"

"No. Just through the foot."

They were silent. She remembered the night they had driven to the factory and her father had gone inside, the dark sullen man who had driven the car across the field and the quarrel afterwards, the cool way her father took command.

"I feel so sorry for that other poor fellow they killed," her mother said. "Trying to get work in times like these and then to be shot just when he gets a job. . . ."

"Communists," Digby said. "Every time."

Her father said heavily, "You don't know how I feel. If they'd come into my own house and shot my wife and daughter I wouldn't feel any different than I do."

After dinner she waited restlessly until Walt finally came, half an hour late, taking off his raincoat while he told her briefly, "I won't be able to go, Carl's got some work for me later on."

"Has anything happened?"

"No. They're still there. They shot another cop."

[338]

He moved nervously, paying no attention to her when she looked at him.

"Mr. Digby's here," she said in a low voice, motioning toward her father's room.

"Yeah. I heard he got here."

"He's in there now."

He nodded again. "Carl hasn't come?"

"No."

He said abruptly, "I've got to get out of this. Christ, you don't know. They didn't kill that guy. The cops killed him. Thought he was a striker. Now they pin it on a guy I know." He pulled a newspaper out of his pocket and gave it to her. STRIKERS STORM FACTORY, she read. SMASH MACHINES: ONE KILLED IN RIOT. For a moment she was disturbed at his intensity and stirred by some new note in his speech; she thought that he looked thin and worried. But a moment later she thought, *What business is it of yours?* sick of his melodrama and his gestures that made her so nervous.

"It isn't your funeral."

"I know this guy Winters. I used to work with him."

"Well, Lord. . . ."

"He didn't do it! You understand? He didn't have anything to do with it!"

"He's responsible. . . . If it wasn't for him."

He said "Oh," impatiently, and moved away.

She cried in anger, "Oh, you make me tired!"

"You make me tired," he replied.

"Oh, I do?"

"Yes."

"Oh," she said with dignity. "Oh."

He looked at her, cold, nervous, his face troubled and young, his clothes seeming to fit him awkwardly, his head thrust forward as if his collar hurt him—"I'm sick of it," he said passionately. "You hear that? You know what that means?"

"Oh, God," she said. "I don't know what's happened to everybody."

"Everybody's nuts," he said. "Everybody's gone nuts." The word seemed to give him a bitter pleasure; he repeated it like some senseless curse dragged up out of fatigue and bewilderment. "God," he said, "suppose everybody just went nuts and went running around and yelling and screaming; suppose everybody just lost control and began running around. . . ."

She looked at him.

"Oh, don't worry," he said. "I'm not going to."

A moment later he said in excitement:

"Think what a mess it would be. Everybody screaming and running around bumping into things. . . ."

"Oh, cut it out!"

He nodded without resentment, almost as if he agreed with her. Then he asked, "What's the cop car doing here? They afraid for Digby?"

"No. It's Mr. Keenan."

"Chief?"

She nodded, still watching him uncertainly, confused by his jerky speech and his nervousness.

"What's he here for?"

"I don't know. That other strike. . . . It's something. They're afraid to do something because of that other strike."

Then she did not understand him at all. He sat down and looked at her, his face twisted and cunning and his lips tightening over his teeth. He said flatly, "You don't trust me."

She felt a tug of revulsion at the physical ugliness of his expression, then a vague beating fear like the fear she had felt that night on the tideflat only sharper and more poignant, less tangibly connected with anything real around her. "Oh, Walt," she said in misery, "what's the matter, what's the matter?"

He repeated it. "You don't trust me."

"Yes I do."

"No. Nobody does." He rubbed his hands together, the taut expression still distorting his features. "Listen," he said. "I know that guy. I used to work with him. I know what they're going to do."

The bell rang. Carl came in, his pear-shaped face dark and anxious. There were two workmen with him, ill at ease and staring in the front room, standing back shyly when Carl spoke to her.

"I'll tell papa you're here," she said, ignoring Walt as she opened his door and told her father they were waiting. But then when she saw him look at her with a stricken and baffled appeal on his features she relented and called to him before he went inside. He stepped back and she said with a rush of emotion she could not understand, "If you want me to I'll be out in your car when you get finished. If you want me to."

He looked doubtful.

"Walt," she said. "I'm worried, worried."

"Why?"

"You never asked me. It's the first time you haven't."

"Ask you what?"

"You never asked me if I had."

He looked at her. "Oh," he said. "Well, did you?"

"Not yet."

He said brutally, "Jesus, you ought to know enough by this time . . . I can't do everything."

At first she was shocked. She tried to figure him out, in a rush of panic; it would not work any more. Like a revolver that turned out to be empty when she pressed the trigger.

"Never mind," she said. "I'll be in your car."

She smiled at him. He went inside and a few moments later the chief of police came out of the smoke-filled room, his face set and angry, closed the door behind him and went outside without speaking to her. A few moments later she let the reporters in.

This madhouse, she thought.

Her mother came to her, as she knew she would, begging to be told that there was nothing wrong with her meal and nothing disturbing in her father's sudden outburst. "I was never so embarrassed," she murmured. "Never."

"Oh, mother," she said. "Please."

"Never," her mother repeated softly. "Never in my whole life."

9. WALT

WHEN he went inside Digby was sitting back heavily, his vest unbuttoned, a large cigar between his lips. "Well, Mac," he said. "One thing, I can see you have to get a new chief of police in this town."

"We can't get a new chief of police without getting a new mayor."

"Well, get a new mayor."

MacMahon's study contained his desk and his hunting equipment. There was a rack of high-powered rifles at one end, and a stuffed cougar that MacMahon had shot at the other end. The cougar was mounted on a mahogany slab in a snarling attitude, and bits of its tawny hide had come loose and one of its glass eyes was missing. MacMahon sat at the desk with the cougar behind him. As he talked he rattled his fingers nervously over the surface of the desk.

"Ah!" Digby said.

He stiffened suddenly, extended his neck, opened his mouth, and belched.

"You know Carl," MacMahon said. He gestured toward Walt and Bullett and Morley. "These are men from the plant."

Digby nodded to them. MacMahon stood up and paced restlessly across the floor, moving with cautious, jerky steps, jiggling each foot, before he placed his weight on it, as though he considered the rug a thin ice that might break through.

"Sit down," he said abruptly.

They sat down.

Digby watched MacMahon's careful pacing for some time. He relaxed in the chair, with his legs spread wide and his hands resting gently on his paunch. His large, serene face relaxed into a sort of bloated contentment, and his eyes partially closed. In appearance the two men were much alike, except that Digby was a trifle heavier and a few years older than MacMahon, and his features could relax more completely than those of the younger man. The larger pouches under his eyes, also, were of a grayish festering color which contrasted oddly with the flush on the rest of his face.

"Well," he said. "Been having a little trouble, I understand."

"Well, yes," Carl replied. "In a way, yes."

As the silence continued Carl added, "In another way, no."

Walt stared at Digby. This was the man who owned the factory. This was the man for whom they worked and who, when the trouble threatened his property, hastened by plane and train and fast motor halfway across the continent. And as though conscious of his scrutiny, Digby frowned importantly and drew deeply at his cigar.

"You need a new chief of police," he repeated.

And Carl replied, "That's easier said than done."

MacMahon teetered uneasily over the floor. "If they had broke into my own house I would not feel any worse than I do this minute." He looked at them sadly. "If they broke into my own house and shot my wife and daughter."

"I'm no fool," Digby said.

In the pause he could hear the rain drive against the windows. The blue thin cigar smoke swayed in the troubled air.

"You got Communists in there," Digby said. "You won't have any peace till you get them out."

MacMahon replied stubbornly, "It's the same old bunch. Our men won't have anything to do with outsiders."

"Communists."

"No."

Carl said, "Hagen's a Communist. Winters is a Communist."

"No," MacMahon said in a choked voice. "They wouldn't take that second cut. They want Carl out. They want us to take back five or six men we let go."

"Communists," Digby said. "Why didn't they ask for the factory. . . ." He turned on MacMahon. "You've got to clean them out if you have to get a whole new crew. You won't have any peace till you do it. You've got to clean them out like—" he hesitated, waving his cigar to fill up the gap in his words, "like you'd clean out a nest of cockroaches. We got to economize. We got to cut down. We got to retrench and economize all up and down the line or we go to the wall and we can't afford trouble every month or so from them."

He turned to them, "You men haven't been cut," he said. "We've tried to play fair with you. Now we want you to do something in return. You know what's happened. If we had a decent police force in this town it never would have happened. But we've got a bunch of thieves and grafters in office you can't do a thing with, spending the people's money and not giving a thing in return, not even able to keep up a semblance of law and order and letting people run wild—there'll have to be a change from top to bottom. That's all there is to it."

He was silent; the long speech seemed to exhaust him. They waited for him to tell them what he wanted them to do. But he seemed to have forgotten, his anger at the politicians leading him off the subject, and he brooded for a long time with his eyes intent on the floor.

"The way I look at it," MacMahon said miserably, "the country's unsettled."

"Where are those newspaper men?" Digby asked. "What happened to them?" He cried out in another rage, "What do we have a police force for? Why do we pay taxes?"

No one answered him. Walt looked around him. He saw Morley sitting on the edge of his chair, the muscles of his cheek twitching beneath the skin; Jug Bullett looking stolid and doped and MacMahon moving grudgingly over the rug, Carl

[345]

standing tense and nervous in the middle of the room.

Digby sighed, a look of pain crossing his features. He ran his hand under the top of his trousers and caressed his belly. "I ate too big a dinner," he said.

He got up and walked over to the gun rack, taking a rifle off its stand and balancing it. He held it before him loosely, closing his eyes professionally so he would be more sensitive to the feel of it. He tossed it to his shoulder a few times, tilting his head to one side each time that he tossed it, as though he were listening to some hidden sound it made. He did this for each of the rifles in the rack. "You've got some nice weapons here," he said at last. He picked up an evening paper from Mac-Mahon's desk and walked into the bathroom. "I'd be better off," he said, "if I didn't eat such hearty dinners."

They waited. "The police won't go after them," Carl said nervously. "They're afraid of that strike at the Superior." He looked at them questioningly, trying to guess if they understood him. "We got to have men we can depend on," he said.

Walt felt a vague and sickened weakness. He heard the rain, he saw the drifting cigar smoke, he thought of the factory washed by the storm on the tideflat, the people inside. When he looked at MacMahon and Digby he was still conscious of their voices and their aged appearance, their heavy bloated bodies and the pouches under their eyes like bags of decaying flesh. He was still conscious of this, still thinking: These are the people we do it for. These are the ones. He heard Carl saying carefully, "Now we've made up a list of names. These are all people we can trust. They'll all be armed. Now we want you men to go with them. You'll be perfectly safe." MacMahon teetered back and forth across the rug; down the hall the toilet flushed, a subterranean gurgle. For this, he thought. For these people.

10. Johnny

AFTER dark the storm eased off. The strikers had gathered in a tight group around the flashlight, collecting near the drier where they had an open path to the head end of the mill or to any one of a dozen doors that opened out on the tideflat. Besides they knew of other exits, places they had found when they were working where they could sneak out when they wanted a minute or a chance to grab a smoke. Vin Garl and Winters and Sorenson talked to them.

Vin Garl said, "What do you want to do? We can get out of here now if you want to. In ten minutes we could be out of here and I don't think we'd have much trouble getting home. They may have a few bulls planted along the road, but most of us have crossed this God-damn flat so many times we know it by heart and I think we could get past them."

He looked around to see if there was any response. No one interrupted him.

"We can do that," he went on. "We've scared hell out of them already and nobody's been hurt yet. If we don't go there's pretty sure to be hell popping tomorrow. I don't think they'll come after us tonight. They don't like it in here in the dark. But tomorrow, if we stay, they'll either shoot us out or do business with us. There's a chance they may do business with us. They know if they come in here they got a fight on their hands; they're scared to death of them walking out at the Superior and at Maloney's Number One and if there's a fight here, if they get too tough, it may pull them out there. Maybe they'll figure that if they settle with us it'll pull them mills out, and maybe they'll tear into us with everything they got to try to scare hell out of them at the Superior and try to keep them from walking out. If they do, if it turns out that way, Centralia and Everett won't be anything to what'll happen here."

Vin Garl waited again. The light was resting on a ledge in the wall its beam masked so that only the dull reflection went back on the faces of the men. There was still a little steam up and it was warm in the middle of the building.

"I doubt if they'll shoot us up. Maybe they will. I think they'll settle. They've got a big export order to finish. We busted their scab crew. They'll *never* get a scab crew in here again; they couldn't raise a crew now to come near this factory inside two hundred miles of here. And they know it. They know if they want to finish that order, *we*'ll have to finish it. And then it's only two months, three months till election and they won't want to make any trouble unless they have to. So it'll cost them something if they shoot us up and if they do it, it'll be because we're setting a bad example. It drives them nuts. They'll be jumpy for a year. They won't only bear down on us, they'll bear down on guys that never even heard of us and you'll see they'll be making a drive on the vags in Seattle and Portland tomorrow. . . . And remember, even if we *do* sneak out of here now we haven't settled anything. We've busted a million of their laws. Probably there's warrants out for half of us. So if we do sneak out, before we decide, remember we won't be able to come back on the line tomorrow the way we have been."

Sorenson said, "I didn't want to come in here. If I'd known what this was going to lead to I'd have never got started on it. From the first I tried to smooth things over. I tried to get to MacMahon when they wouldn't talk to any of us. I tried to get you to propose that we let Carl stay and just make it that none of us lose our jobs and half the cut put back. But no, nobody would listen and here we are. Now there's been a man killed, there's been shooting and people have been beaten up and still you can talk about staying here and having more trouble in the morning."

He looked at them accusingly. He turned toward Vin Garl.

"He tells you they got a big export order that has to be finished. We don't know what they're doing with that order. If he'd been here as long as I have he'd know they always say every big order is a rush order. We don't know how much a rush it is and how much they're just saying it's a rush so we'll have to highball it. We don't know whether they'll settle with us or not. All we know is, if we stay it'll be more serious than anything that's happened yet, and it won't only be somebody we don't know being shot."

Waino said, "We ain't crippled, are we?"

"Shut up," someone said. "Let him finish."

He went on bitterly, "Everything's been left to a few men who didn't care what they did. You turned over everything to them and they've got you in one mess after another. They made MacMahon sore right away so he wouldn't even see the delegation. They talked wild until they got the whole town down on us. Instead of trying to figure out some way of settling with MacMahon, all they could think of was getting *another* strike at the Superior. They banked everything on another strike and they didn't get it and even if they had it would only have led to more trouble. We can get out of here; I say let's get out while we can."

"You left out something," Vin Garl said. "I thought they was coming out at the Superior. Yes, I still say they are. And if they *had* walked out, MacMahon would have settled with us. You think it don't mean anything to them to have five hundred men out here, a thousand out on the other side of town, five hundred out in the South End? You think that don't keep them on the jump? They don't know what's happening; they don't know but what *every* mill is going to walk

[349]

out. But you notice as soon as we went out they eased up at the Superior and they postponed their cut at Maloney's."

"Where are we getting?"

"I say, *now* let's talk business with them. Now we're in their God-damned factory. We busted their scab crew. We're here where we can stop them from trying to work a hell of a lot easier than we could stop them by walking back and forth on that God-damned picket line, and yes, if we want to, if they make us, we can keep this factory from running for a hell of a long time. *Now* let's go to Digby. We can tell him this, we got some cards to play now that we didn't have before—take out your efficiency man, take back the men he canned, take back the cut, and we'll stay right here and start work to-morrow morning!"

Winters said quickly, "It's slacked off a little. Why don't we send out and get fifty-sixty men and bring them back here. And leave it this way. Anybody wants to leave can get out. There's nothing stopping anybody from getting out. Send out after the guys that didn't get in and the guys that wasn't down on the line. Let somebody go see them fellows at the Superior and find out what they figure on doing. And tell them up in town what happened—we ought to get a big crowd down here tomorrow morning."

"Don't worry," Vin Garl said. "There won't be a mill on the harbor that won't be short-handed tomorrow. . . . Probably they'll try to keep them off the tideflats."

As Johnny walked down to the other group he heard Soren-son cry out, "If you hadn't beat up that cop I'd say all right!" Down toward the head end there was another cluster of men where Dwyer and his father were talking. In the stockroom there was a group watching the cops in the office. Already some of the men had gone out under the factory to try to find out what was happening to the people who had been in the cars when the factory was rushed. A few had left as soon as it got dark to go into the poor section and tell the people what

[350]

was going on, but so far none of them had got back. Johnny heard someone call out to Sorenson, "Nobody's stopping anybody that wants to leave!"

"We didn't beat him up! We took his gun. You think we wanted to let him keep it?"

Sorenson said, "I'm trying to tell you you don't know what you're getting into! Nobody's been hurt yet. So you think you can get away with anything. Listen to me! The quicker we get out of here the better off we'll be. I don't mean sneak out! Let me go talk to them. Let me go talk to that cop. I was talking to him when you started raising hell. He'll talk to me and I'll tell him we just wanted to get in out of the rain, we thought he meant we could wait till the storm blew over, now the storm's over, let us go our way. . . ."

They began moving out toward the stockroom.

"You God-damn fool, they'll lock you up if you go out there."

"Leave it to me."

Sorenson walked ahead, the crowd tagging along loosely, still puzzled and uncertain. Vin Garl called urgently to Dwyer, "Come here Frank."

"What's the matter?"

Johnny stumbled off through the darkness after Sorenson. "Let him go," Dwyer said. "See what happens."

Vin Garl called out, "Don't all you fellows get around that door!"

Out in the stockroom the men who were watching the cops stopped them. They had pushed the truckloads of doors together until they blocked the aisles.

"Where you going?"

"Talk to them," Sorenson said. "Let me by."

After a moment they let him pass, but stopped the men who followed him. Standing behind the trucks Johnny could see the faint light that seeped in around the door. There was a small swinging door in the middle of the large door that closed the main entrance of the factory. Sorenson pushed it open and stepped out into the blinding light concentrated on the loading platform. He squinted his eyes at the spotlights and held up his arm. There was a shot; the small door banged open. Sorenson dove back inside. The little door jumped as the shots struck it, banging open to its full swing and snapping back on the rebound until another shot drove into it. Sorenson ran back to the trucks. Somebody yelled, "You hurt?" and he gasped, "No!" as he came back into the crowd. They all backed away from the door. The shots stopped. In the silence the door swung idly for a moment until the wind caught it and slammed it shut. When it was closed, with the light on it, the needle streams of light came in through the new holes. Then from inside the factory somewhere there were a few answering shots. The spotlight of a car went out; then another. They heard the sprinkling glass.

As he went back inside someone caught him.

"Johnny?"

It was Waino. "Yeah?"

"We're going to town. You want to go?"

"Who?"

They pulled away from the crowd. Waino explained hurriedly that they would be rounding up some of the men, to sneak them in under the factory. With the sound of the shots still pounding his ears he could scarcely hear. Waino explained that Vin Garl wanted to get in touch with somebody, a lawyer, he knew; the other guys who went out were supposed to get in touch with him but none of them had come back. He saw his father swinging his flashlight and hurrying toward Sorenson, and he tried to get out of sight because he was afraid his father would not let him go. Vin Garl was waiting for them beside the conveyor. He did not have time to think whether he was afraid; they slipped down the conveyor at once, splashing into the slime under the factory, the two Finns breaking the way through the brush. He had a moment of uneasiness for fear he was going to miss something by leaving; then as the water rose

[352]

up to his knees and the wind chilled him he thought with regret of the warm steam pipes of the factory. He was soaked through before he reached the tideflat and there the fresh rain hit him. They hid behind the pilings while Vin Garl crept out to see if there was anyone posted on this corner of the tideflat. The reflected light from the police cars spread over the railroad tracks and the weeds beyond them.

Now the night turned into another nightmare, and when they finally broke away and raced along the shadows of the brush, he had a nightmare feeling that he was running hard without getting anywhere, his feet sliding on the sloppy ground, the branches of the shrubs slapping back across his face. They made for the road that reached to the last houses along the edge of the flat. Looking back he could see the lights of the police cars concentrated on the door of the factory. Since he could see the ground faintly under his feet he felt exposed and naked and his skin tightened as he imagined one of the cops in the cars seeing him, the spotlight moving across the tideflat, cutting the dark like a knife. Vin Garl and Waino had to wait for him, and as he stumbled in and out of the drainage ditches he kept thinking, It's easy for them; they're used to it, until they reached the road.

There was a police car parked at a street intersection. Beyond it, where a well-used path went into the tideflat, there were several cars and under the first street light they saw a group of men standing in spite of the rain, looking off toward the factory.

They dashed across the street and into the alley between the houses. The rest of the night, it seemed to him, they were running into shadowed yards beside the dwellings where people were asleep, ducking out of sight when the police prowler cars splashed along in the street. In an alley in the poor section they found a battered old Ford and started it, reconnecting the wires across the switch and pushing it down a slight slope until it started. It rattled and blew; the motor kept missing because water had poured in on it and Waino urged it along gently, choking it and racing the motor when it showed signs of dying. Johnny sat between them, drenched and miserable, shaking with cold and fear. Then he thought of being in bed, but when he said so Vin Garl said, "Don't worry; they won't be sleeping tonight either."

They drove up the back streets, trying to miss the prowler cars, figuring out what they would do if they were stopped, a story that sounded plausible, when they should try to make a run for it. They went up to Hagen's first, but there was a prowler car parked near the house and they rattled past it, trying not to show any interest, and turned around the block. At the end of the next street there was another prowler and in the glimpse they got it seemed to be starting toward them. Waino turned out the lights of the Ford. He whipped it into an alley and back toward the main part of town. Everywhere in the poor section the lights were on in the houses. Where the mill yards began they let Vin Garl out and then circled around in the deserted streets, trying to find an opening so they could get in and borrow a less conspicuous car. In the main part of town the cops stared at them. At last they saw a light in Gil Ahab's shack and left their car there, exchanging it for his second-hand truck that was covered with religious posters and slogans, *Millions Now Living Will Never Die!* Gil Ahab preached in some little church where most of the ceremony consisted of waiting until some member of the congregation was seized with the gift of tongues. To every new man he passed out his pamphlets, and during the lunch time he would set up his charts, some of them about the pyramids and some of them long scrolls with the dates of the greatest happenings in the world, showing how it had all been pointed out in the Book of Revelations. They broke in on him, telling him why they wanted his car, and he dressed and prayed, getting down on his knees while they waited in embarrassment. For some reason that memory stayed in Johnny's mind more clearly than anything else, and long after the rest of it had become a confused blur he could remember them standing in the miserable room, looking at the religious posters that dotted the walls, the stacks of books and pamphlets, and heard him calling on God to give him guidance. "You've got to get down on your knees," he told them when he had finished. "You've got to take the humble way. That's what it means when it says it is harder for a rich man to enter heaven than for a camel to get through a needle's eye. The needle's eye was the name of a gate in Jerusalem; it was so small the camels had to get on their knees to go through. You've got to get down on your knees. You've got to take the humble way."

They felt safer then, thinking no one would stop them, two kids and a religious nut, as they drove around and collected a crew. They went up to where the prowler cars were thick, and Waino drove slowly past them, watching while the cops leaned out to read the banners: *Jesus Saves! Millions Now Living Will Never Die!*

JOHNNY dried his clothes on the steam pipes as much as he could and then wandered through the factory, talking to the guards at the doors, sneaking up to the loading platform to watch the cop cars still going and coming, talking to people he had never seen before who now greeted him like an old friend. While the first excitement had died down a little, there was still the drive of new threats; and they pounced on him particularly, as they did on all the newcomers, so they could tell him again what had happened. Excited and happy he moved through the dark factory, and found Ellen at last sitting with some of the girls at the outskirts of the dim light from a flashlight. It was near one of the steam traps and it was warm; he sat down beside her without thinking about it long enough to be uneasy.

"Where were you?"

"I was home. I just got here. We crawled under the factory."

She said, "I looked for you. I thought maybe you got caught when I didn't see you."

"No. We went out after some more people."

They were silent for a moment. The girls and the women talked in low voices, fatigue now showing on their faces and in their speech. Ellen started to tell him what she had done, how she had run into the office and been chased out again, but she broke off abruptly. "You're cold," she said. She put her hand on his. It was warm and soft; she held her palm against the back of his hand for a long time.

He had been shivering occasionally before, partly in excitement, partly with the cold; now his teeth began to chatter.

"Is it still raining so hard?"

"Yes. Hard as ever."

They waited. Her hand touched his again where it rested on the burlap sacking. The edge of her palm touched his.

Presently she said, a little stiffly, in a low voice, "It's warmer over by the press."

"Where?"

"Over this way."

They felt their way into the darkness, holding hands so they would not get separated.

"Those old hens will talk," she whispered once with a nervous little laugh that seemed completely unlike her usual voice.

They found the exposed steam pipes by the press and sat down. She pulled her hand free. On one side of them the huge cylinders of the press rose up, and on the other the naked pipes sent out their waves of warmth. They could hear occasional voices and sometimes Dwyer or someone else who stayed up all night passed with a flashlight, going out toward the outposts.

"Isn't this a good place?" she whispered.

"Yes."

They were silent for several minutes. They sat with their backs against the cylinder and their feet out toward the steam pipes. He spread the burlap out over the floor.

She put her hand on his again. "You're not so cold now," she said.

"No."

She started to draw her hand away, but he held it. She did not move. He put his arm around her and kissed her. Her arm went around his neck, and in a moment they had pushed away from the cylinder and were stretched out on the floor.

[357]

They struggled for a while, panting and pushing and pulling at each other, and once she freed her lips to whisper, *Don't roll into the pipes!* He was too excited to answer her or to do anything but try to caress her more ardently, but again and again she stopped him with quaint questions and promises. "Promise me you'll be careful," she said at one moment, and he promised recklessly. And at the very last she pushed him away and sat up, saying *Listen!* with a trembling intensity. "Yes?" She kept him away. *"Promise me,"* she whispered.
"I will, I will!"

"No, listen. Promise me you won't talk about me."

"Oh, that's easy," he whispered, *"Why didn't you ask me something hard?"*

12. Hagen

THE fights started on the tideflat. All morning long the crowd grew. Even before daylight was complete they could see the shadowy figures behind the massed lines of the police. At dawn they could see the tideflat sheeted over with water and as the headlights of the police cars grew pale and weak they could make out the silent crowd forming. Beyond the flat the mills began to loom up out of the brown morning light and then the outlines of the buildings in town and then slowly the hills that repeated all the way inland to the mountains. The rain had washed the air and cleared it of smoke; for the first time in weeks, as the light grew strong, they could see the mountains.

All morning long they waited in a growing tension as there was no word from town and as the police and as the swarms of new men, not in uniform but carrying rifles, began to spread out on all sides of the factory. Beyond the tracks near the loading platform the main force of the police was located, the cops standing in groups, talking aimlessly, swinging their clubs as they waited. Now and then a police car darted off toward town. No one asked the strikers to leave. No one from the company came near the factory. Down the road, they could see, the cars that tried to reach the factory were turned back. Beyond the first line of the police the prowler cars were parked at regular intervals, and behind the cars was the dense and growing crowd.

All morning long they waited, and then Dwyer and Hagen went out to see if they could talk to Carl or MacMahon or Digby. That was all. As they went down the steps to the parking space before the factory, a fight somehow started in the line near them. Dwyer stopped, uncertain, and Hagen moved back to the foot of the steps. The cops began swinging their clubs. The ones in the prowler cars leaped out and ran into the mass of men. There was a shot in the crowd and the bullet drove into the factory wall. Dwyer leaped back on the loading platform. Hagen looked at the crowd where the fighting was now general, where the men were beginning to scatter. There was another shot, and this time he went down, falling at the base of the steps while on the tideflat the men began fighting back.

13. Johnny

JOHNNY had gone out on the tideflat with Waino to see what was going on, crawling under the factory and through the brush to come out into the crowd. He was to locate anybody he knew and lead him back inside, but when he came out he got separated from Waino and found himself in the blue line of the police. It stretched around the crowd like a rope. There was a cleared space, a hundred feet across, between the police lines and the cars and the second line before the factory. There were only a few workers where he was, a lot of people from town, a few heavy strangers with reporters' cards in their hats moving through the lines.

A cop stepped up to them, lifting his club and letting it swing. "You can't get through here," he said. As he pushed Johnny back one of the reporters walked up and studied Johnny carefully. The reporter was a thick, heavy-set man, wearing a brown suit and a brown felt hat. He was chewing absently on the stub of a cigar. He squinted his eyes as he looked at Johnny, and whenever Johnny looked away he saw that the reporter was still there, looking at him.

His heart had begun to pound. Beyond the cops he could see the crowd inside the factory. Most of them were inside the main entrance or standing on the loading platforms or in the empty box cars. There was no talking anywhere. The wind that came in with the tide cut along close to earth, flattening the shrubs and bull rushes and tugging at the legs of his overalls.

Most of the crowd were strangers. There were a few faces he recognized, a few men looking anxious or surprised or with a habitual expressionlessness on their features—an expressionlessness he had come to regard as familiar and to adopt himself, seeing it as one of the answers of the workers, one of the protections that made them indistinguishable and inconspicuous, one defense against the insults and orders of the foremen. He tried to join them. Someone touched him on the arm. Waino was standing beside him again. "Follow me," Waino said, looking toward the factory. "Stay a ways back."

In a few moments Waino edged off into the crowd. Johnny waited. One of the reporters bumped into him. He turned around and pushed Johnny savagely, *"Watch what you're doing!"* he said. Johnny tried to edge away; he saw the workers near watching him. The other heavy-set reporter moved toward him. He backed away, lost himself in the crowd, and found Waino again.

"They got us spotted," Waino said. "A bull tried to pull me in."

They were under the factory when they heard the shots. When he got up in the factory, far behind Waino, he saw the men crowding at the entrance and dropping down off the loading platform, climbing down to the tracks or dropping from the box cars, edging out into the cleared space or waiting in a straggling line to draw in the ones who reached the factory. A little way ahead of him two of the reporters were holding a worker and slugging him as he struggled, their great flushed faces fierce and brutal and distorted with the strain of their blows. In a blur of movement he saw one of them bring up his knee, and a spasm of pain across the worker's face, and then a crowd of men from the factory rushed in and drew the worker back to the factory. Johnny groped over the roadbed and found a rock twice as large as his fist, his heart lifting with its weight and the solid feel of it.

Now all at once there was a pause in the fighting. The two crowds had joined at the factory. He was a hundred feet from the building, and there were a few others, scattered and bewildered, still farther on toward the place where the police were massed together around their cars. As he started to back toward the factory, afraid to turn his eyes from the savage blue figures, he saw some of those before him stop in their tracks; he heard them give a cry and he saw the anguished looks on their faces as they turned. Off in a cleared space, at one side of him, one of the police was holding Ellen by the arm, twisting her arm as he pushed her toward the factory. The cop was intent on what he was doing; he did not see that he was separated from the rest of the police or that all of the workers were watching him. Ellen gave a cry as he twisted her arm; she tried to struggle with him, turning and striking blindly with her free arm. Somehow she hurt him, or he saw that he was alone, for when he tried to free himself, and she continued to struggle, he brought his club down carefully and deliberately across her head and shoulders, holding her with one hand while he chopped the club down steadily as though it were a hammer and he were driving a spike into her back. Then there was a cry from the crowd.

The cop did not see the crowd until it was on him, and then he went down, head over heels, with his club flying twenty feet from the impact when they struck him. In a blur of movement Johnny saw the crowd go past like an avalanche gaining in power as it fell. For a moment he could see nothing but the figures shuttling past him; then he heard the shrill whistle of the police and the cries of the men. One of the police cars came driving straight toward him, splitting the crowd, but before it reached him it dropped into a ditch, and while the wheels spun and it paused, the crowd closed around it again and in a moment it was lifted clear of the ground and thrown on its side. He saw one of the police stand up as the car paused, tugging at his revolver, and then make a wild grab to get his balance as the car was tossed aside as though it were some flimsy object, a twig or a leaf in the path of a winter flood. Then he heard the tearing sound of shots, a sound like the breaking of glass, only louder and more fearful, and in a moment the crowd began to move away.

For a time he ran around blindly, clinching the rock in his fist, and each breath sending its knife into his side. He had a chance to throw the rock when he came on two police who had cornered a man near the office. He threw it, waiting till he was quite close and until a moment of clear vision outlined the broad back so clearly that he could not miss. One of them began to chase him. He tried to race back into the crowd, but the crowd had scattered in all directions, and everywhere he looked he could see the police and no clear spaces between them. Someone made a dive on the cop who was chasing him. The cop sprawled on his face, his breath rushing from him in a groan.

Vin Garl jumped up and grabbed Johnny's arm and jerked him around behind the office. They sprinted toward a small door of the factory. When they got back to the main entrance a few men had got back on the loading platform. The tide-flat was still in confusion. In a few places there was still fighting, but mostly the workers had got free and the police were trying to head them off, trying to round them up in the narrow space between the fireroom and the factory.

Winters came up the steps. The blood was running from a cut on his mouth.

"Do something," he said. "Start them this way."

Vin Garl said, "What? Call them?"

"No, good God, let them get away! The cops—do something to draw the cops here—break the windows, something! Give them a chance to get away!"

Winters ran on to another group. "Then get out of here," he called back. "Hit the brush."

Johnny was watching the tideflat, and trying to get his breath. The car sprawled on its side looked like a crippled animal, and one of the cops was still standing beside it, holding his hand on his forehead. He could see the crowd drawing together again, and the cops drawing together too.

One of the men tried to reach one of the windows to break it. He climbed on a pile of doors and poked at it ineffectually. But Vin Garl had grabbed him by the arm again. "Here," he said feverishly. "This ought to make a noise." He put his shoulder against a pile of doors loaded up on a truck, ready to be pushed into a box car. They leaned on it together and pushed the truck off the platform. It fell with a roar and the doors spread out over the tideflat like playing cards. Johnny ran to the end of the platform and looked out; he could see some of the cops looking back toward the factory. *They're stopping!* he yelled. *They're stopping!* Vin Garl and the other man pushed another load off the edge. As it crashed on the load that had already fallen the sound rose like an explosion. Johnny saw the cops turning back toward the factory and heard the shrill scream of their whistles. One of the police cars started back for town.

Then they ran back through the factory, dodging through the alleys and down the conveyor until they reached the hiding safety of the brush.

For a long time Johnny could scarcely see. For a long time he did not know what had happened. He followed Vin Garl through the barbed wire of the brush, blindly, his fears like bloodhounds at his heels. In his imagination he pictured them coming out into a cleared space where the police would be waiting, the savage men with guns and clubs who thought nothing of smashing a man's face or of driving a spike into a

[365]

girl's back. The brush bent under the wind. It was thick and closely packed, and although he scratched himself as he broke through, and sometimes was stopped in an agony of fear, it seemed too thin and frail a screen to hide him, and his heart quickened at every gap in it.

Before him Vin Garl ducked his head and broke through the tangle, holding up his arms to protect his eyes. His shirt was plastered to his back with sweat, and the skin was scraped from one arm below the elbow, leaving a red and swollen sore. Once he turned around to curse Johnny because he was so slow. Sometimes they heard someone in the brush near them, and then they froze into silence, not knowing whether the sound came from someone they could trust or from someone hunting them with guns and clubs. Sometimes their imaginations pictured someone in wait for them when all that they saw was a blot of deeper shadow, or a cunning arrangement of the branches and leaves of the brush. Sometimes the brush clawed at them like a live thing, trying to trap and hold them as they tried to get free. Before they were out from under the factory they could hear the police overhead. Then as soon as they could no longer see what was happening their imaginations, released from the checks and guidances of their eyesight, raced on feverishly and gave them terrible pictures to torment them; and then they thought of the workers who could not get away, of their being torn to ribbons by the police, and of the police catching them alone, separating them and beating them in their fury. The memories of the few minutes of violence fed their imaginations; they remembered the coarse blotched faces of the police, distorted with fury as they swung their clubs or ran after the few who were separated and lost, and the dull sickening smash of the clubs on human flesh. . . . So they rushed blindly through the brush, afraid of what might be ahead of them, and sick at heart with their fear for the ones who had been left behind.

When they came to the edge of the water, and dropped silently over the bulkhead and hid themselves in the driftwood that was piled on the narrow beach—then Johnny gave way and cried with his fury and his helplessness. *"Oh, bastards!"* he said, over and over, *"Oh, bastards!"* while the acid tears streamed down his face and he gasped with each breath he drew. But Vin Garl sank down in exhaustion and stared dully at the gray water. Now his face was drained of all expression as his weariness had torn all emotion from him; his high cheek bones seemed more prominent because the flesh was drawn tight and bloodless across his cheeks, and his eyes were narrowed and somber. Now and then he touched the raw gash on his arm. For a long time after Johnny had controlled himself neither of them said anything. They waited to recover from the shock of the attack, until the minutes and their little safety and the broad normal world would dilute their memories and make them seem less terrible, until the terrible crash of clubs on flesh and the tearing sounds of shots and the broken screaming would seem less real and the anguish less intense, until at last they would get strength enough to talk to each other. Down the harbor, toward the edge of town, they could see the mills at work, the smoke brushing across the grimy buildings and the pennants of steam flapping in the wind. The flat and sunken tugboats pushed through the water, and the bridges opened and closed, and when the wind shifted they could hear the low persistent throb of the mills and the whistles of the boats; they could see the lines of steam rising and hear the sound of the whistles a long time afterwards.

At last Johnny asked dully, "What will we do?"

"Stay here," Vin Garl said. "Till it gets dark, anyway."

Johnny remembered the terror that had clawed at him and felt a weak relapse into his memories. When he closed his eyes he could see the big cop holding Ellen, swinging his club down hard, an intent and serious look on his face, as though he were chopping into a tough piece of wood, and the crowd drawing itself together before it moved forward in its fury. He could see it clearly, the pain and horror on Ellen's face, the calm absorption of the cop as he brought the club down methodically on her head and shoulders, and the stunned silence of the watchers. . . . The water here came almost to the bulkhead. The driftwood crowded the narrow beach and extended for a hundred feet into the water. The branches of the trees and the roots of the washed stumps rose over the surface of the gray water, more and more scattered with the distance from shore. Behind the bulkhead the brush rose in a mass. Down the beach, toward town, a dark figure dropped down into the tangle of driftwood. He was a worker; Johnny could see his torn shirt and his loose coveralls. He looked around indecisively before he sat down on one of the logs.

"Another one," Vin Garl said.

They walked stiffly down to the worker. He was terribly beaten on the face and head. His hair was matted with blood from a cut on his scalp and his eyes were almost closed from the welts on his swollen cheeks. He said nothing as they approached, only holding himself with an inflexible, automatic alarm, ready to run again. The three of them sat down together. The rain still fell irregularly, the showers sometimes marking the surface of the harbor like a screen stretched over the small waves. Gradually the newcomer got his breath. He lifted his head painfully. "You know how to get out of here?" he asked.

Vin Garl nodded. "What are they doing back there? They still there?"

"They're all over the place."

The new man spoke with an effort. He slid down beside the log to protect his back from the rain.

[368]

Vin Garl said, "We'll wait till dark. Then we can go down the bulkhead till we hit the road."

"Who'd they shoot?"

Vin Garl nodded toward him. "His Old Man." Johnny looked up. "Christ," Vin Garl said. "I thought you knew. . . . I thought that was why you were crying."

They looked at him. "Bad?" he managed to say.

"I don't know."

The rain fell hard, drenching them while they waited, not like rain but like some new and terrible weapon of their enemies. He tried to crowd under the driftwood and Vin Garl put his hand on his shoulder, "Come on, son," he said gently, "don't cry," and then they sat there listening to him, their faces dark with misery and anger, listening and waiting for the darkness to come like a friend and set them free.

Note on the Text

This text of Robert Cantwell's *Land of Plenty* is a photo-offset reprinting of the first printing (New York: Farrar & Rinehart, 1934).* No editorial alterations of any kind have been made. The following substantive emendations have been recommended by Mr. Cantwell:

xiii. 4	1932 [1933
xiii. 5	1933 [1932
xiii. 15	1931 [1933
28. 17	threshing [thrashing
88. 30	going [doing
115. 9	would for [would go for
152. 16	warn [warm
186. 14	meaning [demeaning

The nonsense word "blubl" at 289.19 is intentional.

---

* The English issue (London: Bell, 1934) consisted of the American sheets.